To Izzie,

My yoga buddy,
& dancing queen!

READING
BETWEEN
the
LINES

Jo Merrett

With love,

x x
x

Published in 2017 by WEbook
Albury Court, Albury,
Thame, Oxfordshire, OX9 2LP

www.WEbook.com
The Social Network Where Writers Get Published

Text © Jo Merrett 2017

A CIP catalogue record for this title is available from the British Library
ISBN: 978-1-910571-89-7

For all the women of the world who think they can't.

You can.

One

Chief Reporter, Aidan Tindall, is single-minded, serious and intensely aloof. He is also the current subject of my personal, sexual obsession.

I came three times this morning thinking about him. With two fingers buried deep in my pussy, the other hand circling my clit, I'd leant against the shower wall and let my mind's eye wander all over the torso I imagine exists beneath those crisp, expensive shirts.

Looking at Aidan's empty chair, I suck thoughtfully on the end of my pen and feel a shiver run down my spine. My nails tap impatiently on the desk, and I heave a frustrated sigh: bored, bored, bored.

Casually, trying not to be spotted, I sneak a glance at my watch; five whole minutes until I can justifiably clock off and the weekend can begin. I peek furtively over the top of my monitor towards the News Editor's desk, while my fingers dash out a Google search: *Cocktail bars, London*. That'll make it look like I'm still working, and I can still get a head start on the weekend.

Friday afternoons are always a drag. This week's paper is already on the stands, and although it's nice to have things on the back burner to fill column inches for next week, no one's seriously hard at work past 3pm. I look around the open plan office, now bathed in a golden, late afternoon light, and watch the dust molecules float through the air as the summer sun streams in through the partially broken blinds.

Two journalists' empty chairs are pressed hard up against the desks. To my left, Aidan's desk is spotless: a few pens neatly lined up next to a small pile of ordered notepads, and a scribble pad in perfect parallel with the edge of the desk.

By contrast, Anna's workspace could best be described as a dustbin. A random clutter of chewed biros, discarded fag packets, chewing gum wrappers, several reporter pads in disarray, and strewn across the desk, a balled up scarf and a tangle of hair bands. Ew. I screw up my nose in distaste. I'm not a clean freak, but the area should come with a health warning.

Half of the reporters have already gone home, but it's not my week to knock off early; someone has to man the decks in case all hell breaks loose. Perhaps a masked terrorist runs riot through Staines town centre, threatening to blow up the Elmsleigh Centre... You never know these days, the crap that's unfolding across Europe. Realistically though, dog shows and petty council skirmishes are the bread and butter of a two-bit paper like, *The Staines and Egham Express*. The chances of something remotely interesting happening – especially on my watch – are less likely than Ed Sheeran turning up and asking me to sing a duet on his next album.

That makes me chuckle. Pete, the News Ed., looks up from

the other end of the room, a pile of papers stacked up in front of him like sandbags in a trench. I raise my eyebrows and give him a confident nod. Oops, don't want him knowing I'm only killing time. I close down my browser just in case Pete walks down this end of the room. Turning my snigger into a cough, I stare intently at the blank screen as if an undesired wheezing fit has torn me away from a massive scoop.

I check the time again: two minutes. *Ugh.*

It's not always going to be like this. Well, hopefully not, anyway. The aim is to do a few years on a local rag, then try and blag my way onto a national. Or maybe grab a job at a regional news agency before trying for shifts at one of the daily newspapers in London. Aim high and hope for the best, that's my theory.

Someone's got to get these jobs, why not me?

Mum and Dad tried warning me: it's tough trying to make it to the top. Everyone and their dog was doing a media degree or journalism course when I set my cap at a reporter's job.

"It's not what you know, it's who you know." Dad had preached, "And you don't know anyone! You're not going to end up being the next Kate Adie, you know."

Says who? I love my dad but he's not always right, even if he thinks he is. Kate Adie was a no one once, wasn't she? There are jobs to fill and they need writers. I'm as good as the next guy, aren't I?

So when *The Express* invited me to interview after fifty, yes, fifty – read it and weep – rejection letters, I was brutally honest about my motives.

"Why do you think you'll make a good reporter?" David, the ruddy-faced, middle-aged Editor had asked, clasping his hands behind his head as he tipped his seat back onto its rear legs.

"Because I'm really nosy, and I like to know what's going on before everybody else." I had eyed him defiantly.

Cocky I'd say, and a bit too flirtatious, but it bloody worked! My bolshiness paid off. I got a call the next day telling me the job was mine if I wanted it. Result.

They paid for my training: law, shorthand and general government, all on one day a week at a college half way round the M25 – joy on a Friday afternoon – and were now, two years on, letting me try my hand at a few features. This was something I was, despite my initial misgivings, proving to be rather good at. Writing a double page spread had seemed like a monumental task at the beginning, but it turned out, the more you write, the easier it becomes.

It's local news stories that I still spent most of my time writing though, and the dull nature of some of them meant the end of the week couldn't come fast enough.

Five o'clock – whoo-hoo! I am OUTTA HERE!

Quickly switching off the computer, I swipe my phone, notepad and collective biros into my oversized tote, grab my blazer and raise a hand in parting to Yvonne, the Wraysbury reporter who's hunched behind her desk, phone wedged under her double chin, studiously scribbling notes.

"In a hurry, Miss Cleaver?" comes a reedy voice.

Bollocks. I roll my eyes and paste on a smile, then turn to face Pete who is peering over the top of his barricade. Yvonne mutters something indecipherable into the phone and shoots me a dirty look. "Um, yeah, sorry, got to dash, have to hit the motorway before the traffic gets bad." I'm edging my way closer to the door, "My parents are expecting me. Family dinner, you know how it is. Back to Winchester."

Stop waffling, woman.

Pete, eyes twinkling, raises an eyebrow: "Do you now? Well you have a nice evening, but be back up here tomorrow afternoon to cover those fêtes. You've got five this weekend. Don't go running late and do half a job like last time."

I cringe at the memory.

"Yep, got you, best work, on time." Flushing, I muster my best innocent, yet totally guilty grin and clatter out through the reception doors, waving goodbye to David, who's cooped up in his tiny glass coffin of an office, door shut firmly against the world.

Bollocks! I forgot the fucking fêtes. Fucking fuckety fuck! Stupid bloody summer season.

I jab the lift button and wait impatiently.

Every year around late spring and early summer, the local schools and churches start holding their annual fund-raisers. Huge banners for fayres and fêtes suddenly appear on fences across the area, notices fill the 'What's On' section of the local papers, and each weekend it's one lucky sodding journalist's turn to be on call and cover as many of the damn things as possible. This weekend, it's me. Way-flaming-hay.

A second later the doors swing open and Gemma, my mate in advertising, sweeps out, "You lying fucking bitch, Kate!" she grins, tossing her mane of dark chestnut curls over her shoulder. "Do your mum and dad know you're using them to lie to your boss?" she laughs, arching one perfectly threaded eyebrow in mock disgust.

Gemma is one of my best friends, and the reason I'm in such a hurry to leave. She turned 25 yesterday and is throwing a party tonight.

"What am I meant to tell him Gem? That I've done fuck all but surf the net for the last two hours and I need to get to Topshop before it closes so I can buy a pair of heels? Yeah, Pete'll understand that." I shake my head and roll my eyes.

"But you already have about three hundred pairs of shoes, Kate." sighs Gem, knowing full well she's exaggerating – I only have about one hundred – and, buying shoes is an addiction: I can never get enough. "Plus, it's only a house party, it's not like you need to dress up."

I roll my eyes again.

The lift doors open and we traipse inside, squeezing up against a group of suits. *The Staines and Egham Express*, isn't big or important enough to warrant its own premises, and leases a single floor in an office block filled with other, non-descript businesses.

"When have I ever gone out for the night and not worn heels?

And, more to the point, when have *you*?" I hiss.

Anyway, it's not like Gemma won't look absolutely drop dead gorgeous. I swear this woman wakes up with a blow dry, perfect skin and immaculate make up. Plus, she has almost as many shoes as I do. The doors open and we go our separate ways.

There are now just two and a half hours until the party starts, and thirty minutes until Topshop closes.

Half an hour later, I'm back in my slightly shabby Ford Fiesta, along with a brand new pair of grey suede strappy heels; some long, drop-dead gorgeous, silver spikey earrings, and a Venti double shot latte. I'm starving, but it's no good eating this late in the day, not if I'm going to fit into my best skinny jeans and still have a chance of pulling. Thankfully, the coffee curbs my hunger pangs and by the time I get home it's gone 6pm.

Great, it looks like no one's in. Let's grab a shower and get this night underway.

I pour myself a long, cold gin and tonic, kick off my shoes and carry them, the glass, my bag, and my new purchases up to my room. As I reach the landing, a miniature human whirlwind, barely covering himself with a tiny towel, hurtles into the bathroom, making me shriek.

Grabbing onto the bannister, I manage to save myself and the G'n'T from falling back down the stairs, though some of the ice cold liquid spills over my top and trickles into my bra making me take a sharp breath.

"Alfie! For Christ's sake." The bathroom door smashes closed, but not before revealing a flash of his doughy, hairy arse.

Urgh, moron.

"How long are you going to be?" I yell.

Silence.

"Alfie! How long?" I hammer on the bathroom door. "I have to get out and I need the shower... Alfie!" *Knob.*

Sighing, I walk into the bedroom, dump my stuff and open the door of my worn, overstuffed wardrobe. Instantly shoes, bags and belts tumble out. Kicking them to one side, I rifle through a heaving pile of tops and lie the one I'm looking for - a black, semi-sheer, fitted T-shirt with leather trim - on the bed, along with my favourite indigo skinny jeans, and empty my new shoes out of their bag.

Tugging a facial wipe from the packet, I wipe away the remains of the day's make-up. My fitted, green cotton shift dress winds up in a crumpled heap on the floor, before my conscience kicks in and I chuck it onto the overflowing wash bin in the corner of the room.

Unwinding my hair from the tight top-knot I've taken to wearing at work, I rub the back of my neck. *God that feels good.*

I had planned to jump straight in the shower and take my time over doing my hair and make-up, but the water's still running. Christ knows how long he'll be, or if there'll be any hot water left.

My eyes wander to the open drawer of the bedside table where I can see the white, shiny plastic of my vibrator. I rub my tongue lightly back and forth along one of my front teeth.

'Damn that cold tonic', I think as it sends a tingle through my nipples. I shouldn't really. I mean, there isn't time, but...

it's not like I can get into the bathroom anyway.

I crawl over the bed on my hands and knees and pull it out of the drawer. As I run my hand over the thick, bulbous head, smoothing my fingers along the velvety silicon shaft, I tighten involuntarily and a sharp pulling sensation begins to tug low in my groin. Suddenly, the bathroom door-knob crashes loudly onto the other side of my wall, making me jump.

"Kate! Shower's free!" Alfie bellows at me, thumping on my door as he saunters back to his room at the end of the corridor. "Floor's wet. Sorry!"

Little shit.

Reluctantly, I put the Rabbit back in the drawer and grab a towel off the chair. If I'm going to knock 'em dead tonight the cheap thrill'll have to wait...

The heavy, throbbing bass line pulsates through the door before I even push it open. Gemma's parties are legendary and she always invites her neighbours so noise complaints are at a minimum. I quickly rummage in my Ted Baker bag, check my lip-gloss, smooth down my top and jiggle my tits up.

Perfect, let's go.

Elbowing my way through the throng of people packed into the tiny vestibule, I spy Gem across the living room wrapped around a tall, lean blond with a crew cut.

My heart stops. Shit, no. He wasn't meant to be here. The beat in my chest quickens as the bottom of my stomach literally falls away. I can't breathe.

THE BITCH!

In less than half a second, Gem catches my eye and waves me over, her new best friend glancing over his shoulder, taking a long swig of beer. It's not him.

IT'S NOT FUCKING HIM!

I feel light-headed with relief. *Oh thank Christ.*

Blinking back the tears prickling at the back of my eyes, I paste on a massive grin and stride over.

"Babe, looking good!" she smiles. Untangling herself from her buff companion she reaches across to an enormous ice bucket, pulls out an open bottle of Veuve Cliquot and pours me a healthy measure. Thrusting the glass at me, she kisses my cheek. "Isn't he fit?" she whispers into my ear.

I'm not sure if it's the relief or the long pull of champagne, but I feel ridiculously emotional. Smiling weakly, I say in a strangled voice, "I thought it was Aidan." Tears are prickling again. What the hell is wrong with me? Get a grip. Gem stares at me, glances at her man, now throwing back handfuls of peanuts while fondling her tit with his free hand, then back at me.

Disengaging herself, she tucks the bottle of bubbly under her right arm and – ignoring lover boy's protests – steers me through the thronging crowd towards her bedroom.

"I'd never do that, Kate," she mutters behind me, "I couldn't! You know that, you daft bint!" She looks hurt, confused even.

I'm taking deep breaths now, in between the icy swigs of champagne, nodding at people smiling hello to me as we weave between them across the room. "I know Gem,

I just…" *Keep breathing; look normal.* "It's driving me crazy, you know?" *This is ridiculous.* "Gemma, I'm fine…"

I'm lying, of course.

Retrieving a key from her bra and unlocking the door – even party-loving Gemma's astute enough to keep her bedroom off-limits during a knees-up – she pushes me inside and shuts it firmly behind us, dulling the din. I feel silly now.

"Gem, really I'm fine."

She tops up both our glasses and fixes me with a gimlet stare; Gem's vivid green eyes are like lasers.

"Aidan's not even here this weekend, Kate." she says sternly, "He turned down my invitation weeks ago and you know that. You're getting obsessed, hun."

"I know," I say miserably, staring into the bottom of my glass. I'm so pathetic. "I can't help it Gem. If I don't say something soon, I'm going to go insane. He's just so hot! But he acts like I'm barely there. It's infuriating… and it turns me on so much." I add meekly.

What an idiot. How crazy do I sound?

Gem is grinning at me. She thinks I'm nuts, I can tell. "Seriously Gem, the cooler he plays it, the more I really want him. If I say something, I'm sure he'll just laugh in my face, and working with him, well that would be mortifying."

"Then do it, ask him out." Gemma smile softens, and she wraps her arm back in mine, "He can only say no and you can live that down. You're a big girl!"

"Hmm, maybe." I ponder.

Asking a man like Aidan out for a drink is not really my thing. It's a bit… conventional. I run my finger thoughtfully around the rim of my glass. The teeniest bud of an idea is beginning to form at the back of my mind and I bite my lower lip as excitement thrills through me.

Feeling better, I grin mischievously. "Come on, let's get back to the party. All that champagne won't drink itself!" Squeezing Gem's hand, I open the door and we merge back into the bedlam, buzzing with the shriek and chatter of excited, inebriated guests.

A red-haired girl is singing a Pink song on the Sing Star (really badly), while trying to balance on Gemma's coffee table.

Christ, what time did some of these people start drinking?

Gemma's deep aqua and bold crimson walls create a fantastic backdrop for a party. Work colleagues, neighbours, and some of her old friends from her university days blend seamlessly into a melting pot of booze and laughter. Hours pass before I even think about Aidan again.

Seven (or more) glasses of fizz later, I'm in the kitchen, slightly worse for wear, wedged between the washing machine and a remarkably strong, denim clad thigh belonging to a 26-year-old tree surgeon called Mark, who Gemma knows from her college days.

Ooh, champagne head!

I blink two or three times.

I think I need water.

Mark took today off work apparently and drove up last night (clearly trees can wait), spending most of the day in bed while Gem was at work. I'm reliably informed that all this rest means he won't need to sleep again until tomorrow night and has more energy than you can shake a stick at.

Why are some men so cocky?

He's not really my type: Lightly tanned from spending every weekend (and evening, he tells me), over the last month on a surfboard, he's also a little shorter than I'd normally go for. In my new heels his eyes are just level with the bridge of my nose, and judging by the knackered looking VW camper parked outside that he's clarified belongs to him, money and prospects are not his prime concern.

My mouth's beginning to feel sticky. I really need that water.

The biggest problem I have with Mark is his hair. It is the longest hair I have ever seen on a man with the exception of a heavy metal musician, and I've never met one in the flesh so that doesn't really count. As a rule, I don't do men with hair longer than mine. I prefer a short back and sides.

Oooh, I'm feeling quite sick now.

"I just need to get some..." Still pinioned against the kitchen cabinets because he won't move that leg, I can just about twist round and, leaning backwards and sideways at the same time, reach the cold tap.

The hem of my top rides up, exposing my bare waist and Mark brushes his fingers lightly over my skin. A tingle shivers through me. Nudging the tap on I fill my glass and down it in one.

Oh, that feels better already.

I steady myself against the kitchen worktop and look at Mark. He is really quite attractive, with a strong jaw, enhanced by a light smattering of very dark stubble, piercing blue-grey eyes and full, soft-looking lips that I am becoming more and more inclined to kiss.

The insistent thigh is now firmly wedging itself higher between my own, and God it's strong. I can feel the definition of the muscles through the material, and that's not all. Glancing downwards, the outline of a generous, nicely firming up erection is beginning to become quite visible and he thrusts his hips forcefully towards mine. Jesus! Is it getting hot in here or is it just me? *Ooh, deep breath Kate, deep breath.*

It does seem to be a promising cock. Oh to hell with it. I can overlook the hair. I stop resisting and pull him in for a kiss.

Letting Mark prise my lips apart with his probing tongue, I give into the sensation that coupled with the copious amounts of champagne I've drunk is giving me serious head spin.

Oh he's a good kisser.

We're still necking like a couple of teenagers as we fall out of a cab thirty minutes later. I fumble with the key in the front door, which is no easy feat as the bulb has gone in the porch light and none of us can be bothered to replace it. Mark's tongue is still swirling like caramel in my mouth, affecting my powers of control and inhibiting my concentration. I force him away for long enough to drag him up the two flights of stairs to my room.

We fall through the doorway and on to the bed, kicking the door shut behind us.

My heart is racing and I'm panting like I've just been sprinting. He looks at me like he wants to eat me alive, and I suddenly feel like I'm going to laugh out loud. I think it's the hair. Smothering the urge, I pull Mark's soft, already half-unbuttoned, white cotton shirt over his head and catch my breath. I certainly don't feel like laughing any more.

He might be short, but he's beautifully made.

I swallow hard and run my hands over his large, well-rounded shoulders, then down his strong arms over every vein. His skin feels tight, baked golden by the sun. Propped up above me, resting on his hands with outstretched arms, long, dark hair falls over his shoulders and down onto his chest. I want to run my hands right up into the thick of it and take great handfuls of it. It must be like running your fingers through coils of rope.

A sudden thought catches me unawares: this must be how it feels for a man when he gets close to a woman. I feel like I've swapped roles and the very thought of it does surprising things to my body.

I reach my hands up, but Mark stops me in my tracks holding my arms and laying them with careful force over my head, whilst catching a hold of my top and peeling it up. He leaves it wrapped around my arms like a truss.

Though not completely restricted, I like the way it feels and lie still while he reaches underneath my arched back to expertly undo my bra. I hear my breath quicken in anticipation as he slides the straps down over my shoulders, but he doesn't remove it. Instead he lays the flat of his palms over the cups and presses the lace into my breasts, rolling it over the skin in slow, circular movements. The material is abrasive. Its roughness exaggerated by the sensitivity of my nipples as he circles it round and round, over and over again, until my head is spinning. This is unexpectedly distracting. The intense scratching on my nipples is now triggering feelings way down, lower in my body, a delightful tugging deep inside me. My pants are soaking wet.

I can't stand not touching him anymore. Pulling my arms free of my top, I rip the bra away and toss it to one side. Reaching up towards his head, entangling my fingers in his hair, I tighten my grip, tug his head backwards and pull myself up, pressing my hard nipples against his chest.

I'm so turned on its almost painful. I feel like I'm swimming in a sea of toned muscle and thick, shiny hair. It's intoxicating. Mark's hair is beautiful. It's a rich brown colour, but streaked blonde by the sun and with a slight wave – probably from all that salt. I must ask him what conditioner he uses.

What the fuck? Where did that come from?

His hands are scrambling to undo my belt, and then my jeans, easing them and my knickers down in one go. I wriggle out and kick them off the bed, turning my attention to his lower half, but Mark's already wrestling his jeans off and when he lowers himself back down onto me there are just his trunks between us.

His weighty thickness strains through the thin cotton and instantly becomes saturated by my own wetness. He moans, pressing his lips into my neck to give me soft butterfly kisses, interwoven with sharp little nibbles over the sensitive skin behind my left ear.

Now it's my turn to moan: a soft guttural noise escapes my parted lips as Mark stretches his fingers down over my stomach, lower, tangling his fingertips through the small strip of hair, cupping me, sliding one finger into my slickness.

Go on baby, don't stop now.

Mark sinks two fingers deep inside me and I draw a sharp

intake of breath.

"Is that good?" he whispers in my ear.

"Uh-huh." I'm panting, "Yeah, keep going."

He works his fingers in and out of me, rubbing my clitoris with the pad of his thumb. Already I'm rocking my hips against him.

Dragging my fingers down his chest, I rake my nails lightly through the scattering of hair that tapers over the muscles on his stomach, disappearing into the waistband of his pale blue trunks. As I dip my fingers underneath the fabric and stretch it away from his flat, bronzed stomach, the perfect round head of a beautiful cock springs free, rising above the material. He's so hard the top of him nudges his belly button in a perfect round 'O'.

Oh, yes please.

I lick my lips. I don't know if I want to suck him or fuck him. Frantically, I lower his trunks the rest of the way down and hold him firmly with both hands, one stacked above the other.

"God that feels good, Kate," he breathes, while pumping his fingers in and out of me in a delicious rhythm. I'm pressing myself into his hand and my gasps are coming quicker now. I let go a second, suck the thumb of one hand and holding him firmly, roll it over the fat, purple head of his cock, two, maybe three times while gripping him snugly. A seed-pearl of sticky liquid oozes like a tear from the tiny, mouth shaped entrance and I have a burning desire to bury the tip of my tongue in him and suck it up.

Suddenly neither one of us wants to wait a second longer.

I release him from my grasp and he sucks his fingers greedily, closing his eyes, tasting me, before bracing himself on one elbow and taking hold of himself in the other hand.

I grab a condom from a bowl next to the bed, rip it open and pass it to Mark, who unrolls it quickly over his length. He moves forwards, lowering his hips until the head of his cock is poised at my entrance, meeting my moistness with his thick girth. He goes to plunge into me but I brace him with my thighs, hold him still for a moment. I love this split second, this feeling of fullness right at my opening. Sex, but not sex. Possibly I like it more than the fucking itself.

I take hold of his hips and rock him in and out, a fraction of a centimetre, teasing him, but revelling the sensation just inside me. Then, as always, the moment passes and I want him buried up to the balls in my pussy. Now.

I relax my thighs, let my hips fall open and Mark crashes into me, his hips colliding with mine.

"Fuck, yeah," I shout out, balling my hands in the sheets.

Oh my God. Nothing beats this feeling.

I move both hands to his backside and dig my nails into his taut buttocks, pulling him deeply into me, sucking him up inside my body. We're both rocking now, hips smashing together, finding their rhythm; limbs tangled, tongues meshed together, hands groping.

It's frantic sex, not love-making. There are no hearts and roses; just pure unadulterated fucking, and I love it.

The solid base of Mark's cock rubs against my clit, intensifying the pressure.

God I'm close.

"Holy shit... keep... don't stop," I pant out orders: "There, stay there, keep fucking me, don't stop," I grab his hips and hold him where I need him, thrusting upwards. I tighten my arse and feel my legs stiffen. The pressure builds, stronger and tighter.

"Come on Kate, cum." Mark pleads, kissing me deeply, his mouth over mine and it tips me over the edge.

I cum in waves. They wash over me, splinters of light fracturing my vision, my breath coming ragged and fast, blood thrashing in my ears.

Yes, yes, yes! Oh. God... yes!

Warmth overtakes me, and the spasms are still coming as I feel Mark go rigid. His hips jerk twice, three times, as he floods inside me with great heaving, racking breaths.

Barely holding his own weight on his elbows, we're both spent; our breath slows back to normal, Mark still half hard inside me. He eases out and rolls over, carefully removing the condom, folding it in a tissue from beside the bed and dropping it into the wastepaper bin before collapsing next to me.

"Oh Kate, wow, that was..."

"Ssshhh, mmmm," I reach for the duvet underneath me, lift my backside and wriggle under the covers. "That was great... good..."

Drowsiness is drifting over me now. The evening, all the champagne, and the sex: it's caught up with me and I need sleep. Mark flicks off the bedside light and crawls under the covers, wrapping himself around me. I wriggle backwards, spooning comfortably, and fall fast asleep.

Two

Fuck! Fuck! Fuck! You idiot, Kate.

I swing the car into a space, grab my bag, and run as fast as humanly possible in four-inch heels. I hate Mondays. Thank God that Boots is only downstairs from the office. I leg it to the make-up section, grab the red tube of Maybelline and take it to the till. How the hell have I managed to leave the house without mascara on?

After waking up yesterday morning with the mother of all hangovers, the result of spending Saturday night at a London cocktail bar, followed by a third session of very nice sex with Mark (the second was on Saturday morning, in case you were wondering), I'd gone to bed at 8pm last night and had a full eleven hours in bed, so I couldn't blame lack of sleep for this colossal oversight.

In the two and a half years I've worked at the paper, I have never turned up without a full face of make-up. Not wearing mascara is the worst. My eyes are a decent blue and they're quite a nice almond shape, but without mascara they're nothing.

I'll never forget asking my mum when I was sixteen if she

thought I was pretty and she answered: "You're not typically beautiful, but there's something quite attractive about you when you're made up." And she's absolutely right. No man has ever told me I'm beautiful in my whole life.

In my late teens, I spent the night with a lad I'd had a huge crush on for ages. As the sun came up, I was wearing just his half unbuttoned, oversized denim shirt. I asked him what he liked about me, to pay me a compliment, if you will. Such was my gauche inexperience around men.

After studying my face for a couple of seconds, then in panic looking me up and down, he said finally: "Um, your legs are nice. Long, like."

So, I may not be a beauty, but with make-up I look pretty damn good, which is exactly why I need an emergency stop in the ladies before I even step foot in the newsroom. I didn't forget because I'm tired. I forgot because I'm distracted and shitting myself. Painting my lashes, I notice my hand's trembling and my heart's beating a tattoo in my chest.

Breathe Kate, breathe.

After my little chat with Gemma on Friday night and two days of rather satisfying sex, I've decided to knock this Aidan obsession on the head one way or another by talking to him at lunchtime, and the notion is scaring me witless. But when I set my mind to something...

Lashes up to par, I step out of the loo and into the office. The dowdy receptionist is already at her desk, watering her spider plant.

"Morning, Jenny," I smile woodenly, and out of courtesy. *Boring cow.*

About 19, she was one of those girls who dresses like her mother and looks down her nose at women like me: women who know what they want and will do anything to get it. I turn the corner to my desk, snatching up today's Sun and head for the staffroom. I need coffee.

"Morning Kate, those fêtes go alright?" Pete's on my case nice and early, keep smiling.

"Yes, all done." I say brightly, "We got a load of great pics and you'll have copy before lunch."

Pete runs a hand through his thinning hair and leans smugly back in his chair before continuing:

"Clive tells me you were a bit worse for wear Saturday afternoon. Threw up in the bushes round the back of Frederick Furnivall Primary School?"

"I did no such thing," I deny indignantly, tossing my fringe out of my eyes. *Bloody sneak.*

Clive Reed has been chief photographer on the paper for the best part of thirty-five years and loves lording it over the younger members of staff, despite being one of the laziest people I know. Trust him to drop me in it. "I had a bit of a headache and felt a little dizzy so I nipped around the back of the beer tent to sit down in the shade for a few minutes," I lie. "I think it was the heat."

"It was a beautiful weekend," drones Pete, "I got a bit of golf in, and the wife and I drove down to Barton-on-Sea for a walk along the coast. Lovely views of the island from there…"

Nodding and feigning interest, I edge away a centimetre at a time. Pete's phone rings and I take my chance to scoot off, dumping my bag on my desk en route to the small kitchenette.

I flick the kettle on and dig my 'Shopping's My Drug' mug out from the pile of freshly washed crockery. Anna's already there and she's just made herself a cuppa, judging by the used teabag and dirty teaspoon sitting in a puddle on the work surface. I raise my eyebrow, pointedly eyeballing the mess but Anna doesn't even notice, so I give up, flopping down on a grubby orange plastic chair. She grins at me, sipping her tea.

"How was Fête-gate?"

Queue an eye roll.

"Same shit, different day. I can't believe I ever enjoyed it."

A year ago I was lapping it up, getting out in the local area, proudly introducing myself as the *Chertsey and Weybridge* reporter. Now I'm feeling thoroughly disillusioned. I just want something a bit more challenging out of the job.

Anna wanders back into the newsroom and I flick absent-mindedly through *The Mail* glancing at the headlines.

I'd felt rough as a butcher's dog by the time I got to the third fête on Saturday afternoon. A night of drinking, lack of sleep and passionate sex, followed by brilliant 27°C sunshine and a field full of screaming kids was more than I could handle. I'd needed to scoot into the bushes and throw up the iced latte that had been swimming around my stomach since late morning.

Three pints of water, a bacon sandwich and a nap later, I felt a hundred times better and headed into London for another night of partying with Gemma, Mark and some city friends.

We'd enjoyed a fabulous evening. After some great tapas

at Salt Yard on Goodge Street, we headed to a trendy little basement bar, The London Cocktail Club. I hammered the margaritas all night before catching the last train home and fucking Mark until the sun came up.

Thoroughly spent, I slept the sleep of the dead. It was gone noon before I surfaced from bed. Even then it took two Alka Seltzer, a generous squeeze of milk thistle, a hot shower, a full English and a bag of mini Dime bars before I felt vaguely human. When I'd woken up, I had the bed to myself; Mark had clearly headed off home. He hadn't drunk as much as me. Not judging by the rock hard erection he'd displayed so spectacularly when we went to bed, and the fact he'd climbed behind the wheel of his camper van to head down the M4 before I was even awake.

Spooning instant coffee into my mug and pouring hot water on top, I add a splash of cold water and leave the staff room.

He's here.

Sitting with his back towards me, Aidan's square shoulders hunch over his desk and stop me dead in my tracks. My stomach lurches. I feel sick as my pulse begins to race and adrenaline floods my body.

Considering I see him five days a week, I should be used to this by now, but every time is like the first. A crazy thrill rushes through my veins and I feel light-headed.

Today though, knowing what I'm going to do later, I feel like turning tail and running as fast as I can in the other direction. Instead, I force one foot in front of the other and concentrate on steadying my breathing.

"Morning" I rasp. Ooh that was far huskier than I intended.

Aidan barely looks up from his notepad and grunts, "Alright."

He's slung his leather reporter bag over the back of the chair and is waiting for his computer to warm up. Over the weekend he's had a haircut and his dirty blond hair is buzzed really short. I have a strong urge to rake my nails down the back of his head and actually have to restrain myself from reaching out a hand. Balling my hand into a fist I sit the coffee down on the desk and perch on the edge of my seat.

While pretending to fish stuff out of my bag, I glance up through my (newly made up) lashes and study him discretely: I take in his crisp white shirt with the spread collar, his broad shoulders encased in a slim-fit, charcoal-grey, Ted Baker suit. He is wearing a pink and orange, narrow pin-dot tie, slightly loosened at the collar – something I find incredibly sexy – revealing a lean neck and strong Adam's apple, but not awkward and protruding like some men. I look at his sharp, stubbly jaw and defiant chin and above it – oh God – his sensual, sulky mouth, and eyes so blue they're criminal.

I'm starting to get turned on just looking at him and he can't even be bothered to look up from his reporter's pad.

What am I doing?

I tear my eyes back to my computer, now fired up, and thumb through the pages of my notepad, looking for the weekend's notes.

Wow, my shorthand from yesterday afternoon is pants! I was still feeling pretty ropey and stayed as briefly as possible at the two church fêtes I was scheduled to attend.

Sighing, I start writing up my report. Face painting, teachers in stocks, a tombola, bottle stands (why do I always win a shit bottle of Asti Spumante?). It's all charity this and fund-raising that, pretty dull and not why I went into journalism. I think it's time I started to spread my wings and look a little further afield. Rupert, who was chief reporter before Aidan, got a staff job at *The Daily Record* almost two years ago, and said he could probably get me some weekend shifts later on in the summer. Rupert's a good bloke. A bit earnest and worthy, but loosens up after a few drinks, and it's good of him to offer to put a word in for me. Maybe now's the right time to remind him:

I'LL DO IT YES. LET ME KNOW WHAT THEY SAY. THANKS. X

The morning drags on. Yvonne's back from the daily police press briefing, Aidan goes out to meet a contact and I take a long-winded call from a parish councillor to check I'll be at the local planning meeting tonight.

A contentious proposal to build more than 200 homes with access through a quiet cul-de-sac is up for approval, and if it's thrown out it will put an end to more than a year's campaigning by local residents. Whatever the outcome, unless a bigger story breaks this week, the result will make front page and I'm desperate for a lead story so I have to be there.

I've written up two articles, one on the local market being threatened with closure, and the other a piece about a parent-run craft workshop for kids across the summer, plus the weekend reports, which Pete seems happy with, thank God.

Aidan has at least acknowledged my presence this morning, deigning to answer me in short, monosyllabic or sarcastic answers when I ask him how the stag weekend was and if he'd got the message I'd left about the time change for Thursday's coroner's inquest.

It's not that he always ignores me. Far from it. We do have a bit of banter and exchange the odd comment; sometimes even a conversation, about work. He takes the piss out of my compulsion to work out five times a week, and I belittle his football obsession, making demeaning comments about his team, West Ham. I'd go so far as to say that there's some occasional mutual flirting. In all honesty, I can't deny I've made the odd suggestive comment.

I sometimes suggest that he swims with me after work and see who has the better stamina, which is met by anything from amused curiosity to bored refusal and complete disdain.

Occasionally he infers his limited interest in me might go beyond a working relationship. Those times he catches my eye, holding my gaze just that little bit too long, or when he appraises my body, making me squirm in my seat. On those occasions I switch my attention back to my work, blinking at the screen, swallowing hard, pretending to focus and try to ignore the warm blood pooling in my groin.

It's like there's this unspoken power struggle between us, as if we're playing a game where no one's explained the rules; like kids in the playground where we both want to be top dog. I'm shaking my head at what I'm about to do as I come back in to the office with a second cup of coffee. I drink far too much of it these days, but it staves off the constant hunger. God I hate those naturally slim people who don't have to watch every mouthful they eat, or work their arses off just to keep their weight down. I'll probably have put away four or five cups of the stuff before going home tonight.

It's 11.15am.

My stomach's churning and my legs don't feel like they belong to me. I hold the cup with two hands, as I don't trust myself not to spill the steaming liquid all down myself.

Anna's gone down to the shopping centre to carry out a vox pop and both photographers are on jobs. It's just Aidan and I at our end of the room. Sitting down, I take a deep breath.

"What're you doing at lunch?" I blurt out looking directly at Aidan. My heart's hammering in my chest.

"What?" he looks at me, astonished that I would ask him. I mean, we've never so much as ridden in the lift together, and for two years he's managed to avoid every social occasion we've ever been invited to. He's never been to any post-work drinks, nor attended Christmas parties, and he even claimed to be double-booked on both Rupert's and Josh, the part-time sports reporter's, leaving dos.

He says it's because he doesn't like mixing business and pleasure. But that's just fucked up. I mean who doesn't go for a drink with a colleague on a Friday night? I'm sure he secretly shoots down the pub at lunchtime with Clive but doesn't want to mix with the rest of us. My invitation must have shocked the shit out of him.

Wait until he hears the rest of my proposal.

"Lunch. What're you doing? Are you getting a sandwich?"

I stumble on faking bravado I'm not feeling. "Have lunch with me. Come for a picnic." Not that I'll be able to eat a thing. "I want to ask you something, and I don't want to do it here." I go on, looking directly at him, just the hint of a smile playing on my lips.

The confusion has been replaced with a glimmer of intrigue. Amused, Aidan asks, "And where do you suggest we have this picnic?" He utters 'picnic' like you might say the word 'piles'.

"Down on the grass, behind the Legion."

It's hardly Hyde Park, but hoards of locals flock to the little patch of grass in the town centre during the summer. Not remotely glamorous, and more dust in areas than grass, there are some park benches, pretty flower beds and shrubbery that provide a mini oasis for office workers looking for somewhere to eat their sandwiches and catch some rays during the working day.

"I'm going to go get a salad and I'll meet you there. 12.45?"

Aidan studies my face for a moment, looking for something, a sign maybe that I'm winding him up. But evidently he sees something that makes him decide to take a gamble. Either that or curiosity gets the better of him because he agrees.

"Alright."

He says it casually. A throwaway comment delivered nonchalantly like he's not really fussed, but I know the suspense must be killing him, me turning the tables on him like this. If he wasn't interested he would have dismissed the suggestion out of hand, and then laughed in my face. Anyway, there's a tell-tale muscle twitching in the right side of his face where he's gritting his jaw, belying a hidden tension.

For the next hour we sit in silence as I work on a story about a police charity parachute jump to raise money for a local animal sanctuary. It takes all my effort not to look over at him but I couldn't be more aware of his presence if I was sat on his lap. At 12.30 I pick up my bag, grab my phone and walk out of the office without even glancing towards him.

I head in to the mall and blindly pick up a salad and a bottle of water in Boots, although I have absolutely no appetite. Checking my reflection in the mirrored wall behind the counter, I look fresh faced and perfectly made up, if a little flushed. It passes for blusher and I'm thankful that I don't suffer from that coarse redness some women experience when they're stressed. I fumble with the money at the till, dropping coins everywhere. "Sorry," I mumble, scrambling on the floor for runaway change. As I pass a handful of loose money to the assistant I notice that my hand is trembling a little. 'Relax Kate, you're only going to talk to him,' I scold myself. But my psyche mocks me for deluding myself.

Passing Topshop, Gap, and Zara, I'm oblivious to the window displays that normally call me like a homing pigeon, luring me inside to spend money I can ill afford.

Emerging outside, I turn left enjoying the sun on my skin. I love summer. Winter, the cold and the rain, the short days and lack of sunlight make me miserable, and I'm sure I have that SAD syndrome.

I come outside every lunch-time when it's hot. I know it's probably bad for me, but I slather on factor 30, close my eyes and soak up the sun in my own little world for an hour. I'll likely be more wrinkle than face in thirty years but I simply can't resist it.

The green opens up in front of me. Sticky-fingered children run around shouting and laughing, ice-lollies melting down their arms, and men sit awkwardly on the grass, suit jackets discarded, shoes kicked off and shirtsleeves rolled up. I have no idea if Aidan will actually turn up. Maybe he has no intention of coming at all.

Over the other side of the green it's less crowded and there are some bushes and a couple of willow trees. A young shop girl wearing a pair of Dr Dre Beats headphones sprawls out in a sunny patch, laying on her jacket, and sitting a little further away to the right on one of the park benches, a middle aged woman is reading a chick lit novel.

I walk around the teenager to the left and sit down beneath one of the trees. I don't normally sit in the shade but today I'm glad of the cooler air and something solid behind my back. I still have no appetite and there are butterflies are doing an Irish jig in my stomach, but for the sake of wanting something to do I pull the prawn salad out of my bag and peel back the film lid, tipping the Thai dressing over it. Then I lay it down next to me and open my bottle of water, sipping it nervously.

"That looks grim," Aidan growls, as he sits down opposite me, opening a brown paper takeaway bag and pulling out a huge loaded burger and a carton of extra-large chips.

Startled, I spill a little water on my legs and I'm gratified to notice Aidan's gaze linger on my thighs as I wipe them dry with my hand.

"At least it won't kill me, not like that." I counter, nodding to his congealed lunch, although the chips do smell amazing. Aidan grunts but not harshly and I can see he's amused as he tucks into the burger, a smile dancing on his lips. I pick at my salad and we eat in silence for the next thirty seconds. "I didn't think you'd show up." I blurt out, spearing a prawn. I'm stalling for time. Aidan finishes chewing and eyes me carefully as I take another forkful of salad.

"Do you wish I hadn't?" he teases and looks at me with those blue eyes. Oh, those deep blue eyes, rimmed with long blond lashes. I could step into those cold blue pools and lose myself forever.

"No. Far from it," I lick the sticky, spicy dressing from my upper lip, lingering a little longer than strictly necessary. Aidan inhales a little too sharply. "Aidan I want to fuck you and I think you want to fuck me too."

There. I've said it.

He's shocked; there are no two ways about it. I don't know what he was expecting but it wasn't that. My heart is hammering inside my chest and I'm a lot calmer on the outside than I am inside. He puts the burger down on the bag, still looking at me. I can't possibly predict what he's going to say next but I'm preparing to look like a complete twat.

"Do you now?" he asks, amused. He's regained his composure quickly but I still don't know which way this is going. There's a long silence during which we look at each other, waiting. "Yes, okay. I wanna fuck you," he finally states, with a level of arrogance that equals my own.

Oh God, oh God.

HE. WANTS. ME. TOO.

This might actually happen. I feel quite dizzy and my mouth has gone dry.

"But it's complicated," he warns, "I'm seeing someone."

What the fuck? Oh. I wasn't expecting that.

"Since when? You've never mentioned going out with anyone?" I'm shocked. Of course he refuses to tell me anything about her. "Well how long have you been with her? What's her name?"

"I told you, I keep business and pleasure completely separate." he says aloofly.

I might be wrong, but I think fucking me is probably going to seriously compromise that ethic.

"So how's this actually going to work?" Now I've put it out there I'm curious where we go from here. I mean, telling Aidan was one thing, and finding out he feels the same way is a bonus, but if I don't actually get to take this man to bed sometime soon, then what's the point?

The thought frustrates me and I want to push him for something more concrete. He eats the last bit of his burger, lets me finish his chips and getting up, brushes himself down – I could help him out there, I know exactly where my hands would go.

"We'll sort something out," he insists, like I've arranged for him to come and tile my bathroom. He's brushing me off now, pushing me away again. For a few short seconds back there I had the upper hand. Then we were equals. Sitting together, sharing something intimate and personal, it was like he'd opened up to me, and shown me his cards. Like I got to see the real Aidan, the one he leaves at the office door every day. But that's gone now and he's not willing to share anything else today. "I'll go back first," he instructs. "Give it ten minutes then come back." He walks away, leaving me frustrated, annoyed, elated, aroused, and confused, all at the same time.

Why are nearly all parish councillors over 60? I know that older or retired people have a bit more time on their hands, but attending council meetings is like visiting an old people's home, except, I bet in a home they stay up longer and have more fun than the councillors do. My girlfriends joke that when I'm old enough to be in a home, I'll be forever pulling the emergency cord and waiting, inappropriately dressed, lying prone on the floor, for some fit young orderly to come and help me. They reckon I'll try to pounce on a defenceless twenty-two year old lad at least once a day until I'm asked to leave by the outraged management and my embarrassed children.

It's almost 10pm and the local borough council meeting is showing no sign of ending anytime soon. The large, hexagonal room is packed with county councillors and concerned local residents, members of the relevant parish council, the press and a neighbourhood watch representative, all jammed into the viewing gallery along the edges of the room. In the middle are concentric rows of wooden benches like you might find in a modern church, equipped with lights and microphones – it looks like a miniature version of Strasbourg's European Parliament. The borough planning committee members have been debating the pros and cons of the development for hours and I'm struggling to keep focus.

I smother another yawn.

Normally I'd have tonight's meeting in the bag, boring as it is, but my mind keeps wandering back to my lunchtime liaison.

It's really thrown me, Aidan revealing this other half – some mad wife in the attic, perhaps – that I'd had no idea about. Not that I should be surprised. I don't really know anything much about the gorgeous man's private life, although I've spent many a fun hour thinking about him in the confines of my bedroom.

Grinning to myself at the filthy thought, I catch the eye of lecherous old Councillor Hopkins and quickly look away.

A girlfriend. That could really put a spanner in the works regarding the extra-curricular activities I had planned for the two of us. Although... he was insistent that they were only 'seeing' each other, whatever that means.

After I'd got back to work this afternoon, I kept my head down, tapping on the keyboard. I limited myself to glancing through my lashes every five minutes, taking tiny peeks at Aidan who was buried in his work. It felt as if lunchtime hadn't even happened. Did I hallucinate the entire thing? What if he doesn't mention it again? I'm not sure that I want to go through the agony of raising the subject a second time.

Anyway, I'm going to look like a right sad case if I seem too needy. Like I've got nothing better to do than pester my colleague for a hook up.

I force my attention back to the room and the matter in hand. Geoffrey Reeves, ward councillor for the proposed housing development is recommending a vote to reject the application on the basis that the traffic implications had not been thought through sufficiently. Councillor Reeves, a burly, shaven–headed, former fire fighter with old Navy tattoos and a penchant for brown suede tassel-topped loafers, had indicated, off the record, that he was staunchly against the developers plans. While he couldn't openly support residents without the risk of jeopardising his place on the planning committee, he's spoken up this evening in favour of the locals, backing their claims that the new road would destroy their community.

Greenline, the developers, held a charade of a public consultation more than a year ago, where they claimed to be sympathetic to public emotion, and vowed to take local views into account. Despite this, they appear to have ridden roughshod over the feelings of locals and parish councillors and ploughed ahead with their application. The vocal councillor has ridiculed the statistics listed in Greenline's supporting documentation regarding projected traffic movements. I think he's about to sway the committee's decision towards refusing the proposal.

"Alright, Councillor Reeves, that's enough talking thank you, let's just go to the vote. Everyone's made their point and we're just repeating ourselves now," orders Councillor Norris Hanworthy, the stuffy, no-nonsense committee chair, puffing himself up. "All those in favour of Cllr. Reeves' motion please raise your hands." A quick headcount. "And against?"

A murmur ripples around the bystanders in the room like a Mexican wave, while Cllr. Reeves scribbles in his notepad, confers for a moment with the birdlike, beady-eyed clerk, and announces: "Twelve councillors voted in favour of the proposal to reject and one against, so that proposal is unanimously carried. The committee rejects the application."

A huge roar goes up from the residents and parish councillors slap each other on the back, congratulating each other in undisguised glee. Councillor Reeves winks at me across the room and I gather my things together, heading outside to interview the spokesperson for the local residents association.

Barry Chapman, the parish councillor who rang me this morning, heads me off at the stairwell and starts pumping my hand up and down.

"We did it Katherine, we did it!" he chants, delighted at the win. He is an overbearing, sweaty man who tries to move in for a hug but I see it coming and step backwards, pulling my giant tote bag between us for defence. "Thanks for all your support," he gushes, "we really appreciate all the coverage that the paper's given us."

I brush off his gratitude – I appreciate all the headlines the story has given me and it is, after all, what we journalists do – but I register a glow of pride deep inside and realise that I do still get a small, but notable sense of satisfaction from helping people. Yes, journalism still turns me on, but I need some bigger issues to get my teeth into.

I hang around for twenty-five minutes getting quotes from the key players in the story. Some homeowners, the neighbourhood watch guy, and Cllr Reeves all clamour to talk to me before heading to the Horse and Hound to sink a few before last orders. I could do with a drink too but decide that one probably won't be enough after the day I've had, and I have to drive, so I call it a day and head home.

It's gone 11pm by the time I get in and I'm shattered, so after pouring a large glass of Sauvignon Blanc, I pull on a little red vest and pant set and climb into bed to drink it.

I make myself a nest of pillows and cushions and curl up inside, sipping at the ice-cold liquid. It's been a very funny day. I want to feel pleased with myself, but the brief moment of elation I experienced at lunchtime has been replaced with dark clouds of confusion and I'm not sure what to do next.

Aidan's an attractive man and I know what I want to do with him, but it's not yet clear to me yet what I want or expect from him.

Mmm, this wine tastes good.

If he is seeing someone but she isn't his girlfriend then it's okay to get involved with him, right? I mean, maybe they're having an open relationship and she sees other people too… but if he's saying it's tricky because he's with someone, she must mean something to him, otherwise why did he tell me about her? He could have said nothing.

It infers he wants 'us' – if there is going to be an 'us' –to remain a secret, and that means I probably shouldn't even get involved… but that means not screwing him, and that's something I don't want to contemplate.

Oh God, this is too confusing.

It's late and the wine has made me drowsy. I need to put it out of my mind for now and sleep. Finishing the glass, I switch off the light and promise myself I'll clean my teeth for twice as long in the morning. I'm asleep within seconds and endure a fitful dream of angry residents waving billboards and irate girlfriends banging on the door

Three

The following morning, I have one arm out of my jacket and half a slice of toast and marmite between my teeth when Pete perches on the edge of the desk and informs me that I need to get over to Kingston Magistrates' Court to replace Anna, who's called in sick.

Twenty-three year old Chelsea striker, Robbie Dixon, is up on a speeding charge, although he's expected to get off lightly, as has been the trend for cocky, super-rich, egotistical footballers recently. It will make a great story for the Surbiton edition, regardless of the outcome. I grab my keys off the desk and head for the door.

"Oh, and Miss Cleaver, we're expecting a large turn-out of anti-speeding protesters down at the court, especially after that child got killed on the same road last year. They've been campaigning for a reduced speed limit down there for two years and this court case is bound to bring them out in force. It could get a bit heated.

"I'm sending Aidan down there with you. I've called him and he's waiting in the car – you can get a lift. He's parked in the bus lane downstairs. Chop chop."

WHAT?!

I stand like a rabbit in the headlights, toast halfway to my lips, mouth ajar, completely shell-shocked. We never go anywhere in pairs and now today of all days Pete is sending us out... together! In the same car?

"Come on Kate, don't just stand there! What're you waiting for?" He shakes his head and shoos me off with a rolled up copy of *The Mirror*.

I scurry away, first dropping my keys, then my mobile and finally, clutching my belongings, jump in the lift (why do I always drop things when I'm flustered?). I lean my clammy forehead against the cool mirrored walls and catch sight of my reflection. My dark brown hair, streaked with blond, has come loose and is scrunched up against the glass. Some of it's stuck to my forehead. I look stunned and terrified all at the same time and I'm furious that this has thrown me so much.

Pull yourself together Kate, for God's sake! I wrestle the rest of my hair free from the topknot and quickly tie it back up. I am so pathetic it's infuriating.

Right, let's do this.

I sashay out of the automatic doors in my cream strappy wedges and walk the fifty metres to Aidan's black VW Golf GTi, jumping in just as the number 34 comes round the corner. He pulls away before I even put my seat belt on and for a minute neither of us speaks. The silence is deafening. It's closing in from all directions and I feel like I'm being crushed.

"Is this going to get weird?" I blurt out, staring out of the passenger window. I don't want to look at him. We've never sat this close before. Knowing that if I reach out I can touch him is doing strange things to my insides and sitting inside such a small, confined space isn't helping. Opening the window without asking, I take huge gulps of warm air into my lungs like I'd just surfaced from deep water. Despite the Mediterranean temperatures outside – it's just gone 9am and it's already twenty degrees – the air on my face feels good and revives me.

"Don't talk shit, we've got a job to do so let's do it," Aidan doesn't take his eyes off the road. Looking at him now, I take in his navy suit, lilac shirt and pale blue tie, lightly tanned hands firmly on the wheel. I decide to take his lead and pretend yesterday didn't happen.

Aidan hates small talk so I keep the conversation to a minimum, about the court case and the footballer. He can recite the guy's credentials to date and explains who might be there from his management to prevent us getting a quote.

We leave the car in the multi-storey adjoining the court and head into the modern, glass-fronted building housing the magistrates' court. We have to push past television cameras and reporters stationed outside. Three courtrooms lead off from the airy mezzanine level foyer, naturally lit by vast lantern skylights. The cases are pinned up on noticeboards outside each one.

I find Dixon's case and we file into the relevant courtroom with the other press, and some curious members of the public who have been waiting excitedly outside the magistrates' court until it opened. The case is scheduled first, no doubt to rid the building of the amassing media circus. Madness has overcome all and sundry and there's a hum of expectation.

Even the normally dowdy court clerk has stepped up her make-up. She's wearing a dubious shade of bright purple lipstick I've never seen on her before, and quite frankly it makes her look like one of the undead.

Not being a footy fan, I'd had to google Dixon and I was pleasantly surprised by his appearance. Even so, when the man walks into court with his brief and no management I'm taken aback by how good looking he is in the flesh.

At about six foot two, with closely cropped hair and skin the colour of milky coffee, he has the most beautiful bone structure and striking green eyes. As he steps into the dock I can't take mine off him.

Rumour has it he's been asked to front the new Davidoff campaign, and I can see why. For a few seconds I even forget Aidan's sat next to me. I must have glazed over because I jump suddenly as he jabs me in the ribs with a sharp elbow. He hisses at me to concentrate and doesn't look amused at my new-found attraction.

Whooooo! I think my interest in the footballer might have actually pissed him off. Maybe he's more into me than he's been letting on. *Interesting.* I let the thought dance around my mind for a few seconds before backing it into a corner and focussing on the case.

The procedure's standard. All criminal cases start in a magistrates' court and more than ninety per cent of cases will be resolved there. The more serious offences are passed on to the Crown Court, either for sentencing after the defendant has been found guilty in a magistrates' court, or for full trial with a judge and jury. The court clerk reads out Dixon's name and address and he confirms it, then he's asked how he pleads to the charge that he was caught on a speed gun doing 77mph in a 50 zone on the A308 between Hampton and Sunbury in November last year.

"Guilty." He states calmly, looking directly at the grey haired, bespectacled chairman sat between his two colleagues on the bench. There are usually three magistrates and I think these three have a collective age of over 200. One is an Asian man in a navy turban, easily in his early eighties and the third, a po-faced elderly woman with silver helmet hair and a sober blue and cream scarf wrapped around her throat, presumably to conceal a turkey neck.

The prosecution lawyer sets out his stall, efficiently relaying the facts to the court before calling the police witness who backs up the accusation with his version of events. Throughout this the footballer keeps his head bowed, staring at his hands; bet he wished he'd kept his eye on his luxury Bentley's speedo now. Super-rich players these days appear to live above the law and when they're hauled up in court it comes as an unwelcome reminder that they're just spoilt, glorified schoolboys having a kick about for a ridiculously inflated salary, and they're no better than the rest of us.

This isn't a trial and Dixon's admitted guilt so there's a strong chance that he'll lose his licence, considering the excessive speed and especially as it's not his first offence. However that would clearly be an undesirable outcome for a Premier League footballer, and he's evidently paying his solicitor huge bucks to ensure that doesn't happen. The defence lawyer concedes that his client has committed a serious speeding offence but urges the bench to consider points rather than a ban, as Dixon needs to drive regularly to see his children who live with his former partner in Manchester.

Mitigating, he tells the court that travelling on public transport would be impractical for someone of Dixon's status and that more points on his licence would act as an incentive to drive within the law, because any further offence inside three years would mean an accumulation of 12 points and a 12-month ban.

"He has," he intones seriously, "made a herculean effort since this offence to comply with the speed limits, using his cruise control whenever possible. Having had a driving licence since he was 17, he is bitterly disappointed by this latest misdemeanour."

The three magistrates confer for a few minutes, whispering to each other, glancing from time to time at the dock. I know what's about to happen before it does. The usher orders Dixon to stand and the chairman speaks: "The defendant has admitted guilt and we have listened to all the evidence presented today.

"Mr Dixon we know that you were just two miles over the ACPO guidelines when you were caught speeding. Taking into account the impossible circumstances you'll face if we ban you from driving today we have decided to fine you £500 and you must pay £90 court costs and a £50 surcharge. You will also receive six points on your licence."

Robbie Dixon sombrely nods his head at the bench, then flashes a megawatt smile at his solicitor and looks relieved, but there is a chorus of disapproval from the public gallery and someone shouts, "It's a disgrace!"

Things are going to kick off with the road safety campaigners and Aidan scoots out of the court to get the first reactions as the public file out, but I make a beeline for Robbie Dixon as he leaves the dock. Up close his beauty is even more intimidating and I have to force myself to find my voice.

"Mr Dixon, Kate Cleaver from *The Staines and Egham Express*. Mr Dixon, you must be relieved you didn't lose your licence." He looks down at me through his thick eyelashes, clearly glad the proceedings are over, and seems to be about to speak. That is until his weasel-faced lawyer needles his way between us and ushers his client away throwing, 'No comment' at me and four other journalists from *The Surrey Comet*, *The Kingston Guardian*, as well as *The Mirror* and, *The Sun*.

I guess I'm not surprised; they never let you talk to famous clients. To get a word out of someone in the public eye you need to catch them on their own, without a Jack Russell from legal or management snapping at your ankles. Just as he leaves the courtroom, Dixon turns and winks at me.

Whoa! Cheeky sod!

Sarah, *The Comet* reporter, catches my eye. "I would," she says saucily.

"So would I," I laugh back at her. She's alright, Sarah. We often bump into each other over here or at the Coroners' Court next door. Not like that serious, toffee-nosed cow from *The Guardian*, Janice, who never hangs around for a chat after a job and wears tan tights like my mum used to in the eighties! Even now she's looking down her ugly hooked nose at me.

I find Aidan outside taking notes as one of the campaigners, a bookish looking man in a suit, brandishes a huge placard and drones into Aidan's ear: "...huge infringement by someone who clearly had no regard for other road users."

A small crowd, waving posters and photographs of the young lad who had been killed by a speeding motorist a month before Dixon was caught, has followed the footballer to his solicitor's black Range Rover. They're shouting at him as he climbs in beside the driver. Cameramen film the protesters and the player, whilst journalists fire questions at him before he closes the door on them. He's left the Bentley at home in case he got disqualified. Smart move. That and the fact he might've had no hubcaps left if this crowd are anything to go by. The ignition starts and behind the blacked out windows Dixon is driven away, no doubt to celebrate his lucky escape. The mob disintegrates and I interview the mum of the dead boy for her reaction to the verdict. Needless to say she's outraged and I get some good sound bites. I meet Aiden back at the car once he's finished up.

"How'd you get on?"

"Fine," he says, unlocking the door and taking off his jacket, before throwing it in the back seat with his bag.

Will I end up in that seat one day?

The traffic starts to build up as we approach Hampton, but unusually doesn't clear after the lights. I check my phone and the queue runs all the way to the M3.

"Take a left here." I say quickly, "We'll go back on the smaller roads via Sunbury, Shepperton and Chertsey."

We head along the road by the river and Aidan tells me about the quotes he got. We end up bickering amiably about footballers and the outrageous money they get paid. Aidan thinks it's justifiable – they are near demi-gods in his view – whereas I think they're just egotistical tossers with delusional self-belief. He seems to enjoy the banter; he's a good laugh when he lets himself go a bit.

"Why do you never come out for a drink after work?"

"It's not my thing," he bristles. "I've got mates already, I don't need them at work too."

Well that tells me! Is that why he accepted my frank proposal? If I'd invited him out for a drink or dinner would he have said no? I'm pretty sure of it. Just fucking me offers him a commitment-free, purely sexual relationship without compromising his, 'no friends from work, already seeing someone else' existence.

We're approaching Chertsey.

"Turn left here," I say.

"Why? The office is right."

I look straight ahead, motionless except for my right hand, which I place lightly on his left thigh, my fingers curling around the muscle and I squeeze gently. It's barely perceptible. He follows my direction.

"Now turn right and then take the second right at the roundabout." My voice is calm but thick with desire and I snatch a quick glance at Aidan's face. The faint trace of a smile plays around his lips and he's driving without arguing.

He pulls into a small close and I direct him to a car park space in front of a three-storey mid terraced house, removing my hand as he switches off the engine and looks at me for the first time.

"This is where I live. Coffee?"

"Kate, we need to get back," he warns but he's still smiling, "Pete will be on the warpath."

"Just text him and tell him the traffic's bad. He won't even know what time the case finished. We've got time for a coffee." I plead. Without saying a word Aidan removes the keys from the ignition and takes his seatbelt off.

I unlock the front door and go straight up to the kitchen on the first floor, turning on the kettle and rattling around in the cupboard for mugs and the coffee. There are no teaspoons in the drawer so I fish around in the dirty crockery piled in the sink and rinse one off. God I live with some dirty bastards.

Apart from Alfie, who is an 18-year-old barman, I share the house with 26-year-old Jasper, an accounts manager who has the room next to mine, and Smithy, a labourer whose bedroom is next to the utility room on the ground floor. Being the lone female, I think they imagine I'll eventually tire of the mess and take on the household chores. Not a chance in hell. I wasn't put on this earth to scrub floors and wash dishes.

Aidan wanders through the living room and looks out of the window to the primary school playground that backs on to the garden. The kids are running around and screaming like banshees.

"How do you take it?"

"Milk and sugar." he drawls, "How do you take it?"

Holy shit. My heart beats that little bit faster. Saying nothing, I hand him the cup and our fingers brush together. Tiny sparks of electricity are shooting through my head and stirring something primal in the pit of my stomach.

"Come on, I'll show you around."

Holding tight to the mug, I lead the way up the second flight of stairs towards the bathroom and bedrooms. I open the door to my room. Inside, the late morning sun floods in through the open window and the blue cotton curtains blow gently in the summer breeze. My room is larger than the other three, but I figure I pay for it so why not enjoy it.

The double bed is in the centre of the room, dressed in a brilliant white cotton duvet and scattered with jewel-coloured cushions in assorted shapes and sizes. To the right, near the wall-length window is my white wooden dressing table. Its surface is cluttered. An array of perfume bottles, brushes, and lotions jostle for space alongside jewellery, hair accessories and a cacophony of other essentials.

I have an easel near the window on the other wall, complete with one of my paintings, plus a large vintage chaise-longue in lime green, strewn with jumpers, yoga pants, knickers (oh crap) and a lilac cashmere throw. On the other side of the bed, opposite the window, is the biggest wardrobe I could find that would fit into the space. Taking up the whole of the left hand wall, it was second hand and battered when I got it, but I spent an entire week rubbing it down and distressing it to suit the feel of the room.

I sit down on the far side of the bed still sipping my coffee and watch Aidan. He wanders around looking at my things, stopping and picking up an earring, running his hand along the velvety arm of the chaise longue, studying the painting.

"You have an interesting room, Kate," he seems, surprised. "I mean the house is… bland," he shrugs, "but this room is…

well, it's very you. As if you've brought it to life somehow, kind of, lit it up from inside."

I laugh. I can't help it. That was unexpectedly, poetic?

"It's just my space. I like things to mean something."

Am I still talking about the room?

"Why don't you sit down?" I put my coffee on the bedside table – a vintage wooden fruit storage crate upended on its side and converted into drawers – and gesture towards the bed. Aidan hesitates, glances across at the chaise longue cluttered with my things, then sits down next to me on the duvet.

I take his cup. His fingers, long and cold, meet mine and tiny currents like sharp metal filaments filter through my blood, racing round my body. Despite the heat, I'm shivering and a hard ball has screwed itself up tightly in my stomach. Steadily, slowly, I lean in towards him, not taking my eyes from his. I place one hand on the bed between his knees, the other, fingertips resting on the cool cotton cover, and inch my way forward, stopping just short of his face. My mouth is level with his.

His breath is coming faster now, in short, shallow bursts. His lips have fallen slightly open, and his bottom lip is pink and shining, wet in the middle. I can sense the rise and fall of his chest just centimetres from mine and feel my nipples harden as if they've been capped with ice. His impossibly blue eyes hold my gaze. We're both motionless and time falls still.

A fraction of an inch at a time, I press my lips into his. They're soft and give under my pressure. Chaste for a split second, we stay like this, savouring the sensation of skin on skin. Then I run my tongue over his teeth and he lets me in, returning his tongue in my mouth, licking, sucking, and biting. Oh, he kisses just like I hoped he would, it's intoxicating. He pulls me in, draws me onto his lap, eases my legs apart. I'm sitting astride him now, the skirt of my pale blue shift riding up high. Any pretence of modesty was lost earlier in the car when I slid my hand between his legs.

Large, smooth hands roam up and over my bare thighs, then down towards the cheeks of my backside, peeking out from the risen hem of my dress. I feel him hard, beneath me. *Yes, go on, don't stop.*

We're kissing more frantically now; my mouth is fighting with his, my hands roaming over his chest, his shirt straining over his pecs. I want to own him, devour him, and make him mine. The irritating bleep of a text dashes the silence. "Ignore it," I breathe.

"Kate," he mumbles into my mouth, pulling away, "Kate, we can't, not today." He pushes me off and leans backwards, panting. "We have to get back. Stumbling towards the door, he pulls the phone from his pocket. "I need a leak… though I'd be better off with a cold shower." He looks down at the tipi beneath his zipper and a smile dances on his lips. "Just give me a couple of minutes. I think I'm going to need to sit down."

Rolling back on to the mountain of pillows behind me, laughter bubbles up. I can't resist that man. I stare at the ceiling, catching my breath. If only we could skip work and spend the afternoon in bed.

I prop myself up on one elbow and catch my reflection in the mirror; the colour in my eyes is popping and sparkling with excitement, tendrils of loose hair have tumbled free and I tuck them back up, and secure them with a clip.

Standing, I smooth my skirt back down and walk over to the door. Aidan walks back in holding the mobile, and leans against the doorframe, looking me up and down.

God he's sexy.

"It was from Pete. He said he doesn't know what the fuck we're doing but to get our arses back to the newsroom before he sacks us both."

"Come on then, what are you waiting for?" Cool as a cucumber, I place my hand against his trousers and feel for his cock, holding it for a moment. His response is immediate, "Sadly, this will have to wait." A groan escapes him as he follows me back down to the car. He's serious now.

"This goes no further Kate. No one at work knows, right?" I agree.

I don't know what the policy is for inter-staff relationships but I seriously doubt they would encourage casual knobbing between their employees.

Sitting two metres away from someone you've just snogged, groped and want to fuck while maintaining a dignified, not to mention professional, exterior is a major turn on. I've never had an illicit encounter with a work colleague before, but I can highly recommend it for brightening up what would otherwise be a dull, run-of-the-mill, uninspiring day. Aidan and I must have looked at each other every thirty seconds since we got back and I'm finding his presence both distracting and majorly stimulating at the same time.

Finally clocking off around 5.30pm, I drive to the sports centre to let off some steam with a much needed swim. Today's really messed with my head and I relish the chance of some mindless, repetitive lengths of the pool. There's something comforting about seeing the same stretch of water open out in front of you, knowing it's going to take the exact same number of strokes until I turn back round again.

Aidan and I didn't say a word to each other all afternoon, yet the lack of conversation coupled with the knowledgeable looks only fanned the flames of my desire. I can merely imagine what they were doing to him. I'm sure it's no coincidence that he didn't step away from the desk all afternoon, and when Clive asked him to join him for a fag outside it clearly pained him to have to say no. I can only hope he was able to stand up and leave after I went home, or perhaps the poor guy's still trapped at his desk with a hard on right now.

My swim over, I haul my tired body out of the pool and go to the lockers for my shower gel and towel. Taking them into a shower cubicle, I dump them on the little wire shelf and peel off my costume, enjoying the torrent of warm water that runs down my neck and over my shoulders.

What the hell am I doing?

If you play with fire you get burnt, everyone knows that. There's just something about Aidan that draws me in, like a moth to a flame. If getting burnt is part of the deal, then count me in.

I lather up the shower gel and rub it over my skin, working my way downwards until I'm smoothing it languidly between my legs. *Oh yeah, that feels...*

I've been wet since lunchtime and I'm so charged up I'm not far off cumming. There's someone in the shower next to mine, I can hear the water and swimmers are flip-flopping back and forth just inches away. Two lifeguards are the other side of the door talking about last night's England match.

The soap has made me even more slippery and it feels too good to stop. My fingers make fast little circles, working quicker now, plunging inside me, lost for a second and then back to their furious pace. I'm building up a steady rhythm, increasing speed, chasing down the pulling sensation inside me. So close I'm almost there. Bracing my legs against the sides of the wet shower trough, I lean back on the flimsy plastic wall for balance, legs apart. Reaching out my free hand, I grasp the tap for support as I cum in short, sharp waves, biting back cries of relief. My knees almost buckle beneath me but I save myself – just as well as there's a gap between the door and the floor. My heart's racing and I'm still panting silently. My legs are leaden and suddenly I can feel every one of the fifty lengths I just swam.

Instead of feeling good like I usually do after tossing off, I feel, I don't know. Dissatisfied? Frustrated, even. A sensation I never experience post-orgasm! What the fuck is going on?

Bringing myself off usually relaxes me, leaves me feeling fulfilled. It helps me sleep and even makes me feel better if

I'm not well. Christ, they should prescribe it on the NHS. But tonight I feel hollow. Why?

'Because you'd rather have been fucking Aidan,' screams the voice in my head, like I'm stupid.

Oh go away - I'm too tired to do this tonight.

Blocking out the internal noise, I let myself into the house and go and open a can of tomato and chilli soup. I've no appetite for real food despite the energy I've burned this evening, and even though the heat of the day lingers I need something warm and comforting. Sometimes salad just doesn't cut it.

Jasper's watching Property Ladder in the living room, but I'm in no mood to make small talk. Smiling hello, I take the dish up to my room and kick off my Converse trainers.

Snuggling up on the chaise longue, I pull my legs up and wrap the throw around me, balancing the soup on my knees.

The trees between the school and the garden are almost golden in the evening light and leaves gently dance in the breeze. I love my tranquil haven.

As I blow on the soup, I replay the events of the day. It seems strange Aidan was here, in this room, just a few hours ago. The duvet is still crumpled where we made out. The thought gives me goosebumps and I sink lower under the cosy blanket, comforted and protected from... I don't know what. Aidan? His girlfriend? My own feelings? Something stirs inside that promises more than just a quick bunk-up, but I don't trust my own judgement right now.

Love? Am I looking for love? I don't think so, at least not with him. My last long relationship ended just over a year ago, and really messed with my head. Rob and I had met at university and we'd been friends for a long time before I made the first move during a movie night at his house, four months before we graduated. Having spent three years away from home enjoying no strings sex with casual flings and one-night stands, I suddenly fell head over heels in love. Rather than continue to shy away from commitment, I threw myself headlong into the relationship. So when it ended acrimoniously in March last year, I was devastated. I was so in love with Rob I'd had thoughts of marriage and kids in my head, even if it that was a long way off. He'd had different ideas though and without mentioning anything, applied to teach sailing to kids in France, leaving behind a secure job at a design company.

"I just want to do something else with my life, to travel and meet people before I settle down." he'd pleaded, as I'd sobbed uncontrollably on his bed. "It's not that I don't love you. I do. But this is too much at the wrong time. I never planned to fall in love while I was at uni. I've always wanted to work abroad while I'm young, but I didn't want to leave you. So I took the job and thought I could make it work." He'd dropped his gaze, looked down at his lap. "But I can't. I need to do this now Kate, before I start resenting you for holding me back."

He said I could go with him and find work, just chuck in the job and go, but I refused. It wasn't part of the plan. Not if I wanted to keep moving up the career ladder, and that wasn't going to happen if I turned my back on the only paper in a year to offer me a job. Besides, I knew it wouldn't work and he'd finish it with me anyway. So we split up, and I'd spent two weeks crying in private and putting on a brave face in public. Sometimes it would get too much at work and I'd hide in the ladies' loo, crying silently in the cubicle, and then spending twice as long repairing my face.

That was how I got to know Gemma. She came in one day when I was looking blotchy and without asking what was wrong, put her arms around me and gave me a huge hug. Of course that had set me off again, but it was nice having someone, another woman, to confide in. Since starting the job I'd spent all my free time with Rob, who had gone back home after uni and lived twenty-five minutes away in Windsor.

My best mate, Stella, was working for a computer giant up in Manchester, meaning we only got to see each other a few times a year and I've always had more male friends than female anyway – 'friends with benefits', Stella says. That afternoon, Gemma had dragged me down the pub after work and we'd got absolutely slaughtered, cementing the start of a valued and long-lasting friendship.

With time, the pain had lessened and I'd started socialising with Gemma and her friends, hooking up occasionally with men, like Mark, who I met at a party or a club.

For a few months before he'd gone away, Rob and I had still got together too, for booty calls. That was a mistake.

No matter what anyone ever says, sex with your ex never works, especially if one of you (me) is still in love with the other one. I was deluding myself that it was no-strings screwing and that it was fine by me. It wasn't though, and I was relieved when he left for Europe last summer so I could put all thoughts of him to the back of my mind.

Thinking about Stella reminds me I haven't spoken to her this week. Laying the empty bowl on the floor, I pick up my mobile and speed-dial her. After the third ring she picks up, breathless:

"Ah, yeah, hi."

"Hi babe, bad timing?"

"No, it's fine, I just got back. I ran home from work. God, it's hot out there."

"Even in Manchester?"

"Ha ha, no it's snowing. Yes, even up here! Come and find out. At least you won't have to sleep with your hat on like you did on your birthday!" We both laugh.

When I was up there in March it was particularly cold and despite wearing two layers of thick pyjamas and a winter duvet over the airbed I still missed the warmth of my comfy double, so I grabbed my woolly hat and gloves and Stella found me in the morning tucked up like an Eskimo.

"Do you want to grab a drink, or a shower? I can call you back?"

"Mm, no, I've got a bottle here, straight out the fridge. Mmm, hang on, oh that's better." she guzzles, sighing. "Uh, I'm gonna lie down on the grass and cool off. So tell me, how was Gem's party? Did you pull?"

The woman's incorrigible! No 'how are you's?', or 'how's work?', just 'dish the dirt and spill ya dirty secrets!' I give her a blow-by-blow account of the weekend, keeping it brief about work and telling her everything about Mark - no skimping on the finer details. We've been like this since we met at sixth form and Stella even went to university near me – I was at Bath, she was at Bristol. Nothing's sacred or off limits when it comes to her.

"Sounds like a good way to spend the weekend hon'," she declares, " ...and Aidan? What are you not telling me about that hunk of spunk in the office you fancy?"

How does she do it? It's like she was born with sixth sense. I was going to spill anyway. But how does she sniff these things out without me saying a word?

"Things have, um, progressed in that department, shall we say."

"Over the weekend too? Wow, you've been a busy girl!" Stella's impressed.

"No, not then."

I relay all the facts from the last couple of days. It seems so trivial compared to what happened with Mark. I mean, effectively Aidan and I had a conversation and kissed. That's it. Yet it feels so much more significant.

'It's because you want it more', whispers my sub-conscious.

"It means a lot to you, doesn't it?" Stella says, softly, "It's because you want it more." I smile. She really does know me, this girl. Better than I know myself sometimes, I think.

"I miss you Stel." I don't need to tell her she's right, she already knows.

"Me too, babe."

"So how's Mikey?" Stella's been going out with Mike for the last 18 months. He's a sports physiotherapist from Salford and they met through his sister, who works with Stella. His opening line to her was, "You should let me get you on my couch and work out some of that stress." I'd nearly pissed myself laughing when she told me. I can't believe she fell for it.

"I made him work for it afterwards though." she'd said at the time. He's alright, Mike. He's a good laugh, works hard and treats Stella like a princess. Plus she's crazy about him. I've got a good feeling about the pair of them and I think they'll go the distance.

"He's good. He's just applied for a position with Chelsea, so we might end up down your way if things go well. If he gets it, I'll put in for a transfer and we'll look for a place in town. We've been talking about moving in together for a few months, but we might as well hold fire until we know about this job." She's happy and there's a ring of pride to her voice. "Stella that would be great, oh my God it would be so nice to have you closer again," I feel unexpectedly emotional. "If you come back down it'll be like the old days. I'm taking you both out to dinner the moment you're back."

"Hold your horses," she laughs, "he's not got it yet. I'll keep you posted, okay? Listen babes, sorry to cut you short but I need to grab that shower now as I'm meeting Mike in half an hour. We'll talk soon, right?"

"Yeah you go, give the big man a hug and a kiss from me."

"Okay, but nothing else, I know how your kisses end up, you filthy wench." I can hear her grinning, "Love you Kate."

"Love you too." I hang up, smiling at her cheek.

It would be great if she did move down. A vision of the three of us, plus Aidan, sitting in a London bar, laughing and drinking cocktails pops into my head. I shut it out immediately.

Jesus, what am I, fixated?

Like he'd ever drink a cocktail anyway.

I'm hot now.

Throwing back the blanket, I pick up the bowl and pad back down to the kitchen, passing Smithy and Alfie who are watching a rerun of last week's Gogglebox.

Jasper has disappeared, probably to his room, but he could be out robbing a bank for all I know. He's polite and sometimes passes the time of day over a bowl of cereal, but I know absolutely nothing about the guy. Not that I'm bothered. I wash my things under a running tap, the mess still occupying the sink and most of the draining board.

"Guys, I'd really appreciate you washing up your stuff after you've used it!" I call out. Smithy grunts and Alfie shouts out, "Yeah, Doll, sure thing." but I think there's probably more chance of me winning the lottery than it actually happening. I take a pot of pre-chopped mango out of the fridge – thankfully it comes with it's own plastic fork - and fill a pint glass with water and some ice. "Seriously lads, it's a fucking pigsty in there," I say walking back through the lounge. "I don't want to become the house nag, but it's really not pleasant." "Yeah, sure." Still staring at the screen.

"I'll tell you what, you do it, or I'll tell the landlord you're dealing drugs, and you've decided to get a dog," I say pointing at Smithy and Alfie in turn. Smiling sweetly I head back upstairs and I can hear a low drone from the sofa. I won't, not for one minute - and I think they know that - but I'm guessing they won't take the chance. The kitchen will be sorted by tomorrow.

Flopping on the bed, I switch on the TV and force my brain to switch off. I need to watch some mindless shit to take my mind off things, so I put on a hospital drama and flick through a magazine until it's too dark to see the words. It's still early but the weekend's catching up with me and I could do with the extra sleep.

I need the bathroom before bed and while brushing my teeth I look at myself in the mirror. I have mascara smudged under my left eye and dark circles forming. I look tired. Stressing out doesn't suit me. Despite what they say, it really doesn't pay to wait and I'm not going to hanging around any longer.

I spit in the sink and look back at myself, 'Just you wait Mr Tindall. Tomorrow you're not going to know what's hit you.'

Four

"Aidan's sick. He's not coming in. Probably caught it off me," Anna snuffles, blowing her nose and shoving a cough sweet in her mouth. "Well, he says it's a cold but it's bound to be man-flu and he'll be off for a week knowing him!" she garbles through the sweet, "Look at me, one day in bed and I'm back fighting fit!"

With that she sneezes violently and wipes her nose with her sleeve. Ew! What was wrong with that tissue she had seconds ago?

"I felt like shit yesterday morning but spent the day in bed and drank whisky, lemon and honey toddies and I feel fine now." Anna sneezes again, this time spraying her desk with a fine mist of spittle, "Well, almost fine, anyway." I cringe inwardly and pull a bottle of antibacterial gel out of the drawer, rubbing it all liberally over my hands, wrists and up to my elbows, dabbing some on my nostrils for good measure.

So once again my plans have been foiled. Thoughts of seducing Aidan will have to be put on hold for now. The paper is out today and that means I have to get started on the next edition. I realised pretty quickly in this job that big stories

69

don't happen very often and it's not always easy to find three pages of news each week. Our main weekly is *The Staines and Egham Express*, but the regional editions each have their own front cover and pages one and two of local news plus the little community stories that fill the 'What's On' section. The remainder of the content is the same across the board.

As chief reporter, Aidan covers Staines and Egham, Anna is the Surbiton reporter, Yvonne is the Sunbury and Walton journalist, and I do Chertsey and Weybridge, hence the reason I found a house share over that way. I thought I might as well live in my patch and get to know the area a bit better. Plus it's nice to nip home and put the washing out on a sunny day, make yourself a coffee and occasionally get your leg over with your ex on company time while you're officially out on your patch sniffing out scoops (oh yes, I did!).

I skim through a parish council planning meeting agenda for tomorrow night, looking for any controversial proposals and mark up an application to build a large five bedroom house on the current site of a small bungalow. I know the road and it won't go down well with the neighbours. Could provide a few paragraphs, at least.

The rest of the day drags on, and I shoot out to my patch after lunch calling in at the local police and fire stations, council offices, shops, cafes and community centres. Catching up with the locals for a coffee and a chat is the best way to keep my ear to the ground and hear of anything that might make good copy. Plus it's a good way to fill the 'What's On' columns with scheduled car boots, jumble sales, charity auctions and bungee jumps, plays, sporting events, dog shows, musical productions and every other community activity you could think of. This is how I spend most of my days, talking to people on the phone or face to face, reporting for an article then writing it up back in the office. It's the real reason I went into journalism; I didn't have a burning ambition to make a difference, but I'd known I wanted a career to get me out into the world meeting people and I loved to write so it seemed like a natural choice.

In my careers meetings at school I'd been adamant that I hated the idea of a desk job, doing the same, repetitive tasks every day. What could be better than leaving the office, when the rest of the working world is trapped behind a desk, especially on a beautiful, warm summer's day like today. It feels like such a perk. Even on a cold, crisp day in the middle of winter it's good to get out. I remember driving out to Kempton Park Racecourse last January and taking scenic photographs of the great expanses of fresh snowfall.

Maybe it's just me, needing to get out and take some deep lungfuls of air that haven't circulated through twenty other people, then been churned through the air conditioning. Sometimes on a Sunday if I've slept late and it reaches 4pm without me leaving the house, I'll suddenly feel as if the walls are closing in and I have to get outside or I'll go crazy. Yes, it's definitely in me to escape. I think I must have been a traveller or a pioneer in a previous life.

By Friday I'm expecting Aidan to be off until after the weekend, so I'm taken aback when I come into the office after a breakfast meeting to see him sitting on the edge of the newsdesk, talking to Pete. He catches my eye as I saunter past but carries on his conversation, seemingly cool and collected. I'm anything but, and instantaneously feel heat pricking at my cheeks. The air of confidence I feel in every other part of my life; the self-belief I project when I'm doing my job; the control I exhibit in the bedroom, it all evaporates the minute I'm in his presence and I find this lack of self-control infuriating.

I can still feel the way his tongue caressed mine, and the touch of his firm hands around the naked skin of my thighs.

I have to push the images away and force my attention back to the jobs I have scheduled for today. Mainly writing up the events of last night's meeting and this morning's interview with a woman trying to raise funds for her disabled nephew by doing a charity cycling trip from John O'Groats to Land's End.

But first, I need coffee.

I often stop off for a latte on the way in, but following a particularly nice breakfast this morning at a little café I know in Egham, I'm too full for milky drinks, so I head into the kitchenette to make a black coffee. I'm still staring at the powder in the bottom of the mug, making little patterns in it with a spoon, when I feel warm breath on my neck and my knees go weak.

"I nearly lost my train of thought when you walked in," Aidan voices quietly, "I thought maybe you'd got ill as well and had the day off." He's placing one hand over my backside now, cupping around my cheeks, his fingers curling underneath, towards my dark crevice. "But when you walked in, all I could think about was ripping that pretty blue dress off of you, pushing you down and fucking you, there on the floor, in front of everybody."

The hairs on the back of my neck are standing on end and the tips of my ears tingle. As quickly as he was there Aidan has stepped away again, keeping his distance in case anyone else walks into the room. I'm holding onto the work surface so hard my knuckles are white. Not trusting myself to speak or turn around, I pour water over the coffee but have to steady the kettle with both hands.

That was unexpected!

At least now I know he feels the same way I do. After seconds that linger like hours, I turn to look at him. He's flicking through the sports pages of the paper as if nothing untoward had passed.

What is he playing at?

I finally trust myself to speak: "You're feeling better then?"

"I'm not as bad as I was yesterday, or Wednesday. I was feeling fucking awful then. I still feel a bit rough."

"You shouldn't have come in," I sympathise. *'But I'm glad you did,'* I think. What I actually say is: "You should have stayed at home, tucked up in bed with a cup of Lemsip."

"I don't have any Lemsip," he croaks.

"Aw." I pout in mock sympathy, "Maybe I should have brought you some." There is a wicked glint in my eye and he looks up at me quizzically. "I need to get on," I take my coffee and go. "Can't stand here talking all day."

Games, all the time, bloody games.

The rest of the day is quiet. I pop out for lunch and lie on the grass where I met Aidan. Basking in the midday sun I delude myself that the benefit to my mental health far outweighs the damage I am doing to my skin. I daydream he might join me, but the hour passes uninterrupted and I reluctantly gather my things together and go back to work.

It's my week to leave early and Aidan's turn to cover the fêtes. I usually love going home early on a Friday, but today I'm tempted to stay here a bit longer, just the two of us. It'd be quiet, and we might get an opportunity to talk, properly, but Anna's staying too and I don't fancy her eavesdropping on us. Reluctantly, I bid a communal farewell to the office and leave, heading to the supermarket for some nice weekend treats.

I'm good with my diet all week and stick to healthy, fresh, low-carb options, but at the weekend I sometimes splurge on pizza or an Indian and indulge in something sweet; it's always chocolate. I grab a basket instead of a trolley – may as well tone my arms at the same time – and pick up a couple of fashion and celebrity magazines as something to read in bed. Then I choose a chicken and pesto pizza, some pasta salads, cherry tomatoes, a bag of rocket and two luxury bars of 85% dark chocolate, one loaded with pistachios.

I throw some Fever Tree tonics and a couple of bottles of Sauvignon Blanc in the basket, some more pre-prepared fruit, and then on a whim chuck in a family-sized bag of hand-cooked potato chips, although I'll have to run twice as far on Sunday if I eat them all.

I've run out of painkillers so I pass back through the toiletry department, picking up a new moisturiser en route, and then I see it: small and green with yellow and red printing. I bite my lip, smiling to myself.

I couldn't, could I?

It's like my fingers are on autopilot, acting on their own as I pick up the box and pop it in the basket. Then I go back to the pre-packed section and grab some sushi - the pizza will have to wait until tomorrow. I'm going to need something less bloating now.

Back home, I unpack and pour myself a weak gin and tonic with lots of fresh lime and drink it very quickly. The sushi makes a light, but satisfying meal and I'm tempted to open the wine, but it's not chilled enough and I'm planning to drive anyway so it stays in the fridge.

Running the shower to warm up the water, I brush my teeth and wipe my make up off. Then I peel off my clothes and step under the torrent of water, feeling it sluice away the dirt and grime of the day. In the middle of my stomach, just under my ribs, there is a tight ball knotting itself up, but I ignore it and run through the motions of washing my hair and body, devoting far too much attention than required for such menial tasks. Distraction is a funny thing.

I shave my legs all the way up to my hips and bum, whip them under my arms and then take great time and care doing my bikini line, all the way down between my legs, leaving my regular small landing strip and whisking away every single stray hair until the rest of me is smooth as a billiard ball. I turn to the mirror on the wall, lifting one foot up on the sink, opening my legs wide and scrutinise my appearance.

Yes, that will do very nicely. Very nicely, indeed.

A dash of serum and a blast with the hairdryer sees my hair falling in soft natural waves over my shoulders. I'm lucky with it. Thick and heavy, my hair is down past my shoulder blades and it used to be poker straight, but has developed these pretty little kinks recently that I quite like. I colour it a deep brown, with random blond streaks and it's always ridiculously shiny, even though I do nothing to look after it. I pull it back into a simple ponytail with a hairband, apply two coats of mascara and a flick of eyeliner and I'm done – the look I'm going for is casual, not overdone.

Picking my underwear carefully, I pull on a pair of denim leggings and a black fitted vest top, throwing an oversized thin cotton sweater over the top and adding a pair of flip-flops. No, it looks all wrong. Kicking the shoes off, I root around under the bed for my battered, navy leather ballerina pumps. Yes better, much better. I pick up my things off the dressing table and after slicking on some nude-tinted lip balm, take a last look at myself in the mirror. I take a deep breath and smile at my reflection, "You'll do."

Five

It takes five minutes to drive to the other side of the High Street. I pass the mini-supermarket, the petrol station, and the bakers that sell amazing croissant-doughnut hybrids filled with a different, delicious filling every Sunday (and my downfall after a heavy night's drinking).

I pull up in a little side road between Costa Coffee and Serendipity, the beauty salon where I get a full body massage twice a month. My heart is hammering in my chest now and my palms are sweating.

Christ, Kate, what are you doing?

Locking the car, I walk past three little red brick houses to a small semi-detached cottage with a green painted front door and a gravelled driveway alongside. I crunch up to the side door, past the black Golf and, taking a deep breath, knock on the white paintwork. *Bollocks, bollocks, bollocks.* I feel like turning on my heel and running, but at the same time I have no intention of going anywhere.

The key turns in the door and as it opens I quickly tuck both hands behind my back. He is stunned to see me.

"Seeing as you're still feeling a little unwell, I brought you something." I smile devilishly, biting my lip with nerves, barely able to contain myself, "But you have to choose a hand.

Which one? Right or left?" Aidan's clear blue eyes are clouded with confusion but he plays along anyway.

"Er, right?"

I offer him my right hand and unfurl it slowly. There in my palm sits two sachets of Lemsip, slightly crumpled from being clenched too tightly. He gets it straight away. Raising his eyebrows and smiling he accepts them from me.

"What's in your left hand?" He already knows the answer.

Without taking my eyes off his face I open my fist to reveal two shiny Durex packets and I find myself chewing harder on my lip. Still grinning, he says, "You'd better come in."

He stands to one side and ushers me though the back door. I find myself standing in a tiny outhouse piled high with crates of beer, muddy trainers, coats and jackets and piles of recycling, leading to an only slightly bigger, and infinitely messier kitchen.

Clutter covers almost every inch of the sand-coloured laminate work surfaces; dirty plates, empty beer bottles, half a loaf of bread, cutlery, unopened post. Aidan opens the fridge.

"Do you want a drink?"

I nod, "What do you have?"

"Beer?"

I usually avoid beer for the empty calories, but tonight I'll make an exception.

I lay the condoms on a tiny space on the work-top. Aidan looks at them, then at me, but says nothing. I take the bottle into the living room where a football match is on the television. Aidan sits back down on the sofa where he's clearly been chilling out. There are three empty bottles and a pizza box on the coffee table.

"Is this a bad time? I know how seriously you take the beautiful game," I mock.

"You're fine, but I'm not turning it off."

"Ok." Silence.

"Your girlfriend, the woman you're seeing..." I start to ask.

"It's fine, she's away. Sit down." He pushes a stack of newspapers off the sofa and throws a sweater across the room to make room for me next to him. I sit and study at him as he looks back at the screen.

He has changed into an ancient looking pair of blue-grey Diesel jeans, a blue faded cotton T-shirt with a Native American motif on the front, and he has bare feet. Even they are beautiful – strong, slim, defined. He has never looked so utterly, deliciously fuckable.

I have to tear my eyes away, aware that I'm letching quite unashamedly. I distract myself by looking around the room. It doesn't seem like the home of two young men. Aidan shares with someone, that's all he's told me. Not his 'girlfriend', he had stressed that. Paintings on the wall depict sheep and chickens. There's a bookshelf of DIY and fishing manuals, gardening books and walking guides. Brass ornaments on the mantelpiece sit alongside an ashtray and some ticket stubs. The furniture is mismatching, the furnishings tired and worn.

"It's my dad's place," he mutters, not tearing his eyes away from the game. "He lives in Spain most of the year, so he let me and Dave move in a few years back. It's a bit knackered but it'll do.

"How did you find me?" he adds, rather too casually.

"You told me you lived here, remember. When I started at *The Express*, I said I'd moved to Chertsey and you said you lived here too." I pick at the label on the bottle, taking another sip of beer, "Then another time you said they'd put a Costa right at the end of your road so I just drove down here and looked for your car. I took a chance."

"Right," he's looking at me now, in a way that's making me squirm.

"Do, you wish I hadn't?"

"No." he says hesitantly. The match finishes and he switches off the set, turning to face me, "But you shouldn't have come here like this you know. What if my girlfriend was here?"

"I thought she wasn't your girlfriend?"

"She's not, well, she is, kind of, but not really. You know what I'm saying. If she'd been here you'd have got me in a lot of trouble."

I pause, the glass neck of the bottle hovering at my lips, "I can go if you like."

Please say no. Please say no.

Aidan reaches over to me and removes the beer from my hand, sitting it on the table next to his. He tucks one knee underneath him and, resting an arm on the sofa, leans over and gently cups my chin in his hand, rubbing his thumb along my jaw. My scalp prickles and electric sparks shoot along my spine. Tilting my head to one side, I press my face into his hand, revelling in his touch.

He snakes his arm around my waist and pulls me with force along the sofa into his body, before grinding his mouth down on mine. It's brutal, almost aggressive, and a stark contrast to the affectionate way he just stroked my face. Stubble grazes my skin as he forces his lips over my open mouth. His body feels hard beneath the baby-soft fabric of his t-shirt.

The mass of contradiction sends my senses reeling. He smells of the sea, of peppermint and orange blossom, and tastes of beer and the faint tang of cigarette smoke.

I run my fingers along the back of his head. His hair is so short there it feels like velvet – I've fantasised about stroking this hair for months and now it's almost too much to bear. My other hand lingers over the muscle rippling across his back, smooth to the touch beneath the soft cotton exterior.

He has me, still pressed hard against his chest. The rise and fall of it mirrors my own. I groan and hear the sound, as if it were a stranger's, vibrate through him and fall upon the silence of the room. Aidan wraps his arms around my shoulders and back, exploring the skin there. He buries his fingers higher into the nape of my neck, tangling them into my hair and kissing me passionately.

Suddenly, he wrenches his mouth away and moves his grip back down my arms. He has a tight, almost painful clasp on my triceps as he pushes me away and holds me at arm's length. He is studying me, drinking me in and the look on his face is terrifying, like a man possessed. I don't know what he's thinking, but bizarrely I like the way it makes me feel. Scared and turned on.

"Aidan," I whimper.

"Don't talk," he says, quietly but with a hard edge that makes me want to do exactly as he commands. He tugs my top up and over my head and throws it unceremoniously over the back of the sofa. Trailing one finger, then another down my arm, he strokes the inside of my elbow and lifts my wrist to his mouth to suckle on the translucent skin there.

His hand moves to my waist, fingering the ribbed fabric of my vest and pulling it up a little to expose the soft skin of my stomach. My instinct is to suck it in, both for reasons of vanity (I wish I'd trained harder now), and because his touch makes my gut contract with pleasure and excitement. Circling the metal stud in my belly thoughtfully with his forefinger he traces a line downwards, finally sliding it into the waistband of my leggings.

I inhale sharply and he looks up, pausing motionless.

This.

This is why I came here tonight.

Only a fraction of a second passes but it feels like an eternity. I can hear the blood rushing in my ears and feel the *thud, thud, thud* of my chest.

Still watching me, the hint of a cruel smile playing on his lips, he inches the fabric away from my skin and peels it downwards.

I fight to regain control and let my breath out slowly, steadying my gaze and meeting his eyes head on, willing him - no, daring him - to continue. His fingers accept my silent challenge as they find the top of my knickers. Aiden considers the black and nude lace appreciatively, running his tongue across his lip.

With two hands now, faster and more impatiently, he edges the jeggings down over my hips, shuffling back to give me room to untuck my legs so he can slide them all the way off.

He takes hold of my hips again and brings me still closer. His face is right in front of mine, our noses are almost touching, and his warm breath is on my skin.

Maintaining his hypnotic stare, he slips one hand inside my pants, burying two long, hard fingers into the silky rectangle of hair and rotates them agonisingly slowly. I start wriggling my pelvis against him but his firm hand holds me still.

The way he is watching me, gauging my response and studying my face for a reaction is unnerving, but incredibly arousing too. His hand ventures lower still, pressing his middle finger between my soft folds, finding the spot that is screaming out to be touched, then slides further, into my warm wetness.

I exhale a long breath and let my head fall back, my body held up only by his strong grip and my fierce grasp on the back of the sofa. Oh, this man. He can take anything he likes and I will give it up.

I have to tighten my hold on the furniture as he releases me and moves his free hand to the back of my head, forcing my tongue back in his mouth. He is kissing me furiously, still stroking my hot spot with a relentless rhythm.

"Aidan… can we… go upstairs," I'm panting out the words in between laboured breaths and consuming kisses.

"Your housemate… what if he…? *Oh…*" I moan as he intensifies the pressure. "Aidan, please…" I plead, trying to untangle myself.

"It's fine, he won't be back for hours yet," He sucks on my bottom lip and works his fingers faster.

Oh wow. Wow. Maybe just a bit longer…

No, focus!

"Aidan, you can't know that for sure." It's a wrench but I circle his wrist with my fingers and hold it steady, "I don't want you to stop but I don't want it, here, like this." I gesture at the sofa.

He sighs and reluctantly releases me from his grip, then does something quite unexpected but unbelievably hot; he raises his hand to his mouth and sucks first one, then a second finger, long and hard.

Oh my good God. That was hugely erotic.

"Come on," he grabs hold of my hand and tugs me up off the sofa, as I scrabble for my leggings on the floor. The stairs are narrow like the house, and I bump off the wooden cladded walls. It feels smooth against my bare thighs and it hits home: I'm wandering around my colleague's house in my knickers. He just had his fingers inside me and I'm about to screw him!

This.
Is.
Crazy.

Aidan's room is spacious and airy, though it's getting darker as the light fades. He lets go of my hand and crosses round to the other side of the bed to switch on a small lamp.

The bed is unmade, with a plain cream duvet cover and a pile of pillows heaped on top, but it looks clean and smells nice.

I let the leggings slip to the floor and we look at each other for a long few seconds. Then, in unison we move on hands and knees over the bed. I launch myself at him, tearing at his t-shirt, ripping it off in a frenzied attack; devouring his sullen, angry mouth.

My lips move to his neck; then to his lean, defined chest, lightly covered in fair, blond hair.

Seeking out his small and hard, pale pink nipples with my tongue I pull one into my mouth, sucking and teasing it with my teeth, rolling the other one between my fingers. Small moans of delight escape Aidan's mouth and I drag my free hand from his muscled back, filling his mouth with my fingertips. He sucks on them, mimicking the action of my own mouth.

I want more. I want to see him, smell him, consume his entire body. I nibble and lick his upper, then lower torso. His belly is flat, becoming almost concave as I get lower. The hair, coarser there, is bisected by a battered leather belt.

I bury my nose into his downy chest and inhale deeply. He smells amazing, of the sun on wooden decking and warm evenings on the beach.

The metal buckle jangles in my hand as I wrestle it open and attack his flies. Each button takes me closer to making him mine, if only for tonight. His fingers are buried in my hair now, not pushing or pulling, but definitely creating tension; tugging gently one moment, holding me down the next. I like the feeling of being under his control, even though I'm resisting. *Will there always be this power struggle between us? It's still here, even in the bedroom.*

Aidan helps me slide his jeans off, revealing a slim but strong pair of thighs. He's not stacked like Mark, but has better proportions in his leaner build. There isn't an ounce extra anywhere on his body and his muscle has a beautiful toned definition to it, making it look as if he's been carved from marble. Despite his lack of bulk, he is distinctly ripped and I need a moment to drink in his beauty.

"What?" he asks, his voice husky. Kneeling on the sheets in just a fitted – and boy, I mean tight – pair of dark grey trunks, he is perfect and I want him with every fibre in my body. I sit back on my heels, my thighs spread wide in front of me and slowly, deliberately, lift my vest top up and over my head, shaking out my hair over my shoulders.

We are both down to our underwear now and it gives me a sense of equality I haven't experienced since our lunch in the park. The confidence I'm used to feeling in bed with a man, which has been noticeable by its absence so far this evening, returns with a bang.

I reach behind myself and unclasp my bra, the straps fall over my shoulders and I let it tumble into my lap. My chest rises and falls and I'm trembling. There must be half a metre between us and the charge is electric.

"Fuck me."

He doesn't need asking twice and moves swiftly. Raising me up, he sits me against the headboard propped on pillows and pulls my legs out in front of me before lowering my knickers a few inches. This time I don't stop him, I help him, tearing the scrap of black lace down to my knees, wriggling out of them, widening my legs, making space for his fingers.

Oh, yes.

I press my weight through my hands into the bed, throwing

my head back and circling my hips. I want him inside me so badly, but this feels too good to stop.

With his face now between my hands, I kiss him long and hard before reaching for his shorts. I dip inside to grasp a hold of the huge erection that's been tantalising me since his jeans came off. Like the rest of his body, his cock is long, less stocky than I'm used to, but still gratifyingly solid as it fills my hand.

I skim the trunks over his glorious, pert buttocks, keeping one hand firmly wrapped around him, pausing to lick and suck my palm until it's warm and wet, then I stroke his length, rhythmically, purposefully, causing him to groan out, "Oh Kate, Kate, ah…"

I increase my grip and speed for a few minutes, before slowing it right down to prolonged, deliberate movements.

Removing his hand from me, I flip over onto my knees, lower my head to his groin and nibble softly on the taut skin of his lower belly, lapping at the soft downy hair that covers his obliques.

He has the distinctive athletic V-shape you see on sportsmen and models, a physical arrow pointing towards my kind of treasure. I tease him, kissing all around but never touching him there. "Please Kate," he mouths in barely a whisper, taking his weight on strong arms, his thick muscular thighs folded beneath him and that rock hard cock straining skywards.

My hair falls forward, enveloping him with a softness that makes him cry out as he takes a hold of his cock through my chestnut curls, but I bat his hand away, refusing his request, and take my teasing kisses lower still, lapping at his groin and his thighs, nipping at the muscle, finally drawing my tongue over the tight skin of his balls.

"Yes, there, that's good. Ohhhh!"

He's panting now, the tip of his cock jerking with excitement and frustration. I relent and give him what he wants, drawing my tongue up his smooth shaft while kneading the softer skin of his inner thighs with my hands as he moans and thrusts himself closer.

Lazily trailing the tip of my tongue around the rim, I circle him once, twice, and slide him into my mouth, sucking deeply, swirling on the withdrawal, before plunging down again, over and over.

He loves this and so do I.

Unlike some women, I adore giving head. It gets me so wet. I fantasise about blowing one man while being fucked by another. Perhaps the fantasy is better than the reality; maybe I'll never know.

Replacing my mouth with my hands, I move back up to kiss him again but he pulls away and kneels on the carpet, hooking his fingers in the crooks of my knees, sliding me across the sheets until my backside is balanced on the edge of the mattress.

Pulling my legs apart, Aidan dips his head between them and echoes the path I carved out minutes earlier, kissing my legs, sucking and nipping on my inner thighs, following those damned sensitive love lines all the way up and pausing every few seconds to watch my reaction.

The insistent teasing finds its mark and I'm writhing

around, yearning for this beautiful torment to stop yet urging it to last. "Please Aidan," I breathe. It is my turn to beg. I direct his head, and more specifically his mouth, to my throbbing core. I wrap my fingers around the back of his neck and pull him in closer. He obliges without hesitation, pressing his lips to my warm wet slit.

Oh God, yeah, there, kiss me there!

My mind loses focus for a second.

Arching my spine, I tilt my hips further so he can sink his tongue deeper, up to the root, his mouth spread wide over my openness. Warm blood pools in my groin, sending my head into a spin and my hips circle involuntarily, of their own accord, grinding my pussy into his face.

I suck air in sharply through my nose and let it out slowly through my mouth, like an erotic yoga lesson, focussing all my attention on the activity between my legs. The tension is building and I know that I'm going to cum if he continues.

"Stop." I try to shimmy away, but his mouth clings to me like a limpet. "Stop, I want to fuck you first."

Nothing.

"Aidan, I'm going to cum if you carry on." He momentarily pauses, and looks up at me, eyes twinkling.

"I'm going to make you cum and then fuck you."

He buries his head again, alternately sucking my clit and licking me out. The feeling's insane and protesting is useless; I'm already beyond the point of no return. Clamping his head between my strong thighs and with no thought for his need to breathe, I crush his face hard into me, rubbing my clit into his mouth, taking what I want. I get tighter and tighter, and then the release comes suddenly, in a rush of powerful convulsions, tumbling one after the other. I loosen my grip on him, my arms fall to my side and my thighs fall adrift. Aidan surfaces, gasping for air.

"Oh God, that was amazing. Oh my God, oh. Are you ok?" I pant, propping myself up on one elbow, but he doesn't answer. His chest still heaving, he reaches by the side of the bed and tears open the wrapper of a condom.

Expertly pinching the end, he rolls it on and clambers between my open legs. There isn't much room so I edge backwards and he follows me, crawling like a desperate animal, bringing his hands down on either side of my body.

He is kneeling over me now, his legs pressing my thighs apart and his distended cock stands hard and proud, engorged almost painfully by a driving need, tantalisingly close to my pussy. Looking at me again, registering the wanton lust that must be written all over my face, he nudges his hips forward, rubbing the fat head of his cock over my sensitive clit.

I cry out as a shower of tiny sparks course through my body and my hands ball into fists. He shifts his body and drags the thick glans of his penis down over my entrance, taunting me, teasing me, just how I like it.

No!

I rally myself from my post-orgasmic stupor. This is not the way it's going to happen.

Quick as a flash I wrap my legs around his, sit up and push my left hand into his chest, pivoting on the other arm and twisting my hips, flipping him onto his back. He's taken aback by the speed of my assault and the strength of my thighs – thank you yoga – and lies there stunned.

"What are you doing?" he pants.

"I'm going to fuck you, like I said I would," I say, matter of fact but with a devilish grin that tells him he's going to enjoy this.

Pressing him down into the bed, I rise up off his body. My fingers curl around his stiffness and lift it up and away from his stomach as I position myself over his bulging head. I lower myself, bit by bit, until he's embedded in the entrance to my wet cunt.

He watches me. My eyes half closed, my lips parted, as I savour the moment, enjoying the anticipation of pleasure still to come.

"What do you want, Aidan?"

His eyes spring open: "You."

"Tell me what you want me to do to you."

He's raising his hips, trying to nudge himself further into me but I lift myself higher, controlling and limiting his movement.

"You. Know. What. I. Want."

His speech is stilted and a single bead of sweat rolls down his forehead. The tension is killing both of us but I won't give in.

"Beg me. I want you to ask for it."

"I want you to fuck me Kate." he rushes, "Please, fuck me now."

Those few words are enough and I plunge down, impaling myself on him, forcing us both to cry out in an exquisite combination of pleasure and relief. There are no half measures.

I rise up, almost all the way off of him before slamming

back down, hard into his pelvis, rubbing myself into the rough hair around his cock that grates against my sensitive skin.

I curl my nails into his chest, leaving small red wheals across the surface, and Aidan moans his appreciation, revelling in the pain.

I'm sucking him up inside my body now, leaning right over his face every time I lift myself up, my hair trailing over his lips and eyes; he blindly reaches up, tangling his fingers in my hair, around the back of my head.

"God, you're hot. I'm going cum soon if you keep riding me like that."

I smile, "I want you to."

"Seriously Kate, I'm pretty close… but I want you to cum over my cock. Use your hands to bring yourself off."

I shake my head and keep crushing myself into him, making little snaking movements with my hips.

"I don't need to," I'm distracted by the yearning, tugging in my groin.

"You don't want to cum again?"

"No, I don't need to use my hands." My breath is coming thick and fast.

"You can cum just by fucking me?" Aidan pants, surprised.

"Uh-huh, and I'm close, oh God, that feels so good."

I've got quite a rhythm going, pressing down hard, precise movements, dragging my clit over him, pulling sharply up his full length before sinking down again. The feeling is intoxicating. It's never felt quite like this before.

I don't know if it's the culmination of months of anticipation or days of flirting but every fibre in my body feels like it's on fire.

"Do it," He says, the strain showing on his face, "I can hold on a bit longer."

I almost don't hear him, I'm so lost in my own world, "I'm nearly there, don't move."

I rock myself over Aidan and he tightens his grip in my hair, pulling my head backwards. Oh wow, I don't know why that should feel so good but it seriously arouses me and my stomach is turning somersaults.

"Do it again," I gasp, feeling myself on the brink.

"What?"

"My hair. Do it again."

He tugs my head back, "Like this?"

Oh, there it is again, "Yes, yes, like that, don't stop."

The sensation is overwhelming. I can feel the orgasm building at speed and with one last tug on my hair and rock of my hips I crash into free fall, my pussy twitching around his hardness.

I cum in long, hard wracking sobs, wringing out every last drop. I'm aware that Aidan's on the brink of his own orgasm. Taking a firm grasp on my hips he pulls me down hard onto him, bucking his body up to meet my thrusts and lifts me clear off the bed.

Shouting out, his jaw taut and eyes closed, he stills for a split second before emptying himself, rammed tight up inside my body. Watching him cum turns me on even more and I roll my body around on his, feeling the familiar heat building a third time.

"Don't pull out of me, I'm gonna cum again." I mutter, writhing around on top of him, gyrating in circles, feeling him still hard up inside me. Relieved of his own frustration, he lies back and watches me, fascinated as I work myself into another series of shuddering orgasms. "Oh yeah, oh God, yes," I bury myself into his chest, gulping snatched breaths, my pussy still pulsating around him, "Oh, that was good."

Rolling off him I collapse face down on the mattress, stretched out, moaning contentedly. Aidan disposes of the condom and climbs on top of me, carefully spreading his weight, so as not to crush me and kisses me near my ear, "Better?"

"Mmm, yeah, sorry about that," I smile into the sheets, "I can get a little greedy sometimes."

He laughs, warmly, "Three times, Kate, two of them while fucking me! No one I've been with has ever done that. Not without a little manual help."

I laugh too, "You've been fucking the wrong women."

"Seriously, most women need a little help. How come you don't?"

I turn slightly, leaning on one elbow so I can see his face and he shifts his weight to one side; our legs are still tangled together.

"I've been making myself cum since I was twelve but didn't have sex until I was 19.

"My first time was great - it was a one night stand, a really casual arrangement that suited us both - but I couldn't work out how to translate what I did with my hands into what I needed someone else to do. And I didn't have the confidence to touch myself during sex, so I faked it. But it was still a fun night."

Aidan is looking at me intently, "So what changed?"

"A couple of months later I hooked up with a friend of a friend, a fresher. We hit it off and went back to mine for some no strings fun.

"I was straddling him, like I did with you. I hadn't said a word, I don't know how he knew. Instinct I suppose. We were having sex and I guess he saw the frustration in my face. I mean, eight years of giving myself orgasms on demand and suddenly nothing?

"I told him that I could make myself cum, but... I don't know. I was self-conscious I guess. God, he was amazing. He lay there and told me to use him, in any way that I chose to, to do whatever I wanted. He was fine with it.

"So I did. I worked him like he was a life size vibrator, a human dildo just there for my pleasure. I jiggled and shimmied and rubbed myself up and down on him and he just lay back and enjoyed the ride.

"I felt that familiar build-up and knew there and then I was about to cum. So I did. Again and again and again. I think I came about five times that night. Once I knew how, there was no stopping me."

I smile, "Louis – that was his name - he just lay back and enjoyed the show. It was like the more times I came, the more pleasure he got from it. I guess if it wasn't for him I could still be faking it today!" I shudder, "God, awful thought! I owe him a huge debt."

Aidan's impressed, "How many times have you made yourself cum - during one session?"

"Seriously?"

He raises his eyebrows, looking amused.

I look at him from beneath my lashes, "Eight times."

"Eight? Jesus woman, you're insatiable!" He's laughing now, his arm draped loosely over my waist, "I want you to fuck me and cum more than that."

"What? No Aidan!"

"I do."

"What is this, some sort of competition?"

"Kate, seeing you take control like that, it drove me insane. You're so hot."

I wrap my arms around my head, burying my face and mumbling into the sheets.

"What?"

I lift my head and look at him with one eye, barely open, "I said, maybe. Okay?"

He grins.

I yawn and stretch out, starfishing over the bed, moaning softly, "Right now I just want to close my eyes…"

Aidan eases himself back on top of me, interlacing his fingers with mine, nuzzling my neck, "You're really quite sweet aren't you? I've never seen this side of you before. "But you can't stay. My housemate will be home soon and he's not too discreet. You're going to have to leave."

What the actual fuck?! Did I just hear him right?

"Are you serious?"

"Afraid so babe, he knows my girlfriend too well and loose lips and all that."

I shrug him off and sit up, wrapping the duvet around me. So now she's his girlfriend again! Suddenly I feel uncomfortable. No one has ever asked me to leave minutes after having sex.

I'm not sure if I'm outraged or just disappointed.

"Would you… will you come back to mine?"

He looks up at me and I have no idea what he is thinking. His beautiful face betrays no trace of emotion. It's impossible for me to read him.

"I dunno Kate, I've got to be up early, I've got the fêtes, and stuff to do…"

He's stalling. Is he regretting it already?

"But they're not until lunchtime at the earliest."

Tears start to prickle at the back of my eyes. I know I look desperate.

"I can always run you back over here first thing." My mouth seems to have developed a mind of its own and is running away with itself. An uneasy silence descends on the room. "Look, if you don't want to come back, just say." I squirm.

Aidan looks away.

Throwing the covers aside I jump out of bed and start searching for my underwear, "It's fine, don't worry about it, it was just an idea." The words tumble out and I feel my cheeks redden as I locate my bra and scramble under the bed for my discarded knickers. I need to get out of here.

I perch on the edge of the bed and pull on the pants, reaching for the vest top, on the floor, but Aidan grabs my wrist, "I'll come with you."

I try to shake his hand away, "You don't have to it, it's okay. I get it."

"No, no you don't." He sits up and slides towards me, running his index finger down my cheek, and over my lips. "I wanted you tonight, Kate, and this has been… better than

I imagined, but I'm seeing someone and, going back to yours, spending the night, it seems… this sounds stupid, considering what we just did, but staying at yours, seems… wrong."

"It's fine, it was a stupid suggestion anyway…"

He presses his finger into my lips, silencing my protests, "No, listen to me. It does feel wrong, but I'm gonna do it anyway, because the thought of sleeping on my own tonight is worse than the thought of cheating on her."

He leaps up and pulls his clothes on while I sit motionless in my underwear, utterly confused. "Come on. Let's go!" he throws my vest and leggings at me, "Your other top's downstairs. Turn the light off when you're done – hurry up!" He hurtles out of the door and I dress quickly, crawling over the bed to the lamp.

"Do you have anything to drink at yours?" he calls upstairs.

"Yeah, some wine – white – and gin and tonic!" I come downstairs and pull on my top, slipping my shoes back on, as he opens the fridge, pulling a face.

"Hmm, not really my thing. You alright with me bringing some beers?"

"Yeah, sure."

I grab my keys and walk through the kitchen, turning to face him at the back door.

"Aidan, if you don't want to come with me I…"

He cups his hand around my chin and silences me with a long deep kiss that tugs at my groin.

"Let's go."

Six

Back at mine, Smithy is sat watching *Dr Who* DVDs in the dark. He eyes Aidan suspiciously and acknowledges me with a gruff, "Y'alright?" as I troop past him to the kitchen fridge for the bottle I stashed there earlier.

"Is he always like that?" Aidan asks when we're up in my room.

"Mainly, yes." I pour myself a generous glass of wine. "He's a bit of a Neanderthal, but he's okay. Keeps himself to himself and pays the rent on time." I lie down and Aidan cracks open a beer. Lounging on the bed next to me, he kicks off his trainers. I want to curl up next to him but it feels a bit weird. He hasn't tried to touch me since we left his and I don't want to come across as too clingy. I feel like I already did that by asking him back.

I drink the wine quickly, pouring another glass as he cracks open a second beer. This is a bizarre scenario and I don't think it's crazy to suggest we're both a little nervous. Despite committing three intimate acts together, four if you include kissing, he still feels like a stranger.

Aidan asks me about the painting on my easel; it's one I started years ago and have recently been reworking. It's a view from an island in the Med, where I spent a couple of memorable summers during Uni. It's no Van Gogh, but I like it.

"So how about you Aidan? What do you do when you're not at work? I don't really know anything about you, do I?"

"Yes you do. You know I like beer and football and sleeping with you." He peels my top down away from my shoulder and starts kissing my neck.

"Aidan!" I pull away, "I'm trying to talk to you."

He seems genuinely interested in what I have to say, and he's easy to talk to but the moment I ask him anything remotely personal he clams up.

Undeterred he slides a hand up my top, cupping my right breast: "Mmm, did I mention you have lovely tits." I sigh and lean into his caress. It's late and I have a gorgeous man in my bed – one that I have wanted for a very long time. Conversation can wait.

It's slower this time, less rushed. We take the time to explore and savour each other, each finding pleasure in the smallest of details; a defined muscle, the fullness of a lip, the jut of a hip bone. Layer by layer, inch by inch, we undress each other slowly, feeling the way, from top to bottom then back again.

Inhaling his scent, I relish the feeling of his skin on mine and we immerse ourselves in a tangle of limbs. When my turn comes I'm alight with desire and completely lost in my own emotion.

He slips on a condom and fucks me, agonisingly slowly at first, every long, drawn out thrust, taking me closer, then faster and more passionately until I am crying out in complete abandonment. After the first time I cling on, wrapping my legs around his thighs, raising my pelvis to meet his and forcing myself against him, to steal a second, then a third orgasm, one after the other, each building on the last.

He rolls me over without pulling out of me so I'm straddling him and folds his hands behind his head: "Go on."

He's referring to our earlier conversation. Smiling silently I push all my weight into my hands and raise myself off of him, sucking him up into me, clenching him inside, then agonisingly slowly, sink down again. I repeat the action over and over again until there is nothing left in the room but his cock and my pussy.

I picture him in my mind's eye, shining with my juices as I pull away from him, straining to plunge back into me, his fat, purple head jammed hard into my wet sheath, and the image sends me over the edge yet again.

Shuddering and gasping for breath, I ride him into my fifth and sixth orgasms, each one sending violent tremors though my body, each one giving me temporary reprieve but leaving me still wanting more.

He is struggling now to contain himself. His knuckles are white, his balled fists hold tightly to the sheets and his relaxed disposition is long gone; he is holding back his own orgasm with great difficulty. "You want me to stop?" I pant, already jerking my hips towards number seven.

"No," his voice is thin and strained, "I'm gonna hold out as long as you can keep going."

I don't answer. I'm already bucking my hips in ecstasy. As he pulls my mouth into his and weaves his tongue around mine another, stronger orgasm shakes me with its strength. "Oh, oh, that doesn't normally happen."

"What?"

"That was huge." I'm panting and rocking myself gently now, "Usually the more I have, the weaker they become. But that... that was different. Bigger." I'm flagging now and all my strength is beginning to ebb away. I'm reaching saturation. "Come on, I want you to cum," I beg.

"No." he is moaning softly, "That was eight, I was counting. Cum again." His breath is coming short and ragged now.

"Aidan, no. It doesn't work like that." But he's circling his hips, thrusting up into me, oh dear God. I can feel it building from nowhere. I honestly didn't think I had it in me. My body is working on its own now, furiously pounding against his cock. "Hurry up, I don't think I can hold on." He grits his teeth and with a firm grip on my hips, rolls them around in a different rhythm.

"Don't," I cry urgently, my hands flying to his, knocking them away and taking back control. My breathing is laboured now, so is his. We're heaving like we've both run a marathon but the final moments are eluding me while his are just seconds away. I mash my clit into him, frantically chasing down that golden feeling.

Suddenly his hands fly to my scalp. He plunges two hands into my hair, grabs fistfuls and winds it around his knuckles. I arch my neck and instantly cum in short, sharp, almost painful spasms as he finds his merciful release and floods inside me, biting back cries.

We are both totally and utterly spent and I fall on top of him. Wrapped in his arms we both pant, hearts racing in unison.

"That. Was. Incredible," he finally says, a full minute later, when our breathing has returned to normal.

"Mmm?" I murmur, as sleep descends on me.

"You. The way you can cum like that, one after the other. You're incredible. Jesus, I wish I could do that."

I lift myself off of him and carefully remove the condom, wrap it in a tissue and throw it in the bin by the bed. Dragging the duvet over me I luxuriate in its warmth, letting sleep drift over me.

Aidan laughs, "Look at you, you just wanna go to sleep. You're not even bothered about snuggling up like some women are. You just take what you want, roll over and go to sleep."

"I don't hear you complaining," I mutter.

He laughs, "Kate, you're a man trapped in a woman's body."

I smile with my eyes closed, "It has been said."

He kisses me and I part my lips, taking his tongue into my mouth, sliding my hand to the back of his head. Disengaging himself he says calmly, "You know what? I'm going to let you sleep and walk home."

What?

My eyes fly open and I stare at him, not trusting my own hearing. "Sorry?"

"I'm just going to head home. You don't need to get up." He edges out of bed and starts gathering his clothes.

I am literally dumbfounded. What is this guy's problem?

"But we came back here so you could stay over. You said that you didn't want to sleep alone." He is already half-dressed.

I have absolutely no idea what to say. I sit up drawing the duvet around me and watch, tight-lipped, as he zips up his trousers and pulls on his trainers. He leans over to kiss me but gets a mouthful of hair as I turn my head away.

"Babe, don't be like that. I just think it would be better tonight if I go home and get a good night's sleep – and you're obviously knackered. What's the problem?"

'What's the problem?' Really? Is this man for real?

"I don't want to fall out with you Aidan," I say tightly, "Maybe it is better that you go."

He turns my face towards him and kisses me briefly on the lips. Gesturing towards the two bottles on the dresser he says, "This was fun. Keep the beers," and lets himself out.

I have no idea how long I sit staring at the closed door after he left. I'm not sure I even have the right to feel upset. We're just two colleagues that are hugely attracted to each other and have ended up in bed, right? It's not like this hasn't happened before; I've had sex with men and they haven't stayed. But this feels different. For some stupid reason it hurts that he doesn't want to be here. Maybe it's because on previous occasions they were guys that I didn't know and would never see again.

'Or maybe it's because you want more than just the sex', a small voice in my head says, knowingly. Angrily, I switch off the light and lie down.

Whatever the reason, I really do need some sleep and I don't want to think about it anymore tonight.

Seven

I wake early after a restless sleep to the sound and smell of a summer downfall. It's been weeks since we last had rain. The pungent, earthy smell of petrichor permeating the air is almost pleasurable, but it's undermined by a miserable, grey bleakness that has sucked all the joy out of the sky.

A bit like my bittersweet encounter with Aidan.

I should be lying here basking in the glow of last night, revelling in the memory of mind-blowingly great sex. On the contrary, the arousing thought is soured by Aidan's ungainly, swift and altogether determined exit.

The temperature has dropped slightly with the change in weather, but it's still balmy outside, so I scrape back my hair, pull on a vest and a pair of shorts, grab my iPod and a bottle of water, and set out on a run to clear my head.

Clicking the front door shut, I gasp as the first fresh raindrops hit my face and trickle down my chest. Jogging gently to the end of the road, I pick up pace as I criss-cross through the housing estate and run down the high street, deliberately not looking left as I pass Costa.

Heading out into the countryside, I leave footpaths and tarmac behind me, choosing neglected bridleways and quiet forest trails. Wet woodland and soggy fields become my running track. A distant hum from the nearby motorway is a backing track to my playlist.

The rain runs in rivulets down my face, plastering my hair to my head and clothes to my body. It's a welcome distraction. The rain is both a cleansing atonement for the sins of the previous night, and a therapeutic accompaniment to the rhythmic beat of my feet.

I run for an hour, and when I finally get home I'm pleased to find the tension in my shoulders has abated. I feel more alive than I did when I first woke up.

While I'm in the shower the rain stops and the clouds drift away to reveal a fresher, bluer sky than we've seen in days and by mid-morning it's really warm again.

I heap a bowl with fruit and muesli, topping it with a huge dollop of natural yoghurt and an indulgent squeeze of agave syrup. Taking a towel out into the garden, I lay it on a soggy garden chair propped against the back wall and curl up in the cosy suntrap.

I'm feeling better about last night. I've distanced myself from the momentary hurt and confusion I was feeling when Aidan fled. I think things were magnified because I'd wanted him for so long and I hadn't expected the sex to be so spectacularly good. I smile to myself remembering how warm his body felt on mine. My insides tighten involuntarily at the thought of orgasm after orgasm rippling through me as he lay back and watched. I have little doubt he will be able to think of much else today and, guilt aside in regards his unfortunate girlfriend – poor cow – I'm sure he will also be wallowing in the pleasurable memory.

I drop the bowl into the overloaded sink – sod it, let someone else wash up my shit for a change – and nip upstairs to pull on a floaty maxi dress and apply some light make up. I'm meeting Gemma for lunch and when it's warm I don't like to be heavily made up during the day.

As there's no further rain forecast for the rest of the day I decide to leave the car and walk into town. It's turned into a really beautiful day and a gentle stroll will help prevent me from stiffening up after the run.

I'm not meeting Gemma until one and it's only ten thirty, but I fancy a mooch around the shops and I don't want to be cooped up in the house on such a nice day. What with covering the fêtes and sleeping late for the last two weekends, I haven't been out enjoying the warmer weather much. It feels as if early summer has passed me by.

The Ceanothus are out in force now. Glorious flowers in complementary shades of purple and blue line footpaths and poke their heads over garden fences. I revel in the warmth of the sun on my back, and shiver as it reminds me of the heat of Aidan's body pressed against mine.

It's a strange morning. My usual passion for retail therapy is lacking and I find myself drifting from shop to shop, aimlessly browsing the racks without any purpose or enjoyment. Eventually I abandon the pointless activity in favour of a large mug of coffee and a sunny part of town.

I've bought a paper, but give up on that too. Instead, watching the world go by becomes a better way to spend the time - especially with my wandering mind constantly returning to last night. By lunchtime I'm glad of the distraction from some sane company, and greet Gemma like a long lost relative.

"Ow, hey, take it easy!" she squeals, laughing as I envelop her in a huge bear hug, almost knocking her floppy straw hat off and strangling her at the same time.

"Oh, I'm sorry, sorry. I'm just feeling a bit…" I wiggle my hand about and Gemma's expression changes in an instant.

"Kate?" She's serious now. "What is it? Is it your Dad?"

"No, no nothing like that. It's nothing, I'm just being stupid." She beckons the waiter over and orders two gin and tonics - doubles - and shuffles her chair close to me.

"What is it? Tell me everything."

I take a deep breath. I want to tell her, I really do, but there is something preventing me from spilling all. It's the work thing, I think. I mean, going on about Aidan before the event actually happened was one thing, but sharing the juicy details after I've done the deed seems, well it just seems risky.

"Well, the thing is I met someone, a while ago, in a bar…" I relate the events of last night, bit by bit, omitting names and places, details that would impart information I'm not yet willing to share. The drinks arrive and I pepper my story with long, hard pulls on the strong, icy cold spirit.

Gemma's sips slowly on hers, her eyes widening as I reveal my role as seductress, the rampant sex that followed, his haste to get me to leave, the second helpings back at mine, and his hurried departure.

The waiter approaches to take our order, but she impatiently waves him away, urging me on. When I've finished, she sits back in her chair and drains her glass, banging it down hard on the table.

"Kate Cleaver, you dark horse. Why haven't you mentioned this guy before? What's his name?" She seems quite put out and fires a volley of accusing questions at me: "You haven't breathed a word about him until now. How come? I thought you were hung up on Aidan. And you shagged Mark the weekend before last! Jesus woman, you don't hang about do you?" I shrug, and shake my head, a half smile playing on my lips, "It's early days yet. It doesn't mean anything."

"Doesn't it?" she interrupts.

"I know you Kate, and you're pissed off that he took off like that. Whatever you say, you like this guy. I can tell."

We order a lunch of tapas and chat over a bottle of wine. I feel bad I'm not being straight with her, but I don't want to say I bedded my colleague right now. Plus if she knows he did a runner she'll start shooting him filthy looks at work and he's going to know I blabbed. Somehow I don't think Aidan's the type of man to appreciate being the subject of girl talk. At least not in this way.

"I've never been hung up on post-sex small talk and cuddles, but I thought he'd at least stay until the morning." I smile weakly, "I do like him, I mean not seriously but you know, enough to think it might go somewhere a bit further than a casual shag. I thought he liked me, but now I'm not sure." I play with a scrap of flatbread left on the platter, "I should have expected it I suppose, I mean, considering."

"Considering what?" she asks. I avoid her glance and

gesture to the waiter.

"I fancy another glass of wine, do you? Shall I get a second bottle?"

"Considering what, Kate?" Gemma's tone has changed. There's a steely edge to her voice. I signal for more wine – I need it even if she doesn't.

"He's got a girlfriend," I murmur, looking down, brushing imaginary crumbs off my lap. When I look back up Gemma's just sitting, staring at me, eyebrows raised, lips pursed. "Well go on, say something." I feel like the child who's just got caught stealing sweets from the top shelf.

"What can I say Kate, that you don't already know," Gemma says in a resigned tone. "You're looking for trouble babe and it's not likely to end well." She smiles and reaches across the table to grab my hand. "But if anyone's going to go out looking for trouble, it should probably be you. I think you can handle it."

We drink the second bottle of wine and order a huge portion of dulce de leche cheesecake to share and two dry lattes, as we while away another hour chatting about men.

By the time I go home, I feel decidedly more blasé about the entire situation. If Aidan wants to keep things casual then so can I. No one promised me the big love story. Yes, I was offended that he walked out in the middle of the night. It really wasn't very good form, but then neither is fucking your workmate behind your girlfriend's back, so I don't know really what I was expecting. Hearts and bloody roses? No.

There might have been something incredibly intense between us last night, which I mistakenly believed held the promise of a deeper connection, but perhaps it was just very, very good sex. Either way, if I want more of it I'm going to have to learn to change my expectations and play him at his own game.

I can do that. I've turned casual sex into an art form over the last few years. This should be easy.

Game on.

I'm almost asleep later in the evening when my phone vibrates. Drowsily I open the text:

CAN'T SLEEP. CAN SMELL YOU ON MY SHEETS
WISH I COULD STILL TASTE YOU TOO.

I switch the phone off. Sod him. Let him think about me. Soon he won't be able to think about anything else.

Eight

Two weeks and eight texts later – none of them acknowledged by me – I'm hanging out in the local cop shop, taking down details of a gang attack on Saturday night. It's been a fairly uneventful weekend crime-wise and this looks like it's as good as it's going to get for today's briefing.

I came straight here this morning and haven't seen Aidan yet. Remarkably, I've been totally chilled about the whole thing considering my early angst. My about-turn after lunch with Gemma not only lasted the weekend, but the fortnight too and my resolve has gone from strength to strength.

I can tell from the messages he's been sending that my sudden radio silence has piqued his interest and our encounter continues to play on his mind.

I don't know if it was just guilt that sent him home that night, or a bizarre fear of some kind of commitment, although it's not as if I've actually asked him to make any choices. In the cold light of day he seems far keener than he did when he left, and if I'm to believe his impassioned pleas he is more than definitely up for a rematch.

I finish at the police station and walk back through town towards work. It's always dead on a Monday morning, and once the workers have scuttled into their offices there are only bored mums with dawdling toddlers and cranky senior citizens trailing round the shops. I drag my feet too; I'm in no rush to type up yet another tedious story about small-time crime in a dull and dusty backwater. Even the thought of playing mental footsie with Aidan isn't enough to get me to hurry back.

It's not been all that uncomfortable at work, considering how things could have panned out. Aidan tried initiating conversation a couple of times, when he was absolutely certain no one was listening. He asked why I'd been blanking his texts, and if we were cool after, 'Everything… you know?' I blew him out with a breezy, 'Sorry I forgot to text you back,' and, 'Probably best keeping things casual, considering.' (YOU'RE IN A RELATIONSHIP!!!) kind of way.

He seemed a little taken aback at my new-found coolness, but I laughed it off with an: 'It was, what it was, wasn't it?' and, 'It's not like I was going to propose or anything, just chill out!'

The situation between us has definitely improved since that night. Things are back to being normal, fun and flirtatious even, only in a better and improved way - without the slightly off-hand, distant behaviour he used to exhibit towards me.

Post-sex Aidan is now regarding me with discreetly concealed but definitely existing - dare I say it - affection… Our secret liaison has created a bond that, even in the absence of an actual 'relationship', lends my working day a frisson of excitement.

He might not have openly arranged to meet up again, merely preferring to text-pester me with messages like: 'I WANT YOU' and, 'I WAS THINKING ABOUT YOU IN

BED LAST NIGHT'. But his more considerate and consistent attention - making me coffee for example, or, asking if he can get me something for lunch - has made me feel more wanted than I have in a long time. Plus, the thrill of knowing that I've had this gorgeous man sitting not three feet away, more than fans the flames of my desire on a daily basis. I know in my heart - and my groin - that he won't be able to hold out much longer, and when he does cave I'll be ready.

My phone vibrates in the back pocket of my slim-cut trousers. Sliding it out I flick the sound back on and open the text. It's from Rupert:

FIRST SHIFT A WEEK SATURDAY.
DON'T FUCK IT UP.
GOOD LUCK. R

Oooh. My insides lurch and I need to catch my breath. A weekend shift at a national. Suddenly I'm really scared. I'm not ready for this? Why did I seriously think it would be a good idea to make such a big jump so soon? I haven't even worked for a regional daily newspaper, let alone a national news agency.

I feel sick and a bit light headed. With no time for breakfast this morning and a five-mile run first thing, I'm in dire need of an instant sugar fix. I duck into the nearest coffee shop and order a grande latte with a skinny lemon muffin to go.

I don't know why I'm so shocked. I mean, I did ask him to fix me up with shifts. But now he's only gone and bloody done it, I'm not sure it's what I want.

'*Of course it is!*' shrieks my inner voice. '*It's natural to be nervous, you'll be fine*'. I know I should listen. I need a new challenge and it'll be good for me career-wise to put myself out there. It is what I've always wanted, after all.

Already devouring the cake, I collect my coffee and hurry back to the office. My chilled mood has evaporated and I'm desperate to tell someone my news. As I rush in to the office, I almost bowl Pete and David over as they are heading out of the door.

"In a hurry again Miss Cleaver?"

"Oh hi Pete, er yeah, just eager to get this report written up," I gabble, edging past his bony frame in a green checked flannel shirt and worn suit jacket. "David," I nod a curt hello to the editor, who smiles his usual, amused, lopsided grin and stands aside to let me through. I'm not really sure what he really thinks of me. I mean, I'm pretty sure he likes me, and he seems pleased with the job I've done for the paper. A small part of me thinks he might even fancy me. I've caught him looking a few times at the shorter, tighter outfits I've worn.

Just for the record, that is something I never ever intend to find out for sure.

Making sure that they have well and truly left the building, I stick my head over the office dividers towards advertising looking for Gemma, but she's not there and her bag and coat have gone. "Is Gemma out on calls?" I ask Jenny.

She pretends not to hear me and carries on typing some unimportant crappy memo while I tap my fingers impatiently, before she deigns to answer without even looking up.

"Yes."

Well that was worth waiting for.

"How about those two?" I gesture over my shoulder towards the lifts.

"If you mean Mr Atkins and Mr Rodgers, they've gone to a meeting of the Small Businesses Forum at the town hall, and won't be back until mid-afternoon." She says it in her snooty-nosed, fake secretarial voice.

Right, okay then – mardy bitch!

Without thanking her, I cross the office and round the corner to the reporters' desks. They're all empty except Aidan's and it feels a bit like the Marie Celeste.

"Hi," I smoulder excitedly as I bend over, tucking my handbag under the desk and thrusting my tightly encased, pert arse in his direction. He smiles appreciatively and raises an eyebrow, "Hello, Kate. Looking good."

"You noticed. Thanks." I grin, "Where are the girls? Both on their patch?"

"Mmm, yeah."

"Then come to the kitchen, I've got something to tell you." I hurry into the adjoining room. When he doesn't follow me thirty seconds later, I stick my head back round the door and hiss: "Aidan, pssst. Come on, and close the door."

Reluctantly, he scrapes the chair back and follows me in, running his hands through his hair. God he's hot.

"I'm not closing the door," he mutters.

"Well push it to a bit then," I duck past him and shove the door a little, leaving a small gap. Spinning round I blurt, "You can't tell anyone this but Rupert's got me a shift on Saturday. It's my first one. Oh my God, I can't believe this is it! What do you think?"

Pressing my fingers to my lips, in case I've already said too much, I smile at him wide-eyed with excitement, feeling like I'm going to burst. My nerves have all but evaporated and now I'm just thrilled. He folds his arms across his broad chest and leans sexily against the wall. "Get you. Nice one."

He's not a man of words, well not spoken ones anyway. I blather on: "God, I was so nervous when I got the text but I really think this is what I need. It's time for a change. I've been thinking about this for ages. I'm really up for it."

"Are you now?" he drawls, amused and smirking at me. "I wondered why you were all flushed? I thought I might be causing it." Languidly he draws one finger down my cheek. I grin back at him batting his hand away.

"No, Mr Tindall, you have absolutely nothing to do with this whatsoever. Keep your mind on the conversation and your hands to yourself."

This is about me, not him. God this man is so vain. But I'm fighting a losing battle because, despite his earlier reluctance to find himself alone with me on office territory, he clearly can't control himself now. Sliding two fingers inside the sleek waistband of my trousers he tugs me closer to him and repositions his finger on my cheek, this time tracing a line as far as the corner of my mouth before rerouting his direction along my top lip.

We're standing so close I can feel his sweet, slightly smoky, breath on my cheek, scalding the skin as it touches me. Pressing his fingertip to my lips, he drags it downwards by a centimetre and pulls my lower lip into a pout, before gently inserting it into my mouth.

I suck tentatively, unsure what the other hand is doing as it slides past the waistband and into the lacy top of my silk knickers, lower and lower. I gasp in disbelief as he presses his middle finger home, still looking at me with a distinct amusement.

This is mad. I should really stop him, I know, but it feels so, so good!

There are half a dozen people working just a few metres away – they might be over in the advertising side of the office but that won't stop them using the kitchen - and I'm standing here with my deliciously attractive colleague's finger firmly ensconced in my pants, bringing me off as I speak. God help me, I need to exhibit a little self-control here but oh my lord, that is so, *oh…*

Panting slightly and with my head spinning, I reach for him drawing his mouth closer to mine but he abruptly pulls away.

"No."

"Aidan?" I'm confused and try it again.

"Kate, I said no." he says firmly, still rotating his hand while I squirm.

Okay, I have no idea what his problem is. He shrugs and removes his hand, and I'm both relieved and disappointed at the same time.

"I'm not kissing you in this office." he states matter-of-factly, then inserts his finger in his mouth and sucks off my wetness with a contented groan.

Speechless, I stand there uncomfortably, thanks both to

my indignation and the puddle that's slowly forming in my pants.

"So you mean to tell me you can stand there with your finger in my pussy while the rest of the paper works, but you can't bring yourself to kiss me. Oh for fucks sake Aidan, I give up!" I hiss in frustration.

"It's very simple, darling," he patronises me, "I'm not walking out of this room covered in your lipstick so everyone knows what we're up to."

"But you can walk out of here wearing my pussy juices round your mouth, right?" I turn on my heel and swish back past my desk, scoop up my bag and march angrily towards the exit.

"Are you going back out already?" Jenny bleats pointedly, her voice thick with disapproval.

"No, Jenny. I'm sat at my desk writing a huge scoop and this is just a hologram you're looking at." Rolling my eyes at her, I crash through the doors and jab the lift button aggressively.

Arseholes and morons. That's who I'm surrounded with. Roll on the weekend and hopefully the start of a new life.

Nine

I manage to avoid Aidan for the rest of the day by staying out on my patch until well after lunchtime. When I do return, he's ventured out himself. I know he's got an interview scheduled for late afternoon so the chances of him coming back in today are slim to non-existent.

I head over to the gym straight from work in the hope that pumping some iron will burn my frustrations off.

It's not that Aidan has actually been that out of order. If he doesn't want anyone to raise suspicions at work, he's right to draw the line and admittedly it would be ridiculously unprofessional if someone suspected we'd been kissing. But his decision still seems preposterous in light of the actual circumstances. It would be audacious to suggest our behaviour had been anywhere close to verging on appropriate. In any way, shape or form. However, while he seemed perfectly happy to commit an intimate sex act on the premises, kissing me appeared to have been a step too far. He can deal with sex, but not the intimacy.

Following an hour of hitting the weights, hard, I grab a quick shower and drive home. The house is deserted, just how I like it, and since our little 'chat' the boys have kept the kitchen relatively clear of debris. I make myself a protein shake and sort out my towel and sweaty gym gear, taking it to the utility room on the ground floor.

After putting it on a quick wash, I begin to head back upstairs but pause at the sight of half a dozen porn DVDs strewn across the desk and floor of Smithy's room. He rarely shuts the door, let alone locks it.

Glancing at the front door, I edge my way into the bedroom. Considering he's a slob throughout the rest of the house his bedroom is pretty tidy. Unlike most men his age who are renting a room in a shared house, it smells remarkably fresh. Sleeping so close to the washing machine must make him keep up with the laundry!

I sit down on the clean, grey sheets of his single bed and peer at the cases: 'A Tale of Two Titties', 'An Inspector Calls', 'Double D Desperate Housewives'. Jesus. Really?

Rolling my eyes, I reach for the one furthest away on the floor, carefully noting it's position, so I can return it to the exact same place, 'Three Men and a Little Lady'. From the badly pixelated image on the front cover this is clearly no story about raising a child and the woman involved is anything but a lady!

My earlier encounter with Aidan has played on my mind - and body - all day. The faint twitch in my pants has become a lot stronger since getting home. I'd welcome some immediate relief and the porn would definitely help. I would steal it and take it up to my room, but my bloody DVD player conked out at the weekend. A devious thought enters my mind. *Oh no, no, no, no. I can't do that.*

'*Oh yes you can*', says the little devil on my shoulder.

Really? Should I?

The boys are always back late on a Monday. Alfie starts his shift at 4pm and works through until midnight, Jasper grabs something to eat with his girlfriend and they go straight to their amateur dramatics club, and Smithy helps his mum teach karate to a room full of under-16-year-olds.

I dash upstairs quickly and slip off my clothes, pulling on a soft, grey jersey robe. Lifting my old vibrator from the drawer (I've run the new Rabbit down and forgotten to charge it) I scurry back down the two flights of stairs and into Smithy's room, shooting back out to the front door, to put the safety chain on – just in case!

Sliding the DVD into the slot, I switch on the TV and press play. Instantly, terrible, cheesy music starts to play and the scene opens with a pretty, 20-something blonde woman, dressed in uniform, running a feather duster over the bedhead of a dreary motel room. Whizzing the film forwards, I see two repair men hurtle into the room with a ladder and a tool-box, while a window cleaner appears outside. Wow, Smithy clearly appreciates the bargain basement, budget porn movie. Pressing play just as all parties start removing their clothes, I activate my ancient Rabbit; it buzzes weakly with a lacklustre hum. Bollocks. I must have run the bloody batteries down… I don't have any more.

Disappointed, I pause the screen and go to remove the DVD when, out the corner of my eye, I notice Smithy's bike in the hallway. I slide open the case of the bike light.

Bingo! Four AA batteries to replace the duds in my dildo!

Job done, I press play and settle back onto the bed, sliding one hand inside my robe to pinch and tease my right nipple as the other repositions my vibrator. The woman on screen - let's call her Roxanne - sucks off first one, then a second handyman. I don't know why they bothered with the toolbox, as firstly they didn't even open the damn thing and secondly, it appears that they keep their most useful (and frankly more impressive) tools about their person. The window cleaner watches through the window, pulling his seriously large cock out and rubbing it vigorously while he enjoys the floor show.

Repair Man One is the first to fuck Roxanne while she lays back, propped against the pillows tossing off Repair Man Two and rubbing his well-veined dick against her face and mouth. When they trade places, Repair Man Two flips her on her knees and she blows her previous lover, getting spit roasted in true porno tradition. It's then that she spots the Peeping Tom window cleaner and predictably invites him into the proceedings.

Yes, the storyline's shit and the acting's fake. To be fair, I usually prefer reading well written erotica than watching a cheap porn film, but there's something about watching this woman writhe around with three fit and toned men, each bearing huge cocks, whilst jerking off in my flatmate's room that really turns me on…

I cum quickly. It's hard and fast. My inner muscles contracting around the vibrating column, my legs splayed wide on the duvet. A second intense orgasm follows and I'm left panting and trembling as I come down from my high.

Standing the dripping toy on its end, I eject the film and place it back in the box before laying it carefully on the floor, exactly where it was, straightening the bedding and replacing the batteries in the bike light. I'm about to go back upstairs when I hear a key in the door and the jangle of the chain as someone tries to get in.

"Shit, who's put the lock on?" I hear Smithy's gruff tones as he wrestles with the door.

OMG! Glancing at the still wet vibrator in my hand and back at the door I freeze like a rabbit in headlights, not knowing which way to turn. I decide to creep back upstairs, hoping that Smithy won't see me through the frosted glass in the front door. Then I'll come back down feigning drowsiness, and make out that I was asleep.

With one foot on the bottom step, I feel my heart leap into my mouth as from above the sound of footsteps signals someone else lumbering down the second flight of stairs.

What the fuck?! There was someone in the house the entire time? Holy crap.

In an instant I spin round and leg it along the hallway into the utility room, blood rushes in my ears and palpitations crush my chest. I duck behind the door, there's no time to close it properly.

In a split second Alfie crashes downstairs and whips the chain off the door.

"Alright mate? Dunno who put that on, I thought I was the only one in."

He scratches his head, confused as Smithy shoves his way through the door. " 'Fought I was out there all night, innit?" he barks, crossly, as he kicks open his door that I've left ajar and lobs his kit bag on the floor. "I'm gonna get these overalls in the wash. Got anything you wanna chuck in there mate?" he asks Alfie, pushing the utility room door open.

"Oh, hi?" I blink, as the two lads stand in the doorway, clearly taken aback by my presence. "Do, do you want this?" I stammer gesturing at the machine, "My lot's just finished."

"Kate?" Alfie asks, startled, "When did you get back? Why was the chain on? Why didn't you answer the door?"

"Mmm? I say vaguely, "Sorry, what?"

"The door, doughnut!" Smithy spits, "Someone put the chain on. I was yelling.

"You must've heard me."

I hug my washing to me apologetically, the hidden, hard plastic of the vibrator burning into my skin below my robe.

"Sorry, no. I think I've been listening to my music too loud while I'm running. I didn't hear anything.

"I did put the lock on though. I was going to jump in the shower in a minute and I feel weird walking about the place half undressed when I'm here alone. Uh, how come you're both back? It's Monday…"

Smithy pushes past me and starts loading his clothes into the machine, "Mum's got flu so she's cancelled tonight's class."

I look at Alfie pointedly.

"Oh, I swapped shifts with Jase, so he can go to that Ed Sheeran gig on Thursday night. Pain up the arse really, I wanted to watch, Game of Thrones.

"Still, he did cover for me when I needed that appointment at the clap clinic last month."

"Right."

Cringing, I squeeze past the boys and out into the hallway

with my hidden booty.

"Oh Kate, hang on a minute, what's that?" Smithy says, sharply. Slowly I turned to face them, cheeks burning, sure that I've somehow been caught out. Gingerly dangling a tiny scrap of black lace between his finger and thumb, Smithy proffers my g-string, clearly dropped in my haste to hide the dildo beneath my washing.

I snatch it up quickly mumbling thanks and hurriedly walk away. "You alright Kate?" Smithy laughs, enjoying my discomfort. "You're looking a bit red in the face there, love."

Little does he know the real reason for my embarrassment, I think to myself, swearing there and then never to take another risk like that again.

Relaying the details to Stella later on the phone, it seems a lot funnier than it did at the time.

"And you couldn't toss off in your room thinking about lover boy?" she chuckles, clearly rolling around with mirth at the other end of the line.

"Yes, of course. It just seemed like a good idea… *at the time*." I add, also giggling.

"What like heavy petting in the office kitchen?" she exclaims, with sheer disbelief. "Kate, how the fuck do you get yourself into these situations? And twice in one day!"

"I have absolutely no idea," I confess, "but I have no doubt whatsoever that it is completely and entirely, utterly my fault!"

"You are simply a very, very naughty girl, Kate," she laughs wickedly.

This, as she says, is of course true.

Later, I'm lying in bed thinking of all the crazy things I've done so far in my - still relatively short - life. They're mainly sexual, although not everything is to be fair.

Once, while I was still at university, I 'kept' a guy at my house for two weeks just so I could have sex on tap. I don't mean I kept him there against his will. Although admittedly he did almost miss his train home once a few weeks previously, when I tied him up and rode him, despite his pleas to be released (he loved it).

No, by 'kept' I mean that I paid for everything so he would stay with me. Craig was a surf bum from Cornwall, staying with a uni mate who worked in the union bar. The night before he was heading home we got it on and the sex was electric. We stayed in touch, with me ringing him every night on the student paper's phone – 'abuse of privileges' was what the editor called it. Man, was I abusing that phone in more ways than he realised.

We had phone sex late one night when everyone else had gone home. I lay on the floor touching myself with my legs up the wall while I listened to his breath grow shorter and shorter as he came.

He came up to see me a couple of times – long distance booty calls – but each Sunday night it became more frustrating to let him go, until I suggested he stayed a bit longer. "I can't, Kate." He protested, lying in bed one day, stroking his hand down the curve of my arse. "You know I need to work; I need the money." Craig worked part time in his uncle's surf shop. He wouldn't be missed if he took a little time off, and his uncle would let him play hooky for a while during the winter, but he couldn't afford it.

"I don't need much, just the waves and my beer, and something to eat. But a few days off makes a huge difference on the peanuts Uncle Pete pays me." He smiled, cupping my lower cheek with his fingers. I shuffled up on one elbow and scooted over him, wrapping one leg around his and pressing my body against his chest.

"What if," I began slowly, rubbing myself against him, "you stay up here with me and I pay for everything: food, beers, eating out. Everything."

"Oh. I don't know, Kate…" he started, but I silenced him with my mouth.

"Everything is on me." I murmured in between kisses as I ran my hand lower down his body: "Everything."

Bingo. He stopped resisting.

Holding me firmly around the waist, he slung me up and over his hard cock. "Alright you minx, you've got a deal," he groaned and gave himself up to me.

The fortnight he stayed was incredible. I remained true to my word and had picked up the tab the entire time he was there. In return my student bedroom had been transformed into a giant shag pad: studies and lectures went out the window and daily chores were neglected in favour of hours of sex. This was interspersed by quick and easy post-coital meals and drunken, hazy nights out in clubs and bars - followed by yet more sex.

Days and nights had blended together into one long, fun-fuelled frenzy and we'd done everything under the sun, until

I made the cardinal mistake of breaking our pre-agreed rule: this was just casual fun and no-one was going to get serious.

Well, that was me fucked.

My feelings had been changing for a few days and I'd known it. I'd planned on keeping it to myself, but you know how it is. You're having one of the best weeks of your life, things are going well with a guy your friends love, he's a bloody sex god, and you've just had your fifth orgasm in a row... blah, blah, blah. You get the picture:

"Oh God, I love you," I'd panted, as I fell back onto the bed, still perspiring from an amazing shag. My hand had flown to my mouth, but it was too late. He'd said nothing for a moment, then gently tucked a stray strand of hair behind my ear.

"Oh Kate," he'd said as he looked at me sadly, "Kate, Kate, Kate." I'd closed my eyes, knowing what was coming.

Before the afternoon was out, he'd packed. I mean, of course I'd made excuses, said I hadn't meant it, that 'it was fine' and that we could 'go back to the way things were before'. But it made no difference.

He was right, I suppose. I had meant it – I'd fallen a little bit in love with him. He left that evening and I never heard from him again. I sometimes wonder where he is now.

Dragging my thoughts back to the present, I sigh and turn over in bed. I don't know what it is about men, but I'm beginning to think I've got a serious addiction to them.

I wonder, if that is true, will Aidan be the one that ends in an overdose?

Ten

On the morning of my first shift at *The Record*, I'm up way before my alarm goes off and frankly I'm a bag of nerves. A quick, hard sex session is the best way to deal with that but seeing as firstly, I am not in a relationship, secondly, there doesn't seem to be a man coincidently lying in my bed and lastly, I'm still out of batteries (my memory's like a sieve these days; I wonder what's distracting me?)

I'll have to make do with strong coffee, a hot shower and power make-up. You know, power make-up? When you take a long time to apply a flawless base, the perfect brow, detailed eyes and finished with glorious lips? Well that, plus a well tailored, slim fitting dress, paired with a fine pair of shoes and I feel utterly in control again.

I leave the car at the station and take the train in, grabbing another coffee and a takeaway porridge to eat as I cross town. Canary Wharf is all gleaming steel and glass.

I crane my neck and look up towards the top of the buildings: my future is up there somewhere.

Because I have no pass, security has to call up to the twenty-eighth floor for approval. They let me through to one of the high-powered lifts that speed me up to the floor for *The Record*. It's an airy, modern space with a long, high solid desk. The entrance is adorned with giant, framed images of the top front pages, and senior staff posing in war-torn locations.

Dean Oliver, head of features, bustles out of a door, proffering his hand in greeting.

"Hi, you must be Kate, I've heard a lot about you," he grins, warmly. Tall, thick set and bespectacled, he looks nothing like I'd imagined. Rupert had said Dean was dynamic, witty even, and a bit of a ladies man, something at first glance I can't see. But he seems friendly and puts me at ease by inviting me into the office and introducing me to some of the commissioning editors.

I'm to sit at one of the writer's desks, alongside theirs and next to Sara, one of the other staffers working this weekend. The open plan office takes up half of an entire floor of the tower, and has floor to ceiling windows that must run around the entire building. From where I'm sitting, towards the centre of the room, I can just about glimpse the breath-taking views of the capital as they stretch into the distance.

"So, I've got a few cuttings that I could do with you following up," Dean says, while absent-mindedly scratching his dark (dyed?) hair with the end of his biro. "I know they're a little dry, but we need to see what you can do.

"Rupert's impressed with you – says you're a natural and a fast learner. Anyway, take a look. If you can start with the one from today's *Mail*, about how bad Madonna's feet look in those shoes – we're looking for something along the lines of, 'see how awful, misshapen or old these celebrity body parts look, despite their anti-ageing regimes'. Got it? Photo desks over there!" Gesticulating wildly towards the corner of the room, he goes back to his desk.

Right. Ok.

Glancing desperately at the decidedly blank computer in front of me, I decide to leave it alone until I've tackled the image department. Removing a pen and pad from my bag, I stroll over to a messy desk, cluttered with photographic paraphernalia.

"Um, hi?" I say to a broad-shouldered, redheaded man sitting with his back to me, scrolling through a screen of images, "I'm Kate, I'm on a shift. Can you help me?"

Spinning round on a swivel chair, two amused looking, piercing blue-green eyes engage mine and a lilting Irish voice asks: "I don't know darling, can I? It depends what you're wanting."

Oooh dear.

Suddenly my insides have liquefied and my legs feel like they're not going to hold me up. Steadying myself with one hand on the desk, I tell Mr Damian Lewis lookalike (who it transpires, is called Will) about the feature I'm writing, and that I have no idea how I'm going to find the pictures I need.

"Sure, that's what I'm here for love, come on take a seat… what's your name?"

Pulling up a chair, I force myself to sit further away than I really want to – mind on the job, Kate, mind on the job – while Will clatters on the keyboard, pulling up the files he is looking for.

Stroking at the stubble on his sharply chiselled jaw, he nods at the screen, "There's quite a few to run through, shall I leave you to it?"

Please don't go, stay right here.

"Sure that'll be fine," I smile sweetly, "but what do I do with them once I've found the right ones?"

"Just stick them here in this file," he indicates to the screen and walks over to another computer. "Give me a shout if you get stuck!" he calls in his beautiful, melodic accent.

Or, if I instantly require emergency mouth to mouth, I think to myself.

Pushing all thoughts of Will and his hypnotic voice to the back of my mind, I settle down to trawling the hundreds, maybe thousands, of images stored on the system; saggy gizzards, grotesquely veined hands and huge bunions seem to be the order of the day.

These photographs, some posed on the red carpet or outside exclusive nightclubs, others snatched by the paparazzi, highlight ghastly flaws in the otherwise honed and toned, groomed and beautiful men and women; actors, musicians, and supermodels alike. It's quite reassuring that these icons of stage, screen and catwalk are actually human after all, but part of me feels a bit sorry for them at having their freakish body parts exposed to all and sundry.

I spend the next thirty minutes browsing and selecting the right images while making notes about each case study; who they are, where the picture was taken and what ageing attributes they possess.

When I'm finished, I thank Will and reluctantly drag myself away from his Gaelic godliness, returning to the desk I've been allocated for the day. Kindly, Dinah, the staffer working this weekend, logs onto the computer for me and runs through the basics of starting a new document, saving it to the correct file, etcetera. I'm a self-confessed technophobe and although I learn fast I despise having to pick up personalised systems when I start a new job.

'Yes, but get it right now, and with any luck your next job will be HERE,' an optimistic inner voice whispers. Shaking off the idea just in case it jinxes things, I keep my head down and plough on with this, and then the other, small stories that I get given. I'm primarily a news reporter at *The Express*, but I have written a number of features over the years.

One of the hardest to write, but the most rewarding, was a one-to-one interview with a rape victim. I wasn't sure I had the skill or experience to do her story justice, but she told me afterwards I'd handled it sensitively and that she felt a burden had been lifted, just by sharing her story. That is why I wanted to become a journalist.

I'm just coming to the end of the cuttings when Dean hurtles up to me brandishing his notepad, "Kate, we need you to go out. David Kentish's been rushed to hospital with a suspected heart attack. We're a bit short staffed and news haven't got anyone to send. Can you can head out and see what's happening?"

Christ. David Kentish is the charming, debonair, always outspoken Minister for Health – how ironic. A bit of a silver fox, even in his early 60s, the former actor and author always had a reputation for drinking and smoking too much, along with a string of broken marriages behind him.

When the fifth Mrs Kentish came along, three years ago, a petite, raven-haired yoga teacher in her late twenties, she transformed the ageing, slightly overweight MP, and is credited for his rapid rise through the ranks to a cabinet position.

Now Health Minister, Kentish is famous for practising what he preaches, extolling the virtues of clean living and meditation, and quite frankly exasperating his former luvvie friends, who remember him as party-loving Dave, who could drink anyone under the table. There was national outrage when he secured his current position and *The Mirror* ran a campaign calling for his resignation, in which one after another of his former colleagues came out with tales of gluttony and debauchery from the good old days.

Dean hands me a piece of paper with the hospital name on it and takes down my mobile number. "Stay in touch and I'll get news to send someone down there as soon as they can." Walking away, he adds: "Oh, good stuff on that celeb piece, by the way. I'll bring it up in conference first thing Monday."

I quickly wrap up the boring piece I'm doing about new vacuum cleaner technology, gather my bits together, head downstairs and make a beeline for the tube. Doubling back, I dash into EAT for a salad to eat on the way – two meals on the hoof today, what would my trainer say? She's always banging on about eating consciously, savouring every mouthful and sitting at a table for meals, making it 'an occasion.'

Yeah right, who has time for that? 'Oh sorry boss, I'll follow up on that urgent news story after I've sat down for my 30-minute lunch break'. Ha!

St. Thomas' Hospital is a sprawling mass of modern buildings on the banks of the Thames, right opposite the Houses of Parliament.

Mr Kensit was rushed straight here after he collapsed during Prime Minister's Question Time. Apparently, Helen Johnson, the Prime Minister herself, got down on the floor to give him immediate resuscitation, but the Clerk of the House ushered her off her knees and took over until help arrived.

When I jump out of the taxi in front of the hospital's A&E department, there's already a media frenzy unfolding. Television vans belonging to the BBC, Sky and ITV are jostling for space out on the street and a police officer is trying to keep control in the lobby, alongside a frazzled looking security guard.

I sidle up to a couple of reporters and ask if I've missed anything. "Not yet," rasps a short, gravel-voiced woman aggressively, stubbing out her cigarette and immediately lighting up another one.

"Oi, excuse me luv', no smoking on the premises," shouts the defeated looking, weedy security guard from the doorway. His courage has clearly been bolstered by the presence of the police, so the irritated journalist tuts and edges her way – only just - onto the street.

"They say there's no news as yet," a kinder reporter, greying at the temples and wearing a coffee stained shirt, tells me.

"We think they're going to make a statement soon."

I perch on the wall opposite and call Dean.

Two hours later, my bum's gone numb and I'm glad of the large water bottle I picked up with my lunch. I've already eaten the apple I slipped in my bag first thing and my eyes are starting to glaze over.

The snappy reporter is sat next to me kicking the worn heels of her knee length boots against the wall. She must be boiling, but shows no sign of overheating. In fact with her jet-black bob and pale white complexion she looks like one of the Adams family. If it wasn't for her puffing her way through an entire pack of fags I'd have had serious doubts that she was breathing at all.

Just when I'm beginning to fall asleep, there is a stir in the crowd and a senior medic comes to the hospital door. Quick as a flash, my fellow journos heave en-masse towards the entrance and I'm left craning my neck at the back trying to hear what he's saying.

Okay, here's the thing: I passed my shorthand exams first time, albeit with the most horrendous hangover following a misspent afternoon at the races, however, I don't know if it's the pressure of the first big job, or the fact that I'm standing right at the back, but when the statement's over I don't even have two whole lines written on my notepad.

The crowd disperses rapidly as reporters drift away to call editors and file copy, but I just stand there paralysed with fear, knowing that I'm in some serious shit if I don't do something fast.

Panic-stricken I look around me. Foxy Roxy, the chain-smoking bitch is on the phone and ignoring my pleas for help and Trevor, the kind reporter's disappeared somewhere, no doubt to file a perfectly decent story.

Feeling myself welling up, I clock the Sky team bustling away with their recording inside the distinctive TV van. Their recording! Yes, that's it! I dash over and, almost in tears now, explain I'm on my first shift and I've seriously fucked up.

To be fair, I guess it would sound funny to them because they can't stop laughing and invite me to sit in the van while they run through the tape. I start scribbling, eternally grateful.

Bless them, there is a god after all!

And you know what? I got it down word for word during the first playback. The TV guys are saying I can watch it again but I'm absolutely fine now. I have no idea where it went wrong earlier but I'm putting it down to nerves.

Relieved, I call Dean and file the copy back to the office. He's pleased with the job I've done and asks if I'd be happy to work another shift at the start of next month. I agree happily and, at Dean's insistence, head off home. I live west of London and Canary Wharf's in the east, so at gone 6pm there seems little point in me returning, he says. They've allocated a news agency to the job, who'll stay camped outside until the wee hours, just in case there's another update overnight.

It's been a good day, no, make that a great day, but I'm shattered by the time I get in and want nothing more than a long soak and an early night.

The house is eerily quiet, which is a blissful change. Surveying the debris cluttering up the bathroom and flickering in the candlelight, I wallow up to my neck in hot, scented water, holding a generous glass of wine.

Irritatingly, the phone buzzes. *Damn, forgot to put it on silent.* Reaching one hand out and mopping it on a towel, I open a text:

HOW DID IT GO? A

Sighing and smiling to myself at the same time, I take a large mouthful of the wine and text back:

IT WENT WELL. REALLY WELL. THANK YOU

Kiss or no kiss?
No kiss.
Seconds later it buzzes again:

X

Really?!
I give up. What does that man want?

Eleven

The summer months on a newspaper are known as 'silly season', for none other than the fact that the world and his wife are away on holiday and there isn't really much going on. From schools to Parliament, everything grinds to a halt in this country and the regular bread and butter that we rely to fill our pages all but dries up.

The first two weeks of August, Aidan has time booked off and I don't hear from him once. Several times I've been tempted to pick up the phone and text him, but I don't know enough about his plans to take the chance. If he's away on holiday with his girlfriend, getting a random text from the girl in the office (who he's shagged) could be more than awkward, and he wouldn't thank me for it.

Stupidly, I've booked time off work coinciding with his return, so that means almost four weeks without seeing him. I don't know whether to laugh or cry. I'm sure the break will do me good, yet I can't help but miss him and therefore spend a lot of time obsessing - mainly about fucking him.

Having spent most of my meagre income on new shoes, clothes and cocktails, plus a bloody car that won't stop breaking down, I can't actually afford to go away. Mum and

Dad have taken the tent to Spain and said I'm welcome to join them, but at 25 I really think there are some things you have to draw the line at.

So, I spend the first week chilling out, sunbathing in the garden, reading and generally doing nothing of much at all, which is kind of how I like it. The weather's kind to me, and by the time I drive up to Stella's on Friday morning, I'm pretty tanned and notice I'm more relaxed than I've been for a long while.

I haven't seen Stella since March and I can't wait to catch up properly. As soon as she knew I was off work she begged me to come and stay - wouldn't take no for an answer, in fact.

"You're coming up here KC and that's the end of that. I'll send Mike down to kidnap you and drive you up here in the boot if I have to!" She'd hollered down the line ten days ago.

I'd agreed. I had no intention of not accepting her offer, and was desperate to come, but Stella being Stella always anticipates a problem before there's even a whiff of one: "Not turning me down for lover boy then?" she asked sarcastically.

"Not remotely," I insisted, truthfully. "We are very much not an item and it's highly unlikely that we ever will be. It was an office shag and that's probably what it will stay."

"Probably?" She persisted.

"Fuck off Stella," I laughed, "We'll talk when I see you, but there isn't really much else to say."

She's taking a half-day and meeting me for lunch at a tapas bar in the Northern Quarter. I drive straight to hers, leave the car there and take a cab to the restaurant. When I arrive, Stella's already there sipping red wine and laughing with the waiter.

She's dressed in a bright red, fifties style dress, adorned with a bold poppy print that clashes gloriously with her auburn hair. From looking at her you would never guess that my best mate spends her days in a conservative navy skirt suit and plain blouse, tapping away at a computer.

"What's this, dress down Friday?" I joke, as Stella leaps up, squealing as she almost sending the wine flying and envelopes me in a blowsy cloud of her trademark Estée Lauder Gardenia fragrance.

"Cheeky bitch! I changed before I left! God, I'm glad you're here, I've missed you." I untangle myself from her embrace - and her petticoats - and sit down, beaming.

"You've missed me? I've missed you more like! Stell', you have absolutely no idea!" And, although she actually does, because we talk on the phone all the time, and she also completely gets it every time I call her with a mini-crisis or a drama, it feels really therapeutic to sit down with her face-to-face and talk out the whole debacle.

Not that she gives me an easy ride. Over the next three hours, accompanied by a myriad of little dishes and copious amounts of wine, Stella 'what ifs' and 'buts' and 'I don't thinks' through our entire debrief of my complicated on/off, one-night-stand/friendship with benefits.

Like I said, my fabulous bestie can spot a problem at twenty paces, hell she'd probably find the downside in a £90 million lottery win, so she's having a field day pointing out everything that can and will go wrong if Aidan and I take things further. But she has a wonderful knack of doing it.

Somehow, from Stella it never comes across as criticism. Not once, despite all the crazy, impulsive, irrational decisions I've made, has she ever told me outright that I'm wrong, or that I've behaved stupidly:

Not when I lost my virginity to a much older man on a one-night stand, which was only days after imploring her to help me get hold of the morning-after pill in a completely unwarranted panic following a bodged attempt at sex with a short-term boyfriend/waste of space. Not when I went home with the womanising barman with the disgraceful reputation who I'd been crushing on for months, and with whom I enjoyed two rampant sex sessions with - only to have my heart broken. And not when I carried on sleeping with Rob after we broke up and lied to myself, and to her, that it was just sex.

Nope, Stella is one of those rare creatures that I'm privileged and so, so lucky to have in my life; a wonderful best friend to whom I can tell anything and everything, without fear of rebuke.

We pay the bill and bid the extremely tolerant and browbeaten waiter goodbye. He has more than earned his excessively generous tip this afternoon, and in high spirits, with slightly blurred vision, we stagger our way onto the street, where - like a knight in shining armour - Stella's eternally patient and good-humoured boyfriend, Mike, is waiting.

"Mikey!" I shriek, ruffling his hair and half falling into the back of his Ford Focus ST, "How are you? Still as gorgeous as ever I see." He grins lopsidedly in the rear view mirror.

"Hello Kate," as Stella squeezes her underskirts into the

front seat and slams the door.

"Darling," she greets him loudly in exaggerated tones, smoothing down her starched cotton skirt in an overly large gesture and sitting bolt upright, under the pretence she's sober. "How wash your day? Ishn't it nice to shee Kate again?" And she plants a big, wet kiss on his amused mouth, leaving a smudge of bright red lipstick in her wake. He laughs and cups her cheek affectionately.

"It was fine gorgeous, but obviously not as good as your afternoon, ladies."

We drive the short distance back to Stella's flat, where her flatmate has thoughtfully left a bottle of wine chilling and a note, saying he was sorry he'd missed me but wishing us a great weekend and he'd see me on my next trip north.

"Aw, I can't believe Jamie's not here," I pout, "you didn't say he was going away this weekend."

"He's gone down to Brighton, to Anton's," says Mike, "He's so loved up, isn't he?" Stella nods, kicks off her shoes and dumps her bag on the edge of the kitchen table, which immediately falls on the floor. Stella looks at it and shrugs, "He shez he might be the one. How he can shay that after just shix weeksh I don't know," and she collapses onto the large, grey squishy sofa and promptly falls asleep.

Mike and I smile at each other. It's not that long ago that I remember her waxing lyrical to me about this wonderful guy she'd met and how she thought it could be for keeps - and that was only a month after she and Mike met.

I unpack my stuff and take a shower. By the time I come out, Stella has woken up, finished the large glass of water that

Mike made her drink and is lying prone on the sofa, getting a fabulous foot massage by the sounds of things.

"Aw, God, that's so good, don't stop… there, right there, keep it there," she groans.

"Ugh guys, get a room will you?" I laugh, plonking myself down in the battered red leather armchair in the corner of the room.

It's a draughty old building, with unreliable heating and second rate double glazing, hence the freezing cold stay back in March, but Stella and Jamie have made the place homely, with an eclectic mix of second hand and Ikea furniture, oversized plants and fairy lights round the bay window and the feature fireplace. The comfy, battered sofa is scattered with different size cushions and the walls are adorned with framed, arty prints of Jamie's own work.

A fashion photographer's lowly assistant, he still doesn't get much opportunity to produce fabulous paid-for work that gets published, but the stark, almost clinical, behind the scenes images he captures on every shoot bely a raw talent just waiting to be discovered.

"How's the clinic Mike?" I ask, pouring myself a moderately small glass of the wine, "Did you finish early today?"

"I did my lovely, just so I could come and rescue you beautiful ladies from yourselves," he jokes, getting a foot in the groin from Stella.

"Ow, careful love, you'll put me out of action!"

"Then you'll just have to teach me how to massage it better," Stella winks at me, sitting herself up, her hair sticking out wildly, and her eyes sparkling, "Anyway, can we just tell her now please?"

Tell me what? My gaze flies towards her left hand. I couldn't have missed it, could I? Nope, no ring. Maybe he's asked her but they haven't bought it yet.

"Go on." I ask feeling excitement bubble up inside me, "Tell me."

"Well," Mike starts, "do you remember…"

"He got the job!" Stella screams, "At Chelsea! We're moving down to you! And we're moving in together at last! Oh dear, that wasn't a good idea." Falling back down on the sofa, she holds her forehead, "Darling, could you get me some painkillers please." Mike chuckles to himself, stands up and walks into the kitchen, affectionately rubbing her hair on the way, "Serves you right for stealing my thunder, babe." I clap my hands in excitement and sit down next to Stella, wrapping my arms around her, in a giant bear hug. "Oh my God, that's brilliant news! Mike, well done, wow, this is huge.

"You're moving down south – at last!"

Stella smiles weakly, still rubbing her temples, "What can I say, you beat me down Kate. I said it'd happen eventually."

"No, what you actually said was you'd be here six months because there were openings coming up in London, and Manchester was a temporary stop gap," I laugh, poking her in the arm.

It's been a standing joke between us since she got the job. We'd never been more than a half an hour train ride away from each other before, and when she was recruited for this job she assured me it was only short term.

"And it would have been as well," stresses Stella, "only once

Cassie introduced me to Mike and things started to develop, then I didn't want that transfer to London."

"I know, I know, you put him before me." I sigh, mock sobbing into my sleeve. Stella shoves me back and Mike pretends to cuff me around the head, while giving Stella her requested dose of pills.

"So what are you going to do? Get a transfer? Are there any jobs down there Stel'?"

"Actually there is one," she enthuses, "I've known Zara, in the London branch, was pregnant for a while and she's due in a few months. I had a quiet word with Nathalie in HR, on the down low – she owed me anyway because I looked after her at the Christmas do last year when she threw up on shots, and made a pass at the MD – and she's earmarked the position as mine.

"They'll throw it open for interviews but she reckons it's in the bag. I got my transfer application in two weeks ago and should hear something next week. I've even been checking out flats already."

It transpires that Chelsea's training ground is out near the pretty Surrey village of Cobham, but Mike wants to be based a little nearer the city as their ground is in London. Stella rattles on excitedly as she opens up her tablet and shows me some of the properties they have been looking at buying online. I curl up on the sofa, watching her flick through open plan apartments, modern studio flats and converted churches. This is what Stella has been waiting for her entire life.

Her flat's cute and she couldn't have found a more perfect flatmate than Jamie, who's kind, caring, reliable and really great fun. But this is what she's been waiting for all this time; the chance to settle down and make a real home with Mike.

He's always been a sure bet – getting a job on campus straight out of university and then starting up his own clinic with his dad's help three years ago. Plus, he's ambitious and hard-working enough for her to know that he would never let her down. In short, he's a direct link to the life Stella's craved since her dad walked out the day after her seventh birthday. Stella's mum, Ava, worked her fingers to the bone to keep food on the table and a roof over the heads of Stella and Tanner, her little brother, by holding down two cleaning jobs and part-time admin work.

Her dad pissed off with a woman he met during his frequent visits to the pub, and although he turned up with the obligatory Christmas and birthday presents over the years, he very much became a Dad in name only.

Unlike some women whose fathers walked out on them, Stella hadn't become cynical, resentful and untrusting of men. She wasn't shy of commitment, or had fear that loving someone would inevitably lead to them leaving her. She didn't sabotage relationships before they even got going in a twisted self-defence mechanism. No, Stella is as loving and giving as any girl in a relationship could be; and she's finally getting the chance she deserves, to settle down in a home she can truly call her own.

'Unlike you,' a bitter voice echoes in my head. 'You have flitted from man to man since you discovered your sexuality at 17, and apart from Rob…'

Shut up, shut up, shut up!

I close down the irritating noise and devote more attention to the property search. Grudgingly, even I have to admit that it's true though. I was smitten with Rob while we were together, devoted to him even. But, that relationship aside, I have well and truly played the field these past seven years and I don't seem to be any closer to making a relationship work now, than I did at the beginning.

If anything it's me: the product of a stable upbringing, loving parents and secure home, who has trust issues around men, and absolutely no logical reason for it.

I spend the rest of the weekend pondering this thought and wrestling with my conscience. Stella and Mike are dizzy with their plans and we have a fantastic time eating, drinking and making merry, but when I load up the car on Monday evening following an early supper, Stella touches me on the arm and holds out a hand for me to take.

"It's okay." she says gently, squeezing my fingers warmly, "You'll sort it out."

Good, pure-hearted, insightful Stella. Her kindness brings tears to my eyes and I pull her close, burying my face in her hair, breathing in her familiar scent.

"I'm glad you're going to be near me again," I mumble into her shoulder, "I need you around to stop me fucking up all the time." Stella pulls back from our embrace, holding me at arm's length and wipes away a stray tear as it trickles down my cheek.

"Kate, nothing I can say or do ever stops you doing anything you really want to do," she laughs, "and you don't fuck up. You're just being you. If you were any different, you wouldn't be Kate - and we all love Kate." Swallowing back tears, I hug her again and rub the incessant tears from my eyes. Mike comes downstairs with my ghd straighteners, which I'd left in the bedroom, and also gives me a hug.

"Christ Kate, you'll leave your bloody head behind one of these days! What're you like?" Punching him playfully in the stomach, I grab the irons and chuck them on the back seat with the rest of my junk.

"But then I wouldn't be me and you wouldn't love me so much!" I joke, winking at Stella. She throws her head back and roars with laughter, as Mike looks at each of us in turn, confusion written all over his face before he heads back inside throws a last wave over his shoulder.

"He'll never get us," says Stella, "I absolutely love the bones of the man and I can't imagine being with anyone else, but doesn't matter how long we're together, we'll never have what you and I have, KC."

Smiling, I climb behind the wheel and three point turn the car, beeping my horn and waving madly as I yell, "I love you," all the way to the end of the street, while Stella does a crazy dance in the middle of the road, oblivious to the man in the white van, who waits patiently for her to finish.

I have a subdued journey home, in part due to the emotional moment we've just shared, but it's tinged with a spark of joy that soon that my favourite person in the whole world won't be 80 miles up the M1 and then some. I'm shattered by the time I pull up outside my house, but optimistic that things might actually turn out all right after all.

I text Stella, letting her know I'm back safely. She messages back a few minutes later:

GOOD. COUNTING DOWN THE DAYS TIL
WE'RE DOWN THERE. LOVE YOU X
PS: YOU'RE NOT A QUITTER, SO
DON'T START NOW XX

She's right, you know: I never quit. All through school and the bullying; through college and the sarcastic bitches who started out as friends, but ended up turning on me; at university, when my housemates made out we were looking for a house together, but then signed a lease without telling me.

Throughout it all I never once folded or gave in. "Don't let the bastards get you down," my dad had said over the phone when once it had all got too much.

And I didn't. I drank a lot, had one-night stands and threw myself into everything I did with a gung-ho attitude that basically said: 'Bring it on!' By believing that failure wasn't an option, it simply wasn't. And, if I didn't succeed first time, I just kept on trying until I did.

'So why are you giving up on Aidan now?' that bitching voice in my head harps on. Feeling my hackles rise and my resolve harden, I mutter through gritted teeth: "I'm not."

And for the first time since this episode has begun I actually, truly and wholeheartedly, believe myself.

154

Twelve

Achoo!

I gingerly dab my red-raw nose and ball up another soggy tissue, throwing it in the overflowing bin next to my bed. I am officially the world's worst patient (aside from my Dad, whose toleration levels are even lower than mine) and flu-style colds are the absolute worst!

I woke up the morning after leaving Manchester with a swollen head and streaming nose and spent the next three days lying in bed, watching Pretty Woman and Dirty Dancing on repeat, and generally feeling truly sorry for myself.

Due back at work on Wednesday, I'd rung the office first thing, croaking my apologies and grovelling that I'd try and make it in before the weekend; but following a couple of sleepless nights smothered in Vicks and dosed up to the eyeballs with painkillers and cough medicine, I knew that going in this morning was a bad idea. Missing a Friday at the end of the school summer holidays was no major deal. The other guys would chip in their time, finding a few half-baked stories in my patch and continuing the cover they'd provided while I was on holiday.

I take another nap, and by midday I'm pleasantly surprised

to find I'm actually feeling 50 percent better. Dragging my still-aching carcass into the shower, I stand for a long time beneath the gushing torrent, enjoying the cleansing feeling of steaming, hot water sluicing over my head and body, washing away the germs and grime of the last few days. It does the trick and after slathering myself in body butter and pulling on a soft, clean pair of cotton pyjamas, I gently rough dry my hair until it lies thick and shiny over my shoulders and I feel almost well again.

I eye the pile of dirty clothes sitting in a basket in the corner and sigh. I was going to get up and do the weekend's washing on Tuesday, but when I'd woken up sick it had slipped my mind. Galvanised by my shower, I resolve to tackle it immediately and heave it down the two flights of stairs, bundling it into the machine before slogging my way back up to my room.

Collapsing on the bed, I flop against the pillows, shattered by what feels like the superhuman strength I've just exhibited. What is it about being ill that, even when you're feeling better, you do one small thing and you're fucking knackered?!

Lying there for another couple of hours I nibble on the fruit, nuts, Babybel cheeses and crackers that I'd brought up to my room before my shower. I haven't eaten anything but soup and porridge all week and I think my stomach might have shrunk – bonus! My washing is probably well and truly finished but I really can't be arsed to trek back downstairs and lug it all back up. I might pull out the sick card later when the boys are home and see if one of them will hang it up for me – although I'm not thrilled about the thought of them manhandling my smalls; especially after Smithy's shenanigans with my knickers last month during porn-gate, as Stella has so eloquently nicknamed it.

Thirty minutes later, I've almost dozed off when the doorbell rings. It's pretty faint up here and at first I'm not even sure it is our bell, but whoever's ringing it's persistent because it becomes non-stop, and is now accompanied by knocking.

"Okay! I'm coming!" I yell irritably through gritted teeth as I pad barefoot down both flights of stairs with as much energy as I can muster. Fucking delivery men! Jesus, do they do this when no-one's here? Hammer on the door for ten minutes, winding up the whole street and then leave the parcel with an annoyed neighbour? No wonder Janet, the grumpy woman next door, always looks so pissed off when I show up with a delivery note and a sheepish smile.

"I said I was coming." I snap shortly, throwing open the door in fury, stopping abruptly in my tracks, my rant petering off and my mouth ajar, as an amused Aidan stands coolly outside the front door, one elbow propped against the door frame and his jacket slung casually over his shoulder.

"Are you still coming or have I missed out?" he smirks knowingly, brazenly looking me up and down, mentally removing both items of clothing with his eyes, and appreciatively licking his lips, "Because I know that once is never enough, so if you'd like any company while you come again, you better invite me in," he adds.

I stand there, completely shell shocked for a couple of seconds. Why is Aidan Tindall standing on my doorstop at 3.30pm on a Friday afternoon? Then, hearing the door open on the other side as Marian leaves on the school run, common sense gets the better of me. Tugging him by the arm, I drag him inside the house and slam the front door.

"Whoa, hold your horses babe, watch the shirt." He wrestles himself from my grip and dusts himself down, in an exaggerated fashion.

"Aidan, what the fuck are you doing here?" I hear myself croak in far too husky a voice.

"Well that's a nice way to talk to me when I've come to see how you are?" he complains, starting to mount the stairs, regardless of my incredulous stare and the question. "I come all this way to see you because you're 'sooo unwell', but when I get here, not only are you clearly not ill at all as you're looking abso-fucking-lutely edible in those cute little pyjama shorts, but you're also bloody rude to me." He glances over his shoulder, looking down my skimpy top, and smirks to himself as I self-consciously hold my hand to my chest, feeling stupidly embarrassed. It's ridiculous, considering our previous encounters.

He flops down, crossing one leg over the other; an arm flung over the back of the sofa, and watches me squirm uncomfortably. I wish I'd worn more substantial nightwear.

"Are you going to make me a cup of tea or should I make it myself?" he asks in a cocky manner.

Saying nothing, I purse my lips at his cheek and walk slowly, calmly into the kitchen. I try hard to regain my composure whilst holding the kettle under the tap.

I wouldn't normally react like this, but Aidan's really thrown me by turning up unannounced. I'm not sure I like him on my territory when it's not on my terms.

'*Noooo you silly cow*', the assertive voice in my head shouts, '*you can pack that in right now!*'

Wow, that was a bit harsh. But, you know what: she's right.

With two long, and slowly forced breaths, I take back control. I have no idea why he's here, and I don't really care right now. What I do know is Little Miss Timid-Pants can do one because Little Miss Seductress is going back in there. Just as soon as I've boiled this bloody…

Oooh!

The coarse fabric of his trousers presses unexpectedly into the soft skin at the back of my knees as his groin crushes my barely covered behind, grinding my pelvis into the hard surround of the sink. The blood in my head does a sweeping 360-degree spin and I inhale sharply; involuntarily. A hand skims down the inside of my arm, down towards my wrist, and he interlocks his fingers with mine, sliding them together, lubricated by the water I'd spilled when I dropped the kettle.

Intoxicated by the surprise assault and powerless to resist, I let my head fall back, leaning into his long, hard body as he snakes his mouth around the side of my face, along my jaw, leaving little butterfly kisses that burn my skin, and send a hotwire of flashing sparks straight down to my loins.

I move to turn and face him, but he resists, pinning me firmly against the cupboards. His mouth moves down the velvety skin on my neck and his free hand winds its way into my pink broderie anglaise, cupping my breast and pinching the already tightening bud between his finger and thumb.

I moan out loud, making him take hold of my chin and

almost painfully twist my mouth onto his, crushing my lips with a kiss so overwhelming I'm whimpering by the time we both come up for air.

Releasing me from his grip, but still pushing me against the cabinets, Aidan moves swiftly. He drops to his knees and pulls the tiny, boxer style bottoms to my ankles, gesturing for me to step out of them.

Almost as if in a trance I pull one foot, then the other free of the stretchy fabric and stand naked from the waist down. He pulls my legs wider apart and tugs my arse a little further into the room, pushing me forward until I'm bending over the sink. The stainless steel feels cold through the fabric of my top. He stays there for second or two, motionless, looking up at my crack; no doubt savouring the sight of me standing there, defenceless and on show to the world.

There's something incredibly erotic about this situation: me standing in the kitchen in broad daylight with my pussy exposed, and him kneeling fully dressed between my legs. Feeling vulnerable, yet without the slightest inhibition, I sense the first ebb of my juices trickling slowly down the inside of my thigh, then his breath teasing the fine hairs on my skin as he stretches out his tongue and laps the tiny rivulet away. I gasp, my inner thighs shaking with anticipation as he clambers to his feet.

His belt buckle jangles as he unbuttons the fly of his trousers and the fabric rustles as they drop to the floor. A packet tears open somewhere behind me. Wordlessly, he takes hold of my hips and crashes mercilessly into me in one sweeping thrust.

I'm literally seeing stars behind my closed lids. There is

nothing in the room for me except my dripping cunt and his throbbing cock. Gripping tightly onto the back ledge of the draining board, I brace my legs against the frantic rhythm of his thrusts, steadily increasing in speed until my knees are bashing painfully against the knackered cupboard doors.

Aidan's dick feels as if it's doubled in size as he hammers inside me, almost lifting my body off the floor with the intensity of his thrusts, and I have to reach one hand back to take hold of his hips and steady him:

"Slower," I gasp, the first word either of us has uttered since he asked me for that cup of tea. Breathing heavily, he pulls my body up and away from the surface, so his shirt is pressing against my bare shoulders, and buries his face into my hair.

The cool, crispness of the linen feels good against my skin. Sliding a strap down over my shoulder, Aidan uncovers first one breast, then the other; he takes hold of one with his whole hand as he nips my earlobe with his teeth.

At the same time, shifting his weight slightly so his legs are just inside mine, he begins to move slower, more precisely, each time ramming his huge cock deeper inside me, as he grinds the palm of his free hand against my clitoris. A guttural sound resonates from deep inside, primeval in my inability to control it. He sucks and bites down harder on the tip of my ear, pulling back and driving himself purposefully into me at such an acute angle. If he had a smaller dick he'd be springing out of me on every withdrawal. Tension builds from every angle and I'm completely lost in the moment.

Dizzy with emotion and physically at breaking point, a splintering orgasm crashes through my body and I lose all control of my limbs, relying on Aidan's arms and his strong cock to hold me up. Holding onto the rim of the condom, he eases himself out of me and, weak from exertion, I let him lower me to the floor. As I catch my breath, resting on my knees, he sits back on his haunches then leans backwards onto his hands into the living room, until he is finally lying back on the deep pile carpet. Sliding the condom painfully off his distended cock he looks me in the eye and speaks at last. His voice is hoarse with longing:

"Suck me. Please."

He doesn't need to ask twice. Crawling forward I lower my mouth, take the swollen, angry head of his taut member into my mouth and rub the flat of my tongue up and down the rim. Aidan moans and lets his head fall back on the carpet, shoving his cock deeper between my lips.

I show him no mercy and increase the pressure, sucking hard as I rotate myself up and down and around his tender knob. Taking him deep into my throat I regulate my breathing with this well-practised move, sending his senses reeling. Glancing up and replacing my mouth momentarily with a flick of my wrist I note his fists screwed tightly into balls and his chest and neck reddening, a sure sign of his imminent orgasm.

Plunging the warm, wet inside of my mouth back over him I suck on his dick like an ice pop, this time madly whipping my tongue around his rim, back and forth across the sensitive rib of skin joining his foreskin to his glans. It's all the persuasion he needs and bucking his hips up high into my face he comes in sudden, pulsating gushes, so fast I have to swallow it down in two or three rapid gulps.

Instantly, Aidan pushes himself up and grabs me with both hands around my face. He pulls my lips to his, plunging his tongue inside my mouth and kisses me deeply for a few seconds. His reaction startles me but the snog is good and I'm slightly disappointed when he pulls away.

"Wow, that was... unexpected."

He half smiles and lowers his glance, looking up at me from beneath his lashes, almost, coyly?

"I have this thing. I love to kiss a woman when she's just given me head; swallowed my spunk. I don't know why, it's just something that really turns me on."

I don't know what to say. No man has ever, would ever, want to do that. Most would probably recoil in horror if I so much as suggested it. But, bizarrely, I get where he's coming from. There is something wildly erotic about passionately kissing a man when you can still taste his cum.

"I have to go," he says, buttoning himself up and pulling me in for another deep kiss, only coming up for air when both of us are struggling for breath.

"I really have to go babe, I'm not just saying that. I'm supposed to be calling in at the fire station in 10 minutes – they'll be cutting me out of the wreckage of my car if I leave it any later because I'll be doing double the speed limit just to get there in time." He caresses the side of my face and stroking a thumb affectionately down my cheek says softly, "But it was worth it Kate."

He stands up, leaving me sitting on the floor and walks halfway across the room before stopping. Turning back, he smiles warmly at me, "I really like you Kate, and I want to get to know you better. Really know you. I don't want this to stop."

And just like that, he's gone. I hear his long legs bounding down the stairs two at a time, before the front door opens and slams, but I don't even get up and watch him drive away when I hear the car start.

In fact, I don't even move when the sound of the car has completely gone and all I can hear is the faint buzzing of the freezer, humming in the kitchen. I just stay there, frozen to the spot, staring at the stain on the carpet where Alfie spilt red wine last Christmas during a wild party we threw to celebrate Jasper landing a huge contract with a top department store.

He likes me.

I laugh silently, breathlessly gripping on to the sofa arm for dear life. I feel like I might keel over any minute.

He just said it. He really likes me. He's played it so cool for weeks, barely giving me any sign, other than the obvious – and that was purely physical – that he has anything but lukewarm regard towards me.

I take two or three deep breaths, forcing the rapid beating of my heart to slow down.

I know. It's nothing much. And yes, I'm playing with fire and I'm probably going to get burnt, but reading between the lines, I think he's saying we might actually have a chance at this.

Oh my lord. It feels so fucking good to see just a tiny bit of the big, tall wall, he's put up around himself, fall down. Just to see a chink in the toughened armour he's worn since the day I met him.

Hugging my knees tightly into my chest, I stay there for what feels like an eternity before rousing myself. Shaking myself down, I stroll to the window and look out at the enormous horse chestnut trees on the other side of the road. The giant, hand-like leaves are already starting to turn, their vibrant green colour now sage and browning in parts, and the afternoon sun is noticeably lower in the sky. It'll be autumn before I know it, and then Christmas in a flash.

When you're a child you feel the seasons stretch out endlessly in front of you. Great chasms of time are marked by stupidly exciting occasions, spread few and far between. But as an adult I literally feel like I blink and the world has moved with lightning speed, from crisp, cold, wintery days to fresh spring, into baking summers which arrive suddenly at the foggy mornings and damp, chill days of autumn.

Where will this next period of the year take me?

Part
Two

Thirteen

Unlucky for some, I think ruefully as I look at the blackened number 13 attached to the front of a previously white, semi-detached house.

It's my third shift and I've been sent out to report on a horrific house fire in Lewisham, South London, sadly involving children.

My second day at *The Record* had been uneventful, slightly boring even. I was desk bound all day while Nicole, the staffer, went out on a couple of jobs. I only got to leave the office on two coffee runs to Starbucks and a half hour's lunchtime spent pushing sushi around its carton in Pret a Manger. Nothing I wrote was actually used in the paper and it felt like a washout.

A couple of the smaller stories I'd written from press releases on my first shift also failed to make it into print, but the photo story of wonky toes and dodgy facelifts made an appearance and I got my first byline in a national. I'd been thrilled and went out and bought a stack of copies, posting one under every one of my housemate's doors before they were even up.

Mum and dad were chuffed to bits and cut it out of the paper, sticking it in a second scrapbook entitled, 'National

Papers – Kate's Work'. They'd started keeping a file when I'd joined *The Express*, but soon gave up when they realised I was having a lot of stories in print every week, and there's only so much pride you can take in an article on weed-killer.

Dean had still seemed happy with my progress and had asked me to come back again, so I was quietly delighted. He came flying up to me just before 11am this morning to tell me about the fire and asked if I'd go straight there. Possible fatalities, he'd said, probably kids.

In my hand are a couple of crumpled reports hastily thrust at me by the news editor as I left. It appears the fire broke out just after dawn at the two bed home, although there was no cause being suggested as yet.

A family of five had lived there: three children, Mum and her boyfriend. But on my way here the news ed' called to update me: two of the kids, a girl and a boy had died at the hospital.

I've never actually done a death knock regarding a child. In fact, I've only ever done one, and that was following a coroner's inquest when a company boss killed himself fearing money troubles would lose him the family home. When you work for a local paper, in a parochial suburb, there are not that many reasons to go knocking on the doors of the bereaved.

That one wasn't nice, and I'm told they never are, but I imagine you achieve greater satisfaction if you derive a successful result. On that occasion all I got was verbal abuse and the door slammed in my face from an understandably upset widow, who clearly didn't want to share her views with the local press.

I'm not comfortable with this, but it goes with the territory. There are a couple of other journalists loitering on the scene;

one from *The Sun*, the other from *The Mirror*. They're amiable enough, but we're all in competition to find out as much information in as little time possible, so pleasantries can wait.

A police officer says he can't say anything, but if I wait five minutes his inspector will be making a statement. That's why the other journos are hanging around like loose ends. I don't want to miss the update but it does seem like a real waste of time, just standing here, doing nothing.

Residents in the quiet, suburban side street of Hedgley Road are crowded around gateposts, talking in hushed tones and glancing forlornly towards the burnt out house. The area outside and the adjoining property are taped off, and there are a couple of policemen securing the wider area. A fire truck is still parked outside the fire-ravaged building and fire fighters are tidying up the debris. Keeping one eye on the cordon, I sidle up to a group of neighbours and smile sympathetically.

"This is so sad." One's visibly upset.

God I hate this kind of work. A man and two women, all in their mid to late forties, nod sagely.

"Awful, innit," says the younger of the two women, shaking her dreadlocks vigorously.

"Aye, it's a rum deal indeed," agrees the short, stocky man. I introduce myself and watch them visibly recoil at the mention of a newspaper.

"Oh, look, I don't think we should be..." the older woman starts, dabbing her tears and backing away from me.

"It's okay, I understand this is going to be a really hard time for the family," I interrupt kindly, "and this must be terribly difficult, for any of you that know the little ones."

They all look at each other.

I go on: "Listen, I'm going to speak to the inspector in a minute anyway, and you probably want to think things over. But if there's any possible way that you think you might be able to help me then I don't need to bother any members of the family. Not right now, anyway. Have a think about it." And I hurry back to the security tape, where an officer's approaching.

The officer introduces himself as Inspector Ian Boyle and reads out a written statement confirming what I've already been told: an eight year-old boy and a six year-old girl have died following the fire and he releases their names. The rest of the family were treated at the scene and are not injured. He reiterates the time the blaze seems to have started and appeals for any witnesses to contact the police, adding that early indications suggest the cause might be foul play.

A request that the family be left alone to deal with their loss is met by a guilty exchange of looks between the reporters – two more have appeared, both it would seem from national news agencies. He won't answer any questions and I make a beeline back to my friendly neighbours, who are deep in conversation.

"Y'alright? It's Kate, isn't it?" the older woman who'd been crying asks suspiciously. I nod.

"Yeah, well we've been talking and if it'll help and you don't need to speak to the family then, well, we'll do what we can to give you what you need."

"Thank you," I say, "could I come in perhaps, and maybe do this off the street?" The man, Doug, invites me into his house two doors down and the two women follow, wringing their hands and talking softly.

Doug's husband makes me a cup of coffee, while the dreadlocked woman, Alaya, tells me about the victims. The family had lived on the road for five years, she says sadly.

"Lovely family. Bright young 'fings. It was a joy to see 'em playing out in the street.

"Their youngest, a little boy, was born here three years ago, but the marriage broke up a year later and the mum's boyfriend only moved in eight months ago."

"Dodgy lookin' fella" adds her neighbour, Maureen, sipping at her tea quietly. She lives two doors away from the damaged house and was out at her cleaning job when the fire started. Coming home to the devastating news has been a shock to her and she is taking the news of the children hard.

"How do you mean, Maureen?" I ask gently, pressing her for more details.

"'im, the boyfriend, 'es dodgy. I told the police, people comin' and goin' at all hours since 'e moved in. Reckon 'e'll 'av summat to do with it."

I take a few more notes and finish my cup of coffee, thanking them for their time. "I know it's a difficult request," I add, carefully, "But would you happen to have any photographs of the children? The paper will be looking to print one."

I can't go back without a photo.

They look nervously at one another.

"If the cause does turn out to be suspicious, seeing a picture of the poor little mites who perished might be the difference between someone keeping hush and spilling the beans,"

I explain patiently. "Plus, everyone should see who they are, take a moment to remember these kids."

Alaya stands up and motions for me to follow her.

"We 'ad a barbeque earlier this summer," she says, "invited most the street. I think there'll be some of the kids in those."

We wander across the road, past the news agency reporters, and into Alaya's garden. "Don' seem right, do it?" she asks, looking over at the blackened windows and doors: "I'm forty four now and my kids are all grown up and left 'ome. One's at university and the other's living up in Manchester wiv 'er boyfriend. I think the world of 'em. Those poor parents."

She shakes her head again and lets us both through the front door. We step into a colourful hallway adorned with kitch, the walls covered with snaps of her children at different ages, taken over the years.

"Won't be a mo'," she says, ducking into the front room, and returning a couple of minutes later with an envelope of photos. "Glad I printed 'em off now. New Year's resolution. We all walk around with hundreds of photos on our phone and never get 'em printed, do we?"

Leafing through the pile of pictures she pauses halfway, staring at the image for a second, the colour draining from her face. Fingers trembling she offers me the photograph. I glance down at it:

Two golden haired cherubs look back at me. One is a girl, with long, blond straight hair and freckles, laughing, toothlessly into the lens as she holds a giant, sweet-encrusted whippy ice cream up to the camera. Beside her a fair, shaggy-haired, tanned boy, shirtless and with a slightly grubby face is ramming his frozen treat into his mouth, wide-eyed and mischievous looking. They both have the same almond shaped, bright blue eyes.

"Ollie, and Ellie," Alaya whispers, her voice thick with emotion. I feel a lump growing inside my throat and have to blink back tears that are threatening to fall. We stand in silence for a few seconds.

How can two young lives just get snuffed out just like that? They went to bed last night thinking about the weekend off school. Maybe they'd been nagging about Halloween costumes, or asking if it's half term yet. Then, when the world and his wife got up this morning, they didn't. And they never will. It's too sad, it really is. Sighing heavily, I lie a comforting hand on Alaya's shoulder.

"Thank you Alaya. I will look after it. Would you like it back?"

"Please," she answers, wiping her face with the back of her hand, "I want to keep it. Maybe give a copy to their Mum. Not now, in a while when she's had a bit of time."

She gives me another couple of photographs. This time, according to Maureen, they show the whole family, including Max Jones, the dodgy boyfriend.

Making a note of Alaya's address and taking her mobile number, I thank her again for the photographs and say goodbye. I walk a little further back up the road away from the chaos, the sadness and the ruined home where a family's life has unravelled overnight, before I call Dean in the office and report back. When I mention the pictures he's in raptures and over the moon. "Kate that's brilliant, well done." he enthuses, "Great job. Fabulous scoop and good work getting photos like that."

After filing the story, I end the call and walk a couple of streets to a small greasy café I spotted on the way here. Feeling subdued, I order a large coffee and a large cream horn, the kind my Grandma used to buy me. I take a seat by the window and look out at the buses, cars and taxis moving nose to tail through the narrow street, and at the small businesses sitting cheek to jowl with food outlets and cab offices.

Across the road from the café is a small park, sandwiched between a kebab shop and a 99 pence store. A little boy, no more than four or five is jumping in the piles of orange, red and brown leaves, while his jaded mother sits on a bench wearily looking on as she sips from a polystyrene cup and rocks the handle of a pram, as if in a trance.

It's early October, and despite my previous joy at the end of the summer, nothing more serious had come of the fleeting, infrequent dalliances I'd shared with Aidan. We'd had sex on a couple more occasions and each time it was as amazing if not more intense as the last, but he still refused to go out on a proper date, shunning lunch invitations and suggestions that I cook him dinner after work. He did agree to come out for a drink with me one afternoon in late September, but he texted me an hour beforehand to say something had come up and he wasn't going to be able to make it.

When I relayed the story to Gemma - identities still changed of course - she rolled her eyes and huffed and harrumphed her way through every reason I should stop wasting my time on an attached man and find myself someone decent. And, what by the way had happened to my obsession with Aidan?

If only she knew.

I feel really bad not telling her, and I will spill all at some point in the not too distant future, but with her working alongside us both and not being able to conceal her emotions too well, I really can't afford a scene in the office.

The worst thing is, Gemma's right. I am wasting my time and this isn't going anywhere, but every time I sleep with him I fall that tiny bit further and the thought of never being with him again, in that way, leaves me devastated. I haven't felt this strongly about anyone since Rob, but even if I did decide to give up on Aidan now, I'm not sure I could.

The clouds are a bleak, washed out grey – it's the kind of day that looks like someone sucked all the colour out of the sky while we were in bed. 'Suicide Weather', I call it, because despite the colour in the trees, I know we're only a few weeks away from darker mornings, shorter days and the generally cold, wet winter weather that makes me want to top myself.

What with the tragedy of the fire, and the clouds, and Aidan, I sit pushing what's left of the cake around my plate, brooding into the remnants of my really very substandard coffee.

I want to kiss him again, so badly. Every time I'm not with him I can't tear my mind away from the way his lips feel pressed into mine. Each time I close my eyes I can feel them, soft and full against my mouth, yet strong; and parted - but not too wide - just enough for his tongue to probe gently, then more forcefully, inside mine, over my tongue, slipping and sucking, like he's caressing the very core of my soul.

"You finished, madam?" the waitress' harsh Baltic tones

rouse me from my reverie as she whips away the cup and plate from under my nose, tutting loudly at my cheek for daring to sit so long without ordering more refreshments.

I trudge to the tube and head back to the office, spending what's left of the afternoon tidying up a few menial stories that'll probably never see the light of day.

On the way home I stop and buy a good bottle of red wine, planning to have just one glass with a lean piece of steak and a green salad. I'm in melancholy mood and can't stop my mind from going into overdrive, brooding about the two young children who died, Aidan, and where my life's going right now.

People constantly tell me I'm young and that I want too much too soon. My dad used to say that nothing was ever good enough for me, and that I'd never find satisfaction if I keep looking for the next best thing.

"You want the top brick off the chimney," he used to say crossly, when I'd been on a day out, or given a treat, and still asked for something more. Maybe he's right. Maybe I need to start appreciating what I've already got.

I ponder this while savouring the juicy steak. But there's nothing wrong with ambition is there? Or knowing who you want and not stopping at any cost until you get them?

I'm like one of Thatcher's children growing up in the Eighties, when there was a real sense of infinite possibility, a sense that you could achieve anything if you were prepared to work hard enough. Of course I'm going to aim high and strive for the best.

The evening drifts on with me in deep thought, confused about what I should, and do want, and wondering how long

I'm going to feel this lost for.

It's almost 11pm now and the last track on my playlist finished ages ago. Glancing down at the bottle of Malbec, I realise that I've had nearly all of it and groan at the head I'm going to have in the morning. Pushing my used crockery, the glass and bottle against the wall I resolve to tidy up tomorrow and quickly brush my teeth before turning in.

It's been a strange day, and it's made me look at things differently; sharpen my perspective. Life is short, something the family of those poor kids has found out all too soon. I'll be damned if I'm going to sit back and take the cards I'm dealt. No, first thing tomorrow I'm going to up the ante and take things to the next level.

The world better be ready for me.

Fourteen

Determined that Aidan would be first on my achievement list, I start bombarding him with texts the next morning:

> I DREAMT ABOUT YOU LAST NIGHT

> I WAS SO WET WHEN I WOKE UP I HAD TO FUCK MY VIBRATOR AND CAME HARD. TWICE

> I'M STILL WET NOW AND CAN'T STOP THINKING ABOUT YOU

By the time I'd arrived at work that last one was true, because his explicit messages back to me had left me all hot and bothered:

> I WANT TO SLIDE YOUR PANTIES TO ONE SIDE AND FUCK YOU WITH THEM STILL ON

> YOU WERE SO WET AND TIGHT THE LAST TIME WE FUCKED

> YOU TURN ME ON SO MUCH

I THINK ABOUT YOU WHEN I'M FUCKING MY GIRLFRIEND.

That last one really blew me away. It was some admission and for Aidan, a pretty crazy one. He never talks about his girlfriend. I've never even heard him mention her name. So to tell me something like that, he must have been pretty carried away.

When I got to work he was already there, but we didn't dare look at each other all day for fear of revealing our secret. If it hadn't been obvious before that something was going on, it is now. Anna actually drew me aside in the tearoom and asked if we'd fallen out.

"No, not fallen out, don't be silly," I blushed into my cup, pretending to study the front page of *The Sun* intently.

"He's just getting on my nerves is all." I curse, "Fuckwit. You know what he's like. He's just being a bit of a cock. But it'll be fine. Just ignore him."

She seemed to swallow it and wandered, good-naturedly back to her desk. God, how she's a journalist I'll never know. She never seems to question anything!

That evening, I'm barely back to my car when the first text comes through:

I WANT YOU. NOW

Up at the other end of the car park Aidan pauses with the car door open, and smiles suggestively before jumping in. As he drives past me a second message arrives:

RACE YOU BACK TO MINE

WINNER GETS TO CUM FIRST

The cheeky…!

Leaping into my car, I start the ignition and throw the car through the multi-storey, trying to do the seatbelt up as I fly round the corners, and catch him up at the barrier. His opens fractionally before mine, but I'm determined to win and I keep him right in front of me for the next four miles, constantly looking for an opportunity to overtake him.

It comes at the entrance to a public school, just before the traffic lights on Radcliff Road. Stuck in the inside lane as a people carrier turns slowly into the school gates, Aidan can't go anywhere, but the car beside him, signalling right –for the junction, I thought – suddenly veers into a driveway across the street, leaving the lane clear. Checking my mirror, I instantly pull out and glide past Aidan's Golf, catching the annoyance in his eyes as I accelerate away.

All the way down the High Street it's nose to tail and I'm giving my infuriated, part-time lover, cocky one and two finger hand-gestures in the rear-view mirror. Convinced I've won this, and excited at the prospect of shagging him senseless within the next fifteen minutes, I didn't notice him disappear at first. It's halfway along the main road when I realise he's not behind me anymore.

Puzzled, I weave left and right, trying to see if his car is further back along the street, although I hadn't seen anyone waiting to pull out so I'm confident that no one is between us. Still confused, I draw into the tiny road next to Costa, and am amazed to see Aidan perched smugly on the bonnet of his car, looking pleased with himself.

"How the fuck…?" I start, locking the car and walking up to him.

"Did you forget about Lovers Lane?" he asks, with ill-concealed complacency.

I rub my brow and shake my head. Lovers Lane, of course. How ironic. There's a little one way street, more of an alleyway really, that runs behind the Co-op and in between the old button factory and its warehouse, joining up with Aidan's road, just behind his house.

"Bollocks!"

Laughing at my own irritation and his conceited air, I throw my hands up in surrender and follow him into the house. It's no tidier than last time. If anything it's worse. Aidan clears a pile of motoring magazines and old newspapers off the seat, and pushes a jumble of washed clothes off the arm of the sofa so they land in a heap on the floor.

Before I have time to say anything, he grabs me by the wrist and pulls me in to his arms. He devours my mouth, forcing my lips wide apart, his tongue sweeping violently around, sucking the life from me and crushing me to him.

"I've been hard for you since breakfast, you little minx" he growls, painfully seizing my hand and thrusting it against his groin, where an already rock solid erection is mounting. "Now you're going to pay for your filthy stream of messages, and I'm going to enjoy every minute of it," he laughs, wickedly.

My heart drums in my chest and I give myself up to him,

allowing him to shove my tight little skirt up around my waist and rip my underwear down before throwing me on the sofa. The power he's wielding is intoxicating and I'm more turned on than I've ever been.

Wrenching open his trousers, he lets them hang with his trunks around his knees. He wedges my legs apart and, easing a condom onto his painful looking, tumescent penis, launches himself straight into me, taking my breath away with the intensity of his assault.

I cry out – a mixture of pleasure and, what? Not pain, but shock maybe, that he wants me this badly. Wrapping my arms around his back, inside his shirt, I hold tight, following his movements and allowing myself to be consumed by his passion.

My pussy clenches involuntarily around his thick cock and I can feel him hilting inside me, rocking his pelvis against mine, the day's sexual tension finally finding its release for both of us.

I can't tell where he ends and I begin.

I search out his mouth and he returns my kiss tenfold as he drives my arse into the knackered sofa, increasing his rhythm and moaning into my mouth. I see his face flush and know he's going to finish soon.

"Aidan. Wait, I want to cum and I can't like this." Oblivious, so obsessed with finding his own gratification, he carries on regardless of my needs. All attempts to hold his gyrating hips steady are futile.

Within seconds he's at the point of no return. He looks down at me with an egotistical expression and stammers out, "I, uh, won," coming in a flood inside me.

I'm consumed by disbelief. Taken aback by his audacity and stunned he actually took his own challenge seriously. When he'd said, 'Winner gets to cum first', I didn't think he'd meant it, for God's sake.

My inertia wears off almost immediately and feeling outraged I push him off me and scramble to my feet, dragging my knickers up and my skirt down before locating my shoes which had tumbled off at some point during sex. By now, Aidan's regained his composure and pulling his trousers back up reaches an arm out to me, but I back away sharply.

"Babe, don't be like that, it was just a bit of fun."

My hackles raised, I glare back at him.

"Fun? Sure, fun for you, but I was looking for a little fun too. Or did that just slip your mind?" Smoothing my hair down with my hands, I grab my bag and stalk out of the room into the kitchen. I'm seething.

"Kate, babe, there's no need to be like that. I just owe you one for another day, that's all," Aidan calls after me. I turn on my heel and look him directly in the eye.

"We, Aidan, are very much done. There won't be another day. You can fuck off." And, slamming the back door behind me I march back to my car and drive home.

How the hell I got back, I don't know. I was shaking so much I probably shouldn't have been driving, but I was determined not to break down until my bedroom door was firmly shut behind me.

As soon as I reach my room, I throw myself down on the bed, sob into the duvet and cry my eyes out for the next half an hour.

How could I have been so stupid?

A guy who is cheating on his girlfriend with a girl from the office is never going to turn into good boyfriend material.

Yes, the sex was (usually) mind blowing, and we do have a connection - we do - despite everything. Yet something like today has been coming for a while. I just didn't expect things to blow up quite so spectacularly in my face.

I'm wiped out by tonight's developments and expect to sleep like a baby when I turn in early. Instead, I toss and turn all night staying awake for hours at time, and only snatching twenty minutes here and there. When I do drop off I'm haunted by images of Aidan's face, contorted mid-orgasm, looming above me and can just make out Gemma and Stella to the side of me, shaking their heads and saying 'I told you so'.

By 4am I've resorted to sitting on the chaise longue with a cashmere blanket wrapped around me, watching as dark clouds race across the face of the moon. The winds are up and they're forecasting a storm tomorrow evening. The tail end of Hurricane Glenda that tore into New York State a couple of days ago and is tracking over the Atlantic right now.

I don't think I can face the office tomorrow; the thought of seeing Aidan after yesterday makes me feel sick enough, but the idea of working alongside him, day in day out, for the foreseeable future, well that's worse.

Yes, he behaved like an absolute arsehole today, and yes, the way he treated me is unforgiveable. Yet, a tiny voice I've been trying to block out all night, which can barely be heard above the howling wind and confusion in my head, way, way back in the recess of my mind, whispers: *You still want him.*

That brutally honest side of me that I'd rather just ignore is insisting - no matter how long I promise myself I'll never be with Aidan again - that one day I will cave in and sleep with him once more. Because, I can't not. Because, when it comes to him, I'm weak.

Eventually I fall into a fitful sleep, waking with a start two hours later when the alarm signals morning. I've got a crick in my neck where I'd been slumped against the cushions and the hard padding of the arm rest, and I stand under the shower for ages, letting the hot water pound my sore muscles.

THUMP! THUMP! THUMP!

One of the boys hammers on the bathroom door, telling me to 'Get, the fuck out!' but I ignore him, staring blankly at the stained, chipped tiles, until eventually the water runs cold.

Wrapping myself in a large, fluffy towel I blindly push past Jasper and Alfie, who are fuming, and slam my bedroom door, playing Iggy Azalea on full blast while I get dressed.

'Fuck them! Fuck them all!' I think madly, as one of them – Alfie, I'm sure - lets out a bloodcurdling scream and shouts obscenities through the wall. Let him have a cold shower for a change! I'm fed up of taking their shit and not giving any back.

I grab a yoghurt from the fridge and a teaspoon from the drawer – I'm not using an office one, it's probably contaminated by Anna – and drive to work, avoiding the usual route. Even just driving past Aidan's house is too much for me to bear. My eyes fill with tears and the dull ache that's taken up residence in the void between my heart and my stomach swells way beyond comfortable; it's going to take all my stamina just to get through the day without having a meltdown.

Luckily I still have my interview with previous X-Factor winner, Heather Mantini, to transcribe from the Dictaphone so I make myself a quick coffee, plug in the earphones and glue my eyes to the computer, not daring to look at anyone else, least of all Aidan, when he arrives.

I can feel my cheeks burning as his eyes bore into me, needling me to look in his direction. But as long as I don't let my gaze stray from the screen, I know I'm safe. There's no way he will attempt to actually speak to me about it, not in a really quiet office with so many nosy colleagues.

Keeping my eye on the time, I carry on writing and try hard to concentrate on the inane wittering of 'Have-a-go-Heather', as the national press labelled her when she shocked the nation by winning the competition four years ago.

Never a bookie's favourite, she was more of the comedy act, like Stevie Richie or Chico, and to be fair, I'm not sure even she believed her own hype, but it was one of those years when taste and talent went out of the window and somehow the public were rooting for the slightly over-weight, loveable lass.

Since then things have gone rather downhill. Her first album plummeted and she was dropped by the record company six months later. Public engagements slowly dried up, and last Christmas she ended up in panto with Christopher Biggins and some virtual unknown from *Doctors*.

Things have taken a turn for the better for her recently though. After scoring a victory by winning Comic Relief's Celebrity Bake-Off, Heather's been offered her own cooking column in a Sunday supplement, plus some guest slots baking on Lorraine, a few times a month. There's even talk of BBC2 getting her to front her own show next year, and so the tabloids have rekindled their interest in her again.

Despite the resurgence in her fame, 42-year-old Heather is nothing but loyal; as a lifelong resident of Staines, she remembers the pages of support we ran during her run on X-Factor. Unlike some wannabe popstars that forget their roots at the first sign of success, former supermarket checkout girl, Heather, has stayed in touch with her local rag and always makes time for interviews with us.

I'm almost finished writing up the interview when I realise the time: 11.30am. I've missed my 11am coffee fix. Saving the work, and without looking up, I shove my chair back and walk straight out of the office. I head to the coffee shop in the shopping centre and order a large latte. While I'm waiting I step outside and press speed dial on my phone.

It rings five or six times before anyone answers:

"Hello, *Record* features."

"Hi." I say, clearing my throat, "Ahem. Hi, is Dean there please?"

"Hang on a minute, who's calling?"

"Um, Kate. Kate Cleaver," I add, "I've done a few shifts up there. Is he out of his conference?"

"Kate, how are you? It's Lori," the voice on the other end of the line replies warmly.

Lori Gray, Deputy Features Editor, has been there on two of my shifts and is possibly the kindest, nicest woman I've ever met. By taking the time to get to know me and explaining the jobs thoroughly although she was busy, Lori put me at ease straight away. She even cornered me in the ladies' on my last shift to say I had talent and should persevere as I'd be a credit to the team. I was stunned.

"I'm fine, thank you Lori, really well. And you?" I say, faking a chirpiness, I'm not feeling.

"Ooh, you know how it is, mustn't grumble. Well I would but I'll probably wait 'til later when I have a large red wine in my hand," she jokes, laughing like a drain, amused by her own wit. I smile and take a deep breath:

"Lori, the thing is, and I know it's a bit forward, and I've only done a few shifts, but I'm going to ask Dean if there's a job going, and I wondered, seeing as you've picked up the phone, if you'd put a good word in for me." She chuckles and I wonder if she's laughing at me or with me.

"Honey, I think that's a bloody great idea, leave it with me. Ah, here we go, they've just come out of conference now. I'll pass you over. And Kate honey, don't sell yourself short."

There's a short moment when the line goes silent and I wonder if I've been cut off, then Dean answers: "Kate, hello, what I can do for you?"

Straight in there, with no beating about the bush, I take the plunge and ask him outright for a job.

"I realise it's a bit premature and I probably haven't got the experience you're looking for, but I really feel like I might have what it takes, and I've loved doing the shifts and I think, well you said yourself that you were pleased with me..." My mouth is like a runaway train, over which I've definitely lost all control. I'm filling the silence that persists as Dean says nothing, by inanely babbling on until even I've run out of things to say. There is a pause that feels like forever and I'm about to start talking bollocks again when he pipes up.

"You know it's funny, I was only talking about you yesterday evening to the editor. I said we could do with some new blood and we did lose a writer last month to, *The Mail*. Leave it with me. I'll call you. I've gotta go."

And with that he hangs up. I stand looking at the blank screen of the phone for another thirty seconds until an elderly man in a flat cap and with a walking stick taps me on the shoulder.

"Are you Kate?"

"Mmm, sorry?" I peer at him, blinking. I don't know this man, but he seems to know me.

"Kate? Is that your name, lovey?"

"Yes, how do you know that?" I must still look shell-shocked, because he gently takes me by the elbow and turns me round, to face the coffee bar, where the entire shop, baristas and customers too, are staring at me.

"They've been calling your name for five minutes. You're in a world of your own love." Smiling sheepishly at the old man, I walk back to the bar and apologetically pick up my coffee. I leave as quickly as possible, well aware all eyes are still on me.

As I hurry back to the office, I'm still in a daze. Oh my God, it sounded like Dean was saying they're really considering me for a job. A job at *The Record*!

Fuck!

I mean, I rang to ask him for one, but it didn't enter my head that there might actually be one waiting for me, right now.

Fuck!

I only really rang him on a whim.

I feel sick.

I can't believe this.

Ok don't get carried away, it could amount to nothing… Maybe I could get a place in town, near Stella and Mike!

Stop it, now!

My mind's still whirling as the lift doors open and I step out, almost colliding with Aidan who's clearly on his way somewhere. I recoil immediately, side stepping him with complete disdain, and hurry towards the doors.

"Kate, just wait, please." He sounds, I don't know… unhappy? Pressing my hand to the door, I hesitate and glance over my shoulder, I study his face, taking in his day old stubble, his unusually creased shirt, his furrowed brow and below that, unusually clouded eyes.

He looks… dare I say it - hurt?

I pause, for just a fraction of a second and he takes a step towards me.

No. I'm not letting him back in.

"Fuck. Off."

Leaving the bitter words hanging in mid-air, I push my way into the office and slump at my desk, slopping coffee over my notepad. "You could've got us one," Anna whines, looking enviously at the latte. I suddenly feel exhausted and sick from the events of today and the disaster last night. I pick up the dripping coffee and set it down amid the debris on Anna's desk – in its current state it looks much more at home there anyway.

"Have it," I reply wearily, the joy and excitement I'd felt downstairs obliterated by my confrontation with Aidan. "I don't want it anymore anyway."

Dejectedly turning to my computer I start up a new document and start writing up the NIBS (News in Briefs) I've collated so far.

"Oh, right. Um, thanks," Anna sips at the latte looking at me quizzically over the top of the lid.

"Kate, are you alright?" She asks with concern, and it's actually the first time I've ever seen Anna genuinely concerned for anyone beside herself. She's covered some properly emotional stories since she's been here, and I swear to God she's never shown any real empathy with any of them.

I'm taken aback by her kindness, and annoyingly tears spring to my eyes. My weakness irritates me, and I blink at the screen and snap back: "I'm fine." Immediately I regret my outburst and battle to regain control. A moment later, and this time more kindly, I smile: "Seriously Anna, I'm fine. Honestly. I just had a bit of a rough weekend and I'm still getting over it. I'll be all right when I've had a bit more sleep. Thank you though."

I think I probably will be okay. Dean has given me hope that there is light at the end of this tunnel. If I'm lucky enough to land this position, and I can make it to the next level, it will answer all my problems: goodbye dull and uninspiring job and au revoir Aidan.

My mum always used to say to me that "If' is a little word with a lot of meaning.' Now I know what she means.

Fifteen

By the end of October I've still heard nothing. I haven't got any more shifts scheduled until late November, although Dean did say he'd call if they needed anyone last minute.

That was at the beginning of the month, and since my phone call to him I've had no direct contact with anyone at *The Record* - with the exception of Lori, who texted me to say there was nothing confirmed as of yet, and to believe in the old adage that, 'no news is good news'.

I'm not sure I believe that anymore, but seeing as I don't want to start pestering them and make a nuisance of myself, there's little I can do right now.

Aidan and I have settled into a routine of blanking each other unless we strictly have to speak, and even then it's cold and brief. I don't think anyone's really aware of the issue. He doesn't talk to many people in the office anyway, and when he does it's always short and rarely sweet.

I eavesdrop a lot on his phone calls and make mental notes about his arrangements, mainly keeping track of his interviews and plans to meet with people. I then schedule my interviews for other times so we end up hardly being in the office together.

At first he persisted in texting me several times a day, professing his remorse and offering contrite apologies for his ill-judged behaviour. But I've deleted every one each time without replying and eventually the stream of messages dwindled to a trickle, before eventually ceasing altogether.

Everything has settled back into the same banal existence that preceded our fling, only without the frisson of excitement I'd had back then, and the wondering if anything might come of my infatuation. In its place sits, if not regret - because try as I might to summon up some level of disappointment about the choices I've made, I can't bring myself to feel complete contrition regarding our fling - then sadness, and a degree of emptiness where hope used to be. Waiting to hear from *The Record*, is mind-numbingly frustrating; what I need is a nice little distraction to take my mind off it.

Tom Evans is the dark-haired, preppy sports reporter we share with the *Kingston Herald*, the Surrey Media Group's daily newspaper. He does less than one day a week at each of the three group owned weekly newspapers and two full days at the Herald's offices, plus he attends matches and sporting fixtures on the weekends. He pretty much has no time off at all, but is so sport-mad he doesn't really see the problem in combining work with his passion.

I, on the other hand, finding sport a complete anathema - other than on a purely fitness-related level - have zero interest in that side of our paper, and haven't ever found a reason to make more than small talk with Tom during the brief Friday afternoons he spends at our gaff.

Despite being so fixated with Aidan, I hadn't actually overlooked the fact that Welsh-born Tom is a good-looking guy. It was more that I'd filed him in the, 'gorgeous, but off limits due to the all-encompassing sport obsession slash has mandatory girlfriend, and is therefore taken', box.

Until now, that is.

With Aidan having smashed my rose-tinted glasses to smithereens, suddenly floppy haired, chisel-jawed Tom doesn't seem all that boring or indeed out of reach, at all. In fact, I'm beginning to wonder if I was blind not to notice his startling blue eyes, or the way his cheeky smile lights up his entire face.

Cup of coffee in hand I wander over to him, "Hi Tom, how's it going?"

"You alright Kate? Yeah good thanks. Just tidying up a few things last minute before the weekend." He replies, bashing away on his laptop. "There, all done," he says glancing up as I perch lightly on the desk, the edge of my Lycra skirt-clad thigh, just brushing the very tiniest bit against his hand.

"Did you want a coffee, hon? Sorry, no one ever offers you one do they? We could forget you're here we see you so little."

I laugh lightly and tuck my left hand neatly between my thighs, crossing them over one another and stretching them out in front of me, pressing them together tightly. I'm aware of the effect it's having on Tom.

I have pretty good legs at the best of times, but with all the extra training I've been doing recently to try and block out the non-stop noise in my head, plus the velvety, opaque tights I'm wearing under my oh-so-short teal skirt, they are looking hot right now, make no mistake. Tom's eyes keep darting to where my hand is placed and I think he might be flushing ever so slightly.

"So what are your plans this weekend?" I ask quietly, aware that Pete, who is locked in the office with David for a meeting is glancing my way. Fuck him, it's quiet and I have a great lead for next week's paper already in the bag. "Anything exciting?"

"Well there's racing on at Kempton tomorrow and rugby at Twickenham, so it's pretty full on, and there are football matches all weekend, but I won't bore you with the details," he laughs, "I can see from your face that you're not really interested."

"You got me, I'm just being polite," I laugh too. "Doesn't your girlfriend mind you being out all weekend? You live with her don't you?"

"Yeah, it can get a bit much sometimes. Although she knew what I did for a living when we got together, so I'm not sure she's got grounds to moan." He raises his eyes skywards and shrugs his shoulders. "She's not complaining this weekend though as she's gone on a hen weekend with her mates to Dublin and isn't back until Monday."

Is she now? Well, how convenient.

Pulling a sympathetic face, I softly lay a hand on his arm, "Aw, leaving you home alone! What are you going to do with yourself this evening? Not another football match surely?"

More affectionately than I suspect his girlfriend would like, Tom, pats my hand and smiles, "No, not football, just a microwave meal for one and a bottle of wine in front of a box set, I expect – rock and roll. Living the dream, me!"

"Oh we can't have that." I smile, "Come round mine and I'll cook us something and join you in that bottle, no make it two bottles!" Tom looks decidedly unsure about whether it's good idea and rapidly removes his hand from mine.

"Na, you're alright Kate, I couldn't impose on you like that."

"Bollocks, you're not imposing. My evening was looking pretty much like yours until now. No point in us both sitting there, bored out of our tiny skulls. I can whip something up, I make a mean risotto. What do you say?" He's definitely tempted, I can tell. He wavers, pressing his lips hard together like he doesn't trust himself to answer, and traces small, invisible circles on his laptop with his finger.

"The thing is, I'm not sure, how... appropriate it would be? Me, coming round yours like that, while Bella's away, you know?"

I jump up, "Oh God, no Tom, it's fine. Just forget I said anything. I didn't want to make you feel uncomfortable, Christ, don't worry about it. God, how stupid of me." I back away, calculatedly slowly.

Wait for it.
Wait. For. It.

"It'd be all right if we just went for out for a drink though," he adds, apologetically. Maybe go to the pub, about eight, eight-thirty? What do you think?"

Bam. Hook, line, and sinker - men are so predictable.

"Tom, what a perfect idea. Swing by mine about eight and we'll walk over the road to the Red Lion in Chertsey – do you know it?" I ask, scribbling my address on a scrap of paper.

"Yeah, I used to live over that way when I first moved here. Great, I'll see you then, and sorry about dinner."

"Not a problem, babe," I call walking back to my desk, "I'm off carbs anyway."

Anna looks up from the woman's magazine that she's reading, stretching a grey piece of gum from between her teeth. *Ew.*

"What was that about?" she asks, chamming on it loudly.

"Oh nothing," I reply breezily, "Just letting a man think something was his idea." She stares blankly at me for a moment then returns to a story about a woman that sleeps with ghosts.

I swear, I could literally fuck a man on the desk and Anna wouldn't even notice. Smiling at the notion, I start planning what I'm going to wear tonight. After all, this isn't just going out for a drink.

Sixteen

The doorbell rings bang on 8pm and I take a last look at myself in the mirror. I approve and in a big way.

I went a shade darker during my last colour session and the tone really sets off my eyes. Ringed with dark kohl and shaded to perfection in a whole spectrum of colours from silver to jet black, they gleam like precious stones embedded in the rock face. Even my cheekbones seem sharper tonight – it must be all that exercise. I'm wearing a slate grey pair of super skinny jeans that look like they've been sprayed on, teamed with a loose vest top in a darker charcoal shade, silky to the touch on the front and black jersey on the back.

I zip up a pair of spike-heeled, black suede ankle boots and throw on a tuxedo-style blazer, running my hands through my hair. Perfect. Running a finger around the outside of my nude lip gloss, checking for smudges, I grab my clutch and keys and run downstairs. "Hi, I'm ready. We should go. I won't invite you in, it might look bad," I laugh, shutting the door behind me. Tom rubs his forehead and looks awkward. It's endearing.

"I'm sorry, I had a complete overreaction earlier towards dinner. I should have just said yes. The microwave lasagne was rank."

We both laugh and walk through the narrow alleyway between the houses to the main road, crossing over to the pub on the other side. I take a sneaky sideways peek at him.

He's changed out of the slightly cheap looking, grey suit he wears most of the time at work and is wearing a trendy black, longer length T-shirt with zip details on either side of the hem, skinny jeans and trainers. It would seem that outside of work, Tom is quite the fashionista. "Aren't you cold?" I ask, shivering in my thin jacket.

"Ha ha, no. I've spent too many years on the terraces in all weathers to even think about feeling cold."

We push our way through the smokers that have congregated in the beer garden and into the warm, cosy bustle of the pub, which is heaving with regulars, like every other Friday night. Luckily, I spot a young woman reapplying her lipstick and pulling on her coat so I shoot over to snag us the table. As the young couple stand up to leave, I sit down, earning myself a few dirty looks from a group of girls standing around their handbags by the duke box, clearly waiting for a seat.

"Nothing ventured, nothing gained," I say loudly to Tom, nodding in the direction of the irritated women. *That applies to snagging a man too.* He grins and braves the bar where it is three deep in places.

Watching Tom from across the room, I smile to myself. He really does have a very nice arse, particularly in those jeans. When he returns he's carrying four drinks – two for each of us. "Are you trying to get me pissed?" I joke, taking mine and knocking back a huge glug of delicious ice-cold gin and tonic. Tom laughs: "Steady on, I'm not going back up there in a hurry, it's murder! That's why I bought four in one go."

"God I needed that." I say, taking a deep breath and letting my shoulders relax as I let it out. "It's been a long week." Catching my eye, Tom raises his glass, "To the end of a long week!"

The evening passes quickly and in a blur. Despite his obsession with sport we genuinely have loads in common, from travelling through Europe to enjoying good food, and a bizarre mutual addiction to CSI: Crime Scene Investigations. By chucking out time, we're both slightly worse for wear and neither of us is ready to throw the towel in.

"I've got a bottle of Absolut Raspberry in the freezer, if those bastards I live with haven't nicked it," I suggest.

"Only, of course, if you deem that 'appropriate'."

"Funny!" he remarks sarcastically, glowering at me good-naturedly. Get your jacket on and let's go, tithead! There's a bottle of vodka with my name on it waiting for me at yours."

"Actually it's got my name on it, written in permanent marker," I giggle uncontrollably, draining the last dregs from my glass.

We stagger back across the road, and I let us into the house rather noisily. Grabbing the icy bottle, which has remarkably not even been opened, and two shot glasses, I take one look at the lads sprawled across the sofas in the living room and gesture for Tom to follow me upstairs to my room.

"Sorry, I don't want to make you feel awkward, but you can see the state of the lounge."

"S'fine, don't stress," he says, slurring slightly, pushing me up the stairs and through the door.

We crash in my room for the next hour, me stretched over the bed and Tom slouching on the chaise longue, doing shots, the sharp, clean kick of the strong spirit, punctuated by a sweet berry perfume.

We chat easily and the conversation shifts direction, with Tom bad-mouthing his girlfriend quite a lot for someone who's rumoured to be on the verge of getting engaged.

"I thought you two were pretty serious, I mean, you've got a house together," I say, getting up to open a window. Is it me, or is it hotter in here than it was earlier?

"It's her parents' place. They bought it years ago, when they were younger, and have rented it out ever since. When Bella left university and moved back here, they let her live there, rent free." He replies, leaning back and languidly stretching out both arms, "I ended up moving in when my landlord sold up and wanted me out. I couldn't find anywhere else and 'they' all thought it was the obvious solution."

"And you didn't?" I ask, leaning back against the windowsill, letting the cool breeze drift over my neck.

"Not really, it was all a bit too soon if I'm honest." he says, "As for marriage, there's no way I'm in that league yet. That's Pete stirring up shit, after he saw me in the jewellers in May. It was Bella's birthday and I was buying a necklace she wanted, but he saw me coming out with a bag, put two and two together and got sixty-three.

"Not 69?" I mutter, sitting down next to Tom on the green velvet. Our legs are pressed together and I can feel the heat radiating from his body. He raises an eyebrow and looks at me, holding my gaze for a second or two. I return the look.

Well, well, well, it seems as if Mr Evans is not quite as taken as we all thought he was.

Placing my empty glass on the windowsill, I turn to him

and in a low voice say, "Put your drink down." Without hesitation he sets it down on the bedside table. We both know what's about to happen and it's pointless either of us resisting.

Standing up I undo my belt and jeans and slip them down over my hips, letting them slither onto the floor before daintily stepping out of them. Barefoot, having discarded my boots as soon as I'd got in, I climb onto his lap, placing one knee on either side of his legs and taking hold of the gold painted wooden frame at the back of the seat.

I maintain eye contact as I pull off my top and shake my hair over my shoulders. Underneath, I'm wearing a black push up bra, edged in satin with a lace trim. My summer tan's almost gone, and my pale skin contrasts dramatically against the fabric. In this light, it has an almost ethereal glow and makes my tits look fucking incredible. Tom clearly thinks so, as the moment I take my top off he tears his eyes away from mine and his breathing starts to get heavier.

Still kneeling, my arms either side of his shoulders, I lower my face a fraction at a time until I can feel his breath coming thick and fast on my skin. His pupils are dilated - perfectly round, dark circles in the centre of each pretty blue eye - and, judging by the reaction in his trousers which grazes my inner thighs every time I dip my hips, he is, unsurprisingly, aroused by my spontaneous assault.

Eventually, when neither of us can stand the teasing anymore, I allow my lips to press chastely against his mouth, just the slightest of movements against his skin. I flick the very tip of my tongue over his, a flicker so light that he might well believe he imagined it.

I repeat the move, over and over again, until Tom squirms beneath me, running his hands up and down my back and stroking my spine with his fingertips as if he's afraid to take a proper hold of me.

Pulling away suddenly, I intentionally and without warning grind myself down on to his swollen groin, tilting my pelvis right forward, rubbing up and over him, then maintaining the pressure, rotating my hips in a full circle, sweeping Tom up and away with my actions.

He throws his head back over the sofa and involuntarily raises his hips to meet my thrusts, teased to what must be beyond comfortable, let alone bearable by now. "I want to fuck you, Kate," he whispers, barely able to conceal his need, so intense he's actually shaking. He is that consumed with desire for me my pussy spasms uncontrollably. It's a huge turn on when a man wants you this much.

I smile knowingly, kneel between his legs and undo his jeans, quickly removing them, while he strips off his T-shirt. His skin's also pale, but he has a dark triangle of hair on his chest that descends in a thick line all the way down his firm stomach.

I reach for a condom and, ripping it open instruct Tom brusquely: "Take off your shorts, stay where you are, right in the middle of the seat, and don't move until I tell you to." He smiles wryly and, quick as a flash, has his trunks off and is sat back down awaiting further instruction.

I unwrap the johnny and unroll it over him, quickly and without fuss. Tom's cock is impressively hard and I wonder when Bella last let him fuck her, or if he even wants to anymore. I'd like to blow him – desperately – but he'll only get too turned on and I'm not chancing another man stealing an orgasm from me, leaving me high and dry before I've come. This time I'm in charge and I know exactly what I want.

Shimmying my panties off, I return to my previous position on the chaise longue, take his straining cock in both hands and pull him towards me.

"Wait, can I touch you?" Tom pleads, reaching one hand towards my pussy, so wet by now my knickers are saturated.

I catch his wrist and hold it motionless.

"I said, don't move unless I tell you to Tom."

There's a dangerous glint in my eye and a steely note to my voice that says don't mess with me, but he looks so crestfallen that I take pity on him. Inserting one finger into my sopping cunt I stroke myself, deep inside, for a few seconds, tensing, revelling in the sensation, before drawing it slowly across his open lips, glossing them with my juices, then pressing it inside, slick and sticky against his tongue.

While he moans, tasting me for the first time, I turn my attention back to his soaring cock. Tilting my pussy upwards and over him I sink onto his thickness, feeling myself stretching inside, all the way down his length, until I hit home and can't go any further.

I look directly at him, serious now, and in complete and utter control. "I say where, I say when, and I say how. Got it?" He nods mutely, biting down on his bottom lip, trying to reign in his emotions. He is clearly so turned on: I hope I haven't left it too late.

Taking a firmer grip of the woodwork this time, I raise myself up off him almost completely, then crash back down, pulverising my clit into his wiry pubic hair, feeling the familiar buzz of pleasure as I sweep my pussy in tiny revolutions around his girth. I get lost in a rhythm of movement, pounding up and down and round over this beautiful man's body. Tom wraps his arms around me, holding me close and I lean in and kiss him passionately for the first time.

The added sensation of his tongue in my mouth increases the yearning in my groin and I feel the pressure start to build. My pussy's so wet, there's less resistance and I need to rub myself harder to find the abrasion I so badly need. Tom is clawing wildly at my back and shoulders, lifting himself up to meet my thrusts. He goes to move me backwards onto the couch but I force him back down: "I say where, remember!" I pant out, "And I didn't say move."

"Ok," he gasps, "but I don't know if I can hold out much longer, you turn me on so much." Rising off of him, but not quite, I look down at his cock, taking in the thick fleshy skin, dark and engorged with blood, veins standing out. I lower myself slowly, watching him disappear into me and slide back up, leaving him slick and shining with my juices. Seeing myself fuck him up close like that is all I need to bring myself off. With renewed vigour I take his dick deep inside me and grate my clit intensely against his root until, seconds later I lose control and start to reach my peak. "Oh God, I'm gonna cum over your cock."

My cunt spasms over and over, my body shaking with the strength of the orgasm as it breaks over me, destroying me from the inside out. "Now." I say, weakly, releasing my grip on the sofa, clinging to his shoulders instead, "Now you can do what you want with me."

Tom scoops me up from the seat, still rooted deep inside me and spins me over onto my back. Kneeling on the floor between my legs, he pulls me down tightly over his cock and I wrap my legs around his waist, reaching back over my shoulders to take hold of the upholstery for support. He jackhammers his cock into my pussy, holding my hips and slamming me against the cushions. He's close but I can feel another orgasm approaching. As his face crumples and he lunges forwards into me I tighten my thighs, my hands clamouring for purchase on his arse, and spiral my clitoris into the base of his cock. Waves of painful pleasure come crashing down around my ears as my pussy convulses around his jerking cock for a second time, leaving us both spent and lifeless.

My chest still heaving with the effort, I disentangle myself and flop back onto the cushions, dragging the throw over me. Tom tidies himself up and pulls on his shorts, slipping in behind me, giving me his body as a backrest and folding his arms around mine.

"Is it me, or is it cold in here?" I complain, wrapping the blanket up around us."

"Someone decided to open a fucking window, tithead," Tom laughs, cuffing me playfully around the head.

"I wonder who that was," I smile, burying my head back into his chest as he pulls me closer.

We sit like this for a while, and it feels, I don't know comfortable, I suppose. Eventually, Tom moves.

"I should probably call a taxi. You don't mind, do you?"

He's so sweet.

"No, of course I don't."

"This was, fucking amazing, you're amazing Kate. God, you're fantastic, but…" I press a finger to his lips.

"Shhh, you don't have to say anything Tom. I'm not after anything. This was great, but it is what it is. And don't worry, I won't say a word." He smiles and presses a kiss into my forehead. I kiss him softly on the lips and holding the blanket around me, stand up and close the window. Tom dresses while I call a minicab for him. He says he'll see himself out, which is great because I don't know who is still up and don't really fancy doing the walk of shame in front of the lads.

"The cab's here," I say, walking him to my door. Tom scoops his arms around me and gives me a sweet, lingering kiss.

"You're going to make some lucky guy a wonderful wife one day," he laughs, "the way you…" He doesn't finish, just shakes his head.

"Bye Tom," I grin, "I'll see you next week."

Drawing the soft wool close to my skin, I hop into bed and snuggle down. Despite the vast amount I've had to drink I'm remarkably alert and don't feel remotely sleepy. Turning on Netflix, I select Pretty Woman. Alongside, Dirty Dancing, and, Bridget Jones' Diary, it's one of my all time favourites. Soon I'm lost in the movie, tucked up to my neck in cashmere, duvet and duck down pillows.

When I fell asleep, I don't know, but it was a long and dreamless sleep and the first night in a long time when I haven't woken up once.

Seventeen

I wake late the next morning, sunlight streaming through the open curtains, with the television still on. Blinking in the bright rays, I bury my head under the pillow and groan. I might have been absolutely fine when Tom left last night, but in the cold light of day my mouth feels like the bottom of a budgie cage and there must be an entire Russian army marching through my head.

Blindly, I reach for water and wince as my mobile clatters to the floor. I fumble around for it in the debris of magazines, shoes and discarded underwear from last night. There's a missed call from my mum and two text messages. One's from Stella:

CALL ME YOU BITCH, #SHITFRIEND

Which makes me laugh out loud and then wish I hadn't. The other's from Helen, my massage girl, telling me she can fit me in next Wednesday after work. I'm rubbish at booking appointments with her and when I do finally get round to it, it's always well overdue and hurts like hell. Unlike some people who view a massage as a treat, Helen has the hands of the devil, and although she works absolute magic, she pretty much beats the living hell out of me every time I see her.

It's my own fault really. I put my body through so much, what with the running, swimming and the spin classes, yoga and the weights sessions, that I should go to her far more often than I do, and then my muscles wouldn't end up so fucked.

I scroll through Facebook, reading all my notifications and comment on a few posts. Gemma was out getting trashed again by the look of things; honestly that girl's body should go to medical science one day; she's out every weekend, yet always looks fresh as a daisy by Monday morning. Whereas I, on the other hand, really hit the cocktails or vodka heavily just one night a month and show up to work after the weekend looking like something the cat dragged in.

Finally, I open my emails, deleting all the spam and the M&S offers immediately, without even reading them. One piece of mail catches my eye, no subject line. FROM: *d.oliver@record.co.uk*

That's Dean's email address. Looking at the right hand side of the screen I see the time it arrived: 6.47pm, yesterday. How have I not seen this until now? Then I remember.

I put the phone on charge when I got home from work, forgot to take it to the pub and, not wanting to be disturbed, switched it straight off when I got back. I didn't even think about turning it on again when Tom left. Nervously, my heart rattling in my chest, I open it and start reading. Small black shapes keep spinning before my eyes and I have to stop and rub them before reading the tiny text again as it seems to hops about on the screen:

"...PLEASED TO OFFER...HOPE YOU'LL ACCEPT... LOOK FORWARD TO HEARING..."

Oh my God. Sitting bolt upright I drop the phone and press my hands together in prayer, breathing rapidly through my fingers. *Oh my fucking God.* My mouth has gone even drier than before so I glug down half a glass of water and immediately wish I hadn't. I feel sick. My hands are still shaking as I pick the phone back up and speed dial a number It rings three times before someone picks up.

"Halloo?"

"Dad, it's me."

"Hello me, how are you?" my dad jokes. He thinks he's hilarious.

"I'm fine. Dad, is Mum there?"

"Oh that's nice," he moans, "You don't have a word for your old dad, anymore. I suppose I'm just the man who bankrolled your degree. That's charming.

"I remember I used to get home from work and you couldn't wait to sit on my knee but now…"

"Dad, I do want to talk to you but I need to talk to Mum as well," I interrupt impatiently, anxious to share my news with them, "Can you call her and put it on speakerphone?"

"Linda! Linda? Lin! Are you there? It's Kate, she wants to speak to us both."

"What's wrong? Is she alright?"

"I don't know - she seems upset."

"Well what did she say, Ron?"

All this is going on as I sit in bed, fiddling with the label on the throw. I'm the most excited I've been in ages and feel like I'm about to burst. "Dad, just put it on speaker and stop arsing about!" I snap, rubbing my aching temples.

"All right Katherine, there's no need to be rude," he reprimands, as Mum's still griping in the background. "Just sit down and shut up Lin, I think she's hungover." They go quiet and my blood beats a violent drumroll in my ears.

"Mum, Dad," I start nervously, adrenaline surging through my veins, "I've been offered a job at *The Daily Record*. I'm going to be a feature writer on a national newspaper."

The silence is deafening. No one says anything for a couple of seconds, then Mum starts screaming and Dad's saying, "Well, well, I don't believe it," over and over again. Wincing at the racket, I hold the phone away from my ears until the din subsides.

"Oh Katherine, love, well done." my mum's saying, sniffing down the line, "Ooh, that's made me go all emotional."

My dad in his brusque, detached manner is congratulating me, now he's rediscovered the power of comprehensive speech, "Bloody well done, Kate, I always said you could do it and now you've gone and proven me right. Great job, well done love." This is an outright lie as he's always told me not to expect too much and that the chances of me actually securing a job on a national were next to none, but I'm in a good mood, so I'll let him have that one and choose not to contradict him, this time.

We chat for a few minutes and Dad makes me read out the contents of the email three times, but eventually I get them off the phone. I can't stop grinning. This is what I've always dreamed of, ever since I was in my mid teens - an actual job on an actual national newspaper! I never believed it would happen this quickly though – I mean I've only been a bona fide journalist for, not even three years yet. It's an amazing feeling knowing that I'm already this close to fulfilling my professional ambition.

I won't deny I'm a bit scared too. I think I'm ready for it but this is uncharted territory for me and I'm terrified my self-confidence will be eroded away when I'm asked to write full length features day in day out. What if I can't cut it in the new job? I'm very good at undermining my capabilities when I want to – I think it goes hand in hand with other insecurities that plague me on a daily basis: I'm not fit enough; I'm only winging it at work and one day someone's going to find that out; I'm too fat and not pretty enough, why would anyone ever want to date me? Honestly the list is endless some days

Looking down at the loo paper, I see I've come on and realise how close last night came to not happening. Thank Christ this didn't happen a few hours earlier! It's bad enough that I appear to be picking guys up one by one at the office without showing myself up with an unscheduled bleed mid-seduction. I finish up and grab a quick shower, downing a couple of paracetamol with yet more much needed water and scrape my hair into a ponytail. Dressing in a pair of joggers and a T-shirt, I slip on a pair of navy Uggs and loop my soft grey Zara scarf round my neck, belting a chunky cardigan around me.

Smithy and Alfie are already up, and are watching Saturday Kitchen in their boxers. "Right I need a greasy fry up, who's with me?" I ask, sipping some ice-cold coconut water straight from the fridge.

"Drunk a bit too much last night, did you?" Smithy says,

scratching his balls through his keks. I pretend not to notice.

"Might have, what of it?"

Alfie winks at Smithy and says lecherously, "Not so much that you couldn't stay awake and talk to your friend though."

Smart arse.

I ignore him and grab my keys, "So that's no one then, no? Right full English breakfast for one then, I guess."

Seeing that I'm not going to rise to the bait, both lads leap up. "Hang on, we'll come if you're driving." Alfie yells, running upstairs, like a lunatic, "Just getting some clothes on, wait for me!"

Smithy follows me downstairs, "Yeah, give me five too."

"I'll wait in the car but I'm gone in three minutes so hurry the fuck up," I call, walking out of the front door.

Ten minutes later we're all sat in Piccolos on the High Street, flicking through the morning papers and giving the nice red-headed waitress our order. Alfie appreciatively watches her walk back to the kitchen, elbowing Smithy like a hormonal teenager. Honestly, sometimes it feels more like I house share with a couple of randy primates than two twenty-first century men.

Grabbing a copy of *The Record*, I skim the headlines – another bomb has gone off in France, this time at a packed railway station in the busy suburbs of Lyon – and turn to the centre pages, where there's a feature about three women whose partners left them after they lost half their bodyweight. The journalist who wrote it, Rosa Nepton, has her byline and photograph at the top of the page and as I sit there, looking at it for a few minutes, I imagine my name and picture in its place.

"I'm going to work for this paper," I say proudly, gesturing at the article. The boys are busy ogling a woman with huge tits in *The Daily Star*, and barely look up as I roll my eyes at them. God, how do I tolerate these goons?

"Mmm, yeah?" Smithy says, "If you say so."

"No, I am. I got an email this morning. If I accept, I start on December 1st." Alfie tears his eyes away from the woman's saucer size nipples and looks up.

"Seriously?"

"Yup!" I break into a massive smile and can't help but give myself a self-satisfying hug. Suddenly the tacky rag gets pushed to one side and the boys bombard me with a load of questions: where will I be working, will I meet anyone famous, can I take them with me if I get to interview an England footballer?

I don't think they've fully grasped the idea of writing features for a national title but bless them, to give them their dues they do seem interested and really excited for me.

By the time the food comes I'm blooming starving; the painkillers have done their job and I'm actually feeling a lot better. We eat in companionable silence, the boys relishing their tucker as much as me and we're all groaning by the time we leave. Piccolos are renowned for their portion sizes and although I went for the healthier veggie option in the end, complete with hummous, guacamole and sweet chilli, plus additional crispy bacon, because I'm not actually veggie and just order it because I like it, I still feel like I won't need to eat another thing all day.

When the bill arrives, Alfie and Smithy insist on paying my share in celebration of my good news, which is really sweet but I'm sure is all part of their misguided plan to meet the rich and famous, through my new job – those poor, delusional lads.

The rest of the day passes in a bit of a blur. I sit down to write a resignation letter to David, but after three attempts and my headache coming back I resolve to do it tomorrow and take a siesta mid-afternoon, meaning it's dark when I wake up and it really throws me, not knowing if it's very early in the morning or night-time.

Despite my earlier conviction that I would be stuffed for the foreseeable, I wake up hungry, and beg Smithy to nip out for a pizza. When that fails – the boy is surgically attached to the sofa on Saturday afternoons and would only move if the house caught fire (even then I wouldn't put money on it) – I drag my boots back on and drive down to the M&S garage for one of their sweet and spicy chicken, pepper and pepperoni thin crusts and a bottle of red wine.

Cutting it in half and sticking the rest in the freezer – I'm hungry not stupid – I eat it on the couch with the lads, who have ordered a Chinese takeaway and are watching X-Factor.

They do their usual thing of marking the women out of ten and playing Slag or FAG (which in this case stands for Frigid Or Gay), dividing the women into two categories, those who are gorgeous and clearly 'up for it' – their words not mine – or those who evidently wouldn't put out because they either have no sex drive or are obviously lesbians.

Clearly this game and line of thinking – based solely on

the premise that all men are sex gods and no woman in her right mind would turn one down – usually drives me nuts, and more often than not results in me having a heated debate about sexist pigs and why men and women's sexuality is viewed so differently, even in this day and age.

Did you know, there are no equivalent derogatory terms for the words 'slut', 'slag', and 'whore', to describe men who enjoy the same sexual freedom of sleeping around? I mean how ridiculous is that? Alfie insists this is justified. He says a lock that can be released by many different keys is a shit lock while a key that can undo many different locks is clearly a master key. Alfie is a brainless tosser, which is why some evenings I'd rather sit up in my room on my own, with my dinner on a tray, instead of face this pathetic banter. But tonight I'm in too good of a mood to seek solitude, or even defend my case for equality, so I let the male banter drift over me with an apathy that doesn't go unnoticed.

"Cat got your tongue tonight?" Jasper – usually the quieter participant, bravely asks. I'm sure he only joins in with the others because he's outnumbered, and his girlfriend's not here. If Hazel heard some of the things he comes out with she'd be wearing his balls for earrings.

Once when he used up the last of my luxury Jo Malone shower gel, I was so pissed at him I told Hazel he'd said Amanda Holden was a, 'self-obsessed, glory hunter only after column inches in the media, because she went back to work just a fortnight after giving birth'. She was still screeching at him about respect and women's rights when I went to bed that night. Smirking at the memory, I shove another slice of pizza in my mouth and flick him the bird.

"She's just smug because she's got a flash new job," Alfie bleats, opening another can of lager. "She's going to be doing all them top interviews with celebs and stuff for *The Record.*"

Almost choking on my dinner I wash it down with swig of wine and rolling my eyes at Alfie, explain, "I won't be doing anything like that, dickhead. I'm just going to be one of several feature writers, based for the most part, in the office, writing up features... and other stuff, and that's about it."

But, eventually, you want more than that, don't you? Asks the over-achieving, cocky little voice in my head. If I'm honest with myself then yes, of course I do. But after landing what was to me an impossible job, it seems, well, just plain greedy to be hoping for any more right now.

X-Factor finishes and I head straight to bed. Despite my earlier nap, the alcohol I consumed last night and my late bedtime have taken their toll and I'm absolutely shagged (though only metaphorically this time).

I'm just drifting off when a buzzing signals a text – shit I forgot to turn the damn thing off. I'm tempted to switch it off without reading the message but curiosity gets the better of me:

NOT SURE BELLA AND I ARE GONNA WORK
OUT BUT GONNA TRY. THANKS FOR LAST
NIGHT. YOU WERE INCREDIBLE. TOM X

Smiling to myself I turn it off and roll over. Tom's a sweet guy and whatever Bella's like, I hope he makes the right decision. He deserves to be happy. I just hope he isn't settling for the wrong reasons.

But what are the right reasons? And what are the chances of two people, who are perfectly right for one another, finding each other without having to settle over some things?

I might have landed the dream job, but will I ever be able to say I've had the same luck in love? It's a question that I can't answer right now and sometimes I wonder if I ever will.

Eighteen

Wheezing for all I'm worth, I ramp up the speed on the treadmill for the last thirty seconds and run as if my life depends on it. Oh god, I think I'm going to die.

Five, four, three... come on bitch, you can do it... one. Done!

Dropping back to a jogging, then walking pace, I wipe a towel over my face and take a glug of water. I'm red-faced and sweating, like an overweight pig in a frock, but one look at my pert butt and trim waist and I know it's all worth it.

I have been working out like a demon for the last fortnight. For a start it's leaving me so knackered I'm too tired to lay awake at night brooding over Aidan, who still looks fucking hot but is still a tit, plus I'm leaving in two weeks, so there's not really anything else left to say to him.

Having handed my resignation in, I'm really counting down the days until I don't have to sit next to him every day. He stiffly asked me if it was true I was leaving the day after I told David, and I said I was. Quietly, so nutty Anna, wouldn't hear, he said he was sorry I was going and that he would miss me. When Anna left her desk he even added he had no regrets about what happened with us, but that he wishes it could have ended differently.

I swear to God, it took every ounce of self-control in my body to: 1) not burst into tears, and 2) not read him the riot act there and then, at the top of my voice.

Taking a deep breath I'd simply replied: "It's fine" – it so obviously isn't fine – and asked if we could just drop it please. Then I got up and walked to the ladies loo before locking myself in a cubicle and crying my eyes out for ten minutes. I don't really know why I'm still so upset. I'm mad as hell at myself for letting it get to me in this way – God knows Aidan doesn't deserve this level of attention from my already overworked brain. But sometimes the disappointment just gets too much, and I have to let it all out.

Away from work it's definitely easier, especially when I'm out running or in here working out. Refilling my water, I wave at Justin, the lad with special needs who's working out on the rowing machine, before I cross over into the weights room and dump my stuff on a bench.

Lifting two 10kg dumbbells, I start doing fly arms, five sets of ten, which I'm really feeling following last night's hot yoga. All those planks took their toll and oh boy, this is killing my shoulders now.

Who is that?!

In the mirror, I spot an average height, dark haired guy, with a light dusting of stubble. He's wearing a red leisure centre T-shirt, holding a clipboard and pen and putting a short blonde woman, easily in her sixties, through her paces on the Kinesis machines.

He is ripped.

And I mean, ripped. From what I can see beneath the

unflattering work shirt, he has well defined biceps and strong forearms, a thick neck, narrow waist, and he is really good looking, like seriously beautiful. I'm not sure where he's come from, as I would definitely remember if I'd seen him in here before. None of the trainers are anywhere near as memorable as this fine specimen.

I am so distracted I have absolutely no idea how many sets I've done, so I decide to stop before my arms fall out of their sockets. Switching to the large barbells, I do five sets of deadlifts starting with a 50kg weight and moving up to a 60kg before I finish. Gratifyingly, I catch Mr Hot Muscles watching my arse as I bend forward to put the weight back down.

He disappears up the other end of the gym, but when I go to sign out forty-five minutes later he's back on the desk.

"That was a pretty full on work out – running and weights!"

I smile at him politely – he noticed me running too?

"You're new here, aren't you?" I ask, writing my sign out time in the entry book.

"I am, is that ok with you…" he laughs, leaning over to read my name, "Kate?" Grinning back at him – he does have stunning eyes – I joke: "Well I'm not sure, after all no one told me they were recruiting another trainer and I don't think I'd have approved your application."

Yvette, my gym buddy and BodyBalance partner in crime, squeezes in between the desk and me to sign out. "Stop harassing the guy, Kate," she accuses. "I'm sorry Jack, she does this to every man she meets."

My ears prick up: Jack is it? How does she know that? Yvette and I will be having words. How dare she keep a gorgeous little secret like this to herself. Pretending to punch her in the arm I reach out a hand and Jack takes it.

"Pleased to meet you, Jack. Do ignore Yvette here, she's suffering from the first signs of early onset dementia. Fabricating untruths about her nearest and dearest is her current affliction." The three of us laugh and I say goodbye before frogmarching Yvette to the lockers. "Forgot to mention a fittie had started here did you, you evil wench?" I hiss, tugging my bags out of the tiny cupboard.

"No," she giggles, rescuing her own kit bag and following me to the changing room. "Pete just introduced me to him while I was getting a coffee after Pilates yesterday morning. They were on their tea break. I said to Edna after we sat down: 'Kate'll have her eye on him the minute she clocks him.'" I give Yvette a patronising smile and head for the showers. She's right of course. A fifty-one year-old mum of two boys, both in their early twenties, she knows me inside out and can always tell when I have the hots for someone.

We only met at the gym a few years ago, but during that time we've got to know each other intimately and she's been a real rock when things haven't been going so well for me, especially in recent weeks. In turn she's entrusted me with a few secrets of her own, including a three-year affair, with a man half her age. Yvette's been happily married (she says) since she was just twenty and will never leave her husband. But four years ago she started seeing a guy who worked alongside her at the estate agents.

They started out just rubbing along well together, office banter, that kind of thing, but it progressed to drinks after work and before she knew it they'd slept together.

She didn't tell me at first because I'd met her husband, Barry, and she didn't want to put me in a difficult spot. But after a few drinks at the gym's Christmas party, she confessed all and went on to keep me informed of all the developments. When he finally ended it last January because he'd met someone his own age, she was devastated, and because I was the only other one who knew, it took several weeks of secret lunches and evenings down the pub, while her husband thought she was at exercise classes to help Yvette feel like herself again.

Blow-drying her hair now, Yvette, smirks at me in the mirror. "What?!" I say accusingly, "Go on, spit it out, you know you want to."

Turning off the dryer, she turns to face me and says, "I think you should ask him out."

"What?"

"Jack. I think you should go back in there and ask him out."

"Yvette! I've just met the guy, I can't go waltzing in and suggest a date."

"Why not?"

"Because, well, because…" She raises one eyebrow.

"Because if he says no it'll be embarrassing and I'll have to keep coming here because I can't afford another gym, okay?" I glare at her. But she keeps looking pointedly at me until I shrug and throw my hands in the air. "Fine, you win! I'll do it alright? Anything to get you to drop the death stare, jeez!"

Packing the last of my stuff away I grab my bag and head for the corridor, "But you have to stay here, okay?"

She blanks me. God that woman's infuriating. Ignoring her silence, I head back to the gym where Jack's still sitting at the desk. He's holding the phone and is about to dial out, so I mutter, "It doesn't matter," and turn away. But he puts the handset down and calls after me:

"Kate? Do you need me?"

What a question. Do I need him? He has no idea!

"Um, I was wondering..."

Damn, Yvette.

"Yes?" he asks, looking amused.

Just say it.

Deep breath.

"You don't fancy a drink, do you?"

"A drink? Oh, sorry Kate, but I don't drink. I've given up."

Right. He's teetotal. Of course he is. You don't get as fit as that by necking pints and eating crisps down the pub. What was I thinking?

"Oh God, of course, sorry," I stutter, embarrassed, not knowing what to say. Then I realise he's laughing.

At me.

"I'm j-o-k-i-n-g." he spells it out as if I'm a bit slow, "Yeah sure. That'd be great. When are you free?"

Admittedly it takes a few seconds for the penny to drop but finally I find my tongue. "Um, yeah, um Friday night?" I reply, without even checking my diary. I'm pretty sure I'm not doing anything, but if I get my phone out he'll see how much my hands are shaking, although I don't know why. It's not like I've never asked a man out before.

We agree on a time and a place to meet and exchange

numbers, much to the amusement of the other trainers. I hurry back out to meet Yvette in the corridor.

"What did he say?" she squeaks.

"He said yes."

She squeals even louder.

"Yvette, shut up." I whisper, frowning, "He'll hear you and I've made enough of a tit of myself already. I don't know what's fucking wrong with me."

"I do," Yvette grins, "You really like him. I can tell."

"Oh, shut up woman," I scold her, but a little shiver runs down the back of my neck and trickles down my spine.

Oh god, what if she's right?

What if I'm a mess because I really do like him?

'*Don't be ridiculous*,' my subconscious mocks, '*you don't even know the man*'. But my body's telling a different story: my cheeks are burning and my palms are still sweaty. Maybe my sub-*fucking*-conscious knows bugger all and can do one. All I know is that I'm really looking forward to Friday night.

By Friday it's pissing down with rain and blowing a hoolie outside. I toy with straightening my hair, then think better of it and use my BaByliss Curl Secret for a headful of loose, tumbling curls – at least when I get blown to smithereens I'll still have a look of wanton goddess about me. That, or it'll be like I've fallen through a hedge backwards.

Doing a subtle, smoky plum eye, I pare down the rest of my make-up, finishing with just a slick of tinted lip balm, aiming at pretty but slightly sexy too. Keeping the look minimal,

I choose a loose fitting t-shirt style top, in my new favourite colour, charcoal grey, that sits on my hips and shows off my newly trim figure to perfection. Sticking with high waisted indigo skinnies I pick a black blazer and matching black patent courts to complete the outfit. The look reminds me of something. Then I remember. It's almost identical to what Vivian wears in the final scene of, Pretty Woman, when she's leaving Edward. Damn my obsession with that film!

I've agreed to meet Jack in a bar in Weybridge. It's one I've not been to before and when I step out of the taxi it's absolutely packed. My date is stood just outside on the steps and comes rushing down to the kerb to meet me as I fight to put my umbrella up in this atrocious weather.

"Kate," he shouts over the din: "I'm so sorry, I didn't think about it being this noisy. It was a shit decision, forgive me."

I laugh, "It's fine Jack, it doesn't matter," but he protests.

"No, I want to be able to hear you when you speak. We need to find somewhere else." I nod in agreement and gently taking my elbow – a very gentlemanly gesture that surprises but pleases me – he steers me across the street and down the road to a Slug and Lettuce pub, with about a third less drinkers inside.

Closing the brolly and shaking the rain off my jacket, we go inside and find a cosy sofa for two, right in front of the fire. "It must be our lucky night," I say, sinking down into the warmth of the cushions.

"Well it definitely feels like mine," Jack says smiling affectionately at me. His whole face lights up when he smiles and his gorgeous brown eyes crinkle attractively at the corners.

God, he's really beautiful.

After getting a round in, we sit and chat about how he came to be working at the gym. Originally a computer technician by trade, he grew tired of the desk job and craved something that would allow him to be more active day-to-day. Already a bit of a gym junkie, he decided to combine his passion and work and get paid for something that he really loves doing.

"And how have you ended up here?" I ask, sipping at my raspberry vodka and soda.

"My last place got taken over by a bigger company," Jack answers, "They wanted to bring in new staff and asked me to reapply for my old job. To be honest the changes they'd made weren't really to my liking, so when I saw an advert for this place I thought it would be a good opportunity to move on." He asks me about my career and congratulates me when I tell him about the new job.

"It's a good opportunity, and I'm not pretending I'm not over the moon about it, because I am, but it's not like I'm going to be writing my own column or anything," I explain.

"Do you always do that?" Jack asks, finishing the last of his beer.

"Do what?"

"Put yourself down all the time. It's the third time you've done it tonight and I get the impression you do it a lot."

"Oh." I don't really know what to say. Yes, I always do it, but I've never really thought about why. Stella and Gemma have pulled me up on it for years and my mum's always saying I sell myself short. "Well, it's a bit of a defence mechanism

I guess. Like, I get in there before anyone else has a chance to have a dig at me.

"I think I've probably been doing it since school. There were some kids... well let's just say, some of them weren't actually that nice to me. For a very long time."

Jack's been listening intently through all of this. Now, wordlessly, he slides a hand along my leg, which I've tucked up under me, and over my hand, giving it a comforting squeeze.

Oh wow. My stomach does a flip and all the hairs on the back of my arms and neck stand on end.

"You're amazing Kate, and you've achieved a hell of a lot already. Believe in yourself, and you might find that more incredible things happen to you." There is something about his voice, about his eyes, about that body encased in tight jeans and his incredibly fitted t-shirt clinging to his pecs, abs and biceps that makes me go weak at the knees. I don't think it's just the vodka taking effect.

Just before eleven, Jack says he should really make a move. He is working the early shift tomorrow and needs to be in by six thirty. He lives in Addlestone, but insists on sharing a cab and dropping me off first, despite my house being further away.

When we pull up outside, I'm torn. I really want this man to come inside with me, sleep in my bed and let me screw him until he begs for more. Yet, a part of me, a tiny little, almost insignificant part wants to wait. '*Yvette's right, you do like this guy,*' my mind screams, '*that's why you want to wait*'. Could that be true? If I break with tradition and don't sleep with a guy on a first date, will it change the way this turns out?

Jack's clearly having some kind of similar dilemma,

because he's sitting watching me but not saying anything at all. Eventually I say goodnight and lean into kiss him on the cheek. But he turns his head at the last minute and catches my mouth with his. In an instant every tiny nerve ending in my body catches light. Pressing my tongue into his mouth and my body into his, I feel as if I'm freefalling.

The cab driver has been patient until now but now coughs deliberately loudly and I break away from Jack, flushed with excitement and dizzy with longing. "I'm going to… um," I smile, slightly embarrassed. Normally I'd be dragging him up my stairs. I'm not used to saying goodbye in the back of a car. Gathering myself together, I say, graciously, "Thank you, Jack. I've had a lovely evening."

"So have I." he insists, "We should do this again. Sometime soon." Refusing to take any money towards the taxi, he tells me to hurry inside – it's still tipping it down – but instead I watch the car disappear round the corner and stand out in the street in the pouring rain, feeling the fat, heavy raindrops explode as they hit my face. My hair, at first just damp, quickly becomes soaked through, but still I remain there until the sodden fabric of my jacket moulds to me like a second skin.

When finally I go inside, I peel everything off and throw it straight into the washing machine, and pull on pyjamas I've left drying on the rack. Stopping for a glass of milk on the way up, I look at my reflection in the darkened window.

With my wet hair and cutesy PJs I look about fourteen. The window doesn't reflect the make-up that's now probably running down my face or the fine lines in my skin, just starting to show at the corners of my mouth and around my eyes.

I sigh. There's so little time when we look really fresh-faced and youthful. It seems that almost as soon as we understand what we can do with it, it all starts to fade away.

I really did have a great night with Jack and I didn't want it to end. Maybe, just possibly, I can put the last few months behind me and actually get on with my life, instead of feeling like I'm stuck in limbo, going around in the circles on permanent repeat. *But no – this is it now.* A new job, with real prospects and a new man – perhaps? Maybe even a new home further into town, at some point in the future. I'm getting ahead of myself, but tonight's been such a pleasure that I let myself indulge in a little fantasy.

After all, judging by my previous record you never know how long things are going to last.

Nineteen

My final day at *The Express* is a bit of a farce really. I'm obviously demob happy, knowing I'm out of there at last, and there isn't a lot left for me to do. I scribble up a few minor stories; one in particular is about the increase in graffiti in the Westwood Road shops area. It's so dull I'm surprised I even stay awake whilst typing. Next, I ring around a few of my better contacts and say my goodbyes, popping down to the police station and fire station just before lunchtime.

Fire fighter Steve Jones pouts and pulls a sad face, putting the kettle on for me to have one last cuppa.

"Can't say I won't miss you babe," he says, appreciatively looking me up and down in my new textured body con dress that hugs my curves.

"Behave, and hurry up with that coffee." I warn him, amused at his lack of self-control. Steve and I had a bit of a casual 'thing' eighteen months ago that fizzled out naturally, but was a whole lot of fun at the time.

I was writing a feature about the local fire brigade, which involved shadowing them for a day and taking part in some of their training exercises. When we got back inside for me to interview Steve, as watch manager, the constant flirtation that had evolved over the previous year finally came to a head, with him closing the blinds and the pair of us necking like a couple of teenagers; his hand down my knickers and mine wrapped around a sizeable, delicious feeling cock. It was a bit of fun that was to be repeated over the next few months, every time I needed to head down to the station for a briefing, or just to call by and see if there was any gossip. We had a laugh, but that was it. Steve's married and we never had full sex, although we came close several times. One day we both agreed to call it a day, but we've been close ever since and he's always gone out of his way to help me.

Cupping the mug close to me, my legs curled up on the chair, I listen while Steve tells me about an RTA that happened outside the area in Leatherhead. He didn't attend as it's not their patch either, but says the whole of Surrey Fire and Rescue are talking about it.

"So he wasn't wearing anything on his lower half at all?" I ask, incredulously, laughing hard and trying not to spill my coffee.

"No trousers, no underwear, nothing: just socks and trainers!" Steve grins. "And she has this huge gash to the head where she hit it on the steering wheel when they ran into the road sign. Honestly he's lucky she didn't bite it off on impact."

"I can't believe she was giving him head while he was driving," I exclaim, my shoulders shaking with laughter.

"Don't pretend you've not thought about it, sweetheart," Steve jokes. I refuse to dignify his accusation with an answer, but simply raise my eyebrows and slurp my drink.

Heading back to work, I feel a bit sad about leaving now the time's come. I mean, of course I'm excited about *The Record*, and the thought of staying here fills me with dread, but I've made some really good friends through this job; it feels weird leaving it all behind.

Nearly everyone accompanies me down the pub for a late lunch just after 2pm. The whole of editorial comes down – even Aidan – and the girls from advertising join us, leaving just Jenny to man the phones. Funnily enough she isn't missed.

David buys me a glass of white wine and makes a funny little toast, acknowledging my speedy progress onto a national for someone 'so young', and wishes me the best of luck for my future. Privately he assures me he never doubted my abilities and says he knew I was destined for great things the moment I opened my mouth during my interview.

"You've got what it takes, Kate. Keep your head down, do what you do best and you'll do well at *The Record*."

Pleased by his praise, I go to sit back down with Gemma and Anna, and spy Aidan and Clive sitting at a corner table, knocking back pints with Darren, the Advertising Manager. They're whispering and exchanging amused glances but I ignore them and reminisce with the girls about some of the funnier stories I've worked on. However, when I get up to go to the ladies' Clive gives me a lecherous look up and down, and alarm bells go off in my head. *What are they up to?*

I'm longer than I anticipated because my mum calls mid-pee to tell me that my cousin Laura's gone into labour. By the time I return to my seat, half the guys and girls have gone back, including Aidan and Clive. Gemma says she can stay a bit longer but looks pre-occupied, and when I press her I'm horrified by what she says next.

Tentatively she says: "Kate, can I ask you something?"

"Oh God, what is it? What have I done now?" I giggle, chucking peanuts down my throat, a bit squiffy after three glasses of wine and no real food to speak of.

"Have you slept with Aidan?"

I'm frozen to the spot with my glass half way to my lips doing my best impression of that little shocked emoji with the big round eyes and the tiny straight mouth. "Kate," she says kindly, "If you have I'm not offended that you never told me, but if you haven't I think you should know that Clive's inferring you two have had a thing."

I take a very big gulp of my wine, leaving just a drop in the bottom of my glass and then finish that too.

"I think I'm going to need another drink." I say quietly. Without a word, Gemma gets up and orders another glass of wine, a bag of cheese and onion crisps and a diet coke for herself.

I sit staring at the knots of wood in the table as they swim before my eyes, my mind whirring on overtime. Aidan must have said something. The fucking cunt. And he and Clive were sat with Darren, so he'll have told all the girls in advertising – that's how Gemma knows.

Oh my God, how can I go back to that office this afternoon, with the entire staff knowing about our affair?

She puts my drink down and sits patiently, waiting for me to speak. Eventually, I ask her in hoarse tones: "Does everyone know?" She shakes her head and relief floods through me.

"Darren quietly took me to one side when he left and asked if I knew anything. He said I ought to tell you before it got out. That's if it's true. And judging by the look on your face, I'm guessing it is."

Holding my head in my hands for a second, I take a couple of deep breaths and tell Gemma the whole thing, from start to finish. I tell her about the picnic in the park, about the night at his and how he walked out at mine, about the texts and the kitchen – at which point she audibly gasps – and how he fucked up the last time we had sex. After which she takes a big swig of my wine and says she wishes she wasn't driving because she could really do with a drink herself after hearing that.

"Are you mad at me for not telling you?" I ask, feeling really guilty I haven't confided in one of my bezzie mates.

"No. And yes," she says punching me in the arm, "but I get why you didn't tell me. I swear to God I want to march back and rip his fucking throat out, messing you about like that!"

She's being quite loud and a couple of the old timers at the bar peer over their newspapers, frowning at us. I lay a restraining hand on her arm,

"That's precisely why I didn't tell you," I smile weakly.

"The problem is, I don't know how much people know. What did Darren tell you exactly?"

"Just that Clive's had a few too many and was saying what a sexy girl you were, and that someone in the office was a lucky bastard for getting his hands on you."

"That was it? He didn't name anyone?" I exclaim incredulously, "So why on earth did Darren decide it was Aidan?"

"He said Aidan's normally the first to join in with a bit of banter – apparently he and Darren often go out for a drink after work – but this time he sat there not saying a word, nursing his pint and staring at his shoes.

"Plus, Clive seemed to enjoy making him squirm, digging him in the ribs, asking him if he thought you looked hot in that dress and what you might look like underneath it."

Ew.

The thought of that dirty old bastard talking about me like that makes me feel physically sick, but I'm also grateful that it seems to be only Clive that Aidan's told.

"If only I could find some way of shutting that filthy little pervert up before he blabs to everyone else," I say thoughtfully. Gemma opens the crisps and offers me one.

"Er, no thanks, I feel sick enough as it is." I say, clutching my stomach.

"Well don't be," she splutters through a mouthful of salty snack, laughing maliciously, "because I've got solution that ensures Clive doesn't open his mouth about this to anyone, ever again."

By the time I get back to work, Aidan and Anna have both gone home, which is no great shakes because I'd probably knock his teeth down his throat if I saw him right now, and I'll miss her like a hole in the head.

Clive's tucked away at the back of the room, quietly downloading photographs from his camera from a mayoral event he attended this morning. He came straight to the pub so I knew he'd be busy until close of play today. There's no reason for me to be here now. Yvonne's on the late shift and I only came back to grab my things and formally say goodbye to Pete and David.

Sidling up to Clive, I sit on his desk with my back to the rest of the room and cross one long, firm thigh over the other, making sure my dress is hitched up, high. Sweetly, I tell him how much I've enjoyed working with him over the years and that it's always been a joy to learn from someone with so much more experience than me. He looks chuffed to bits and can't keep his eyes off my hemline.

Then, resting a hand on his shoulder, I whisper that I'm eternally grateful that he's kept the Aidan situation to himself for so long, but that, as an attractive man of the world, I'm sure he's been party to a few office affairs in his time.

He falls for my bait immediately, placing one clammy mitt high up on my thigh, squeezing it painfully. I think I might actually throw up but stick to the plan, picking up the plastic ruler he always keeps on his desk, and flicking it, bringing it down hard on his hand. "Ow, what did you do that for, you little bitch?" he hisses, nursing the bright red welt that immediately springs up on his skin.

"You think that stings, you scumbag?" I whisper through gritted teeth, "You say one more word to anyone about me and Aidan and I'll release a sting in the tail that'll end your marriage for good. "Thanks to a little birdie, I know all about your liaison with Geraldine in advertising at last year's Christmas party." Clive has gone a curious shade of greyish white.

"Wouldn't it be a shame if I 'accidently' let it slip about your little indiscretion, Clive? It's Tolworth Avenue you live in isn't it? Brenda's your wife's name, I think."

Standing up and leaving this odious little man to lick his wounds, I replace the ruler in the pen pot and say out loud: "It's been a pleasure Clive. I'll see you around – don't be a stranger."

Picking up my coat, scarf and hat, and swinging my bag over my shoulder, I take a last look around the newsroom, go see Pete, and then David, who shakes my hand. He covers it with both of his and does not release his grip for a second or two, before looking me straight in the eyes: "Be careful Kate, you're a good journalist but watch your back at *The Record*. I think you can handle almost anything that's thrown at you, but it's a different world up there, and I'd hate to see you come unstuck. I like you too much for that," he adds. I nod solemnly and promise him I'll do my best. His affection is touching and I feel quite emotional as I step into the lift for the last time.

The alcohol I consumed earlier has worn off and I'm feeling a bit hollow and empty inside. Gemma's driving me home and keeps checking that I'm okay, but I assure her I'm fine and I've sorted the Clive situation – thanks to her spilling the beans on Geraldine.

Once I'm inside the house it's clear I'll go to go stir crazy if sit here all evening, so I dig out my swimming stuff and hop on my bike (cycling's okay when you're over the limit, isn't it?), before heading down to the leisure centre.

I've already done twelve lengths when I see him. Strong, defined shoulders slicing through the water, his dark hair slick with moisture, a pert arse encased in tight Lycra trunks.

I take a breather, loitering in the shallow end and wait for him to swim back the length of the pool.

"Hello, you," I say as Jack surfaces and rips off his goggles. There are those eyes again, albeit this time ringed with red pressure marks.

"Kate!" he exclaims, barely out of breath as he stands up and runs a hand through his hair. As he lifts his arm, I'm treated to a full view of his glorious naked torso for the first time. Broad sloping shoulders give way to a strong, well-defined – but not over muscly – chest, covered with a light dusting of curly hair. Beneath sits a beautifully taut, flat and toned stomach with a neat six-pack. From his belly button, another strip of hair leads tantalisingly into his swimming trunks, which sit irresistibly low on his hips. High at the top of his right arm, above the bulging bicep, sits an artistic black tattoo of some circle, tribal thing that extends over his shoulder and part way down his back.

Wow, this man should be given a medal for services to womankind. He could just stand on a corner with his shirt off and raise the spirits of every female that passes.

"How are you hon?" he asks when I don't say anything. I'm literally standing there mouth agape, gawking at him. Pulling myself together, I find my voice:

"Oh, um I'm great, thanks Jack. I just didn't expect to see you here."

"Yeah, thought I'd just get 50 lengths in before my shift. How was the meeting on Tuesday night?"

We'd met for a quick coffee before my council meeting –

our second date since our evening in the pub. The weekend before we'd managed to go for lunch before he'd headed off to a stag do. It was at a local Italian and we'd spent a lovely couple of hours, eating, drinking and laughing – a lot. Something I'd noticed that first night in the pub, was just how easy I felt in his company. He's very witty and has some cracking stories to tell, mainly about things he's witnessed in the gym. It's three dates in and I still haven't slept with him; it must be some kind of record. I feel like a born again virgin and I'm sure I've healed over!

We agree to work out first and chat afterwards as neither of us wants to stop for too long. I push on with my lengths, switching up the stroke and using a float to just work my legs. While I do, I admire Jack's physique as he crashes through the water near me – all strength and power. Finally completing my 40 lengths, I climb out of the pool and stretch my aching limbs before showering.

I'm still rinsing off when Jack enters the room, carrying a towel and a bottle of Molton Brown hair and shower gel. Being a man, he takes so much less time than me, and we finish within minutes of each other, heading to the lockers together. "What time does your shift end?" I ask, pulling my stuff out of locker 165 and promptly dropping a shoe into a puddle on the floor. "Shit." I bend over and pick it up before looking over my shoulder. "Jack? I said when do you finish?"

I catch him standing there clutching his bag and looking at my arse, his eyes full of lust. We both look at each other, not moving, holding our breath and each hoping the other will make the first move.

Grabbing my arm, he tugs me into a nearby changing room and locks the door behind us. He dumps his stuff at one end of the bench and pulls my belongings out of my arms. Then, walking up to me painfully slowly, Jack tucks a hand around the back of my neck and pulls very slightly on the string fastening. It slithers undone, although the bandeau top remains where it is.

My breath's coming faster now and my legs begin to tremble. Leaning my shoulders back onto the cubicle wall I tilt my pelvis towards him and slide my arms up and around his defined shoulders before pulling him in for a kiss. He tucks his wide forearm around the back of my neck, resting it against the partition wall, forming an impromptu cushion for my head. His kisses intensify in strength, but his beautiful mouth is still soft against my skin. I feel like liquid fire beneath him as little by little, I give myself up to him.

"How much do you want me, Jack?" I whisper, as his kisses descend lower, down my neck and along my shoulder to that sensitive spot where the collar-bone dips, and the skin slopes away. Glancing up from beneath thick lashes, his eyes consumed with lust, his voice catches.

"The first time I saw you, I wanted to touch you." My stomach somersaults and my head swims with pleasure. Firming his mouth back against mine he peels down the top of my bikini to uncover my right breast. He edges his tongue lower and kisses the plump skin. Then, he catches my nipple between his teeth, making me bite back a loud groan in case anyone should hear us.

As quickly as he nipped me, Jack begins suckling again.

He licks and tugs in a series of sharp, sensitive movements until the feeling becomes too intense and I'm forced to break away and drag his lips back to mine. By now I'm delirious with pleasure, so when he trails his fingers over my stomach and between my legs, tucking aside my still wet bottoms, and effortlessly inserts a finger inside of me he has to stifle my cries with his tongue. He crushes his mouth hard against mine, swallowing the noise I can't seem to help making.

"God your pussy's so wet," he murmurs as he peels the other side of my swimming costume down whist stroking me rhythmically in tiny little movements that send me wild with frustration. My hands delve inside the waistband of his trunks, releasing his thick, veined cock. I sense the change in his body as he kisses me more frantically now, his shoulders tensing. "Blow me," he pleads quietly.

"Say please," I whisper, grinning.

"Please," he breathes, almost begging, his pupils dilated.

I kneel down on the puddled floor, oblivious to the rough surface and sink my lips over his smooth knob. No teasing, no foreplay: I envelop him entirely, sliding him deep into my warm, wet mouth until my nose is buried in his sweet, straw scented thatch. Inhaling deeply through my nose, I bob my mouth up and down. He's so hard; an iron rod enveloped in a velvet glove, and I can only maintain momentum for half a minute more before wanting his tongue back in my mouth and his cock in my hand.

Standing up, I press my nakedness into his chest, feeling my nipples graze his coarse hair as he holds me closer. His erection presses between us. Reaching down, I gently tug him away from his stomach and tuck him firmly between my thighs, closing them together over him. Tilting my hips back and forth I create an irresistible friction.

Suddenly he moves very quickly, yanking aside the crotch of my costume and manoeuvres the tip of his cock so it rests squarely at the entrance to my pussy. I feel him pressing against me and just about hear the soft, sticky sound above our breathing. Jack looks at me long and hard for a few seconds, his eyes searching my face for something. Approval? Permission? I don't know who moves first but I edge my pussy forward as he nudges very slightly inside me.

This is ridiculously reckless – we're in changing room for god's sake. People are towelling off in the room next door. There are children shouting and screaming in the pool.

And we have no condom.

I hear the blood rushing though my ears like a freight train and my chest rises and falls rapidly as I reign in the desire to call out Jack's name. His cock see-saws in and out of me, at first excruciatingly slow and steady, but soon with an alarming ferocity.

If it wasn't for his strong and steady arm positioned behind my shoulders I'd be crashing back against the wall with every thrust. But each time he enters me he pulls me even closer. His eyes are shut, his mouth tight and his jaw tense.

"Look at me," I whisper. He doesn't hear me. "Jack, look at me." His eyes meet mine and we both smile wicked, amused smiles at each other, revelling in the illicitness of our secret rendezvous.

Pulling out of me abruptly he catches his breath for a second, then asks, "Suck me again?"

He's close, I can tell, and this time there'll be no going back. Wordlessly, I take him in my mouth and blow him long and hard, jerking him off at the same time. In just nine or ten pumps he finishes in strong, powerful convulsions, filling my mouth with hot, salty cum.

Raising myself level with him, I smile with one eyebrow raised and bite my lip. After regaining his composure he smiles back, kissing me and holding me close.

"I should probably…"

"I think you should…" I say, amused and feeling slightly awkward. He grabs his bag and towel and hitches his trunks back up over his hips. "You owe me an orgasm," I joke, quietly, as he goes to open the door.

"I'll bank it for you." he smiles, "Can I have that one on the house though?"

Checking outside is clear he disappears and I lock the door behind me, sinking down on the bench, still shaking. Holy crap, I can't believe I just did that – another Kate-ism to add to my repertoire of sexual misdemeanours!

When I leave the changing room, he is waiting for me by the hairdryers. Tucking a loose strand of still wet hair behind my ear, he looks at me thoughtfully. "What?"

"Nothing. I was just thinking how beautiful you look," he says, which makes me laugh out loud because no one has ever called me that in my whole life.

"What, like this? All flushed, wet hair and barefaced, in trackie bottoms and an old vest top?" I snort, derisively.

"Yes, like this," he says, wrapping both arms around me

from behind as we admire each other's reflection in the mirror. "I happen to prefer you without make up actually, although you look great either way. I did fancy you first in the gym, sweating on the treadmill, without even wearing so much as mascara you know."

"Oh you know your cosmetic products then!" I laugh.

"Seriously, we talked about this," Jack adds, stroking my ribcage with his fingers, "I told you to stop putting yourself down. If I pay you a compliment, you need to learn to accept it." Begrudgingly, I agree to try.

"But it won't be easy changing the habit of a lifetime," I warn him.

We walk down to the lobby together, Jack's arm comfortably slung over my shoulder. He has to go upstairs to the gym and the exit is on my right. "I don't want to let you go," he complains, pulling me closer.

"No but you've got work and I'm fucking starving," I laugh, unwinding myself from his grasp.

"What even after wrapping your mouth round me," he whispers, naughtily. Backing away so I'm not tempted to stay, I press my index finger to my lips, "Sshh," and wink at him.

"I'll call you," he shouts after me and I smile to myself, walking the wrong way, then remembering I left my bike in the racks at the other end of the car park, near the main road.

My head in the clouds, I cycle half way home before realising I've forgotten to turn my lights on and decide I should probably eat and have an early night. I can still smell Jack on my skin and it feels so good.

For the first time in what feels like forever, I fall asleep without thinking about Aidan.

Not even once.

Twenty

Monday morning dawns bright and frosty. December's turned cold with a vengeance and there's a sharp north wind blowing when I leave for the station.

I park in the car park down the road – I'm not paying station prices – but still balk at the price. At nine pounds per day, five days a week, forty eight weeks of the year it's going to cost me more than two grand just to park the sodding car. I resolve to find a way round this pronto, before I end up haemorrhaging my new annual 'Shoe and Nars Lip Gloss Fund' – generously allocated to myself from my newly increased salary – on a small rectangle of concrete.

Warming my hands through my new Jack Wills gloves on a large steaming latte, I mill around on the platform with dozens of other shivering commuters, watching my breath fog up in the icy temperatures. I don't start until ten, but when the train arrives it's still a proper cram to get on and nigh on impossible to find a seat.

I squeeze up onto the large luggage shelf at the end of the carriage and perch between a huge suitcase and a stuffed-to-bursting backpack.

I'm trying to ignore my stomach doing flips, but it's becoming harder to pretend this is just another day in the office. I'd hoped that having done shifts at *The Record* would make this easier, lessen the impact somewhat, but it hasn't made a blind bit of difference. I'm as anxious as I've ever been on a first day, and have already been to the bathroom three times this morning.

Trees and fields give way to terraced housing and high rises as we forsake the Surrey countryside for the suburbs. Battersea Power Station and the huge warehouses of New Covent Garden Market slide past the window. These are eventually followed by The London Eye, which looms into view as we slow down on our approach to Waterloo Station.

Distracted men in sharp suits are plugged into earphones, and women dressed in heels carrying huge, oversized bags, hustle past me. Each is heading for an unknown destination, locked in their world and casting barely a glance in my direction. And why would they? I look identical to them in a smart pair of cropped, textured trousers, black ankle boots and a roll neck sweater. I look every inch the professional, from my check woollen coat to my black, geometric tote.

I jump on the Jubilee Line, and am sandwiched against the doors by the sweaty armpit of an overweight businessman, who's more interested in reading his paper, hanging onto the overhead bar one handed, than my personal space.

Finally the doors open at Canary Wharf and, gulping in great big, deep breaths of cold, fresh air, I walk slowly towards the tower block that stretches up into the wintery sky.

All of a sudden I feel scared. The excitement that's filled me all weekend has evaporated.

Dean's told me I'll get a pass arranged today, but for now

someone will come down and meet me in the building foyer. I report to reception and a petite blonde rings up to *The Record*, asking me to take a seat while I wait.

I don't even have five minutes to watch the other workers scuttle through the security barriers and into the lifts before Marlene, the features secretary, comes to find me. We've not met before as she doesn't work weekends but she seems pleasant. "Hello, Kate?" she asks, "Come this way, and I'll take you up, although I'm sure you know how to get there by now."

The office is still filling up but there are already far more people there than I've ever seen during a shift. Marlene leads me to the features desk where Lori and Dean are wading through today's nationals.

"Kate. Hi, welcome." says Dean, looking up from a copy of *The Sun* and shaking my hand. Lori smiles from the other side of the desk, "Morning, Kate. You made it then?"

I beam back at her, "I did," but I don't get to say any more as Dean's already heading down the other end of the office where features are based. Four writers are already at their desks: a short blond girl with curly hair is flicking through *The Times*; a guy in his mid-twenties is on the phone, and two women, one tall and brunette, the other with a short, elfin crop, are discussing the Emmerdale actress, Tandy Raymond, who went out of last night's Strictly.

Pointing to an empty seat opposite the short blond girl, Dean says, "This is your desk. Mel, this is Kate, she's starting today." Mel tears her attention away from a story about a pit bull saved at the eleventh hour and reaches over to shake hands, "Hi, pleased to meet you. Welcome to the mad house."

Raising his eyes, Dean laughs, "Mel will show you the ropes and I'll get one of the tech guys to come down and fix you up in a bit. We'll get you sorted with a security pass, and you have a medical booked for later on today with Dr Barker."

Stashing my bag under the desk, I take off my coat and hang it on the coat stand over by the wall. Mel tosses me a copy of *The Mail* and *The Guardian* as I sit down. "Here, you go through these. We skim through all the nationals every morning to look for feature ideas to put forward to the desk for conference."

"Yes, thanks, I know. I've done a few shifts this summer." I say, reading the headlines on both. The body of another child has been found in the waters off Greece. The flimsy life raft the migrants were travelling on capsized during a nocturnal attempt to cross the dangerous seas from Turkey. On page three of *The Mail* the story is decidedly more upbeat. Nodding at the photograph of a plethora of familiar faces posed at a press conference yesterday, "I see *What The Servants Heard* is going to be made into a film, at last. Wringing out one last finale to bring the fans – and the money – flooding in, I guess."

Mel laughs because it's well known the popular costume drama that's had viewers glued to their seats for the last seven years, and should have been wrapped up one, or even two, seasons before it finally did.

There'd been wide speculation that a movie would be made one day, but writer and creator, Thomas Rayminster, held out for two years before making yesterday's announcement. Some critics believe it's 'scraping the barrel' and will result in a lacklustre, big budget film that pays mere lip service to the brilliant, original writing and acting seen in the first four series.

"I have an idea for a feature, but the technical department haven't set me up with an email yet. Do you think I should write it down, or just tell Dean?" I ask.

"Give him a call," Mel answers, pulling the top off a coconut yoghurt, "Dial 14 for his line."

Watching her tip a small container of nuts, seeds and oats into the pot – "Breakfast", she mouths at me – I listen to the phone ring three or four times, before Lori picks up, "Dean's phone."

"Oh. Hi Lori, it's Kate,"

"Kate, how exciting is this? I said you'd get here, didn't I? You have to start believing in yourself honey."

"You did Lori," I can't hide the glee in my voice, "I owe you big time. Whatever you said, it worked. But right now I have an idea for conference and no way of sending it to Dean. No emails yet. What should I do?"

"Email him from your phone. No better still, email me and I'll forward it to him, big up your idea."

"But you haven't heard it yet, Lori!" I protest, giggling at her craziness, "What if it's rubbish?"

"If it's from you darling, it'll be bloody brilliant," she laughs and hangs up. I jot down a few words in my email. Off the back of this story we should pull together all the best films ever made from favourite television programmes, complete with a picture from the original series, a still from the film, and some facts about each one. Off the top of my head I can think of about five: *Sex and the City*, *Charlie's Angels*, *The Inbetweeners*, *Mr Bean* and, *The Flintstones*, but there must be loads more. Before I send the email, I flick through the rest of the nationals and add another couple of ideas.

A tall, raven haired girl who was chatting when I arrived comes over to my desk, proffering a hand. "Hi, I'm Sarah. How're you doing?" she asks in a thick Scottish accent.

I shake it and admire a spectacular diamond engagement ring on her beautifully manicured finger.

"That's beautiful."

"Och, thank you, pet. I chose it myself. You cannae trust a man to get something like that right," and she dissolves into peals of infectious laughter, which leave Mel and I laughing too. Sarah introduces me to the other writers. They don't just do features, and they all write for both the online and the print edition. The guy who was on the phone is Ricky, the woman with short hair is Rosa, and then there's Sara and Nicole, who I met over the summer.

Everyone seems quite friendly, asking me about my previous job and what I worked on while I was on shifts here. I'm just beginning to feel quite comfortable when a very slim, sharply dressed, redhead, who I've seen sitting on the features desk next to Lori, walks over and sticks out her hand.

"You must be Kate. I'm Esther Williams. Deputy Features Editor," she says in clipped tones, with a distinctive plummy accent, "I take it you've met everyone now, so maybe you can let them get back to work."

I notice the other writers scuttling back to their desks as this ice-queen forces a thin, brittle laugh, that doesn't reach all the way up to her eyes. Sitting back down, I hesitate, "Um, yeah, sure. Er, nice to meet you Esther." *I think.*

"If you have nothing to do, can you get going on with this piece?" She says snootily, shoving a cutting in front of my nose. "Apparently these statistics reveal forty per cent of people now play this app, Rabbit Valley, during the work day, and thirty-two per cent spend at least an hour playing it on office time.

"We want to find three women who admit they're guilty of the hour a day, one from each of the different age groups, 18-30, 30-45 and 45-60, and we want it by close of play today. Okay?"

"Yes sure, but unfortunately I can't use my system at the moment because no one's given me a login yet, and I don't have an email address or anything. When I did shifts, someone always logged me on with one of the other writer's logins."

At that precise moment, two guys in polo shirts turn up looking vaguely techy. "And now you don't have that problem anymore," gloats Esther, before she turns around and struts off looking smug.

Wow. What. A. Bitch.

"Sorry about her," Mel whispers conspiratorially across the desk, "Esther McAvoy, resident *Record* bitch, snob and all round diva. Did no one warn you?"

I shake my head, pulling a face. "Is she like that to everyone?" I ask, clocking Rosa, peering round her screen, smiling sympathetically at me.

"No, she likes men, so Ricky gets an easy ride, don't you babe? But if you're a woman…"

Mel makes that sucking, whistling noise tradesmen make when they're about to charge an astronomic fee for a tiny job.

"Basically she's a woman hater, which is weird because she's a lesbian," sniggers Ricky, as he opens a packet of digestive biscuits and offers them around. "Is anyone going down to Starbucks before they get out of conference?"

Nicole says she'll go and Mel offers to go with her.

"Why don't you come Kate, you can't use your system yet?" she asks, nodding at the computer guy sat at my PC.

"Better not." I shrug, glancing nervously up at the features desk, "But is there any chance I could use the Internet on your computer while you're out?" Mel agrees and I give her some change for a latte.

While they're gone, I do some research and come up with a few more facts and figures to support the app story. I find that Rabbit Valley, has soared in popularity since its release eighteen months ago, and the numbers of players has exceeded those playing Candy Crush and Angry Birds put together.

By the time the coffee arrives, I'm up and running on my own system and I have emailed all kinds of groups, online gamers, forums and chat pages. I've even put out an appeal on my own Facebook page.

When everyone's back out of conference, Lori comes to see me. "Told you they'd love it. You need to pull that feature together this afternoon."

"Which one, the one about the films?" I ask, wiping foam off my top lip.

"Yes," she calls, walking away, "Get the photo desk to help you with the stills. And well done. Good idea."

Thank God I did something right. It's a good start to the day despite the run in with that witch. Taking another sip of my creamy latte, I watch Lori return to the desk and talk to

Esther. They're like chalk and cheese.

It's really going to be very interesting working here if I have to answer to Esther all the time.

And by interesting, I obviously mean vile.

It's a quarter past five and I've just finished speaking to a woman who admits she's hooked on the rabbit app. Seriously, if any of these women have a job at the end of this, I'd be surprised. She was the third of my case studies and spends the most of her time playing the game. I've already written the other two up and just need to type this one out before I'm done. I've been flat out all afternoon.

I'd decided to plough on with the movie feature first and get it out of the way while I waited to see if any of the emails I'd sent bore any fruit. Fortunately, I came back to my PC to find a whole host of possible candidates and immediately identified three perfect case studies. I ran them past Lori, and then contacted each of them in turn while eating a salad at my desk. I think I only got up three times this afternoon and two of those were for the loo. Finally finished with the interview, I send it through to the desk and reluctantly call Esther on her extension.

"Yes?"

"Oh, um, Esther, it's Kate."

"Is it done?" she snaps.

"Yes."

"Right I'll take a look." She hangs up.

"She doesn't mince her words, that Esther, does she?" I mutter, replacing the handset on the phone and stretching. Ricky laughs quietly, his shoulders shaking.

My back's stiff and I'm not used to turning work over for the next day. Suddenly it's dawned on me what a huge leap I've made from a weekly to a national daily.

Yawning, I realise I'm exhausted and all I want to do is go home and run a bath. It's six o'clock and I have no idea when I'm supposed to clock off.

"You can leave in about half an hour, if you have nothing left to do." says Mel, "But some nights I'm here until gone eight getting a story finished."

My phone rings and I catch Esther looking across the office at me, her phone to her ear. Shit. I pick up.

"Hello?"

"Kate? Esther. It seems fine. Well done. You can go about six thirty if you're done." And she's gone. Lowering the phone, I look at Mel.

"Well?" she says, cocking her head to one side like a small dog.

"She said, 'well done'." Mel's eyebrows disappear behind her fringe and her mouth gapes a little.

"Well, perhaps she's being extra nice because it's your first day."

"Jeez, what's she like on a bad day?" Mel and Ricky look at each other and chorus in unison, "You don't want to know."

Forty minutes later, I'm hugging myself gleefully as I stroll back to the tube station, congratulating myself on what I believe to be a pretty successful day. I pull my mobile out of the bag and call Jack.

"Hi babe," he says answering almost immediately, "I was about to text you. How'd it go?"

"Good, I think," I smile to no one in particular, "I wrote two features and the desk seems happy with them. It was okay. Listen, are you doing anything? Do you want to go out for a drink? I, kind of, feel like celebrating."

"Sounds perfect," Jack agrees, "but do you want to make it dinner as well? I'm starving."

"Sure, good idea. My train gets in at 7.25pm so shall I pick you up around ten to eight?"

"Are you sure? Shouldn't it be me picking you up?" Jack asks.

"Yes, of course, what was I thinking?" I mock apologise, "And while you're at it you can trade me off for seven cows and three sheep and I'll walk ten paces behind you.

"This is 2015, what kind of man are you?" I tease laughing.

"Sorry, I was trying to be gallant," Jack also laughs, taking the joke in the spirit it was intended.

"Thank you." he says, apologetically, "A lift would be great. See you then."

I get to the platform just as the next tube arrives and I'm able to catch the earlier train, giving me fifteen minutes to spare back in Woking.

I nip into the loo to take my hair down and brush it out. I'm glad I washed it this morning now. Studying my reflection in the mirror, I reapply my lippie and add a little dark shading around my eyes, before spraying myself liberally with Santa Domingo by Oscar de la Renta. My roll neck doesn't do me many favours, but I'm wearing a black vest underneath, so I whip the jumper off and decide I don't mind freezing for twenty minutes. I can always wrap my coat tightly around me and ramp the heating up in the car.

Jack is waiting for me out on the pavement as I pull up, stamping his feet and blowing on his hands. As he jumps in he gasps, "It's brass monkeys out there. I was only waiting five minutes as well. It's baking in here though."

"Sorry, is it too much?" I ask, reaching to turn it down, but he grabs my hand and an electric current passes right through me.

"It's fucking lovely, don't you dare. I thought my balls were going to freeze."

"And that would be a travesty," I giggle.

We drive the short distance to a Japanese fusion restaurant in Weybridge. I've eaten here before and the food is fantastic. Jack and I chat for ages about my day, and about his too. I tell him about Esther's frosty attitude and behaviour towards me, and you can see his hackles rising, bless him.

"What are you going to do about it?" he asks, in between mouthfuls of katsu curry.

"Nothing, right now. I'm the new girl and I have to fit in. If that's means bowing to Miss Hoity-Toity then I will, but if it continues I'm going to call her out on it. At some point, anyway."

I pause to eat some more of the delicious sticky, spicy chicken, and Jack watches me, smiling.

"Mmm, what?" I mumble indignantly through a mouthful of food. Wiping the juices off my chin, I feel extremely self-conscious all of a sudden.

"Nothing," he smiles at me, "it's just nice to see a woman enjoying her food for a change. So many girls just pick at their dinner, it's a real pleasure to see you tucking in."

"Ha. You make me sound like a pig in a trough, snout down, bottom up," I laugh, taking a sip of wine.

"Not at all," Jack grins, "Although I'd quite like to see you face down, with your arse up in the air."

I feign pretend shock, before eating some more scrummy food.

"The thing is, I've done all the faddy diets, living without fat, then without carbs… even, without alcohol." The thought of that makes me shudder. "Now, as long as I keep up the high levels of training, eat sensibly all week, and don't go completely crazy at the weekend, I can enjoy decent portions of good, healthy food and small amounts of the really bad stuff. Life's too short to go without anyway," I add, savouring a deliciously spicy prawn.

"I agree." says Jack, "Also, I like looking at you even when you're not eating, in case you were wondering."

I roll my eyes at him and scoop up a handful of delicious salty edamame beans.

We share a dessert and I suggest adjourning to a nearby pub, but Jack has other ideas.

"I've got a nice bottle of wine back at mine, or something stronger if you like."

"But then I won't be able to drive… oh, right."

I'm not sure why I feel thrown. Perhaps it's because it's a work night and I can't possibly turn up to work tomorrow in the same clothes I wore today. Not on day two as well.

Or maybe it's because I still really want this to work and, despite the steamy encounter we had at the sports centre the other day, I feel like this is a significant step, still quite early on. Then I think about how nice it will be snuggling up to Jack all night, and how good it will feel waking up with him tomorrow morning.

'And how fucking great it will be mounting that beautiful cock in the confines of a bedroom where you can really let go and enjoy the ride', yells my subconscious. Bollocks, I'm in! I'll get up early and drive home to change.

"That sound great, let's go," I say rather too quickly than is seemly, but who actually gives a shit. Chasing the incredibly lazy waitress for the bill, I start to shrug my coat on and find myself downing the rest of my – rather small – glass of wine a bit too quickly. I wish I wasn't driving because I could do with a quite a bit more to drink right now. I think I'm actually nervous. How ridiculous is that?

We walk back to the car, Jack's fingers entwined in mine. I'm quite reluctant to let his hand go when we reach the car, but remind myself that I get to touch all of him as soon as we get to his.

On the short journey to Addlestone we carry on talking about healthy eating and fitness.

"So I try to mix it up," Jack is saying, "Cardio, weights, out on the bike and swimming. I'm not a big fan of running though. I don't know how you do it."

"I love the feeling of being out there in the elements, running free, just me and my music I guess," I answer, slowing down for the roundabout into his road. "I'm not a natural, far from it. In fact as a child I couldn't really run at all – my chest would tighten up and I'd find it hard to catch my breath. I swam for a long time, but now I only do it once every couple of weeks, or when I feel like it, it got too boring."

"Well it wasn't boring the other day," Jack says saucily, sliding his hand over my thigh and into the warm gap between my legs. I gasp involuntarily, at the pressure, so close to my pussy and feel myself tighten and begin to get wet.

"It's the second on the left, then right. And keep your eyes on the road, Cleaver," he adds, sounding far huskier than he did earlier, as he slides his hand up to my fly, deftly unzips my trousers and slides one cool hand down the flat of my stomach and into my pants.

I'm gripping the steering wheel so tightly the veins on the back of my hands are clearly visible in the streetlight. My heart rate rises and my breathing increases as I struggle to remain focussed. His middle finger traces a line between my lower lips, lightly but oh, so definitely there and it takes every last ounce of concentration to steer the car safely into his road and park up alongside his Audi A3.

After turning the ignition off and removing the keys, I feel my shoulders relax and I let my head fall back, abandoning myself to the delicious feeling as he brushes against my slick interior. I'm gutted when he withdraws his hand and opens the car door.

"Jack!" I protest, but with a smile. Wickedly, he ignores my protests, steps out of the car onto the pavement, and asks innocently: "Coming?"

"Not now I'm not, no, but I could've done if you'd carried

on," I whine, pouting like a spoilt child.

Ignoring my silly joke, he walks to the front door, unlocks it and waits for me to follow him. I hesitate, one foot still in the car. I don't know why, but I feel like what I do next could change the rest of my life. Is that daft?

Taking a deep breath, I follow him up the garden path and cross the threshold.

Twenty One

Jack's kitchen is all grey slate and bright recessed spotlights. It's immaculate and the complete opposite to the one in my house. I find myself wondering if Jack even cooks in it. I'd been willing to forego the aforementioned drink and carry on where we'd left off but – deliberately, I think – Jack has opened and poured each of us a large glass of red wine. Picking mine up, I gulp down one, then two large mouthfuls – *ooh, I needed that* – and wander back into the lounge, taking in my surroundings as I go.

A large open plan living room leads straight off the front door, with the stairs to the bedrooms set at the rear of the room. I find myself impatient to discover what his bedroom is like; I feel as if it will be very masculine, and the thought this does things to me that I can't process right now.

Perching on the edge of the grey, suede sofa, I kick off my boots, peel my coat off and take a few more fortifying gulps of the smoothly spiced red liquid. Jack is staring at me, an entertained expression on his face. "What's so funny?"

"You are. I gave you five seconds to jump on me once we got inside the door and you've disappointed me, Kate."

My eyes open wide.

"I thought after you responded so quickly to my touch

in the car, you wouldn't be able to help yourself once we got inside, but it seems your self-control is stronger than I gave you credit for. I should be impressed but I'm gutted if I'm honest. I thought I'd be inside you by now."

Oh the cheek of it – that's it!

Unable to stop myself laughing out loud, I pick up a cushion and lob it towards his head. He ducks and quickly puts his glass down, which is just as well, because I proceed to throw every soft furnishing I can lay my hands on in his direction. Then I throw myself on him too, battering his big chest affectionately with my hands.

He grabs hold of my wrists with a single fist and cups my left breast with the other one. Rolling his thumb over the nipple through the fabric of my shirt, I'm so turned on that it's like he's touching my bare skin.

"Jack," I breathe, desperately longing for him to strip all my clothes off and fuck me on the sofa.

"Not here," he says, instinctively pulling me up and into him as he leads me upstairs to the larger of the two rooms.

The walls are painted two shades of grey, and the curtains are almost charcoal with a black strip running along the bottom. Against the back wall there's a bed in dark brown wood, matching bedside tables and a simple, uncluttered chest of drawers. The bed – which is huge – is covered with white pillowcases and a duvet cover in every imaginable shade of grey, with thick and thin stripes alternating down the length of it. Still holding my hand, Jack pads towards it but stops just short turning to face me instead.

"I've wanted you in my bed for weeks," he growls, making

my stomach somersault in delight, and magnifying every feeling enveloping my body.

Tugging me to him, he kisses me fiercely, burying his hands in the loose bun I've secured at the top of my neck. As his kisses intensify, he pulls at it frantically and I help him to release it from its bind. His attention moves quickly to my vest, which he pulls up and over my head letting my breasts spill over the top of my bra. My stomach flutters and my breathing picks up speed as I start to undo my trousers, but Jack's strong hands stop me. "No," he insists forcefully, "I want to undress you… If that's okay." He adds, and I smile my assent.

Jack reaches down for the second time this evening to undo the fastening, while and pull him in close, burying my face in his neck. I inhale his warm, spicy scent and nuzzle the point where his rough stubble meets soft skin. A blue vein runs from his jaw to collar bone and I trace it with my lips, kissing every millimetre as he peels my trousers away, letting them drop to my knees.

Replacing the hand he removed earlier, he cups my mound, first outside then inside my knickers, before pressing his finger against me, working it smoothly up and down the warm, wet channel until I'm not aware of anything except for the movement of his skin against mine. I start to sway, slightly delirious from the incredible surges sweeping through my body. Reaching around me with his other arm, Jack cradles my arse with his hand to steady me, pressing me harder into his finger, a wonderful sensation building in my clit.

I'm impatient and anxious to fuck him and impossibly turned on. I don't want to wait a minute longer than I have to. Unable to bear it, I kick my trousers off and unbutton his shirt to unveil his beautiful body. Next, I rip off his jeans. Beneath his royal blue Superdry trunks, the outline of Jack's erection is plainly visible, a small damp patch appearing at the top, where the head of his cock is leaking. "I want to suck you but I need you inside me." I pant, resisting the urge to drop to my knees and sink my mouth over him, adding desperately: "Now, Jack!"

He pushes me back onto the bed and walks around to one of the bedside tables. Never taking his eyes off me, he takes a condom out of the drawer and tears open the wrapper.

Positioning himself back between my legs, he quickly pulls off his underwear and, looking directly at my lace covered pussy tugs at his red, swollen cock, two or three times, then carefully unrolls the latex over it.

I can feel my juices seeping through the fabric of my white panties as I realise I'm clenching and releasing my pussy while rocking my pelvis back and forth. My need to have Jack inside me intensifies each time I look at his thick, solid cock sticking up at a jaunty angle, now dressed and ready to go.

Kneeling on the duvet between my thighs, he takes his dick in one hand and tears my knickers off with the other, the slim scrap of material no opposition to his desire. I push them further down my legs, releasing my ankles and open myself wide, greedy for him. He halts with the fat, angry head of his cock at my entrance, looks at me one last time, then pushes himself deep into me with a thrust that forces the air out of my lungs.

"Ohh," I moan loudly in rapturous relief as I smash my

groin into his, feeling my pussy stretch around his girth. I'm literally being split in two by his hard rod. *Oh, this man is amazing.* He pulls his full length out, almost to the tip, before driving back into me, very slightly circling his hips, chafing the walls of my pussy, one side at a time, fulfilling an intensely distracting itch.

I'm rolling against him, grinding the sensitive bud of my clit into his pelvis, crushing it against the base of his cock, revelling in the sensations I'm releasing. I feel like I should move, change positions, sit astride Jack, let him fuck me from behind, but fuck it, this feels so damn good I don't want to stop and he's not objecting.

His lips are on mine, furiously bruising my mouth, heightening my arousal, and he's making little grunts which suggest he's as turned on as I am. I rarely cum at the same time as a guy but something tells me that's about to happen. Feeling my belly and pussy tighten together I rub myself three, maybe four more, times against Jack, clinging to his arms for support as he powers into me, and then I feel it. My orgasm creeping, clawing its way closer, within reach, tremors of an almighty collision on the brink, but not quite there.

Jack's fighting to hold back, but he doesn't have to wait much longer as a couple more strokes take me into overdrive and I cum hard against him, my pussy contracting around his flesh.

Finally able to let go, he abandons himself in a frenzy of thrusting, the vein on his neck standing out in stark relief against his reddening skin, sweat beading on his forehead from the strain of holding back while I came. His breath is shallow and fast, and his strong arms are stacked against the mattress, as levering himself into me, he cums in quick, sharp bursts. Still holding his weight up, Jack takes a few seconds to catch his breath and regain his composure, and then he rolls off me, collapsing back on the bed.

"Oh, wow, phew," he gasps, trying to catch his breath. "That was intense, Kate. God, that was, wow." I laugh and wriggle under the duvet, snuggling into the crisp linen and plump pillows. Jack cleans himself up and joins me, gently reaching around my back to undo my bra and slide it down off my arms. "Sorry, I said I wanted to undress you, then only did half a job," he apologises.

"It's fine," I giggle, "I didn't really give you much chance. I was a bit impatient, wasn't I? Sorry."

"Trust me, I wasn't complaining," Jack growls in my ear, nestling up behind me and spooning me. He wraps his arms around me, cupping my breasts in his large hands and stroking my skin as he softly kisses my neck.

"Seriously Kate, that was incredible."

"It did feel pretty good," I admit, relaxing back into his warm, toned torso. His broad chest a cushion for my head and his legs tied up with mine.

I feel like I've come home.

Whoa! Where did that thought come from? I have no idea how those words formed themselves and the independent clockwork whirring around in my head startles me. *That was weird!* Jack hasn't noticed me tense up, so I convince myself I'm just in a post-coital daze and not to worry. It's probably like baby brain – a flood of hormones has just addled my grey matter.

We lie cuddling and talking for a while, and then Jack gets up, pulls on his jeans and goes downstairs for the wine and glasses. While he's there I nip to the loo to tidy myself up. As I wash my hands I study my face. My eye make-up's smudged and my cheeks are all pink, like someone's been pinching them, or like when you've been out in the cold on a blustery day. My lips are bright red and swollen as if I've bitten them, and my hair is tousled and tangled. In short, I look like I just got well and truly fucked.

I jump back into bed as Jack comes through the door.

"God you have a nice arse."

I ignore him, tucking myself back under the duvet and smile as I accept the glass of wine. Jack sprawls across the bed and strokes my toes, which are sticking out from the duvet. "You have very pretty feet, you know. Like the rest of you."

"Thank you," I accept graciously, even though I don't think I'm pretty at all. I also think all feet are ugly, and mine are the worst – like Hobbit's feet.

I never used to be able to take a compliment, throwing it back in people's faces with sarcasm or a self-depreciating joke. But the girls have pulled me up on it so many times, and now Jack's made a thing about it, in the end I've had to accept them, start smiling, and learn just to say 'thank you'.

And it's a good lesson to learn. Since Jack's pep talk, I've actually started enjoying the attention I receive, and if I still don't quite believe some of the comments I get, let's just say a small part of me is gaining some self-belief.

We spend the best part of an hour just lying there,

wrapped in each other's arms, chatting and laughing. Jack had got in bed with me, with his jeans still on, spooning me, stroking my arms and tummy and dropping comforting little kisses on the top of my head. It's funny, but I haven't had this for a long time and I've missed it. I mean, the sex I've had since Rob left has been fantastic (most of the time), spectacular, mind blowing even, on occasion. Suddenly, I flashback to fucking Aidan on that first night, and it makes shiver involuntarily.

"You okay? You cold?" Jack asks, pulling me closer.

"Mmm, a little," I lie, blocking out the unwelcome memory and, pressing myself back further into his hard body, I joke: "Maybe I should put some clothes on."

"Don't even think about it," he scolds, enveloping me further in his strong arms, "I like you naked in my bed, Miss Cleaver." I smile and kiss his bulging bicep, revelling in the attention. But try as I might, I can't escape the feeling of cold water pooling in my stomach.

Why did I have to go and think about him, when I'm feeling so, so... loved up?

This is exactly what I've unwittingly been craving during the last couple of years: great sex and a loving guy to stick around afterwards to make me feel like a million dollars; somebody, who can't wait to curl up with me at night and wake up with me in the morning, without looking for the first excuse to leave after sex.

'Not Aidan then?' Says a little voice in my head.

NO!

I mentally slaughter the voice with a razor sharp knife,

right across the vocal chords.

I want someone who's as comfortable holding my hand in a restaurant or walking along the street as they are going down on me in the bedroom.

I'm determined to shake this silly feeling and I'm mad at myself for letting it infiltrate my brain in the first place. I know I probably shouldn't be looking this far ahead, but I really like Jack and I want to be naked in his bed for as long as he'll have me. Which, because I've not entirely thought this through until now (and the voice in my head has really pissed me off), has quite surprised me. But I'm going to run with it anyway and see where it takes me.

Setting the glass down on the bedside cabinet, I turn to Jack, snaking my arms around his neck and shoulders and lying the full weight of my body against him. I press my mouth into his, kissing him gently and enjoying the way he feels: soft, full lips contrast with his hard jaw and scratchy stubble. My lips part, and I slip my tongue into his mouth, darting it around, wet and warm, exploring every corner, lost in the sweet, sweet feeling.

Jack's hands stray over my nakedness. They slide over my waist and curl around my bare backside. Then he cradles my face between his hands, like you'd treasure a small creature, or a precious stone, and kisses me as though he's transferring life from his body to mine. He groans and shifts beneath me as I feel the tell tale swelling harden beneath his jeans: a blatantly undisguised passion. "I want you again Kate," Jack mutters urgently, wrestling with the buckle of his jeans, "Fuck me. Please. The way you kiss me turns me on so much."

I sit astride him, upright, leaving a wet patch on his jeans as I undo the fly. Together we shimmy them off, me pushing them down his thighs, him kicking them onto the floor. I go to mount him but he balks, stalling my movement by holding my hips. "Wait, we need a condom," he says hurriedly.

"Do we, Jack? Really?" I ask, pleadingly, "We didn't use one the first time in the pool changing room. "I'm on the pill and had my last check up four weeks ago. I'm clean. How about you?"

"The same, only two months ago," he says, releasing his hold slightly, "And I've not slept with anyone else since then."

I smile expectantly at him, "Well then?"

In an action I take as permission, he lets go and slides his large palms along my legs, rubbing them against the firm flesh of my thighs. His thumbs splay between them, applying an unyielding pressure along their insides, right down the sensitive lines that flow directly from my clit.

The feeling sends mini shockwaves through me and the fluttering in my pussy gets stronger. Now he's not preventing me anymore, I slide upwards until my greedy, wet opening sits right above the enlarged head of his cock. I gasp with delight as his velvety smooth skin slides into me and I tilt my hips back, engulfing him up to his balls, revelling in the sensation of having nothing between us.

We stay there for a few seconds, me swirling my hips in little circles like he did earlier, intensifying my own pleasure, and his too it appears, if the dazed expression on his face is anything to go by. I adjust my position, sitting right back, bolt upright and start to raise and lower myself on his firm erection, dipping my fingers into my pussy, exploring the point where he and I join. I slide my fingertips over my taut, slippery skin as it stretches to accommodate him, before rubbing them around his cock and down to his balls, now jammed hard against my arse. Retracing my route, I bring them back up to my clit, swollen and sensitive, ridiculously aroused, and gently massage the plump, sticky flesh surrounding my hard bud. Jack has lifted his head and is straining to see me touch myself. I also look down, and immediately I'm even more turned on seeing his hardness embedded in my cunt, no space between us.

But I want more. I want his mouth where his cock is, kissing me there the way he kisses me on the mouth; I want him to do to my open wetness what he does to my lips.

"Go down on me," I whisper, almost faint with longing, "I need you to kiss my cunt."

Eyes cloudy with desire, Jack mutters, "I've wanted to do that all night." I scramble back onto the bed, my thighs falling open, desperate with anticipation but unwilling to lie back until I've watched him. Propped up on my elbows, I see him crawl towards me, inflamed cock sawing wildly in mid-air now I've unsheathed him.

Licking his lips, the gorgeous man lowers his head and inhales deeply, just inches from my dripping pussy, savouring the smell and sight of me. "God, Kate, you're incredible," he sighs, then adds, wickedly, "and pretty edible too."

Then, unbearably slowly, he presses his mouth firmly against my wetness and French kisses me, exactly the way he devours my mouth, pushing his tongue inside, swirling it around, turning his head this way and that, and sending my mind into orbit. I feel my back arch right off the mattress as I tip my head back and tilt my body into his incredible lips, closing my thighs around his head. He keeps sucking and kissing me, teasing and tugging my sensitive flesh, occasionally pausing to focus purely on my clit, then returning to embrace my hot centre. His attentions are relentless as he laps me intently, leaving no opportunity for me to come back down to earth. I'm in my own little world where I'm unaware of anything, except his probing tongue dipping in and out of me.

I'm vaguely aware of the faint buzz of an impending orgasm, hovering in the peripherals of my mind, and start clenching my buttocks and thighs a little tighter, lengthening my legs and riding the rhythm Jack's created for me. The pressure increases and I'm close enough to feel the beginnings of a wave of sheer bliss washing over me.

"Don't... stop. Keep... going," I pant out, rocking my pelvis back and forth against the constant movement of Jack's flickering tongue. My arms are by my side, the bottom sheet balled in my hands, every fibre of my body tenses and I feel like I'm going to explode. My head thrusts back onto the bed. My pussy strains at his tongue and I freeze, motionless. Holding my breath for a second, time stands still, and I cum in long, strong bursts of pure pleasure. Falling limp, my head to one side and heart pounding, I reach for my beautiful man. He wipes his lips with the back of his hand then climbs up my body, seeking out my mouth for a long, deep, passionate kiss.

Without saying a word, he yanks me up from my stupor and

flips me over, balancing me on hands and knees, separating my legs to make room for him. I sense him there, the hair on his legs barely touching mine, and shivers run through me as he rests his fingertips lightly on my hips.

One hand glides appreciatively over my right bum cheek, smoothing the round of my arse from my spine to my wet, open crevice. Inserting his hand just between my cheeks he gently pulls one to the side, opening me up and exposing my plump, juicy cunt and arse crack to the elements. Without hesitation, he presses his rock-hard cock against my slit and, pulling on both hips now, draws me back onto him. I'm already highly sensitised from my orgasm and feel every millimetre of his length filling me up, from his thick root, jammed up against my arse, to the swollen head battering my cervix, deep inside of me.

The pressure's intense. I'm sure he's bigger than he was earlier, or maybe my pussy's so engorged I'm aware of all of him stretching me open, crammed tightly into my cunt.

I'm still dazed from cumming so I let him take charge, giving myself up to him, letting him fuck me. First hard, then slow. Rocking on my elbows now, my hips push further back so he can lever into me at a deeper angle. He massages my hips and backside, kneading the soft flesh with long, strong fingers. His thrusts intensify and his pace picks up as he establishes the rhythm that's clearly going to take him all the way. I can never normally cum when I'm being fucked from behind, but the tightness in my groin combined with continuous friction sends bursts of tiny, joyful sparks through my pussy, both shocking and surprising me.

Jack launches himself into me with three last, strong thrusts, ramming himself hard up against my arse, his cock twitching and jumping, as he pours himself into me in a flood of powerful gushes.

I sink to my stomach, Jack's still firm erection embedded inside me, all strength has been sapped from my body as he lies down on top of me and tilts my head towards his for a soft, slow kiss. I'm shattered and can barely move, but Jack gently lifts me up, lies my head on the pillow and gets me a towel for the inevitable spillage that will come anytime now. After covering me with the duvet he uses the bathroom, then turns all the lights off and climbs into bed next to me, pulling me close, holding me tight.

I close my eyes and allow myself to drift off, dimly aware of the slow, steady breathing on my skin and the rise and fall of his chest against my back.

'*I feel safe*', is the last thing I remember thinking before I fall asleep.

Twenty Two

I'm giddy with excitement as I glance at the other side of the table, mentally pinching myself. Seriously, my mum will fucking implode when I tell her about this.

It's the second week in December and the fifth annual 'Have-A-Go Hero Awards', created and hosted by *The Record*, is being held in London, with every actor, musician, singer and celebrity worth their salt in attendance.

We writers have been drafted in to carry out the post award interviews with the winners and, as such, are expected to loiter around in the lobby during the three-hour sit down meal and ceremony, "And *not* the bar!" Esther had laboured at the pre-awards briefing. But, after spotting several empty seats in The Dorchester's grand banqueting suite, I'd bitten the bullet and asked Sasha O'Neil, *The Record*'s glamorous and influential Fashion Editor, if there was any reason I couldn't join one of the tables, at least until I actually had some work to do. She was lovely and agreed it was pointless us standing outside if there were places available, and immediately seated me on her table where I'm now perched in disbelief, looking over at the gorgeous Jamie Dornan, a slightly smug-looking Simon Cowell and *Coronation Street*'s former 'bad boy' and heartthrob, Jay Roman, all tuxedoed up, glasses in hands (could the testosterone count be any higher?).

I'd immediately texted Mel, who'd let the others know, and they too have snuck into spare seats dotted around the room. I spot Mel two tables away, to the left of the stage, sitting next to TV fittie, *Happy Valley* and *War and Peace* actor, James Norton. We lock eyes and she grins at me, pulling a, 'Holy fuck this guy's fit, I can't believe I'm within touching distance,' kind of look.

I snort with laughter, cramming my hand over my mouth, before feeling my cheeks redden as the impossibly handsome Mr Dornan catches my eye, smiling at my blatant lack of self-control, his beautiful dark eyes filling with amusement. Quickly looking away, I notice Simon Cowell 'appreciating' first one of the waitresses as she pours some wine at the neighbouring table; then one of the pretty young *Eastenders* actresses wearing a daringly low-cut dress; and finally, bringing his glance to rest on me, looking me up and down, even smiling flirtatiously. Honestly! I have to avert my glance for the second time in as many minutes. Is there no safe place for a girl to look in this room? Taking my gaze above the heads of my fellow diners, I encounter Esther's frosty face shooting me daggers across the room. It would appear that there weren't enough spare seats for everyone and, bearing in mind she would have been bottom of the list when it came to telling each other we could sit down, I'm guessing she's been standing in the shadows since the start of the evening – ouch!

Pretending I haven't seen her – although the look of horror on my face probably gave the game away – I quickly look back at the stage and join the applause as the next recipient makes their way to the stage, where One Direction are waiting to present an award.

The evening unfolds as it should: a mixture of glamour and surrealism, peppered with magic and strewn with disbelief. Humbled by the thoughtful and courageous actions of young children, frail Nannas and ordinary folk alike, famous faces of stage and screen become consumed with emotion. There's not a dry eye in the house for the duration of the night.

The ceremony lasts longer than it does on television, and it could feel like it's dragging on a bit if it wasn't for seasoned presenter and former reality star, Bindi Evans. She keeps the audience eating out of the palm of her hand with her down to earth, northern humour and witty banter.

She's as comfortable with small children as she is with the old and infirm, embracing all of them with a warm hug and genuine affection, thinking nothing of kneeling on the floor, in an absolute floor sweeper of a gown, to reach their level. Unlike some reality stars, who get looked down on by some of their more 'worthy' contemporaries, she is beloved by everyone in the room - even Prince Charles seems taken with her! With the last award underway, I see Ricky and Sarah making their way out of the room and gesture to Mel that it's time to make a move.

We gather in one of the side rooms to interview the winners in full for tomorrow's edition of the paper. Every writer had been allocated winners beforehand, and I've already shot backstage three times this evening to capture immediate reactions from each of mine.

Helen Parkinson, a dinner lady from Stoke celebrated for dashing back into her burning school to rescue a trapped four-year-old boy, was so overcome after receiving her award from David Beckham she was a gibbering wreck, barely able to string a sentence together, let alone give me a cohesive comment. Although, having been required to get a few words off David myself I could empathise with her – he is seriously hot and I fluffed my questions more than once!

Now waiting in the silk draped, marbled-floored reception room, I cringe inwardly as I see Esther bearing down on me, grim-faced and glowering. With no place to hide and already having had a couple of glasses of wine – although no more until after the job is done – I stare brazenly at her and decide to front it out. I'll stand my ground and take her wrath. Let's be honest, what choice do I actually have?

Presenting more bravado than I actually feel, I plaster on a defiant expression – my 'fuck you face', Stella calls it – and look her directly in the eye.

"I hear it was you who asked for a seat at the awards." Esther accuses, caustically. Raising one eyebrow, she awaits an answer.

"I did, yes," I answer, pleasantly but firmly. Offering neither an apology nor an explanation. Fuck her. If she wants to make something of this, she can do all the hard work.

"You're not here to party, Kate." she snaps, glaring at me, "You're here to do the job you're paid for. Nobody else has seen the need to invite themselves to dinner before, not since these awards started, in fact."

At that point the large double doors on the far side of the room open and the award winners, mostly with glasses of champagne in their hands, flood in.

"Perhaps no one had my initiative," I smile sweetly at her sour face, and head towards the first of my winners, a police officer who sat on the icy edge of a multi-storey car park in a blizzard for four hours last January, talking a homeless teenage lad out of committing suicide. "Will you excuse me?" I throw back over my shoulder, "I need to get on with my job, Esther." She's going to have it in for me now, but frankly I don't care. I can't abide bullies, and that's what she is. They made my life hell at school, college and university, and now it would appear Esther wants to do the same thing at work. Some women just don't grow out of that playground mentality. If anything, I pity the damn woman as there's clearly something lacking in her life, or she has self-esteem issues, or something.

I have a nice chat with Derek the police officer, then Helen again, and finally, little Ollie, an incredible six-year-old from Bolton, who raised more than £24,000 for his local hospital after they treated his baby sister for leukaemia. The poor little chap can barely keep his eyes open, but he'd begged his parents to let him be interviewed last to give him time to get as many autographs from celebrities as possible before the evening was out.

His face shines despite the fatigue, and eyes alight, he describes the highlight of his night, sitting on David Beckham's knee while they watched videos of him playing football on his mum's mobile phone.

"I'm jealous," I whisper to Lorraine, his uber-proud mum, "I wouldn't mind sitting on Mr Beckham's knee myself." She giggles and agrees, before whisking Ollie away to their hotel room for his belated, but much needed, bedtime.

I have to scribble up the interviews and send them over to the office in time for tomorrow's edition. We'll be running more in depth pieces over the coming days but it's imperative we carry something on each of the winners tomorrow, no matter how small, as a direct follow up to the evening's ceremony. It will give readers a taste of the heroic acts they can see on ITV tomorrow night when the show's televised.

Stepping out into the foyer, I nip up one flight of stairs and cloister myself in a little nook, overlooking the hotel atrium, and start sending over the copy, vaguely aware of the general hubbub spilling out of the bar below. I've almost finished when I get the distinct feeling I'm being watched. Looking around the mezzanine I find no one but an oblivious seven-year-old being dragged upstairs and vehemently assured the party's most definitely over by her weary parents. Glancing back over the balcony, I notice Mel and Ricky, sidle out of the bar, with a cocktail in each hand, giggling at a shared joke and spying on Ed Sheeran, who's flirting with a blond model over by the champagne bar.

Then I spot him: On the other side of the seating area, tall and clean-shaven, is an immaculately dressed man in a dark suit, white, open necked shirt, and no wearing a tie. His chocolate brown eyes, framed by thick eyebrows and a high set of cheekbones, gaze steadily in my direction.

They belong to the ridiculously good-looking *Hollyoaks* actor, Danny Sergeant, and rest firmly and unflinchingly on my face, as he sips, slowly, at his bubbly. I already know instinctively it's me he's watching, but glance over my shoulder anyway to find – as I knew I would – no one else there. Despite my disbelief, I also know why he's watching me and exactly what he wants.

Looking away, he leans over and speaks to a barman, who pours a glass of champagne and hands it to a passing waitress. Mesmerised, I want to tear my eyes away and hide my face, but feel compelled to keep staring at this beautiful boy, that is until that same waitress taps me on the shoulder and hands me the ice-cold flute of golden bubbles.

I go to thank her, but the words get stuck and I end up rasping at her, nodding my thanks instead. The chilled amber liquid is like a balm to my dry throat, and instead of sipping at it I take two or three greedy gulps, before turning back to acknowledge my benefactor and signal my gratitude.

But he's gone.

Disappointed and confused, my eyes dart back and forth across the entrance hall, scouring the throng of jubilant merrymakers; celebrities mingle with tipsy award winners and journalists, as a general party atmosphere fills the room.

I tip forwards slightly, trying to see underneath the jutting mezzanine floor where the atrium extends towards the vodka bar and the restaurants. But still I don't see him.

Suddenly fingertips brush against my rib cage, making me jump, and a gravelly voice says, "Be careful, you don't want to fall." Spinning round, I almost lose the contents of my glass as those beautiful eyes travel across my face, even more hypnotic up close. "Danny Sergeant," he says smoothly, offering me his hand. I grasp it and shake it vigorously, probably grasping on to it a little too firmly, in a vain bid to conceal just how much I'm shaking.

"Um, Kate. Kate Cleaver." His hand is warm and dry. I'm aware mine is cold and slightly damp from holding the condensation-drenched glass. "I'm sorry," I gabble, wiping my hand down the skirt of my simple, fitted black dress, "It, it's the champagne, it's cold."

'It's meant to be, you daft cow,' I think to myself.

"Not that I'm complaining," I add, hurriedly, "I mean, thank you, the drink, it's great, you shouldn't have, although it is really nice..." I tail off, only too aware of just how much of a prick I'm making of myself. Danny leans sexily against the cool marble pillar, his eyes dancing in amusement, the corner of his mouth twitching with the mere hint of a smile. I take a deep breath and compose myself, smiling assuredly this time, "Can we please start again? I'm Kate Cleaver, a writer for *The Record*. Thank you for the champagne Danny, it's delicious, and very kind of you. I can't think what I've done to deserve it though."

"Do I need a reason to buy a beautiful woman a drink?" he asks, clinking his glass against mine, "Cheers."

This guy's clearly a player. I mean, until now he doesn't actually have a reputation as one but surely it's just a matter of time before we, or one of the other papers, run an exclusive on some woman he's charmed into bed and unceremoniously dumped.

'Yeah, that's right, write him off as a lothario,' mocks the little voice in my head, *'He couldn't possibly actually be interested in you.'* Mentally batting the thought away, I give him what I hope's an enigmatic smile, rather than looking constipated, and sip a little more champagne. I'm very flattered and excited by his attention, although I'm not exactly sure where it's going. Nevertheless, I have Jack now. He's lovely, and gorgeous, and serious about me, and I couldn't do anything to jeopardise that.

But, oh my God this man's absolutely stunning, and now he's saying something to me, so I really have to start tuning into the actual conversation and stop getting distracted by his mouth.

"…doing up here, all alone." He finishes and pauses for a few second, waiting for me to speak.

"Um, I was just finishing sending my interviews over for tomorrow, but I'm all done now and I was about to go down to the bar and meet my colleagues for a well-earned drink." I say cheerily, endeavouring to squeeze past him onto the stairwell. But he doesn't move, meaning my body has to brush against his and his face is just inches away from mine as I leave the seclusion of the little nook. My heart's racing and if I thought my palms were clammy before, they're sweating buckets now. Gently but masterfully taking hold of my elbow, a gesture which sends goose bumps up my arms, Danny steers me towards the stairs.

"Do you mind if I join you?" he asks.

"Er, no. Of course not," I stammer, "but don't you have some mates you want to hang out with?"

"Are you trying to say I've got no friends and I'm desperate?" he laughs, which puts me at my ease and embarrasses me all at the same time.

"No!" I answer, laughing. "But it's just unusual that you want to hang out with a bunch of journalists instead of joining your colleagues, isn't it?"

"Nah, I spend all day with them, and in my experience hacks are a good laugh, can hold their drink and know all the good gossip. Plus, you're gorgeous. Why would I want to walk away when we've only just met?"

I have absolutely no idea what to say to this, so we walk downstairs in silence, with me hanging onto the handrail like a frail old lady and clutching what's left of my champagne as if my life depends on it.

Ricky and Mel spot me as we step into the atrium and their mouths literally fall open. Staring pointedly at them, tight-lipped and trying to implant my thoughts: *'I have no idea, don't ask!'* directly into their heads I edge up to them and through slightly gritted teeth say: "You alright?"

Neither of them says a word. They just carry on looking at me like puzzled monkeys who can't quite work out that there's a sheet of glass between them and the kid with a face full of crisps. I am looking at them so hard it feels as if my eyeballs are going pop out of their sockets. 'Say something,' I will them. Ricky suddenly regains the power of speech, although I soon wish he hadn't. "Kate. Hi, we were wondering where you'd got to. Was everything all right, or did Cruella lay into you? Did you see her face during the awards? She looked like she'd swallowed a wasp. These cocktails are great, have you had one? Oh no, you're sticking to champagne, good idea, wish I had – I'll regret this in the morning. Have you seen Ed sucking the face off that girl from the Calvin Klein ads? I heard he was back together with his girlfriend, clearly not…"

Oh my God man, take a breath!

"Ricky, Mel, this is Danny Sergeant," I interject quickly, before Ricky passes out from lack of oxygen, "Danny these are two of my workmates, Ricky and Mel." He smiles politely and they shake hands while he contemplates Ricky with equal measures of amusement and suspicion. "Danny bought me a drink when I finished filing my copy," I explain, raising the glass like it's evidence, "I was just saying I was on my way to find you guys and Danny thought he might tag along."

"Oh right, yeah sure. The more the merrier," Mel says, smiling a little too widely and trying but failing to be discreet as she dramatically raises one eyebrow at me. "The others are all in there." she says, slurping at her Martini and nodding in the direction of the overcrowded bar, "Except Sarah, who had to get back for the babysitter; and Esther, who's in a shit mood and has stormed out."

"Yeah, I think that's my fault," I shrug, not really giving a fuck right now but suspecting I might change my mind tomorrow morning. I drain the rest of my champagne, which is instantly replaced thanks to Danny subtly gesturing to the barman. "Oh, thank you," I smile graciously, "you don't have to buy me drinks all night, you know?"

"I know, but it's my pleasure," he insists, to which I can't say much, but I smile appreciatively anyway.

We stand chatting for ages. Mel shares some juicy titbits with us about one of the *This Morning* presenters and their sexy shoe fetish, and Ricky spills that he definitely saw Chelsea's very newly married star striker sloping off in a taxi earlier, with his arm wrapped around Tash Taylor's tiny, curvaceous waist.

Tash was last year's winner of The Voice and there'd been fervent speculation in the press that she was gay after pap pictures of her emerged wrapped around the pretty, brunette lead singer of The Chimes at Glastonbury, and then again on a beach in Ibiza. But Tash has always refused to confirm or deny the rumours, instead preferring to tweet mysterious, ambiguous statements like 'Ask no questions…' and 'Que sera, sera.'

Now, it would seem the speculation was misplaced, or the pretty ex-dental nurse swings both ways. Either way, the scandal, as far as I can see, is purely centred on 26-year-old footballer, Jason Butler. I don't give a rat's ass about Tash's sexuality one way or another, and always fail to see why it ever interests anyone. But the allegedly loved-up Mr Butler? Well that's a different story. *Ok! Magazine* ran a 10-page spread on his lavish star-studded wedding to model, Tania Reece in October, after the couple sold them the exclusive rights for a reputed £1.5 million pounds.

Since then, they've been photographed on their honeymoon, back home at their sprawling mansion in Richmond, and at every red carpet event between here and the Moon! The lovey-dovey couple looked as if they were joined at the hip until a few days ago, when Tania jetted off to Barbados with her mum and sister for a pre-Christmas holiday. While the cat is away the mouse has most certainly decided to play, if Ricky's story is to be believed.

"So, I said to Mel I'm nipping out for some fags from that newsagents on Littlewick Street, round the back of the hotel, and when I came out that's when I saw them, bold as brass and giggling like school kids, climbing into taxi."

Ricky downs the rest of his espresso Martini and, having already tipped the wink to our showbiz reporters, disappears outside to chat to some of the photographers.

Mel catches sight of Fearne Cotton, who she interviewed back in the summer and got along with so well that they ended up going for a curry and sharing a cab home. She dashes over to join her and Holly Willoughby, who is already looking distinctly worse for wear, leaving me alone with Danny again, staring into the bottom of my almost empty champagne glass.

"Well, I think I might make a move," I say, smiling apologetically, and reaching for my bag, "I have to get back to Chertsey tonight and I'm back in the office first thing tomorrow."

"Don't go," Danny says quickly, catching hold of my wrist, encircling it with his strong fingers. He's not hurting me – far from it – but his touch still makes me jump and he drops it suddenly, as if my skin is scalding hot. "Sorry, I'd just like you to stay a little longer, if you will. We haven't really had the chance to get to know each other."

I study his face for a few long seconds, chewing on my lip, a million thoughts racing around my mind. Jack has texted me. A couple of times, as it happens. In the first one he asked how the awards had gone and had I spoken to Bindi Evans (his closet crush). I'd sent a 'LOL' and said: 'Yes, she's given me her number and is coming round for a threesome at the weekend'. The second time was just after Danny had sent up the champagne, to ask me when I was leaving and if I wanted to come round to his, because if so he'd wait up for me, despite being on an early shift tomorrow. That was over an hour ago and I still haven't replied. I know I'm stalling and I also know why and it's making me feel like shit.

Danny is still looking at me, waiting for my response.

Slowly, like in a dream where you find yourself naked in the street and no control over your own body, I find I'm nodding and following him into the packed bar. It's heaving with inebriated guests who, now the formalities are over, have apparently thrown caution to the wind and are now intent on getting as drunk as possible in the shortest time available. Of course alcohol was flowing during the ceremony, but with television cameras rolling and speeches to be made everyone was on their best behaviour. Not so much now, it seems.

We edge our way over to the far side of the bar, where there are marginally fewer people waiting, and Danny pals up with one of his acting cronies, forcing his way through the impatient queue of drinkers waiting to be served. I tuck myself out of the way, squeezing in between the wall and David Lewis, the burly captain of the England rugby team who is leading a rowdy drinking game. Along with some of his teammates, there's the retired schoolteacher who spends his days helping ferry the old folks of Wakefield around town, and, oh my God, is that Lionel Blair and Esther Rantzen necking shots?! Shaking my head and laughing incredulously at the ludicrous scene, I take out my phone. The screen is still displaying Jack's last text and I quickly tap out a reply:

THANKS HONEY, BUT NOT TONIGHT.
IT'S GOING TO BE A LATE ONE. I'LL
MESSAGE YOU IN THE MORNING. X

I feel really bad, but I haven't actually done anything wrong. Yet.

So far I've had a drink with a good-looking actor and, given the opportunity Jack wouldn't hesitate to spend the evening boozing with Bindi Evans, but I still feel guilty as sin as I stuff the phone back in my bag.

Tossing my hair over my shoulders, I take a deep breath and try to exude an inner calmness that doesn't exist. Danny's now ordering and nods at me across the room, his dark eyes narrowing sexily, smouldering like they do on screen, and I immediately feel jittery and nervous.

'Done nothing wrong!' my inner voice snorts sarcastically.

Who am I kidding, when I so very clearly want to?

Twenty Three

On a table in the far corner of the bar, Dinner Lady Helen, is dancing on top of a table, an open bottle of champagne in one hand and – is that her bra? – in the other as Barry, her good-natured husband, looks on. TOWIE's Bobby Norris and Gemma Collins are giggling and actively encouraging her antics. "Well, it looks as if someone's having a good time," Danny says, returning with a rum and coke for himself and thrusting a huge cocktail at me. "Salt rim, just like you asked for," he says, as I take a lingering sip of my drink, savouring the irresistible zesty lime and salt combination. God, you just can't beat a well-made 'rita.

"I do love a salty rim," I wink suggestively with a naughty grin. The champagne's filtered into my blood stream now and I can feel myself loosen up and relax. Tiny bubbles of excitement and spontaneity fizz through my veins as the little devil on my shoulder dusts down his fork, readying himself for action.

"Do you now?" Danny grins back at me, clearly amused by my silliness.

"Yes. I like to turn the glass each time I drink so I get a salty mouthful with every sip," I say flicking the tip of my tongue back and forth over the encrusted edge.

This time I keep a straight face but my eyes narrow with amusement and it's all I can do to keep the smirk off my face. I see Danny's gaze riveted on my mouth and I bite my lower lip suggestively before smiling. "Come on, there's a crowd moving out over there and it's too packed here. Let's go." Grabbing his hand, I hold my glass aloft and push my way through the masses, saying hi to interviewees and work colleagues who smile questioningly at me, but I don't pause until I reach the far corner of the room where a small space has opened up.

The bar is a strange shape and the walls taper off into a slight alcove that is recessed behind the high, frosted glass of the bench back, meaning that this corner is out of view of the rest of the room. There's a narrow ledge that runs along the wall and I rest my glass on it while I root around in my bag for my Nars lip-gloss. I unscrew the lid and, without a mirror, run the applicator over my lips. "I never understand how women can do that," Danny says, watching with fascination, "I'd have it halfway round my face by now."

Pressing my lips together, evenly distributing the nude sheen, I say, "My ex-boyfriend hated me doing this in public, but I don't care. There was once a photograph of the Queen touching up her lipstick at the Highland Games, sat in full view of everyone. If it's good enough for her, then it's certainly good enough for me."

"You have nice lips, very kissable, far nicer than the Queen's," says Danny, still looking at my mouth, which means that of course I immediately smile, lick them and then pout far more than I normally would.

"Do you spend much time thinking about how kissable the Queen's lips are?" I mock.

"No, but I imagine I'm going to spend a lot of time thinking about yours," he answers.

"How do you think I might kiss?" I ask provocatively, enjoying flirting with this attractive, witty and interested young man.

"I think you'd give the kind of kisses I might get lost in," Danny says, his eyes dancing a small jig, "I think you'd start off slow and deliberate, pressing your whole mouth against mine like it belonged to me. Your lips would feel soft yet strong and they'd pull me in until I lost control. You'd tangle your tongue against mine so that I couldn't think straight, and it'd turn me on so much I'd need you to stop or make love to me immediately."

He stops talking and I realise I'm chewing frantically on the end of my thumbnail, my breathing much faster than is good for me. Danny steps forwards, further into the shadows, and reaches one arm around my waist, pressing his palm into the small of my back. Pulling me towards him, he slides the fingers of his other hand into my hair, moving his face closer.

His top lip brushes against my cupid's bow, light as a feather and he nudges the tip of his nose against mine, nuzzling, but not quite kissing me. His breath is ragged, matching my own, and his mouth is tantalisingly close to kissing me properly. He backs away, just a centimetre or two, for a split second and my eyes dart around his face, from his eyes, to his cheeks, to his lips, dancing between his features, drinking them in.

His beauty is truly intoxicating.

But, Jack. Oh God, Jack.

I flinch inwardly at the thought, but the dizzy part of me, flattered by this actor's attention, drunk on champagne and tequila, pushes it away to the back of my mind. Danny's leans in again and this time the tiny butterfly kisses – his lips resting on mine – intensify and he crushes his lips into my mouth, bruising them with a ferocity and longing that matches my own. It lasts thirty seconds, maybe a minute at the most, but I can't ignore the nagging guilt any longer.

Tearing my mouth away from his, I steady myself against the wall to regain my composure. Downing the rest of my drink in one, I reach out and stroke Danny's cheek, rubbing my thumb regretfully across his lips.

"I'm sorry, I can't do this," I apologise mournfully, looking sadly at this incredibly stunning man. "I'm seeing someone," I explain, "I thought I could do this, but I can't." And without waiting for his response (because I'm frightened that if I hang around any longer my resolve will weaken and I'll do something I'll really regret in the morning,) I grab my bag and squeeze back through the drinkers, out of the bar and across the foyer, stumbling into the ladies loo.

Remarkably, given the number of people milling around, no-one's there, apart from the diminutive South American toilet attendant, who looks up and nods politely at me before continuing to fold small white towels. I slip into a cubicle and slump heavily on the seat, holding my head in my hands. I feel slightly sick and I'm a bit pissed even though my capacity for alcohol is usually pretty high.

I suspect the nausea is caused by guilt rather than booze.

All of a sudden I feel really tired and don't want to move, but I need to pee quite badly so I force myself back up and lift the lid. After sitting there for what feels like an eternity, the bathroom door crashing open rouses me from my reverie and someone click-clacks hurriedly across the marble floor. The door in the booth next to mine is thrown open and sounds of retching are enough to make me finish up quickly and flush.

I cross the room to the sinks, wash my hands and lean dejectedly against the cold surface. I look long and hard, studying my face in the mirror.

For Christ's sake, what the fuck is wrong with me?!

I have a gorgeous, kind, incredible man at home who's sexy and fit as fuck and clearly devoted to me. I really like him – hell – I could probably fall in love with him if I let myself. That's what I want, isn't it?

Well, I thought it was.

Just this morning I was messaging him all the way to work and mooning over photos of us I took at the weekend. In one he has no shirt on and is standing behind me, his strong, defined arms wrapped around my body, eyes closed, head back laughing. In another, his lips are pressed into my neck yet he's looking into the lens, sexy and full of affection. In a third, we're lying in bed after making love. My skin's flushed and I look relaxed and content, with my head on his bare chest.

Happy. That's how I look. Really, really fucking happy. So why am I here now, having just had my tongue down another man's throat, when I could be on a train home to Jack?

The face looking back at me has no answers. It just looks distraught and full of anguish, like somehow this happened by accident and it was an event outside of my control.

Yes, I can delude myself. I'm young and 'just having a bit of fun', but suddenly it doesn't feel like fun anymore. Danny's seriously hot, and how often do you actually get a bona fide celebrity coming onto you... but if he knew what I'd just done, Jack would be so hurt.

I feel awful. As self-destruction goes I'm damn near a professional at it, but this temptation to stray so early on in the relationship – a relationship that just a few hours ago I thought I wanted so badly – well, it completely blows me away.

Tears are threatening to spill down my cheeks. Tears, which stem from my pathetic, undeserved self-pity and have no right to be there, I blow my nose and give myself a mental shake. "Sort your fucking life out, Kate," I mutter to myself as I pull my jacket on, pick up my bag and head out to hail a cab.

Shit.

Danny's leaning against the wall in the hallway; a worried look plastered on his face. He jumps forward when he sees me and places a hand on my shoulder, gently restraining me.

"Kate?" he says, kindly, "Are you okay?"

I turn around to face him and take hold of his hand, which is still on my arm. Squeezing it I smile at him. It's not his fault.

"I'm fine, Danny. Thanks for asking. I'm just feeling very guilty, that's all. You seem like a really nice man and I'm extremely flattered you're interested in me. I'm amazed if I'm honest. Why would someone like you be interested in me?

But I let my ego get in the way of sound judgement. I can't do this – I don't want to do this – I'm just gutted no hot actors came on to me all the years I was single, that's all." Danny laughs and squeezes my hand back.

"It's okay, I understand. I just wanted to make sure you were alright. It was nice meeting you, Kate… and it was even nicer kissing you," he adds, with a cheeky wink, which makes me smile. He drops my hand and I walk away, only turning back when he calls after me.

"Oh, Kate. You asked why I'd be interested in you. Why wouldn't I be? You're beautiful." I give him a small smile and walk across the foyer towards the taxis waiting outside. Mel, still at the champagne bar, waves at me and mouths, "See you in the morning." I wave back half-heartedly and climb wearily into the back of a cab, sitting in subdued silence and feeling nothing but sad and empty as we cross town. I tip the driver too much at the station. I'm in such a hurry to get home.

The train's packed, but I manage to find a space next to a fat guy with suspicious stains on his cheap trousers who's taking up half of my seat as well as his, and keeps leaning on me every time he drops off. Resting my clammy forehead against the cool glass, I stare out of the window as the bright lights and chaos of the city give way to increasing darkness. Every so often blinding white lights break the inky exterior with a brick and concrete blur as we pass through another station at high speed.

After almost twenty-five minutes, we slow down to a gentler pace approaching Woking station. The illuminated buildings of the retail park, the long stay car park and the little parade of independent shops drift into, and then pass out of, view. At first I think it must have started raining as the shapes outside the window distort and merge into each other. It's only when a tear splashes onto my hand and I run my fingers over my face I realise I've been crying, and I have no idea how long for.

The fat guy wakes up and shifts himself off of me, apologises, then does a double-take and asks if I'm okay. I mumble that I am, but one glance at my grime-covered hands tell me I have black eye make-up streaked down my cheeks. I obviously look a complete state.

Keeping my head down, I clutch my belongings and shuffle off the train and out to the cab rank, waiting in the cold for almost ten minutes before one turns up. It's a fairly short journey back to Chertsey but it feels like forever. My head's banging and I still feel a bit sick. I need water, painkillers and bed, in that order, although God knows if I'll sleep. I certainly don't deserve to.

The lights are still on as we pull up outside. I pay the driver, and dig my mobile phone out of my bag, flicking it onto silent and pressing it to my ear. As I climb the first set of stairs I start talking, muttering a mix of random 'yes', 'no' and 'I don't knows' to my non-existent caller as I walk through the living room, just raising my hand to acknowledge the boys as if I'm in the middle of conversation and can't stop. Safely in my room, I shut the door firmly behind me and drop my mobile on the bed, breathing a weary sigh of relief. I couldn't face making small talk with the lads. I feel mean. I'd promised them a blow-by-blow account of the evening when I got back, but looking the way I do and feeling so shit about my earlier conduct, there's no way I could have sat there chatting without one of them asking what was wrong.

Most of my make-up has disappeared already, but I run a wipe over my face, discarding it carelessly on the dressing table and strip off, dumping my clothes on the floor and pouring myself into a cosy pair of pyjamas. I open a bottle of Evian I'd placed beside my bed before work this morning in anticipation that I'd over do it tonight and lack the discipline to go back down to the kitchen when I got home. It's proven to be the right move, as I have neither the energy nor the inclination to leave this room before morning – or in fact ever again – the way I'm feeling right now. I glug from the bottle greedily, trying to limit the damage from the fizz and cocktails, and wishing in vain that it were as easy to wash away my sin as it is to flush the alcohol from my system. Adding a couple of painkillers to the mix, I force myself to go next door for a pee, knowing if I don't I'll be awake again in a couple of hours.

As it happens, it appears all my precautions are in vain because four hours later not only am I still wide-awake, but I have the mother of all headaches and my stomach is balling up into tiny little knots of anxiety. Why did I have to be so reckless and stupid and jeopardise the first thing that's made me truly happy for a long, long time? All for a cheap thrill and an ego boost.

Irritated by my idiocy and inability to sleep, I angrily turn onto my left side and hear a huge thump as something falls onto the floor. Muttering, I reach down and grope around under the bed, discarding odd shoes and runaway lipsticks until I discover it's my phone that I'd unceremoniously dumped on the duvet when I came in. How it's managed to stay on the bed this long is a miracle, considering how much I've been tossing and turning.

Picking it up, I notice a notification on the lock-screen: it's an unopened text. Still on silent, I didn't hear it arrive just after midnight. And it's from Jack. Feeling sick, from both guilt and tiredness, I read it, tears immediately welling up and a lump forming in my throat.

I CAN'T SLEEP – KEEP THINKING ABOUT YOU. MISS YOU. IF YOU'RE STILL OUT, HAVE A GREAT NIGHT AND CALL ME TOMORROW. STAY SAFE. PS: I THINK I LOVE YOU, JUST A LIL BIT X

Oh my fucking God, no.
No, no, no, no, NO! Not now! Not after tonight!
I'm on my knees staring at the illuminated screen. The words are taunting me, dancing in front of my eyes, tripping through my head. Tears begin streaming down my face and I rock from side to side, hugging my arms around me, trying to make the hurt go away. 'He loves you and you don't even deserve it, you silly, selfish cow,' the little voice in my head mocks, taunting me for my stupidity.

I turn the phone off and throw it across the room before curling up in a ball and tugging the duvet up over my head; I wish I could disappear beneath it and vanish forever.

Of course I'm pleased he loves me. I've wanted it for days,

weeks even, and if I'm honest with myself I've been falling in love with him too, though I'd never admit it to myself so early on. But the joy I should be feeling is marred horrifically by the timing of his announcement.

I'm furious; beyond mad at myself for cheating tonight. I don't even know what made me do it. I can't blame insecurity as Jack's made me feel adored – worshipped even – from day one. And it's not habit either, I've never cheated on anyone else. Yes, I've slept with a lot of men during the last couple of years. But I haven't had commitments with them, so I haven't broken any trust. The guilt is simply overwhelming; I'm eaten up with it among a mess of salty tears and snot. Jack doesn't deserve this. However the thought of telling him, and the hurt it would cause, simply breaks my heart. I'm consumed with turmoil and don't deserve to find a moment's peace tonight, but eventually self-loathing overwhelms me as I sob into my pillow and fall asleep, mentally and physically drained.

Glancing in the small handheld mirror for the umpteenth time this morning confirms what I already know. My face is a puffy mess and my eyes resemble two bloodshot, reddened piss holes in the snow.

Despite a long shower, fifteen minutes beneath cucumber slices and copious amounts of cover up, you can still see that I've done a lot of crying over the last 24-hours.

I ascend into the cold, fresh air at Canary Wharf. Stepping off the escalator, I exit into blinding sunshine that causes me to wince and reach for my sunglasses. After the bright plaza, I'm grateful to get inside the darkened interior of the shopping complex and hurry up the stairs to the lifts. Pressing the button for the twenty-eighth floor, I peer at my off-putting reflection in the mirrored walls with contempt and self-disgust. The doors have all but closed when a large leopard-print tote is wedged firmly between the metal panels, causing them to spring apart again. A bedraggled looking Mel almost falls into the lift, her head a frizzy mass of matted curls and her skin a pallid grey colour.

"You look like shit," she says, staring at me with an ill-concealed sneer.

"That's rich, coming from you," I retort, with some humour, raising an eyebrow at her unkempt appearance, "Your cardigan's on inside out too." I add, helpfully. Sighing, Mel dumps her bag between us and shrugs the thick cream fluffy knit off her shoulders, turning it the right way round before slowly putting it back on as the doors open. I snatch up her bag and push her out onto the landing before the lift goes back down to reception with us inside it.

"Thanks," she says, taking it and peering closely at my face. "Are you okay Kate? Have you been crying?" she asks pointedly.

"No!" I say indignantly, and probably a bit rudely, before I turn away and bustle into the office, "It's just a hangover, that's all. Come on, we're both cutting it fine."

I needn't worry though. Lori's the only person sitting at the desk and she waves amicably at us both, sipping at an

JO MERRETT

espresso and casually flicking through the tabloids. Sarah is the only other person already in and she looks fresh-faced and chilled, having gone home early.

"Ha ha. Late one was it girls?" she chortles on seeing the state of us. I say a silent prayer of thanks that everyone was drinking last night and I can pass my crumpled face off as the result of a heavy night. There must be a God after all!

Sitting down, I pull out a large Evian bottle and sip from it at regular intervals as I start to scan the papers. My phone buzzes for the second time this morning – it's Jack again.

I'd found the first one when I'd switched my phone on earlier this morning. Short and sweet it read:

MORNING BEAUTIFUL. HOW'S YOUR HEAD? X

I hadn't responded.

This one reads:

ARE YOU OKAY? NOT HEARD FROM YOU.
HOPE I HAVEN'T SAID THE WRONG THING X

I'd had three missed calls when I got off the tube too, but haven't called him back. I'm too ashamed of myself to enter into conversation with that lovely man. At the sight of the new message all the raw feelings from last night come flooding back and I have to bite back tears.

"Kate?" Mel is looking at me, a worried look on her face and an edge of concern to her voice. It's enough to set me off, and despite trying to hold it together a big, fat tear rolls rebelliously down my cheek. Mel leaps up and pulls me by the hand, dragging me into the ladies loo before anyone else notices. Checking all the cubicles are empty she wraps her arms around me and gives me a big squeeze, though at her height her head is buried awkwardly in my armpit. She pats me reassuringly on the back. Finally she releases me and stations herself by the sink, folding her arms in front of her. "Go on." she says, "Tell me everything."

I haven't known Mel long but not only is there something in her stance that brooks no argument, but I'm not sure I can get through the next five minutes – let alone the rest of the day – unless I offload on someone. So I open my mouth and start talking. Despite crying and spluttering and hiccupping my way through the next six or seven minutes, I've finally told Mel the entire, shameful, sordid story.

She doesn't say anything, or pull any judgemental faces, but listens without interruption. It is only when I finish by saying, "...and now I don't know what to do," she smiles kindly and starts speaking.

"I can see why you're so upset, and in the same situation I'd probably be feeling equally as bad, but you're human Kate. You've made a mistake, which from the looks of things, you deeply regret. That is the important thing. And," she adds as she takes hold of my hand again, giving it a tight squeeze, "you stopped things before they went any further, which you should be giving yourself credit for, because I was stood with that man last night and if it'd been me I'm not sure I would have been capable of walking away from him – OMG he was seriously gorgeous!"

I smile weakly at her, "Not helping, Mel."

"Sorry, sorry. Back to the point." she giggles, "Look, Jack sounds lovely and regardless of what you say, you clearly do deserve to be with him because if you didn't care then you wouldn't be this upset, would you?"

"Well, mmm." I'm not convinced.

"And it's not like you two are engaged or married or anything, in fact have you actually even had a conversation about being exclusive?"

"Well, no –" I start, only to be cut off again by Mel who's in full flow,

"There you go then, and telling him wouldn't do any good. It would just hurt him and you'd only be doing it to ease your own guilt, which frankly you know you don't deserve anyway, so there's absolutely no point, is there?" She stops for breath but keeps looking at me, expectantly. I'm not sure what to say. She's right of course, about all of it. Jack and I haven't discussed being exclusive. I feel bad because I do really like him, but I was flattered by the attention Danny gave me. She's also right about it just being a snog.

"Well, yes..." I say reluctantly, "I guess, maybe, I could be slightly over reacting, I suppose. It's just that message from him, saying he thinks he loves me. That's when it really hit home how reckless I've been, and what I might lose if I got found out."

"Then you have to make sure you don't get found out, don't you my dear?" Mel says, draping an arm around my shoulder. "Now, I'll head back to my desk and, if anyone asks, say you're feeling a bit under the weather. You clean your face up – I'll get you your bag, shall I?" She dashes out, returning half a minute later with my handbag, a packet of face wipes and my water, "I thought you might want to rehydrate after shedding all those tears," she smiles kindly.

I take a few cool, reviving swigs, then remove my ruined make-up and reapply some simple makeup. I still don't look great, but I've repaired the major damage and I'm feeling a lot better than I was.

I study myself for a few seconds, taking in the calm after the storm. I wouldn't say I'm a drama queen, or particularly prone to histrionics, but I do have a tendency to make things more than they are and I overthink everything.

Rob used to despair of me. He always said I'd focus on the negative at the expense of everything else, and if I didn't hear from him for whatever reason I'd imagine the worst. But he's right, you know. Once he said: "If there's a gap you always fill it with what you imagine I'm thinking, and it's never good. You need to learn to relax and chill out."

Relaxing isn't my strong point though. I honestly can't help it. Even in hot yoga I find my mind wandering during the meditation bit. I do fear the worst – always have done, always will do, I suspect. Although my paranoia doesn't stop me risk-taking, I stew on stuff for ages, letting things go around and around in my head. It sometimes feels as though my mind is a prison with no windows and no doors, and the walls are closing in on me. The feeling that I can't escape my own head is simply the worst.

The door opens and Sara hurries in, setting down her takeaway coffee cup and dashing into the loo.

"Hi babe, sorry, busting for a wee," she calls from the cubicle, "I thought I'd be dead clever and drink loads of water last night and this morning and I've already been to the loo about twenty times!"

I laugh, "Yes, but how's your hangover?"

"Yeah, okay, but I had to get up four times in the night as well and I didn't get to bed until almost three so now I feel like shit 'cos I'm knackered. I can't bloody win."

Still laughing I go back to the office, where Mel has kindly made me a cup of coffee.

"You look happier," she whispers, "better?"

"Much." I assure her, "Thanks Mel. Sorry to be such a car crash."

"Shut up, silly!" she hisses, opening a raw fruit and nut bar, then changing her mind and digging out a packet of chocolate hobnobs from her desk drawer instead. "There are some days that eating clean just doesn't work, and this is one of them," she declares, ripping open the packet and handing three over to me.

"Oooh, you'd better save some of those for me," Ricky groans as he skulks in behind me and collapses into his chair, clutching his head.

"Somebody kill me now, please." Giggling (and secretly relieved I'm not the only one feeling like crap, albeit for different reasons) I thrust the biscuits in his direction and start dunking mine in my coffee.

I pick up my phone and message Jack:

> CAN'T TALK NOW – LAST NIGHT WAS
> GOOD. PRETTY HUNGOVER AND NOT MUCH
> SLEEP. YOU'VE DONE NOTHING WRONG.
> TALK LATER – I'LL CALL YOU X

I send it, then scribble out another one:

> PS: I LOVE YOU TOO.
> I THINK. JUST A BIT. X

Taking a deep breath, I read it again and press send.

"Ok?" Mel asks, through a mouthful of crumbs.

"You know what? With enough carbs and a bit of luck today, I think it just might be," I say thoughtfully, cramming another biscuit into my mouth.

Twenty Four

One way or another, Jack and I weren't able to see each other until the end of the week. I was sent down to Brighton later that day to interview a woman who was retiring after giving birth to 14 surrogate babies, and it ran on quite late. I eventually got home, but not until after 11pm, and Jack was on late shifts the following two evenings.

On the drive down to Brighton I'd resolved to stop torturing myself about the previous night. Mel was right: it wasn't going to help anyone and would cause more pain than good. Yes, I'd decided that what happened at the awards was going to stay at the awards, and I'd already wasted far too much energy fretting about it to waste a single second more. We'd spoken though – a lot. It was as if once the floodgates had come down on our emotions we couldn't get enough of each other. The first conversation had felt slightly awkward, for me at least, because I felt guilty and also because we'd both admitted how we really felt.

"Hello you," Jack had said warmly when I'd finally plucked up courage to call him from a service station on the M23.

"Hi."

"You ok, babe?"

"Yeah, you?"

"I'm very well – very well, indeed! Except for one thing: you only think you love me do you, Miss Cleaver?"

"Um, yeah. But you said it first." I retorted.

"How old are you exactly?" he accused with affection, and added, "It's not a competition, you know." I'd smiled down the line,

"I know. Jack, can I ask you something: do you love me, or are you in love with me?"

"Both I think," he replied, his voice breaking very slightly.

"But just a lil' bit, right?" I joked.

"Totally." He was smiling; I could hear it in his voice.

It was a filthy, dirty night pouring with rain as great gusts of wind buffeted the car – a stark contrast to the bright, cold sunny morning we'd had. As I'd looked out at the almost empty car park, the light from the street lamps streaked across the tarmac and reflected in the puddles, I couldn't have felt happier. While I had been sitting in the car, Jack had said affectionately: "I've known for a while you know. Since the night you stayed at mine, in fact. But I didn't want to scare you. It seemed too soon to say anything."

I hadn't known what to say. I've always done the chasing in every relationship, and liaison, I've ever had. I knew for a fact that I'd loved Rob far more than he'd ever loved me – and I wasn't prepared for this shift. I'm not actually sure any man has been the first to declare his feelings to me, and if I'm honest it scares me a little bit, but at the same time, it thrills me. It's not that I'm afraid exactly, but this definitely creates a change in our relationship, and one I don't know if I'm ready for.

I spent so long hankering after Aidan, and despite it ending badly I still feel like there's unfinished business between us. I don't know if I'm ready to throw myself headlong into another full-on relationship. In the end I told Jack that I needed to get back on the road and I'd see him soon.

That turned out to be two days later, and now pulling up outside his house, I'm actually terrified to go in. ·

Each time we've talked during the last 48-hours, we've not mentioned the "L" word again and things have reverted to normal. I'm not sure why I'm feeling so scared, I guess it's just a big step, and the last time I opened myself up to love it had ended badly. I'm still sitting here, at the gloomy end of the badly lit cul-de-sac, ten minutes later, when Jack's front door opens abruptly and he strides down the pathway in bare feet, brandishing a huge knife. I grin at him and unlock the door.

"Have you come to kill me?" I ask, laughing at the crazy sight, "Because I warn you I've just bought these boots, and if you get blood on them I'll be fucking furious."

He doesn't actually smile at me, but his eyes dance merrily as he rests one arm on top of the car, his huge frame filling the doorway.

"Were you planning on coming in anytime tonight, or am I serving dinner in here?" he asks, looking around my Ford as if he's assessing it for dining potential. I'm laughing helplessly now, and it's a welcome relief from the constant stress and turmoil of the last few days.

"No, sorry, I am coming in, I was just..." I falter, not knowing quite how to put it. Slipping inside the car and closing the door against the cold, Jack perches uncomfortably on the edge of the seat and rests his hand warmly over mine, putting the knife on the dashboard.

"Kate, nothing has to change. Only if you want it to." I turn my hand over so our palms meet and clasp his fingers between mine.

"I do want it to Jack, I really do. It's just. I don't know, I guess I'm just a bit…" He stops my mouth with his, crushing me with a kiss that sucks the breath from my body, hardening my nipples and making me wet.

How does this man turn me on so easily? Christ, I've never been slow to get aroused, but this is fucking crazy, even by my standards. I've been permanently wet for weeks As he pulls away, I moan reluctantly. When he kisses me it's like stepping into a parallel universe where time stands still and nothing else matters.

"I know you're scared Kate, and I know why. I'm not going to hurt you, I promise." Of course it's a clichéd pledge that everyone entering a relationship makes at some point or another and, unless they have the power of foresight, it's not one that anyone can guarantee they won't break. Yet, locking eyes with him, right here, right now, it's like Jack's looking straight into my soul, stripping back everything until there's nothing left except his core and mine. He just summarised precisely how I'm feeling; lock, stock and barrel. It took me so long to get over Rob – and it still hurts now, if I'm honest. I'm not sure I'm ready to open myself up again, and my ego's still bruised and battered following the Aidan situation.

Maybe that's why I let myself go a step too far with Danny – perhaps I'm trying to sabotage Jack and I before it really goes anywhere. If I ruin the relationship before it flourishes, I'm the one doing the hurting and won't become the victim again. *'But you still would be, you daft bitch.'* mocks my psyche, *'You'll simply be both victim and perpetrator.'*

Annoyingly this makes absolute sense and it dawns on me how much I really want to trust this man. The irony is, I've already broken his trust without him even knowing it. In an instant I know I want him right now, in every sense of the word. Scooting across the gap to the passenger seat, I press him back into the upholstery and straddle him, locking my lips with his. I wrestle with his belt buckle and tug his jeans down over his hips impatiently.

"You want to do this here?" Jack asks, nodding at the street and the neighbouring houses. I glance outside. Jack's house is in the corner. To the side of it and behind the car there are only trees and bushes, and while there are properties on the opposite side of the street, the light isn't working this end of the road and so the chances of us being noticed are slim. Besides, I like the feeling we might get caught and I want him too badly to wait.

"Yes," I breathe, trembling and excited. Needing no more prompting Jack's fingers stray beneath the hem of my fitted dress and upwards, along my thighs, pausing to consider the lace tops of my hold ups, then advancing further to the wisp of black lycra, already soaked by my own juices. Having freed him from his shorts, I'm greedily running my hands up and down his hard-on, tossing him off with a crazed enthusiasm that betrays my need to have him inside me as quickly as possible. I reach down and move the seat backwards, lowering the backrest as far as the mechanism will allow, but there's still precious little room for manoeuvre. Jack has wrestled my underwear halfway down my thighs but it's severely restricting my movement.

"Just leave them," I instruct, urgently, "Fuck me with them on. I want you inside me. Now."

He slides them back up but instead of pulling me down onto his swollen cock, he leans forward and reaches past me grabbing hold of the chef's knife from the dashboard. I freeze, fixated on the steely, sharpened blade as he lowers it to my groin. A shiver of anticipation tinged with fear sharpens my desire and my nipples harden into tiny ice-capped bullets again. Looking up, he slides one finger beneath the crotch of my pants, brushing against my wetness, and hesitates.

"Were these expensive?" he asks. Biting down hard on my lip I shake my head wordlessly. I'm lying, they were, but I'm captivated by what he's about to do and more turned on than I've ever been in my life, so I'm willing to sacrifice a pair of Victoria's Secret knickers.

Slowly, cautiously, he raises the knife and slides the blade inside the fabric, pressing the sharp edge into the material, careful not to catch my thigh with the razor point. The blunt spine makes contact with my wet flesh and feels completely alien as the ice-cold metal catches my clit. I gasp with pleasure, and goosebumps cover my body. Jack draws the knife away from me and effortlessly slices through the thin fabric like butter.

Job done, he needn't use it again, but registering the pleasure and fascination on my face, he raises the knife and levers it inside the waistband of the shredded garment. Holding it steadily by the handle, he lowers it gradually and once the point is safely clear, pushes the spine back until the length slides between my folds.

"Oh," I exclaim, arching my back and pressing myself against the knife as he jiggles it against my slit, "Oh. My. God." *This is so wrong, yet feels so, so right. Who knew?*

Severing the elastic so it pings away from my body, Jack gently pulls the knife clear and lays it down in the footwell. Insanely turned on by his antics, I pin him against the seat and lower myself over him, groaning with pleasure as he fills my yearning pussy with his thick, full hardness. Digging the heels of my hands into his shoulders, I sit bolt upright and tilt my pelvis against him, throwing my head back, screwing him hard with just one goal in sight – there's no further stimulation required following this evening's unexpected foreplay.

It's grown cold in the car, which makes me only more aware of the heat growing between my legs as I pump my slippery cunt over his solid prick. Jack's letting me find my own rhythm, but is fighting to control his need; in between kisses he presses his head back against the headrest and the tension shows on his face.

"Do you wanna cum?" I pant.

"Yeah," he moans, rocking his hips beneath me, "but I can hold it a little longer. Take what you need... Just don't be long," he adds, smiling painfully.

He doesn't have to worry – I'm already close and getting closer with each thrust. Resting my forehead against his, one hand embracing his face, I trace my thumb along his cheekbone. I can feel his breath coming faster now, mingling with mine, his lips touching my chin.

"Tell me you love me," I whisper.

"I love you."

"No, use my name."

He grins mischievously: "What's your name again?"

I roll my eyes but can't help laughing, "Babe, my name's babe."

"Yeah, that," he says, grinning, "I love you, babe."

I keep moving, crushing my pussy against his cock. Behind us the headlights of a car turn the corner and pull into the road. We freeze, motionless except for my pussy which is twitching helplessly, beating a tattoo around his prick.

The vehicle turns into a driveway and the driver gets out and goes into the house.

"I love you Kate," he says, seriously this time.

"Oh god, I love hearing that," I groan, rolling my head back in pleasure.

He wraps his arms around me, tilting his hard dick up inside me, burying his face into my chest, "I love you Kate, I love you."

"Oh yeah, that's good, I'm gonna cum, oh yeah, I'm coming. I'm coming now, over your cock," and fucking hell, I cum so hard, shaking as spasm after spasm rocks my body. Seconds later, while my pussy's still pulsating, Jack grabs hold of my arse and plunges up inside me reaching his own climax.

We cling to each other for a few moments, neither of us wanting to move, but eventually I say, "Ok, I might die of hypothermia if I stay out here any longer." At which point

Jack remembers dinner's in the oven and the moment is admittedly lost.

Scrabbling around for my shredded underwear, and the knife, we climb out of the car giggling like a pair of teenagers and leg it into the house before his neighbours spot us.

Jack pours me a large glass of Shiraz and runs me a bath, insisting I warm up properly before dinner. He's made Cajun Chicken, which has survived despite the prolonged cooking time, and will keep quite happily for another thirty minutes in a warm oven, he insists.

Sitting on the toilet cistern with his feet on the lid, his own glass of wine in hand, he watches me submerged in bubbles with water up to my chin and my breasts bobbing on the surface. I sip my wine, slowly feeling fortified by the alcohol seeping into my system and the hot water warming my skin.

"Better?" he asks.

"Well I was feeling pretty damn good in the car, but if you mean am I feeling warmer, then yes, thank you," I grin.

"You're crazy, do you know that?"

"Has been said," I reply, raising my eyebrows.

"We could have easily been seen out there."

"Well I'm not the one who brought a carving knife outside and sliced my knickers off, am I?"

"It was fun though, wasn't it?" Jack says, moving to the bath mat and kneeling on the floor to be next to me. Trailing his fingers through the water, he traces a path along my chest. They dip between my breasts, and he cups one of them affectionately before sliding his palm back and forth over wet skin, grazing my nipple. It perks up of its own accord, and Jack catches it between the flat of his fingers, playing with it thoughtfully, resting his chin on the edge of the bath.

"Why did you want to do it there, outside, I mean?"

"Why not?" I ask, circling his arm and stroking the soft, veiny inside of his wrist. "Doesn't it give you a thrill knowing you're fucking while anyone could walk past?"

"Yeah, but it's a little risky, isn't it?"

"Doesn't that add to the excitement?"

"Sure, I guess so." he says, reluctantly letting go of my tit and standing up. "I've just never had sex anywhere public before I met you, and we've done it twice already. I'm going to start calling you, Dangerous Kate." I smile wickedly up at him and finish my wine. "Right," he says, as he rinses his glass and flicks cold water at me, making me squeal. "I'm going to dish up – you've got five minutes to get out of the bath and downstairs or I'm eating yours too. I seem to have worked up quite an appetite."

"Jack," I say abruptly. He pauses by the door. "I know we've not actually said it, but you and me, we're official right? I mean you want it to be just you and me, yes?" He turns and takes the soft, fluffy, grey bath towel from the radiator and pulls me up out of the water. Wrapping it tightly around me, he pulls me so close that I can see the dark rims of his chocolate brown irises.

"I want you all to myself Kate, and while I've got you I don't want anyone else to have you." Kissing me tenderly he adds, "And there isn't a woman out there who can hold a candle to you, so don't think I'll look at anyone else, because I won't. Now hurry up, or you'll have to eat dinner wearing a towel."

He clatters down the stairs as I pull the plug out and step onto the mat. I have a spare pair of pants in my bag as well as a toothbrush, leggings and T-shirt – Jack asked me to stay again tonight, so I came prepared – there's nothing worse than getting up in the morning and putting on the same knickers you wore all day yesterday.

I think about what he said earlier as I pull my dress over my head. He's never had sex in public? Wow – either that makes me reckless, or... is Jack, perhaps, a little prudish? I mean, I've had sex in all kinds of places you'd consider pretty public: in a cornfield, in the garden of my parents' house, an alleyway behind a nightclub with Rob (yes, I am that girl), even late one night in a children's playground, although that just sounds wrong now.

Actually, come to think of it, all my friends have indulged in a little public sex at least once or twice over the years. So yeah, maybe Jack's admission highlights something revealing about his attitude to sex – I plan to find out more, but not tonight.

I end up spending the entire weekend at Jack's house, only popping home for clean clothes, a few toiletries and my straighteners, plus a rather nice bottle of Sauvignon Blanc I'd been saving for a special occasion.

We spend Saturday evening curled up on the sofa watching films and eating takeaway, then most of Sunday morning in bed, before driving down to the coast and blowing the cobwebs away with a walk along a very cold and very blustery beach.

"Blimey," Stella says, when I call her for a catch up later in the week while I'm on the train to work; I've come straight from Jack's again. "You two are starting to sound like an old married couple. I think you might be heading down the altar sooner than Mike and I at this rate."

"Fuck off, Stel!" I retaliate, a little too loudly, as a pompous looking suit peers disapprovingly over the top of his specs. I ignore his disapproving glare and continue, albeit in a softer voice, "I love being with him Stella. I really do. It's not just the sex - although that's pretty damn hot. It's more than that. I love his company. And being at his house too. He's made me feel right at home. I just want to be there with him all the time, more than I want to be at my place, even."

"Christ, you're loved up," she laughs, but I know she's not taking the piss and she's pleased for me.

"I do love him, yeah. I know its early days to be saying that, but I do and I'm not going to pretend I don't."

"And he told you he loves you first?" she asks, a hint of disbelief in her voice.

"Yes! I know! When have I even been able to say that before, babe?"

She laughs, "That's great. I can't wait to meet him."

Stella and Mike are moving into their new London flat three days before Christmas and we've arranged to go out for drinks next Wednesday, on Christmas Eve, so the three of them can meet.

"I'm so glad you're happy for me honey; Gemma's been a bit funny about it, kind of pessimistic and cynical."

"How do you mean? Stella asks evenly, keen not to judge.

"Well, she's met Jack, and she likes him I can tell – I mean you just know when Gemma doesn't like someone, don't you? But she's been a bit cagey with me recently and when I pressed her on it, you know what she asked? 'How can you be sure that you're in love with him and that you're not just in love with the idea of being in love with him?'"

"Maybe she's just looking out for you." Stella says fairly, "You often say how she looks for the negative side a situation. Perhaps she's just playing devil's advocate before she gives you the thumbs up."

"Mmmm, maybe." I muse, "She was fine with me once we talked about it properly. I brought the subject up, and she did say that as long as I was really sure then she's good with it. You might be right, Stel, she's just doing her thing, I guess."

We say our goodbyes and I let her get back to packing boxes. She finished at work on Friday, and can now devote herself entirely to the move until starting her new position in London in the New Year.

I can't shake what Gemma's said to me though. I've a niggling irritation, deep down in my stomach, that what she's asked isn't entirely devoid of the truth. I mean, I don't think I'm in love with an idea, but if I am honest with myself, I do wonder if part of my attraction to Jack is what I admitted to Stella, about feeling at home at his place.

Rather than being holed up in a room in a soulless

house with people who aren't actually my friends but who, like me, just need a roof over their heads, I actually enjoy 'living' at Jack's. And how can I honestly know how much that contributes towards my feelings about him, about us? I mean people don't live in a bubble. When you get to know and form opinions about someone, you take into account all kinds of things: their job, their interests, their friends and family, their home, their style, well, everything really.

Arriving at work, I push all thoughts about 'us' to one side and force myself to focus on the day ahead. To be honest, mulling it over hasn't made things any clearer at all.

Things are becoming much quieter at work as the holiday season approaches, but there are still a few crazy stories to put to bed before we can all take our feet off the gas and wind down. I spend the day finding cut-price turkeys, Christmas puddings and bottles of champagne for an article on sourcing the best value Christmas dinner and put the finishing touches to a feature about hangover cures.

We have our office party tonight and I'm road testing the milk thistle theory, squirting syringes of it into pints of water all afternoon in readiness for a night in Tinkers, the bar frequented by *Record* staff for post work drinks.

It's fancy dress theme which I abhor, but reluctantly comply with, pulling on a Bat Girl costume in the ladies loo at five o'clock, next to Sarah who's squeezing into a snug 70s style flared jumpsuit, and Rosa who's working a passionate red flamenco costume. With her short, dark hair and Mediterranean colouring she looks just like Strictly's, Flavia Cacace.

"I don't know whose idea this was, but if I find out tonight

I might have to accidently spill a pint over them," moans Sarah, trying to suck her stomach in beneath the unforgiving pale blue satin.

"Where did you get your costume?" I ask, wishing vehemently that I'd decided on a less revealing outfit for my first office party. Basically I'm just wearing a black leotard, tights and a pair of elasticated wings.

"It's my bloody sister-in-law's," Sarah says, tugging on the legs to try and eradicate the camel's toe that keeps persistently reappearing. "She's the same size as me but what she's failed to mention is that she was obviously a whole size smaller when she last wore it! Or it's shrunk in the bloody wash!"

Rosa and I exchange looks in the mirror as we smother inane grins. Trying not to laugh out loud, I zip up my thigh high, heeled suede boots and scrape my hair up into a sleek top knot. A slick of mascara and a dramatic flick of gel eyeliner and I'm good to go.

"Wow," says Mel, adjusting her Wonder Woman headdress as I arrive back at my desk, laden down with my daytime clothes, shoes and make up. "You look HOT!"

"Thanks," I mutter, "but I'm not altogether sure that's a look I should be channelling just a few weeks into a new job."

"Nah, you're fine," laughs Ricky, who is wearing a furry bunny costume. That's going to get pretty hot within about twenty minutes I reckon. Factor in alcohol consumption and I suspect we'll be looking at severe dehydration by close of play. "You haven't seen Dean yet," he sniggers.

I crane my neck, looking towards the features desk but can't see anyone, so I stand up for a better look. Lori is there dressed as Little Bo Peep, complete with toy lamb, and I can see Esther in a blue skirt suit, pussycat bow blouse and huge wig, wielding a boxy eighties–style handbag as Margaret Thatcher.

"I see Esther's not deviated from type," I hiss at Mel, "Still playing the hard-nosed bitch character."

Mel and Ricky snort with laughter but there's still no sign of Dean until, right on cue, the door to the gent's toilets open and out steps the Features Editor, or should I say 'The King' himself?

A rug of thick chest hair escapes from the plunge-fronted, white rhinestone encrusted jumpsuit, while a black quiff wig and huge over-sized sunglasses dominate Dean's face, but it is the clear outline of a rather insignificant looking meat and two veg that completely captivates my attention. Like watching two people arguing in the street, I find I just can't look away.

Ricky and Mel have both buried their heads in their notebooks, stuffing fists into their mouths to avoid outwardly guffawing at the boss, and Sarah's wisely taken herself down to the Features Desk, still hoiking her gusset out of her crotch – perhaps someone should advise Dean to do the same thing.

This leaves me red-faced, alone and speechless, only just pulling it together and dragging my gaze away when Dean comes over to flaunt his costume - and a lot, lot more besides!

"So," he gloats, excitedly, "wadda ya think? U-huh-huh!" and swivels his hips in a jaunty fashion that sends Ricky and Mel into fresh paroxysms of laughter, stifled only by the sheer amount of hand each is thrusting inside each of their mouths. I can see Mel's shoulders shaking out of the corner of my eye, and it's only thanks to the massive sunnies he's sporting that

Dean's both oblivious and impervious to their amusement, as they are fortunately hidden by the wide frames.

I try desperately not to look south, but it's a bit like driving past a car crash on the other carriageway of the motorway – you know you shouldn't look and you slag off every other driver in front of you for doing it and holding up traffic, yet when push comes to shove you can't help yourself.

For the want of something to do, I sit down at my desk and immediately regret it: his cock's now level with my face. Oh my God - what was he thinking when he tried this on? Does the man not own a full-length mirror? Despite his insignificant size, he is running the risk of taking someone's eye out with that thing.

Eventually muttering something about needing to call a case study before the party, I manage to get him to leave. I'm both furious with my colleagues and beside myself with laughter at the same time.

"I'm going to kill the pair of you." I chortle through gritted teeth, wiping the tears from my cheeks, "How could you let me face that without warning?"

Ricky, who's turned crimson with the effort of holding in his hysteria can barely get a word out, but eventually tells me to hurry up and close down the computer because everyone's leaving.

"I can't come yet 'cause I told Dean I've got to make a call," I whine.

"Shut the fuck up and pack up yer stuff." Ricky snipes, standing up and grabbing his giant rabbit head, "He can't see a fucking thing in those glasses, and anyway if we don't go now there'll be no food left. I've heard they've got those tiny, mini sausages we all like," he adds, waggling his little finger for good effect. The three of us convulse with laughter again, and it's a good five minutes before I'm even able to stand up my legs are that weak from laughing.

Dabbing my eyes with a tissue, I look around the office at my colleagues in their variety of costumes. I'm so glad I made the leap and took the risk to join *The Record*, when I did. It's only been a few weeks, but already I feel really at home here. Apart from the Iron Lady down the other end of the room, everyone's made me feel right at home.

'*Now you just have to work out what you're feeling when you're actually at home, and whether 'home' means your place, or Jack's*', says the little voice inside my head. Mentally shutting it out, I close down the computer and grab my stuff.

"Right." I say joyously, "First round of shots is on me."

Twenty Five

Curled up in a tight ball, almost hanging off the side of the bed, I'm dimly aware of a rustling near my feet, and the smell of coffee and something baked wafting up my nostrils. Warm, strong arms envelope me and I smile sleepily as Jack sings: 'We Wish You A Merry Christmas' cheerfully, although remarkably tunelessly, in my ear, his lemony scent washing over me as he plants little kisses over my face and ears.

"Mmmm," I murmer, my eyes still clenched shut, "Merry Christmas honey... I'm just going to sleep for a teeny, tiny bit longer."

"Oh no, no, no. No you're not. Come on, wake up Sleeping Beauty, I have a pile of presents here with your name on it." Reluctantly I peel open one eye, squinting in the lamplight, and peek down the bed. There are indeed several clumsily wrapped gifts, varying in size, strewn across the duvet. Oooh, and is that a stocking I see? Tiredness evaporates immediately and is replaced by excitement as I sit up quickly, smiling like a small child in a sweet shop.

The last time I celebrated Christmas in bed I was still little myself, or a teenager at least, and despite Jack asking me what I'd like for Christmas, I really wasn't expecting anything like this. I look longingly at the gifts, eager to rip the wrapping off, but I need a wee and nip to the bathroom first.

"What?!" I ask Jack accusingly, as I scoot past the end of the bed, lovingly touching the ribbon and shiny wrapping on one of the bigger gifts.

"You, your face." he smiles, "You haven't stopped grinning since you clocked them. You're like a little kid."

"I feel like one," I yell from the loo, peeing as quickly as possible and taking the opportunity to brush my teeth and clear the sleep from my eyes. Climbing back into bed, dressed in my festive red vest and cute Rudolph panties, I plonk myself down between his legs and, as he wraps me up in his embrace, kiss him passionately over my right shoulder, feeling ridiculously happy and stupidly content.

Yesterday's dinner with Stella and Mike went brilliantly, and Stella had texted me last night to give her seal of approval:

OH KATE, HE'S LOVELY, I CAN
SEE WHY YOU FELL FOR HIM.
BE HAPPY. SPEAK SOON. S X

We were only meant to be meeting for a drink, but Jack and I couldn't be bothered to cook and Stella still hadn't unpacked the kitchen.

"What's the point? We're going to Mum's for lunch tomorrow and staying the night; then we're driving to Mike's Mum and Dad's for Boxing Day, so I haven't got to cook anything until at least Saturday," she'd laughed, looking at Mike for support. He'd nodded in agreement then raised his eyebrows at me behind Stella's back, wisely keeping his mouth shut on the matter.

When we'd nipped to the loo in pairs, as all good girlfriends do, Stella had given my hand a squeeze and told me she was sure this was the real thing. "One look at you both and you can see how much you adore him," she'd said, topping up her pillar-box red lippie and giving her petticoats a shake. "I can't believe you're letting Gemma make you doubt yourself. I mean, I love the girl, but she could be a bit more glass half full." I snorted and Stella glared at me. "Alright, I know I tend to err on the side of caution too, but that's just because I like to see the bigger picture. Look, anyone can see you two are in love, it's like you're made for each other. Actually, this how you were with Rob," she added, looking sideways at me in the mirror.

"Stella, don't." I'd frowned, "Don't compare us with me and Rob."

"I'm not, I'm just saying I think you need to stop worrying and enjoy it for what it is. And if you like being at his house it's because he's there with you, not just because it gives you a bit of breathing space from the Asylum." I smiled, amused by her pet name for my house – she's not far wrong. When I'd left that morning Alfie had been tossing Mini Shreddies at Smithy, who'd been trying to catch them in his mouth, while balancing on one leg.

All cosy and wrapped up with Jack – having had fantastic sex with him last night and now waking up in his bed - I couldn't be more sure about how I feel about him. We'd agreed to spend the day with our respective parents, agreeing it was too much, too soon to do the big family thing, but Jack had asked me to stay the night and if we might spend some of Christmas morning together before going our separate ways.

"I wish you didn't have to go," he says now, tightening his hold on me, "If I had my way, you wouldn't leave this bed all day."

"Ah, but then I wouldn't get my Christmas dinner, and that would mean no roasties. I'd be a right old grump." I protest, wriggling free and snatching up the present closest to me, "Now, let me at this great big stack of pressies with my name on."

Jack pretends to wrestle it off of me but relents and tucks his arms around my midriff while I tear the paper off.

"Oh my God a Molton Brown candle, I *love* these."

"I know, you haven't stopped going on about them." Jack smiles, "Did I get the right one?"

"Lime, Basil and Mandarin. Yes! Thank you so much," and I shower him with kisses, marvelling at every little detail, from the beautiful glass votive and luxurious packaging to the hand tied ribbon on the box. "Look, it even comes with its own matches," I squeal. Jack shakes his head and rolls his eyes.

"Women!"

I work my way through the presents one by one and unwrap Hotel Chocolat goodies, the thick fluffy socks I adore wearing on a cold night, a voucher for one of the Champneys Day Spas, and a set of handwarmers – "Because your hands are always like ice – even straight after a workout!"

In the end I'm down to one last gift - a small present no bigger than a bar of soap. Feeling excited, I look at Jack and he pulls a face, wrinkling his nose in a cute puppy-dog fashion.

"I hope I got this right, because I'm not sure I can take it back." Uh oh. I have no idea what he's bought me, but I hope it's nothing mega expensive as I haven't bought him anywhere near this number of gifts.

I read the writing on the back of the sparkly Santa gift tag:

Beautiful Kate, this is how I feel when you're with me. Thank you for being a part of my life. All my love, Jack xxx

Cautiously removing the ribbon, I peel back the wrapping paper, ball it up and add it to the already large pile on the bedside rug. Inside the paper is a small, navy jeweller's box with a logo I don't recognise. I feel Jack tense up behind me as I lift open the lid. There, lying on the blue velvet cushion, sits a tiny pair of interlocking hearts on a white gold chain.

"Oh." I breathe, speechless.

"You don't like it," he says with disappointment.

"No, I do! It's… Oh Jack, it's exquisite!" And I turn to face him, throwing my arms around his neck and planting a huge kiss on his lips. Fingering the glistening metal, I trace around the first heart, then the second, lingering where they join.

"What did you mean, what you wrote on the tag? This is how you feel when I'm with you?" Jack squirms and looks embarrassed. He tucks a stray lock of hair back over my ear, and hesitates.

"You gonna make me say it?" he asks, looking down at his lap. I say nothing.

"Okay, I feel like you've got a little bit of my heart already and I don't want that to change." He looks up, his warm brown eyes deadly serious for a second: "I've not had this before Kate. Not with anyone."

Whoa. That was a little more intense than I was expecting, but good, I think. I stroke his face and look back at him.

"With no one?"

"No one."

I can't help the smile from creeping over my face, like the first fingers of the sunshine stretching over the horizon at dawn. I don't know if it's simply flattering my ego or if it runs deeper, but I like that I'm the first person who's made him feel this way.

"Do you want your Christmas presents now?" I grin.

"At last! I thought you'd never ask!" Jack complains, feigning mock shock - which I ignore - as I reach under the bed for the big silver gift bag I'd stashed away when we got home last night.

"No peeking," I'd said, stuffing it between shoes boxes and suitcases, "or else Santa won't come."

"Er, I think you mean Father Christmas, this is Britain not America," he scolded, slapping me playfully on the bum as I reached under the bed. "And it looks as if he's brought my present already," he exclaimed as he made a grab for me and pulled me down onto the mattress, so he could begin to unbutton the sheer, sleeveless blouse I'd worn out to dinner.

Stripping me down to my underwear he paused to kiss my newly exposed skin every few seconds, Jack had suddenly stopped before removing my knickers. Kneeling between my legs, still in his jeans but with his shirt already off, he looked like a fucking God towering above me, all toned, muscular torso and beautiful looks. Running his hand up my stomach and between my breasts, coming to rest on my collarbone, he'd stopped and looked at me, then asked quietly, barely concealed lust in his voice: "Will you make love to me Kate?"

We'd only ever spoken about 'fucking' or 'shagging' before, and this change of terminology was quite a departure.

"Is that deliberately different use of wording?" I asked, unsure how to respond to his plea. To date, I'd always cringed at the phrase 'making love' as it reminded me of the awkward pre-teen sex chat my mum had given me; this, along with the expression, 'sexual intercourse,' still makes me snigger like a school kid. But there was something about the way Jack had said it that made me feel different.

"Yes," he replied, stroking his fingers down my neck and slipping them inside my black lace bra, making me stiffen and squirm. "You can fuck anybody: someone you meet in a bar, or online, but when you care about someone and have feelings for them, it's never quite just fucking anymore, is it? I want you to make love to me, Kate." I curled my body upwards and cleaved to him, latching my lips onto his and trying to mould myself close enough to become a part of him and crawl into his soul.

"Yes." I'd panted as I came up for air, desperate with desire. "Yes, I'll make love to you, Jack." And without giving him time to respond, I'd flipped him over onto his back and sat astride him, unbuckling the big, shiny clasp on his jeans, pulling them only halfway down his thighs and mounting his straining cock. I lowered myself a tiny bit at a time, and watching his reaction, I never took my eyes off his face.

We'd changed positions a couple of times, Jack remaining firmly inside me as he lifted me effortlessly. His cock firmly ensconced in my pussy, we were bound so close we moved as one. I'd cum a couple of times already, but still had more to give. As Jack was in the final throes, with the first waves of his orgasm breaking, I'd thrust my cunt hard against his groin and rocked myself into a third and last orgasm, my tremors melding with his as we came at the same time. Then we'd collapsed on the duvet, tangled together, spent, exhausted and completely satisfied.

"I love you," I whisper, my eyes half shut, my chest heaving. Gentle lips covered mine in a whisper light kiss:

"I love you too Kate."

I push the peas around my plate absent-mindedly, making patterns in the gravy with my fork.

"Stop playing with your food, Katherine!" teases Mum as she exchanges a knowing look with Dad and nudges Auntie Susan, who almost spills her wine and tuts at her sister in annoyance.

"Aw, leave the poor girl alone," pipes up Uncle Brian, "it's a wonder she comes home at all with the amount of ribbing you lot dish out.

I smile gratefully at him from the other end of the table and lay my cutlery in the finished position on my plate.

"No more, Kate?" asks Dad, proffering the bowl of carrots

and platter of roast potatoes, but I can't eat another thing and the thought of pudding is actually making me feel sick.

"Shall we wash the pans up and stack the dishwasher before we eat dessert, Mum? Bel and Laura can help."

"Is that okay?" I ask my cousins, who are already on their feet and piling up the dirty plates.

"Oh, well if you're sure." Mum says, sounding mildly disappointed that she has to wait twenty minutes before ramming more food into anyone. "But don't be too long, I want to watch the Queen's Speech."

Exactly one year older and younger than me, the girls and I are pretty close. We all grew up together going on family camping trips and days out. Since Granny and Grandpa died, we've been spending alternate Christmases at each other's houses.

Scraping leftovers into the food bin, Bel giggles: "I thought Auntie Linda was never going to shut up about Jack."

"I know, anyone would think I've never had a fucking boyfriend before." I laugh, scrunching up gravy-soaked paper hats and cracker rubbish and squeezing it into the bin next to reams of crumpled, torn wrapping paper. "Can you imagine how she'd have been if I'd actually dragged him here for dinner?"

Taking the plates off her sister, Laura loads them into the dishwasher, smiling wordlessly. The elder of the two, she is the quieter and by far, the more sensible one. When I was home from university, Bel and I used to go dancing and drinking in town and roll in at silly o'clock in the morning, while Laura sat at home and studied.

She's not changed much even now, and shuns going out or buying the latest trends, preferring to save her money instead and dreams of buying her first home.

"So, now the oldies are all in the other room, dish the real dirt on juicy Jack," Bel demands with glee, "I want to know everything."

"Well, you're gonna have to have to wait, aren't you, Jelly-Belly," I shove her affectionately, using my childhood nickname for her, "because I'm not spilling the beans with Mum and Dad within a ten-mile radius. They've got a built in radar and bat-like hearing when it comes to my love life, which is on a need to know basis, and they most very definitely, do not need to know."

Right on cue, Mum walks round the corner and into the kitchen, an empty wine bottle in her hand. "Don't mind me girls, you carry on," she says, singsong fashion, "I just need another bottle of this nice red wine your dad bought, Kate. Now, where did he put it?"

"Oh, do you mean that red wine Mum, in there, on the sideboard, next to the dining table, where you put it before dinner?" I say, sarcastically, pushing her back out of the kitchen. "Nice try, Mum." I call after her, shaking my head. Turning back to the girls I shake my head: "See? Bat-like!"

Jack thinks this is hilarious when I recount it to him in bed much later that night. "I'm laughing with you, not at you babe. Don't you think I got much the same kind of grilling at mine, and the girls were even worse than my mum."

Jack has three sisters. All older and all married with children of their own. It's become their mission in life to fix him up with a suitable woman, according to him. I've actually met one of them: Gina, his eldest sister, goes to the gym, and I've bumped into her several times. When she found out I was the mystery girlfriend, she was all over me like a rash and now keeps giving me encouraging little smiles while I work out as Jack, if he's working, grimaces at me from across the room.

"Everyone loved my watch," he says, twisting his wrist this way and that, proudly admiring the Fossil timepiece with its worn-looking brown leather strap, cream face and blue dial.

"Good," I beam, snuggling closer into him, "I'm sorry it's not something more classy or expensive."

"Hey, don't be a tit, I love it," Jack says, cuddling me close to him, "I love all my presents. Especially the one I unwrapped last night." Laughing, I tilt my head and kiss him softly.

He had seemed delighted with his gifts, despite the fact that I was afraid that they made for rather a boring haul. Buying presents for men is so difficult compared to shopping for women, and I really didn't want to go down the pants and socks route this early on in the relationship. It's rather the kiss of death isn't it, when it comes to love and romance.

Eventually I settled for a bottle of Dolce and Gabbana's, The One, a grey Superdry T-shirt, some luxury gingerbread chocolates and a super cute black and white scarf that the crazy boy's worn all day, even insisting on wearing it in bed now, with nothing else on!

Jack bites into a gingerbread truffle and pops the other

half in my mouth. "Mmmm," he luxuriates in the flavour, "I think this has got to be the best thing about Christmas – you can get things with ginger in everywhere! Gingerbread lattes, gingerbread biscuits, gingerbread chocolates!"

I silence him with a kiss and reach over at the same time, snaffling another truffle. "Oi, what's your game? Cheeky," Jack starts to tickle me and I nearly choke on the sweet treat.

"Chocolate. Chocolate is the best thing about Christmas!" I splutter, trying not to cough chocolate spit all over both of us.

"I can't believe you have to work tomorrow," he says, letting me go.

"I know," I say miserably, sitting up to wash the delicious truffle down with a rather indulgent swig of Irish Cream. "But that's newspapers for you. Everyone wants their copy as usual. Anyway, at least I didn't have to work today, Nicole volunteered for it. "You know we all have to put in one day over Christmas or New Year, that's just how it works, and she's going away with friends, so she wants the New Year off. She doesn't even like Christmas much. She says all her family hate each other."

"I can't imagine not liking Christmas." says Jack, taking a slurp of my Baileys, "That's like saying you don't like puppies or kittens."

"Um, some people don't!" I point out.

"Well, you know what I mean"

Working on Boxing Day will be weird. At *The Express* we used to close for a few days, and being a weekly it didn't really have any impact on the edition. I've always spent both Christmas days with my family, stuffing myself stupid and watching crap TV. As much as I'd like to spend tomorrow with Jack, and I don't relish getting up early in the morning, I'm quite excited at the thought of going into work. And, if it means I don't eat my bodyweight in saturated fat and sugar, it's got to be a bonus, doesn't it?

Curling my arm around Jack in the pretence of a hug, I stretch out and sneak my fingers into the chocolate box again. It's not tomorrow yet and everyone knows you can eat as much as you like on Christmas Day – it's practically the law.

Twenty Six

After adjusting the hem of the black stretch fabric over my thighs, I stand back and scrutinise my reflection. I've gained a couple of pounds since being with Jack, but new relationships can do that, can't they? What with all the eating out and cosy nights in, festive nights out, and Christmas to boot, I'm surprised I haven't put on more. But having a gym trainer for a boyfriend has its perks. Aside from the odd indulgence, most of our home-cooked meals are pretty healthy, with lots of quinoa and courgetti making an appearance, well, when I'm cooking anyway.

Jack's more into having a huge piece of meat or fish on his plate with a pile of vegetables and the odd sweet potato here or there, but I like to play around with food and I'm keen to try out new ideas when I spot them in a magazine, or on the television. Still, we've both upped the training in the last couple of weeks to compensate for the complete blowout on Christmas Day. I swear, by about 4pm, when I managed to squeeze in a mince pie and three Quality Street, despite declaring only an hour beforehand I'd never eat again, I thought my stomach was actually going to rupture.

Now, running my hands over my new curves, I'm not actually displeased with what I see. The bodycon dress, black lace over gold underlay, skims my silhouette like a second skin, high on the neck and thighs, showcasing my toned arms and a reasonably flat stomach, all things considered. I'd have stressed out about the slightly rounded belly a couple of months ago, when, if I'm honest I was probably overdoing it at the gym, trying to block out the stress and heartache from having to work alongside Aidan every day. I'd lost some of that softness that always becomes a woman and was starting to look too thin – 'a little bit Fatima' according to Gemma, referring to the former British javelin thrower, who was always knocked for her masculine appearance.

No, the extra flesh isn't a bad thing, especially in this gorgeous frock. Turning sideways I give my booty an admiring glance: not quite Kim Kardashian yet, but definitely on the way.

"Mmmm, let's not go out," Jack says, coming up behind me and cupping my arse with both hands – he's clearly a fan of my enhanced derriere too – "let me take you to bed and ravage you instead." I giggle and squirm out of his clutches, slipping into my highest black patent shoes and snatching my clutch from the dresser.

"Nope, we're not missing this party for love nor money," I insist, even though the thought of being seduced right now seems wonderfully appealing. Jack looks drop dead gorgeous in a black, crew neck Religion t-shirt, very slim-fitting black jeans and black blazer. "I can't believe Stella's unpacked her home and is throwing a New Year's Eve party ten, no hang on, nine days after moving in – the girl's fucking crazy! A week ago she didn't even know where the kettle was!"

"I get she's your best mate and everything but perhaps

we should give it a miss if it's going to be a bit half-arsed," Jack says hopefully, looking longingly at my tits, one chocolate brown Chelsea boot on, the other still in his hand.

"No!" I reply firmly, brooking no further argument. "Stella's an absolute perfectionist and if she's said she's throwing a New Year's Eve party, then that's exactly what we're going to get, champagne, canapés, fireworks, Auld Lang Syne, the works."

"Taxi's here." says Jack, looking out of the window. "And it's snowing again. Only lightly though. I'll go down and give the driver a shout, tell him we'll be a couple of minutes."

Adding a coat of nude lip-gloss and a liberal spray of Bvlgari's Omnia Coral, I grab my black vintage chenille swing coat and follow him downstairs.

"Ok, I'm ready, how do I look?" I ask, giving him a twirl.

"Like only a blind man will be able to resist you tonight, although…" he hesitates, pulling me close and inhales deeply, "You smell just as incredible as you look babe."

"That's my favourite 'go out and knock 'em dead' perfume." I say nonchalantly, disentangling myself from him and leaving the house so I can pick my way through the snow. "Come on, let's go, before I change my mind and let you take all my clothes off."

"Hang on," Jack calls, locking the front door, "I've never smelt that before. Why haven't you worn it when we we've gone out?"

"I didn't want you to think I was trying too hard, did I?" I shout, grinning mischievously over my shoulder, wrapping my coat round me to keep out the chill. "You might not have chased me so hard and lost interest too soon."

Jack follows me into the cab and tells the driver we need the station. Settling into the back seat he slips his hand between my legs and squeezes the flesh, almost painfully. "You are going to be in so much trouble later Miss Cleaver," he says in a stern voice that tells me nothing, yet promises everything.

It takes about thirty minutes to get to Wimbledon – normally I don't travel from Chertsey because every train is stopper and the route into London would take so long I'd rather kill myself. But this is the better option tonight and we've booked a taxi to bring us home in the early hours.
Stella and Mike's pretty ground floor garden flat is only a couple of streets from the main line station, but in these shoes – 'Kate's silly shoes', Stella calls them – there's no way I'm walking, especially not in this snow, and we take another cab the short distance to the house. It's a traditional red-brick Victorian semi-detached property with high ceilings and period features, not unlike her place in Manchester.
With the money he got for his studio flat and the clinic, they were able to invest in a bigger than average one-bedroom apartment in excellent condition, decorated to a really high standard, and the partially decked south-facing garden is 'beautifully landscaped' according to Stella. Honestly, she's sounded more and more like an estate agent in almost every conversation we've had for the last two months. I feel like I know more about the flat than the people who sold it!

The party's already in full swing when we get there, and the door is on the latch. Despite the number of people crammed inside you can clearly see how lovely the place is, even before she's redecorated.

Off the narrow, cream hallway that runs the length of the flat, the first room at the front the property is an airy duck egg blue living room, with a deep white pelmet that runs around the top of the walls. Stella's huge grey sofa and red leather armchair look as if they've always been part of the décor, and Mike's super-sized HD TV sits comfortably on one of the vast built in cabinets either side of the feature fireplace.

"Oh my god, what did they leave Jamie to sit on?" I say to Jack, even though he's never met Stella's housemate or seen her Manchester pad.

"Well we were going to buy him a few orange crates, but then we settled for deckchairs," Stella teases behind me, holding a bottle of beer and a champagne mojito with my name on it.

"Hello, darling." I gush, giving her a squeeze and relieving her of the icy cocktail, "This is mine I presume."

"Of course, I saw you guys come in." she beams, handing the lager to Jack, and giving him a hug, "Here you go sweetie, get this down you. Well, what do you think?" she asks impatiently.

"Stel, it's lovely." I say truthfully, I'm completely in love with the place. "But seriously, Jamie?"

"Oh, we simply left the furniture from Mike's flat there – he was fine with that – he's not there much anyway, and if things keep going as they are with Anton, he thinks he'll be moving down to Brighton soon." I jump up and down gleefully, well as much as my heels will allow, clapping my hands with excitement.

"I know," squeals Stella, "OMG imagine if they get married – our first gay wedding – what would we wear?!" I laugh, sharing her enthusiasm. It would be so great if Jamie's found 'the one'.

"Hello sexy," Mike's deep voice echoes across the living room, "I see you found the alcohol okay?"

"Huh, cheeky bugger." I tut, giving him a warm hug, "It would have been more polite to ask if I'd found the flat ok."

He shakes hands with Jack, and they immediately start talking about the Boxing Day football matches and the weekend fixtures. Turning back to Stella, who looks resplendent in a fitted, black velvet, vintage pencil skirt cocktail dress that clings to her gorgeous curves, I ask for a tour of the flat.

Leading me back into the hallway, she takes me into a modern fitted kitchen that sits behind the first room and looks out onto the garden, accessed by a discretely placed back door. Behind that, comes a simple bathroom with a plain white suite, and finally a large bedroom with patio doors again leading out onto the garden. The entire property is exactly as Stella described it, and I feel bad saying it, but I do have a pang of envy now I've seen it for myself. It's everything I want for myself: a private pad in Greater London, on a brilliant rail line and a quiet residential street. But on my salary there's no way I can afford even a studio flat, let alone a place like this. Even if I kicked my shopping habit and my coffee shop lattes, I'd still have no chance of investing in a property any time soon. However, I'm truly pleased for my mate, I really am. She's absolutely oozing happiness and I can see she's thrilled to be in this little love nest with the man of her dreams, new job just around the corner, and maybe marriage and children somewhere down the line.

"You deserve this Stella," I say, taking my best mate's hands into mine and looking down at her glowing face – even in her Dorothy in Oz style red shoes, she's still way shorter than me!

"Aw, thank you honey," she smiles, pulling me in for a big bear hug like only BFFs can do.

"This will be you and Jack soon, I can tell," she says in a dramatic stage whisper, getting dangerously close to smudging her red lips all over my cheek.

"You can tell no such thing missy," I reprimand, holding her away at arms' length. "I can, I have psychic abilities, you know that Kate."

"What I do know is you've had far too many of those cocktails young lady," I yell, walking back into the hallway just as the front door bangs open and Gemma and her boyfriend, Matt - the tall blond guy she copped off with at her party back in June – strut into the house, shouting: "It's okay, we're here, you can start the party now."

Rolling my eyes in amusement at Jack as he disappears into the living room with a fresh beer, I wave at Gemma and go to follow my man, but stop and shriek as I spot Jamie and Anton snuggling in the kitchen. They've just arrived, but can't stop as they have another two 'soirees' to attend before midnight. Fancy!

It took ages for Gemma and Matt to get together. Every few weeks they'd get it on during a night out and she'd divulge the juicy details to me in debriefs over coffee, or a bottle of wine, a few days later. I'd said she should just ask him out, but she kept saying it'd never work, what with him being so much younger than her; turns out Matt's twenty-one and Gem's a bit of a cougar. Anyway, eventually they spent the entire bank holiday weekend together on a camping trip at the end of the summer with about twenty other people, and Gemma didn't sleep in her tent once! After that they were inseparable, and they now see themselves as the new Posh 'n' Becks! Admittedly they do make a very beautiful couple.

I spend the night catching up with friends and showing Jack off to anyone who hasn't yet met him, but the evening passes in a blur, much too quickly for my liking, as all the best nights invariably do. Before I know it, Gemma's linking her arm in mine, and Jack's holding my hand, as Mike announces it's almost midnight and gathers everyone in the front room.

Counting down, glasses charged and ready, we're fizzing with excitement; the imminent arrival of the New Year, just seconds away. On the television, ITV relays the chanting of thousands of partygoers - gathered just a few miles away on the banks of the Thames - directly into Stella's living room and we all look at each other in anticipation.

Stella's flushed and happy, Mike looks from her to his mate, Dom, and winks at him, raising a beer. Gemma's making wild gestures and doing something strange with her legs and

I look to Jack, who's smiling at me, his dark brown eyes like deep pools of chocolate, the laughter lines on his face and the occasional fleck of grey in his otherwise lovely dark brown hair.

A ruckus explodes around me; shouting, singing, noise and commotion, but all I know is Jack's lips are pressing against mine, his tongue is in my mouth and his hands are in my hair. We're suspended in a fragment of time, immune from anyone else, it's just me and him caught in a moment, a split second where everything else disappears. Breaking off the kiss, he nuzzles my nose with his.

"Happy New Year, beautiful girl."

"Happy New Year Jack. I love you."

This is it.

It strikes me like a bolt of electricity and I feel time slowing down. I can actually hear my own heart beating. This is what I've been trying to find since Rob and I split up. And I didn't even know I'd been looking for it.

Could he actually be *The One*?

"Whooo Katie, Katie, Katie!" Both girls descend at the same time, squeezing me between them, making me the filling in their 'Gella' sandwich.

"Happy New Year, KC!" Stella screams in my ear, almost deafening me, "I love you babe. We're gonna have so much fun this year."

Laughing, I hug her back tightly, "I love you too sweetie, Happy New Year."

I give Gemma a cuddle too then do a circuit of the room,

wishing everyone the same generic greeting but can't stop looking over at Jack, who hasn't taken his eyes off me. I edge my way back towards the door where he's standing and wordlessly he takes my hand, pulling me through the people massing in the hallway. Small groups are attempting to sing Auld Lang Syne, but forgetting half the words; drunken revellers are propping up the walls as hours of celebrating start to take their toll.

Pushing open the bathroom door Jack tugs me inside, slamming it shut and throwing me forcefully against the wood, crushing his mouth against mine and reaching down to turn the lock. "I told you you'd be in trouble later," he growls and I shiver uncontrollably, weak with longing for only one thing.

Twenty Seven

Smoothing my dress back down, I clean up the smudges of make-up from round my eyes and shake out my hair, freshening up my scent with the tiny travel-size bottle I always keep in my clutch. Jack smirks at me in the mirror: "You can do what you want babe, but you're still gonna look like you just got screwed senseless."

I give him a filthy grin, "Good, because I don't give a flying fuck." Still on a post-orgasmic cloud, I genuinely mean it. I don't care if every person in this house knows we just had sex; they probably heard us anyway. After locking the door Jack had taken total control, ripping my knickers off and pushing up my dress. He bent me over the side of the bath and slammed into me from behind with no need for foreplay; I'm wet and ready whenever he wants me. With my heels still on, my pussy was angled down and away from him, meaning the underside of his cock rubbed deliciously against my clit in a distractingly compulsive rhythm.

"Yeah? Yeah? Do you like that?" he'd demanded as I'd gasped with pleasure every time his length had crashed into me, his balls smacking against my thighs. Bringing me to the brink but knowing it wouldn't get me off, he'd manhandled me to the wooden dresser and lifted me on top so my pussy was flush with his cock. Unable to take his eyes off my wet cunt, he'd fingered me. Tracing my lips with the pads of his middle and forefinger, he dipped into me, then back out, flicking over my clit then opening me right up.

"I love looking at your pussy when it glistens like this, all wet and open," he'd moaned, transfixed by my gaping hole. Holding my jaw, almost painfully tight, he'd kissed me then fucked me hard until I'd cum in short painful spasms, tightening around his ripe cock, before he emptied himself into my tensed cunt while he held me close, his head buried in my cleavage.

Now, giving myself a fresh coat of lipgloss, my cheeks burn as I think of the raw, animalistic way we just fucked. Slipping my shoes back on, I unlock the door while Jack curls a hand around me and caresses my tummy, kissing the soft skin behind my ear.

"God, I love you being inside you." I melt at his touch and lean back against him.

"Good, because I love you being inside me," I murmer as I take his hand and open the door, smiling wickedly to myself at the thought of what we just did.

"Christ, about fucking time, I'm bursting," Gemma, exclaims, pushing Stella, whose arms are full of empties and naked canapé plates, about of the way and past us into the bathroom. As the door closes behind her, she shouts: "Tart!" at the top of her voice, and, of course, I know it's aimed at me. Jack and I look at each other and start laughing, as Stella asks loudly, "Who's a tart?" We say nothing but, looking from me to Jack, then back at me, my mate pulls a 'yeah yeah' face and raises one eyebrow just as Gemma yells: "Kate's a tart. She just had sex in your lav'."

"Of course she did," says Stella looking at me, the hint of a grin on her face. Like naughty school children caught with their hands in the sweetie jar, we cringe. Biting my lip and stifling a giggle, I say, "Sorry hon, I just got the horn real bad."

"Of course you did," Stella grins, heading to the kitchen with her load.

"Is she pissed at us?" Jack asks, blushing slightly at Gemma's very public announcement and grinning sheepishly as some of Mike's friends, who are lapping it up, fist-bump him in admiration.

"Who Stel? No! Don't be daft, she thinks it's hilarious!" I say, following Stella to the kitchen and pouring us both another glass of bubbly. I should probably stop drinking soon or I'm going to regret it in the morning. We've booked to go out to brunch at Piccolos with Jack's best mate, Stuart and his fiancée, Caroline, and I'd like to make a good impression – I've not met them before and I'm eager not to be throwing up at the time.

We both have another couple of small drinks before the taxi arrives at 1.30am. It's not that late, but we've had a great time and I'm almost glad it's time to go home so I can be alone with Jack and not have to share him with anyone else.

In the cab I kick off my shoes and curl up, tucking myself into Jack's side, his arm holding me close, and feel content that it's his bed I'm going home to.

We get back quickly and he pays the cabbie who's anxious to get away to pick up his next overinflated fare. I tuck my arm into Jack's, steadying myself in the fresh snowfall and pick my way slowly up towards the house. Now I've put my shoes back on, my feet are really hurting.

Quite out of the blue, Jack stops me halfway up the garden path and, holding me just above my elbows, peers down squarely into my face and blurts out: "Move in with me." I blink back at him, not quite comprehending, hearing but not processing what he's saying. "You're here all the time anyway, and it just doesn't seem like home anymore when you're not." He's peering at me now, as if trying to look inside my head and figure out what I'm going to say. If only he could see, it would save me from having to find the right words. I feel like insulating foam has wrapped itself around my brain, muffling the connectors that join my thought and speech processes together.

My mouth opens and closes like a goldfish and it must look like I'm in shock because Jack takes my hand and backtracks rapidly, "I'm sorry, it's too soon, forget I said it. I didn't mean to scare you." And it's like the fog suddenly lifts and is replaced by an immediate rush of panic that he'll retract his request. I know what I want to say in my heart, but fear's paralysing me, preventing me from saying it out loud.

"No, no, don't take it back." I hurry to reassure him, "It's not too soon. I'm just, it's just…" Jack waits patiently until I've managed to sift through the words in my head, rearranging them into coherent sentences that I'm actually capable of vocalising. "I'm scared, no, make that petrified, genuinely terrified of getting hurt, like I was before with Rob." I say, teeth chattering despite Jack laying his big coat around my shoulders. I'm shaking but realise it's nothing to do with the cold. It's time to be brave and come clean: "I want to run away when you say things like that, but only because in my head I equate them with the pain I'll know I'll go through if it all goes wrong. But I've had enough of being scared. I'm fed up with holding men at arm's length, or pushing them away with the decisions I make." I shudder at the memory of kissing Danny in London that night and take a deep breath: "I want to feel every day like I do when I'm with you. And if I'm honest, I feel more at home at your house than I have anywhere else during the last four years, if not longer."

"So?" Jack asks hopefully, optimism in his voice, "Is that a yes?"

"It's stupid, reckless and crazy, that's what it is," I say shaking my head, "Jack it's only been a couple of months." Raising my hand to shush him, pressing a finger to his lips, I add, "But yes. It's a yes." And as my answer filters through into his brain, the clouds covering my beautiful man's face lift and the sunny beams of his smile shine through, lighting him up from within. He throws his arms around me, literally sweeping me off my feet, lifting me up, devouring me with a kiss that goes on and on until I push him away and insist he takes me inside before I get frostbite in my poor, frozen, crushed toes.

Kicking the front door shut, he carries me upstairs and, yes it is just like a movie, only without all the huffing and puffing and embarrassment I've faced when other, lesser men have tried the same and failed. He throws me on the bed, and this time he takes it slow. It's nothing like earlier. He carefully removes my shoes and warms my toes with his hot hands until I can feel them again. Then he undresses me slowly and we savour each other, exploring the other's bodies; skin on skin, carelessly making love until both of us are too tired to do anything else but drift off to sleep in each other's arms.

I don't think I've ever felt happier than I do right now.

The rain is lashing down by the time the train pulls away from Woking Station and the wind's coming in gusts big enough to shake the entire carriage. A platform announcement has already warned the stormy weather is creating severe delays on all routes, but nothing can ruin my good mood today. Jack and I slept in late yesterday, sharing a very sexy shower when we did get up, before meeting his friends at Piccolos for a gorgeous boozy brunch full of fun and laughter. Caroline and I hit it off immediately and it was past three o'clock when we finally headed home.

Today, with all the festivities well and truly over, I'd normally feel empty and flat; the bleakest winter months of January and February stretching endlessly before me; the bright, warm days of spring and summer still only something I can dream about. Usually Celebrity Big Brother is the only thing that can raise a smile during this period when everyone's eaten and drunk too much and payday's a mere dot on the horizon. But looking out at the rain-drenched vista, the snow washed away and only the occasional Christmas lights twinkling sadly in their bleak grey surroundings, I can't help but smile, excited about the prospect of moving in properly with Jack. I'm still sure it's insane and Mum and Dad are going to freak when I eventually get round to telling them. Gemma will go into meltdown thinking up reasons it will all go wrong and Stella will be worried it's too soon, and be scared I'll get hurt, but right now I don't care about any of that. I'm wrapped in my own little bubble and nothing is going to burst it.

I'm still grinning when I arrive at work, even making cheerful small talk with Esther in the lift who, despite her sour demeanour, at least meets me half way asking if I've had a nice New Year. Either she's had a really good Christmas or she's too shocked by my sudden warmness to react otherwise.

I stop off at the Features Desk to wish Lori a Happy New Year, and Esther dumps her bag before heading to the ladies' loo. "I've a nice job for you this morning," Lori says, "Rosa set it up before Christmas, but she's off skiing at the moment. Six women are coming in to the studio for a second photo shoot. It's about gaining weight over the festive period. Rosa's done the before pictures and interviews but I need you to do the follow ups."

"Ok, great," I smile, cheerfully.

"Things should start getting back to normal now." explains Lori, "We've got a couple of new journalists starting in news today so it should take the pressure of you guys a bit." Mel arrives looking groomed and polished with her normally curly hair straightened.

"Whadda ya think?" she asks, pointing at her new do.

"Very nice," I say, genuinely impressed at the difference

it makes. Normally Mel arrives looking like she had a fight with a bear on the way to work, but she really does look lovely this morning.

"Jeff paid for me to have it done for New Year's Eve and it's supposed to last about a week."

"I love it." I beam, "Maybe he can treat you to it on a regular basis. Or failing that treat yourself, because 'you're worth it', as the saying goes."

"You seem exceptionally cheerful?" Esther comments, suspiciously and slightly haughtily, as she returns to her seat, "Any particular reason?"

Lori and Mel look at me in anticipation, bright-eyed and curious. Smiling enigmatically, I shrug and turn away. I'll tell Mel - and maybe Lori too - later over a coffee, if she doesn't get it out of me sooner, but I have no desire to share anything with that witch, good mood or not.

Across the office, one of the chief news reporters, Tom, is chatting animatedly to a blonde girl I don't recognise – she must be one of the new hacks who's started. She laughs nervously and I recognise myself on my first day, just over a month ago now, anxious to please, eager to show what I could do, yet terrified I might fail and everyone would find out what a big fraud I was. The thought makes me smile – I'm glad I took the risk to come here, push myself to do something outside my comfort zone.

Beside Tom, a seasoned hack, Gerry takes off his glasses and rubs his rheumy eyes, still hungover from the night before or possibly still even pissed – he'll be back on the lash by two-o'clock at another boozy business lunch that'll go on until about teatime.

Grinning I shake my head – I'd never get away with it but Gerry's old school; a dinosaur left over from the Fleet Street days where stories were traded over a pint, or seven, and as long as the scoops kept coming in, no questions were asked. His days on the paper are probably numbered but he's nearing retirement age and can get away with the kind of conduct that would see someone like me sacked.

Next to him, another new recruit scribbles into his notepad, phone tucked under his chin, a second pen balanced precariously behind his right ear. He hangs up and tosses the mobile and biro carelessly on the table, leaning backwards precariously in his chair, stretching languidly, his hands behind his head. He looks up and around him, then catches my eye, as I stand staring, motionless, in his direction.

Blonde rimmed, deep blue eyes look back at me. Beneath them, a chiselled jaw and a full, sulky mouth. The world blurs around me and falls into slow motion as an icy hand closes itself over my heart.

Aidan.

Acknowledgements

When I said I wanted to write erotic fiction 12 years ago, I didn't realise it would take me more than a decade to pluck up the courage and knuckle down. I knew I could do it, and I definitely had a story to tell, but with two small children to raise, life just kinda got in the way.

Finally when I did bite the bullet I wasn't sure I had what it took. But thanks to the faith, love and backing of loyal friends and family, who truly believed in me, I've achieved my goal.

I need to thank all of the following people:

One of my best friends, Sharon Hoult, who assured me the first few chapters read like a real book and encouraged me to keep at it, and my other girlfriends, Eloise Bruce and Andrea Belcher, who are always behind me, 100%. My gym buddy, Charlotte Parnell, who endlessly encourages me to reach for my goals, even if it is often accompanied by a stream of verbal abuse.

An author friend, I won't name, but who knows who she is, for reading the beginning of the book and encouraging me to continue with the story, despite my insecurities.

My old school friend, Caz Harvey, who thinks what I'm doing is fab, and another old classmate, Tracy Woods, who is without doubt my biggest fan, and has slavishly read every chapter I've ever written, offering me invaluable criticism.

A school mum friend Liz Perera and her book group, who also gave me brilliant feedback when I really needed it, and fellow author, Kerry Gibb, who taught me a lot about self-publishing and gave me lots of encouragement.

The talented and generous photographer/award-winning director, Ian Derry, for creating such a beautiful image for the cover, and his unyielding support along the way.

The lovely Sarah Barnes, who gave her time unselfishly to star as my cover model, and Lock Studios where the image was shot.

Not forgetting the wonderful Brian Hart, of DMCL, Dictating Machine Co. Ltd, who lent me the dictaphone used in the cover image, free of charge at the eleventh hour.

Closer to home, I can't forget the dedicated belief of my parents, Rosemary and Cecil Merrett, who have always had my back. My mum, in particular, has steadfastly refused to read the book until it's published because she had faith it would and that means the world to me.

Huge thanks to my children, Amelie and Tiger, who've had to fend for themselves a lot more recently, while I've been squirreled away at the laptop. You've been brilliant, thank you xx

And last but not least, my husband Chris, who is quietly proud and has allowed me the time to shine, now that I'm ready to sparkle again.

Thank you, Mr Dart, I couldn't have done it without your support. xx

Jo Merrett

Jo Merrett is a former feature writer
at The Mirror, and a mum of two.
In her spare time she writes a blog
about her various passions entitiled,
Fitness, Food and Fiction.
Jo lives with her husband, children
and two cats in Woking, Surrey.

This is her debut novel

@jomerrettnovelist
@fitnessfoodfiction1615

@jomerrettnovelist
@fitnessfoodfictiondotcom

@JMerrett87

http://fitnessfoodfictionco.ipage.com